Kindred Spirits

BAKER CITY: HEARTS & HAUNTS 5

JOSIE MALONE

KINDRED SPIRITS
Copyright © 2023 by Josie Malone

ISBN: 979-8-88653-169-5

Published by Satin Romance
An Imprint of Melange Books, LLC
White Bear Lake, MN 55110
www.satinromance.com

Published in the United States of America.

Cover Design by Lynsee Lauritsen

PROLOGUE

May 2011

"Sir! We need to talk!"

Recognizing the low, feminine voice as that of the new noncom in charge of the warehouse he operated, Captain Rex Sinclair glanced over his shoulder at the woman in camouflage fatigues standing behind him. "No good conversation ever started with those words, Sergeant Ramsey." He gestured to the seat next to him. "Pull up a stool before you tell me what an asshat I am, and I'll buy you a drink. I'm having boilermakers. Want one?"

"No thanks. At least we agree on something, sir. Your behavior is execrable, sir, and unbefitting an Army officer." She sat down next to him, carefully placing her regulation handbag on the bar. She narrowed the electric-blue eyes that haunted him twenty-four, seven and glared at him. "You bailed on me, sir. You know there's an I.G. inspection at 0800 hours tomorrow. You should have stuck around, sir, and helped prep for it, not hightailed it before closing formation."

"I'm getting a divorce, and the call from the lawyer today pissed me off. My going to be ex-wife wants beaucoup bucks. Beyond child support for the kids, she isn't getting a dime."

"Everything pisses you off, sir. Ranting, raging and yelling obscenities at the top of your lungs is inappropriate, sir, when we have work to do."

Rex winced, reaching for the shot glass of whisky in front of him.

1

Sergeant First Class Deborah Ramsey was tired. He saw the exhaustion in her pale, lovely features. She'd undoubtedly been working ever since he stormed out of the warehouse. In the past month, while assigned to his section, she always arrived before he did and stayed long after he left. She hadn't gone to the barracks to change out of her camouflage fatigues before tracking him down at this ramshackle tavern. "You're not letting this go, are you, Ramsey? Are you sure about that boilermaker? You probably need it."

"No, thanks. I'm not drinking whisky and following it with a beer chaser." She folded her arms and frowned even more fiercely. "It's 'sergeant's business' to train junior officers. You know that's second lieutenants fresh out of college. If you need somebody to wipe your tail or your nose, it's not me. Man up, sir!"

He tossed down the whisky and took a hasty swallow of the waiting beer, struggling to collect his thoughts. He'd been drinking since afternoon and now it was well into the night. "Cut me some slack, Sarge. My wife, soon to be ex-wife introduced me to what she said was my six-month-old daughter when I got off the plane three months ago. Made a big splash on national TV."

"You've obviously mistaken me for someone who cares, sir. I don't. Not about your piddly personal problems—"

"I'd been gone for a year and a half. When I had a week's R & R, she wouldn't meet me in New York and now, I know why. She told me she couldn't get anyone to stay with the other four kids, that the housekeeper was away on vacation. My wife lied to me. She was pregnant with someone else's kid."

"Again, I don't care." Sergeant Ramsey held up her hand. "You have choices, sir. Divorce her. Reconcile with her. But stop throwing tantrums. You're grown. Put on your big boy panties and act like a commissioned officer up for promotion."

"And it's an 'embrace the suck' moment, isn't it?" He finished his beer and signaled the bartender for a refill. "You deserve a better C.O., Ramsey. If you want a transfer, I'll sign the request."

"We can't both run away, sir. You requested the job here in Texas instead of returning to California after your last combat tour—"

"Everybody knows my business there. I wanted a fresh start."

"Then act like it." Sergeant Ramsey nodded at the bartender when she approached, carrying another two glasses, his next boilermaker. "What kind of white wine do you have?"

"Put it on my tab," Rex said. "If the sergeant's gonna keep ripping me a new one, she needs dinner to go with it. I know she skipped lunch and I'm pretty sure she hopped supper too. Better give us a menu."

"It's almost 2300 hours," Sergeant Ramsey said. "Isn't the kitchen closed?"

"Not yet. You have ten minutes to select a burger and fries." The sturdy, gray-haired older woman handed over a grease-stained sheet of paper. "Choose fast, honey." She glanced at Rex. "Might want to sop up some of that booze with food, Captain."

"Good idea." Rex waited until they had fresh drinks before he gestured to a table on the other side of the room. "Let's move over there to eat. You can bring me up to speed on what still needs to be done for the inspection."

"It's hopeless, sir." She followed him across the tavern, bypassing the men at the pool table. "I could only clean up so much of the mess in the month I've been at the warehouse. Your previous N.C.O.I.C. retired. Scuttle-butt is he didn't want to put up with you a moment longer."

Rex pulled out a chair and waited for her to sit down. "Unfortunately, there's more truth than fiction to that story, Ramsey. We're both fairly new at this base. How do we salvage the situation?"

"I don't know." She heaved a sigh. "If it's like other posts where I've served in the last ten years, the senior Army officers won't care about the crap-fest in our section. They'll want optimum results whether it's reasonable or not. So, I'll get the proverbial ass-chewing tomorrow. It's annoying, but it can't be helped."

"You've done your best to rectify a bad situation." Rex gestured to her wine. "Drink up. I've got your six, Sarge. I know I haven't been doing my share, but it isn't reasonable to expect us to clean up something this broken in such a short amount of time."

"It's not the troops' fault. They've done their best with the minimal, erratic leadership they've been receiving."

"I know that as well as you do. You need more support from the non-commissioned side of the house, so let's see what we can do to get it."

She hesitated. "I'm not here for much longer, sir. This is a transition assignment. I'll be shipping out to Afghanistan before the end of the year. I don't have my orders yet, but they'll be coming through soon enough."

"You'll be missed." He paused, waiting for their meals to be placed in front of them. "Let's eat and then we'll work out a plan."

"That's do-able, sir."

More than once during the next half-hour, Debbie Ramsey reminded herself to focus on the cheeseburger and fries in front of her, rather than staring at the broad-shouldered, dark-haired man in combat fatigues sitting across from her. *It's not my fault he's a hunk and a half.* She couldn't help admiring his rough-hewn features, the strong cheekbones and, from an earlier combat tour, the broken nose. His previous noncom had told her Sinclair was injured from an I.E.D, but luckily all his troops survived the assault. If they hadn't, she'd have heard about it. Army bases ran on gossip, too.

She hadn't expected him to admit he'd been irresponsible at the warehouse or to buy her dinner. Granted, he was in a 'sticky wicket' as her best friend would have said. Debbie knew that long before she'd heard him shouting at a lawyer through a closed office door today. The conversation ended with Sinclair roaring he wasn't paying his ex-wife the alimony she wanted. He'd demanded DNA tests on all five of the kids she'd foisted off on him, especially the daughter born when he was away for more than eighteen months in Afghanistan, the one obviously conceived when he was out of CONUS and his wife's mind and life.

Debbie swirled a French fry in a pool of ketchup. It wasn't as if Sinclair was lying about his failed marriage. She'd heard yet another sad story from a different noncom. The captain's wife was a serial cheater who'd slept around on more than one base and when her affairs resulted in pregnancies, Sinclair ended up with his name on the birth certificates. Still, he needed to do his job just like she did. If he yelled, 'bullshit' one more time when everything went from sugar to shit in less than a heartbeat, she'd tell him again to freaking 'man up'.

After he slammed down the phone this afternoon, he'd stormed into the warehouse and raged at a civilian driver delivering a load who'd unfortunately parked in the wrong space. The poor woman burst into tears, which meant it took even longer to get the semi-truck moved to where it should have been in the first place. Debbie had stepped in and smoothed over the situation.

It hadn't gained her any points with the man in charge. Everyone around heard another stream of repeated 'bullshits' and 'f-bombs' before he swept out of the building, shouting his favorite words at full volume. She'd worked the rest of the day and most of the night, grateful not to deal with his tantrums or so-called supervision. When she couldn't finish everything that needed to be done at the warehouse in time, she'd decided to tour the small town near the base and track him down at his favorite watering-hole.

"All right. We've eaten." She sipped the remains of her favorite Zinfandel. "What's it going to take for you to step up and do your job, sir?"

"I'll do my best not to lose it from now on, Ramsey." Rex lifted the glass of beer. "I'm worried. I miss my kids. I need a guarantee I won't go back to California. It's hard to deal with Averill cheating on me when I never chippied on her. Not in fifteen years."

"That's a better track record than most men have." Debbie met his golden-brown gaze. He'd shown his vulnerability and she could do the same. "Tell you the truth, sir. I'm apprehensive about going back to the *sandbox* this time. I don't have anyone in CONUS to look after my business matters."

"No family?"

Debbie shook her head. "My grandparents have health issues, and I don't want to burden them. They've been looking after my horses and I'm not sure if they'll be able to handle them for the next year and a half."

He paused and studied her. "Maybe, we could help each other out."

"How do we do that?"

"I need a new wife when my divorce is final in September. If I'm married, I won't do something stupid and get reeled back into more drama. And if I'm your husband, you can trust me to look after your concerns."

"Are you serious?" She stared at him, hoping her jaw didn't hit the table. "Sir, that's the most ridiculous thing I've ever heard. You may want a wife on paper, but I can't see how a 'paper' husband could help me." She paused, recalling her turbulent life before she enlisted. *Then again, it could resolve a few issues I don't like to remember.*

"Well, at least you didn't refuse." He chuckled, finished his beer, and then stood. "Come on, Ramsey. Let's call it a night. I have a few months before my divorce is final and you leave the States. I'll convince you it's a lifesaver for both of us."

"Not happening, sir." Still, the idea made her smile.

October 2011

They'd deliberately honored the thirty-day waiting period required by Texas after his divorce was final before they married. Rather than let anyone know their plans, she'd used two weeks' leave to visit her grandparents before she shipped out. She'd told them about Rex Sinclair, so they'd know how to contact him if she didn't make it home. Then, she met him in Las Vegas.

She'd always wanted an "Elvis" wedding and luckily, Rex was willing to go along with the plan without bitching about the kitschy ceremony or the minister happily singing Elvis songs. Of course, she laughed her backside off when Rex demanded equal time and the opportunity to reserve a honeymoon suite at the luxury *Bellagio Hotel and Casino*. Turnabout was fair play, as the saying went. They'd spent two days together after the ceremony enjoying gourmet meals, gambling, dancing and, of course, making love in their suite.

She always woke up early, a leftover habit instilled in childhood when she lived on her parents' ranch in Montana. Debbie eased out of the king-size bed, leaving him to sleep. She had to pack and be downstairs in an hour to catch the shuttle to the airport. On her way to the ensuite, the vintage sapphire and diamond claddagh wedding set on her left hand caught her eye.

He'd told her it belonged to his grandmother, and she'd made him promise to give it to his 'real' wife, or save it for his oldest daughter, because his granny and Averill were always at loggerheads. After a quick shower, Debbie opted for comfortable civilian clothes, jeans, a light blue sweater, and flip-flops. She braided her hair, added makeup, and returned to the bedroom.

He must have heard her soft footsteps because he opened his eyes and sat up, the blanket still covering his lower body. "You'll be gone by the time I get back to the base, won't you?"

Debbie nodded. "Yes, but I'll call whenever it's possible."

"Likewise."

When he held out his hand, she crossed to him. She leaned down and kissed him. "Stay safe."

"That's my line, Ramsey. I'll see you when you get home."

"You know it, Sinclair." And she kissed him again. "I'm counting on it."

PART 1

SUMMER 2019

CHAPTER ONE

Master Sergeant Debbie Ramsey stopped halfway across the parking lot in front of the warehouse to watch the August sunlight brighten Mount Rainier's beautiful snowcapped peak. No matter how often she'd seen it in the last ten months she'd been stationed at Fort Clark, the sight always made her feel at peace, that everything was right with her world. Yes, she knew the ancient mountain was a volcano, part of the Pacific Ring of Fire and sleeping before it erupted again. Sometimes, she felt like that herself.

She drew a deep breath of the warm afternoon air and continued to stroll toward the large building where she'd work for the next three days until her current enlistment ended. She'd taken two weeks off in April to close the deal on the riding stable she'd bought near Baker City in the Cascade foothills, then taught horse camp for two weeks in June and three more in July. She was running out of leave, but that didn't actually matter since she wasn't staying in the Army.

On Saturday morning, she'd be free to follow what she often thought of as an impossible dream. Now, she had to find a way to share her upcoming departure with the soldiers she supervised. They'd be fine, but what about her commanding officer? He'd certainly notice she was gone when he wanted something. He'd begun complaining about her using up her leave in what he called "dribs and drabs" rather than taking it all at once, but she told him it was easier to pick up the slack after short spurts rather than cleaning up various messes when she was gone for an extended period of time.

Smiling, she hurried up the concrete stairs near the end of the long building. Inside, she paused long enough to remove her camouflage cap. She glanced at the loading area and breathed a sigh of relief when she noted the last delivery of military supplies from the night before had already been stored. One less hassle. She headed for the hallway that led to the offices at the far end of the warehouse.

She'd barely reached the entry door when a familiar bellow assaulted her ears. Debbie grimaced. She'd only been away two hours. How did hell break loose so soon?

"Damn it, Petrie. This is bullshit. Where's Ramsey?"

"She left for an appointment." The other man sounded perfectly calm. "What was I supposed to do when the MP's showed up, Major Sinclair?"

"It's bullshit, Petrie. You're giving me bullshit."

Debbie pushed open the door, glimpsing the vintage sapphire and diamond claddagh ring she always wore on her left hand. She stepped into the large room that doubled as her office and that of the young company clerk who thankfully had a dentist appointment and wasn't here to see the major make a fool of himself again. Silently, she watched the broad-shouldered man in combat fatigues rampage toward her desk, still chanting his favorite word.

A taller, slighter, younger officer with perfectly styled black hair wearing the Army service uniform, their version of a business suit, turned to face her. Lieutenant Petrie annoyed her on so many levels, not the least of which was his insistence on refusing to wear the same uniform—camo fatigues that she and everyone else did to work in the warehouses.

Petrie nodded at her. "Sergeant Ramsey, do something with him."

"Is that an order, sir?" Debbie opted for her most professional tone but didn't wait for an answer. Instead, she walked across the room, stopping where she'd be in the major's way.

For a moment, she allowed herself to admire how he filled out his fatigues and then met his golden-brown gaze when he swung around to face her. "Excuse me, sir."

"Ramsey, where have you been? Don't you know better than to leave a college-trained, moron in charge of my warehouses? He can't even keep the latrines stocked in toilet paper. It's bull—"

"Major Sinclair!" Debbie exclaimed, keeping a straight face. "You wouldn't swear in front of a lady?"

Red seeped into his rough-hewn features, edging the strong cheekbones and from an earlier time, the broken nose. "Sorry, Ramsey. I forgot you were female." Rex Sinclair ran a hand through his short, salt and pepper hair. "Where were you? That damned Petrie—"

"Major!" One of these days, Sinclair might catch onto the fact that she could out-swear any and all of the soldiers working in the supply company, but luckily, he hadn't yet.

"I'm sorry." Rex repeated his apology and fired a glare in the direction of his so-called aide. "Lieutenant Petrie had me called off the golf course. I had to leave the general before we finished our game, and it made me irritable."

"Yes, sir." Debbie sank her teeth into her bottom lip to keep from laughing. "I'm sure the first lieutenant didn't remember how much the general depends on you, sir."

"Watch it, Ramsey." Humor replaced the anger. "I may have been making a fool of myself, but you don't have enough rank to tell me so."

"It's never stopped me before, sir." She met his gaze and smiled up at him.

He wasn't a big man, only four inches taller than her five feet, six inches, but he carried himself as if he were ten feet tall and bulletproof. Just by looking she could tell he was a warrior in every sense of the word, the kind of man who picked himself up when he was knocked down, ready to fight again. At forty-two, he wasn't a spring chicken, but then again at almost thirty-five, neither was she. No wonder she preferred experience.

She folded her arms. "I don't know what's going on here, sir, but I'll take care of it."

"I know you will." He paused. "Where were you?"

"My current enlistment ends in three days, sir. I was at the Recruiting and Retention Office for my appointment with the noncom in charge there. I asked the lieutenant to let you know if you returned before I did, but—"

Rex nodded. "Did you get everything you wanted in your re-enlistment contract? A bonus, a guarantee that you'll stay here instead of being transferred or sent overseas, a promotion? Do you need me to make some calls to ensure you get everything you want?"

"It will be fine, sir. There's quite a bit of paperwork to finish, so I get what I need, but we can discuss that later." Debbie glanced at the junior officer waiting by the door to his office. "Why don't you get back to your golf game? Like I said, I'm here now and I'll stick around to handle any problems that arise."

"All right." Rex frowned before he stepped around her, his attention on the exit door. "Wait for me to make the command decisions, Ramsey. If the general could discuss this in his office, he would."

"But the two of you can't be overheard on the golf course." Debbie inclined her head. "We both know how this game is played, sir."

"I couldn't do it without you, Ramsey." He flashed the sudden smile that always charmed her, although he didn't realize it. "I'll be back for closing formation. If I'm not—"

"I'll handle it," Debbie repeated.

"Thanks, Ramsey. I can always count on you." Rex started for the door.

"If I'd known how important the game was, I wouldn't have had you paged, Major," Lieutenant Petrie said. "I'm glad Sergeant Ramsey was able to use her womanly wiles to calm the situation."

Before Debbie could respond, Rex did with a bark of sharp laughter. "Ramsey doesn't have any of those, Petrie. She's been in this man's Army longer than you have—almost eighteen years—and has more combat experience. When she tells you to do something, I suggest you try listening to her and actually do it before you end up in a pine box." He strode out the door, closing it behind him.

She could tell that Petrie didn't take the major's recommendation seriously. Little wonder, she preferred Rex Sinclair's rugged, rawboned features to the pretty boy glaring at her who figured he was smarter than anybody else on base. The major was a grown man, and he could certainly take care of himself. He'd proven it in more than one warzone, although she'd spent the tour here watching his proverbial six.

It was a deal they'd made eight years ago, covering each other's backs since neither of them had anyone else they could really trust. Granted, he'd have a fit and fall in it if he knew the rest of the enlisted had disrespectful nicknames for the junior officer. Debbie had corrected them enough that they carefully avoided saying, 'petri-dish' or 'that petty looey,' or 'chickenshit loser' around her.

"I'm sorry I wasn't here to help with the MP's, sir." She wouldn't point out he could have contacted her on her cell phone, and she was far closer to the warehouses than the major. "What's wrong? Did one of the delivery drivers get lost on base?"

"No. Two of Major Sinclair's kids showed up at the front gate and the guards brought them here. Since he hadn't left directions for their visit, I had the major paged. Come to think of it, Master Sergeant, there was nothing you could do."

Irritation at his contempt for her position as the ranking non-commissioned officer swept through her. What had this idiot learned in ROTC at college about sergeants and their business? Obviously, nothing!

Debbie struggled to control her temper. *Sometimes, I feel like Mount Rainier, and I just want to explode. Venting isn't enough.*

Three more days. I can deal with this supercilious jackass for three more days. "Thank you, sir. If you'll do the afternoon walk-through of the warehouse now, sir, I'll deal with this situation, sir."

Before he responded, she entered Major Sinclair's office, careful to close the door behind her. She studied the two girls sitting on the chairs in front of the desk, backpacks and two roller suitcases parked nearby. The closer child, a smaller, younger one had ash-blonde hair. She huddled in her seat, clutching a huge toy bear wearing camo fatigues and combat boots. The other girl was older, a teen in fashionably torn, faded jeans, a pink, ribbed, shrunken t-shirt, and flip-flops. She had shoulder-length, ebony curls.

Debbie waited until the pair had finished giving her a solid onceover.

"Hello, I'm Master Sergeant Ramsey. I'm sorry for all the confusion, but none of us expected you. Did your dad?"

"We wanted to surprise him," the younger child admitted.

"I see." Debbie smiled at her. "That's why I didn't put your visit on the schedule for the warehouse personnel. How nice for him."

"He didn't think so," the older girl snapped, all teen angst. Tears sparkled in the dark brown eyes, so much like her father's. "After the cards and gifts, he sends us, he should have known we wanted to see him regardless of what our mother says."

"He has a lot on his mind." Debbie crossed the room and leaned against the large wooden desk. File cabinets lined two of the walls and the blinds were closed on the windows to block the glare and heat. "The general called him this morning with a special assignment and it's all Major Sinclair can think about right now."

"We don't want to bug him." The little girl sniffled, then wiped at the tears trickling from her sky-blue eyes. "It's just that he hasn't called us back and we don't want to go to boarding school. Our stepdad, Gary, was sending us next week. I don't wanna go to New York by myself or be there all alone."

"Oh, my Gawd," Debbie muttered. This added proof to her private philosophy that no good deed ever went unpunished. When Major Sinclair's divorce was finalized almost eight years before, she'd started a mission of sending the five children appropriate gifts because their father didn't. He blamed them for their mother's errors in judgement regardless of how it made the kids feel.

"I don't understand," Debbie said. "Why would your mom let your stepdad make a decision like that?"

"Because Cal left for college last week with Rory and Scott," the blonde explained, picking at a hole in the knee of her jeans. "And Gary says he's done putting up with us."

"Who are they?" Debbie frowned. The names rang a bell, but she wanted to be sure. "I don't recognize those names."

"Our older brothers." It was the brunette's turn. "Dad stuck all of us with names that begin with the letter, 'R', and our housekeeper, Lupe says it's too confusing, so she mostly calls us by our middle names. Except for Rory, who didn't want to be called by his because he knew too many guys named Dave."

"Well, that will make my life easier." Debbie reached for the box of tissues on the desk and passed it to the younger girl. "And you are?"

"I'm Penny. Roberta Penelope."

The older girl said, "I'm Rebecca Evangeline. Vangie."

"Okay. First things first." Debbie waited while Penny wiped her face. "Let's go have lunch. Your father won't be back for several hours, and I run the warehouses when he's away."

"You're not calling Lupe or our mother or sending us back to California?" Vangie eyed her warily. "Why not?"

"It isn't my place," Debbie explained. "All I'm supposed to handle are the major's professional problems, not his personal ones. Of course, if they affect the situation and the enlisted troops here, I'm afraid I do have to get involved."

"And then what happens?" Penny blew her nose. "Do you call Lupe?"

Debbie shook her head. "No. If I'm enmeshed in your piddly little issues, I fix them in my fashion, and you won't like it. Neither will the major. Luckily for you and your sister, I spent almost three years in a boarding school before I enlisted. I wouldn't recommend a place like it for either of you. I learned quite a few skills I'm sure your father would prefer you didn't know."

"Like what?" Vangie stared at her with obvious fascination. "Will you share them over lunch?"

"Don't be silly. I don't know you well enough to tell you how to hot-wire a car or pick locks or shoplift food, wine, and clothes without being caught on film at eleven." Ignoring the astonished giggles behind her, Debbie led the way from the major's inner sanctum to the outer office. She looked toward the opening door and the lieutenant before spotting the stocky, young man who followed him. "Corporal Baxter, what are you doing here?"

Lieutenant Petrie answered for the enlisted man. "I told him to come back after his dental appointment since you weren't here to answer the phones or check in the deliveries. He needs to do his job."

Debbie counted silently to ten while she listened to the company clerk's garbled speech. If she couldn't understand what he was saying, how would anyone else? "Did you bring back the slip from the clinic like I asked, Baxter?"

Baxter nodded and handed her the paper he held. "Doctor said—"

"I can read, Baxter. No need for gibberish." She winced at the sight of his cheeks, swollen like a chipmunk's from the extractions and the bruise on his jaw. "The dentist has assigned Corporal Baxter to quarters for the next two days, Lieutenant. I'm sending him to the barracks. Major Sinclair doesn't want his people to work if they're not in top shape."

"What about the phones? Who's going to answer them?"

"It's why we have junior enlisted, sir." Debbie focused on meeting Baxter's gaze. "Stop on your way out and tell Sergeant Nelson to send someone here to answer the phones and check bills of lading. I don't want to see you until Friday morning and only if you're able to work. If not, call in and rest up over the weekend."

"Thanks, Sergeant Ramsey."

Lieutenant Petrie glowered at Debbie as the other man hurried from the office, before glancing at the teenager and tween beside her. "And what do you intend to do with Major Sinclair's children?"

"They've had a long trip here, sir. I intend to feed them and then take them to their father's house." She looked over her shoulder at them.

Backpack on one arm, suitcase towed behind them, teddy-bear held tight, Penny pressed close to her older sister's side and Debbie realized the girl was definitely still a child, despite her bravado. Vangie on the other hand had on enough makeup for an entire cheerleading squad, plus three pairs of earrings, a ring in her belly-button, as well as a tiny stud in her nose. "Let's see. Penny, you're—"

"I turned nine two weeks ago. Daddy sent me my Ranger Bear. And Van's fifteen. We'll be okay by ourselves until Daddy gets home, Sergeant Ramsey. We've stayed alone every night since our brothers went to Pullman two weeks ago right after my birthday. Mom and Gary went to Hawaii ages ago for an extended honeymoon and Lupe goes home at six."

"Well, that's over." Debbie lifted her chin, measuring them with her gaze. "I don't believe in leaving kids by themselves. Heaven only knows what could happen."

"How do you expect to get them in the house, Master Sergeant? Do you have a key?"

Actually, she did, but she wasn't telling the lieutenant that. "Don't worry, sir. We should be able to get in with the cleaning service or I'll talk to the neighbors. Major Sinclair arranged for one of the local boys to take care of his new puppy and the cat when he's gone."

That issue resolved, Debbie ushered the girls toward the door. "Thanks for being concerned, sir, but I can handle everything. It's sergeants' business."

"What kind of puppy does my dad have?" Penny asked as soon as they were out of the office. "I love dogs, but Gary's allergic, so we can't have pets anymore. Lupe, Señora Gonzales, the housekeeper had to take my cat home with her."

"That's too bad." Smiling, Debbie lowered her voice to a whisper. "To tell the truth, Shasta doesn't belong to your father. I found her in a parking lot last May and I couldn't abandon her, so I brought her home with me. I can't have her in the BEQ, so she lives with your dad."

Vangie's eyes widened. "That's really nice of him."

"It is." Debbie led the way to the parking lot and her 2014 blue Jeep Wrangler. "I don't know what I'd have done if he hadn't come through for me. I couldn't take Shasta to a shelter."

Vangie nodded. "Dogs die there."

"Exactly," Debbie agreed. "No matter how grouchy your father gets, remember he's a good person. He never hesitates to help out others whenever he can. He didn't owe me or Shasta a damned thing after he took in my tuxedo kitten, Bandit. And your dad would go to hell and back for the three of us."

Penny caught her breath, staring up at Debbie. "You just swore, and you made him apologize when he did it."

"That's because she didn't want him to keep acting like an idiot in front of that jerky lieutenant," Vangie explained. "He's as bad as Gary."

"Does anybody like the lieutenant?" Penny asked. "Why don't you get rid of him, Ramsey?"

"I'd like to." Debbie heaved a sigh as she unlocked the Jeep and waited for the girls to climb inside. "Unfortunately, your father has to sign all the paperwork when someone requests a transfer. He thinks he can make a good officer out of Petrie and he's not willing to give up on the man yet."

Vangie eyed her from the passenger seat. "I bet you have a way around that."

"Of course I do, but I only use it for emergencies." Debbie started the engine. "Forgery was just another life-skill I learned at Celestial Faith Girls Academy for Troubled Teens. Now, what do you want to eat?"

While the girls discussed the fast-food options they'd seen on their cab ride to the base, Debbie focused on the traffic. Damn it! She was due to take over the riding stable bright and early next Monday morning when the new session of horse day camp started. She'd planned to use the weekend to move into her new house.

I don't have time to rescue the major's sorry ass, but I'll just have to embrace the suck and do what needs doing one more time. It's sergeants' business, isn't it?

CHAPTER TWO

Rex Sinclair spotted the dark blue, Jeep Wrangler parked in his driveway as soon as he turned the corner. He wondered what happened with the two girls who insisted they were his daughters. They weren't, of course. His ex-wife Averill had never been faithful. Discretion was beyond her, too. The youngest of the girls was conceived when he was away on a combat tour in Afghanistan. Her older sister was born during a tour in Iraq. The same went for all three of his supposed sons.

They married when he was a freshman in college because Averill was pregnant. He hadn't realized she intended to trap someone she saw as a solid meal ticket. The son of a single mother, Rex had never known his own father. Determined not to be like the man who abandoned him before he was born, Rex adored Rory, their firstborn, spending hours with the baby before he shipped out on one of his first combat tours. He'd been pretty sure their second son was his, but as for the third conceived and born while he was away—*I never wanted to see the kind of woman Averill really was.*

He shook his head, trying to forget the painful memories of the humiliating addiction to his first wife. When he returned from Afghanistan in 2011 after being gone for more than eighteen months, he'd been introduced to the six-month-old baby girl on live television. Pride constrained him to file for an immediate divorce. It helped lower the child support payments and kept Averill from receiving alimony when Rex's lawyer threatened to demand DNA tests on all five kids.

Even if I wasn't actively involved in their lives, I never wanted them to know the heartache I did, so I didn't let the attorney go through with it, but it worked to keep Averill from 'nickel-and-diming' me to death.

He forced away the memory of his stepfather who'd favored his own children over Rex, constantly rejecting him. His mother wouldn't allow anyone to use Rex as a punching bag, but what he went through as a child and teenager made military training in college a breeze. *I certainly didn't expect Averill to allow her various partners to mistreat her children. She didn't grow up in a 'Beaver Cleaver' household either.*

He carefully parked his red Ford 250 next to the Jeep. Switching off the engine, he eased from the pickup and strode toward the back door. He stopped at the sound of childish laughter and a young dog yapping. It seemed he had company, or at least Shasta did.

He headed for the fenced back yard, carefully closing the gate behind him. The tri-colored collie mix bounded across the grass in hot pursuit of her favorite flying disc, gleefully carrying it back to the small blonde girl while her older sister waited for a turn.

Keeping a watchful, albeit amused eye, on the trio was the woman who managed the four warehouses for him. He'd rarely let himself notice how lovely she was in camouflage fatigues and combat boots. Although the regs had changed over the years, she didn't opt for a ponytail. She still kept her long black hair coiled into a neat bun on the back of her head, so it didn't interfere with the camo cap she wore.

He didn't think he made a sound, but he must have since she flicked a quick glance over her shoulder at him, amusement sparking in the electric blue eyes. Allowing the girls to continue romping with the puppy, he went to join the noncom. "Ramsey, who's in charge of the store if you're here?"

"Sergeant Nelson texted and let me know the 1400-hour delivery arrived on time. He expected to have it unloaded before the next one came in at 1600. I reminded Lieutenant Petrie to verify the paperwork for the individual Army reserve units coming to receive supplies. Nelson sent the new reservist, Staff Sergeant Hollister to handle the phones and admin duties in the office."

"He's good on the forklift. Why isn't he helping unload?"

"He's been testing the theory all female soldiers are easy."

"Do you want me to straighten him out?"

"Not yet, sir. Let us handle it in the noncommissioned officer chain of command."

"All right, but if you need backup, say so."

"Will do." A quick smile came his way before she concentrated on the girls and puppy again. "I saw to it your daughters had lunch. We made a trip to the commissary and stocked the cupboards here. You've been loading up on take-out and junk food again, sir."

"I'm a grown man, Ramsey." Her regular lectures always amused him, and he grinned at her. "I cook what I choose when I choose."

"You don't, sir."

"It's a matter of personal choice." He changed the subject. "What did you arrange with my ex?"

"I haven't heard back from her yet, sir. She and her fourth husband apparently flew to Hawaii for an extended honeymoon in June. I left messages with the staff at their condo."

"Say again, Sarge." His good humor faded, and he lowered his voice. "I don't think I got that. Where are the girls supposed to be living?"

"At home in Sacramento." Her tone even and far too calm, she continued speaking, but he noticed the clenched fists. "The housekeeper told me the girls are supposed to leave for boarding school next week. Penny, the younger one, is enrolled in upper New York state and Vangie is going to Chicago. Yesterday, was Señora Gonzales' day off and she didn't realize the girls were missing until I phoned."

"Where did she think they were?"

"Visiting their grandmother, your ex's mom at a nearby nursing home."

"I see." Rex watched the plastic toy fly through the air and Shasta tear after it. "Now, what do I do?"

"I took the liberty of telling the housekeeper to send the girls' belongings here, including Penny's cat. It seems her stepfather foisted it off on the woman and she only took it to keep the animal from going to the pound. I also contacted the schools and told them to refund your deposits."

"Wait a damned minute! Do you mean Averill arranged for me to pay their tuition? I'm not separating those kids. Ramsey, that's bull—"

"Major, don't be inappropriate." She gestured in the direction of the girls. "They could hear you. In addition, when I called the last time, I told the condo staff to tell your ex-wife a lawyer would be in touch."

"Ramsey, you overstepped. I don't want—"

"Major, I suggest we finish this discussion where your daughters won't overhear it." The noncom stalked toward the house, pausing on the patio. "Vangie, Penny, your father and I need to talk in private," she called out. "Keep Shasta here and don't let her out of the yard."

"Sure thing, Ramsey." Vangie answered for both of them. "We can stay with you, can't we, Dad? I don't want Penny in New York by herself."

"We'll work out something." Rex tried to ignore the way the two girls immediately relaxed and turned their attention back to the five-month-old puppy. He reminded himself it didn't matter what they wanted. He wasn't prepared to be more than a support check. His career took up all his time. He made sure of that.

He allowed Debbie Ramsey to enter the upscale kitchen ahead of him and closed the sliding glass doors behind them. "Ramsey, those kids aren't mine. You know it. You were there eight years ago when I fell apart and into a bottle. If you hadn't saved my ass, I wouldn't have a career."

She nodded, leaning against the center island. "True, but we don't have to allow the conversation to descend into crudity, Major. You're right. You owe me and you'll pay the debt to them."

"No way! That's bullshit. You're way over the line. You had no business telling my ex I wanted custody or to involve the housekeeper."

Debbie folded her arms and waited. For an instant, the white-gold ring on her left hand caught his attention, but then his gaze met hers. "Major, I've been rescuing your sorry ass long before the past year when I was assigned to Fort Clark. I don't intend to stop now. You don't want those girls stuck in some boarding school any more than I do."

"If I give their mother more money, she'll keep them. Why do they mean so much to you?"

"I don't know them well enough for them to stir my emotions, Major. You're too good a man to punish innocents for the crimes of their mother. She hurt you. They didn't."

"Damn it, Ramsey! I don't *want* them."

"Major, put your 'want' in one hand. Defecate in the other and see which fills up first. You're their legal father. You *will* do what's right."

"Or what?" He glared down at her. The two of them rarely fought. He couldn't believe she was speaking to him in the same tone he'd heard her use on recalcitrant underlings. "What do you have in mind to make me step up?"

"I'll take this matter to the noncom chain of command on base. If I don't get satisfaction from the military side of the house, then I'll start with the civilian. I *will* get you custody of your children, sir."

"That's blackmail. You wouldn't dare."

"Watch me." She lifted her chin and spaced the next words with careful precision. "Furthermore, I'll see to it that what we did almost eight years ago to protect you when your divorce was final comes out. You're an officer in the United States Army, sir. You'll act like a gentleman and behave accordingly, or you'll wish you had."

"You're a witch."

"You bet, sir. Only in my case, you spell it with a B." She narrowed the dangerous blue eyes. "And you don't want to see me do magick, sir."

He took two steps toward her and caught her chin in hard fingers. When he stared down into her eyes, he almost felt like he was drowning. "Be careful, Ramsey. Don't threaten me. I'm not afraid of what you could dish out. The past is a double-edged sword."

"There's nothing you can do to me that hasn't already been done, sir."

"Oh really?" He tipped up her chin even farther. "Are you positive about that?"

"Definitely. I spent nearly three years in a boarding school before I enlisted. I don't care what happens to me." She yanked free of his hold and backed a step. "I've got to get back to work. The girls are staying with you."

"Wrong, Ramsey. As soon as I get hold of their mother, they're going home. Don't worry. I'll see to it they aren't sent to boarding school." He held up a hand to stop any interruptions. "As for you, Master Sergeant, get your reenlistment squared away. The general has a special assignment for me and I'm flying to Texas on Saturday morning. You're running the warehouses while I'm gone."

"And if I don't?"

"You won't like it if I get mad at you, Ramsey."

"I'm not afraid of your tantrums. I've been cleaning up behind them forever. It started when I met you in 2011 and that wasn't a walk in the proverbial park either, not when you spent more time at the Officer's Club than you did at your desk."

"I've never rained all over your parade before. Since I seem to have company, I'll expect you and Petrie to close up shop today. I'll see you at 0600 hours for PT."

"Yes, sir!" Turning, she marched out the back door, pausing long enough to speak to the girls and then petting the puppy.

When he walked out into the yard, the younger girl eyed him. "Daddy, you didn't involve Sergeant Ramsey in what she calls 'our piddly little problems,' did you?"

He had to think for a second to recall her name. "What are you talking about...Roberta?"

"Penny. I like that name better. She warned us earlier. If she has to fix things, none of us will like it."

To his amazement, Rex found himself patting the child's shoulder while the gold, black and white puppy flopped on the grass nearby, chewing on the edge of the heavy-duty doggie toy. "Don't worry, honey. Ramsey always follows my orders."

"Sure." This time, it was the older teen who spoke, barely repressing a smirk. "You shouldn't have pissed her off. Now, we're all in trouble."

Rex was amused at how well the pair of them had come to know his master sergeant in only a matter of hours. "I've worked with Ramsey a long time." He smiled patiently at the two girls. "Believe me, she never loses control."

"Vangie didn't say Sergeant Ramsey would start yelling 'bullshit' like you do, Daddy," Penny said. "And she won't get mad."

"She'll get even," Vangie finished, "especially since she told us she learned how to hold a grudge in boarding school. Did you know she hasn't called or written or visited her family in twenty years?"

"Why on earth wouldn't they want to see her? Ramsey is wonderful even when—"

"She's the one who told them to F. off and die," Vangie said. "She stopped talking to them after they sent her away when she was fifteen."

"Watch your language, Rebecca Evangeline. Don't tell me Ramsey swore in front of you. That's impossible."

The two girls studied him with knowing looks. "Yes, she did," Penny finally said. "But it wasn't until some jerk cut her off in traffic. She cusses worse than Gary's dad and he's a long-line trucker."

"Now, I know you're exaggerating." Rex chuckled. "How did you know where I was stationed?"

"We're not dumb, Daddy. You sent me a card and fifty bucks for my birthday, but I really didn't need an Army Ranger bear," Penny said.

Vangie rolled her eyes. "Then why do you sleep with it, Penny? We almost had to buy it a ticket at the bus station until I promised you'd keep it on your lap, and it didn't need a seat."

"Don't pick on your sister or I won't notice when she returns the favor about your birthday present." The comment was a shot in the dark, but by the way the younger girl wrinkled her nose and the older one glowered, he'd struck paydirt. He'd learn what the gift was later. If he was cautious, he'd also find out why these kids–these two strangers–thought he walked on water and how Ramsey arranged that.

Rex gestured toward the back deck. "Let's put Shasta inside and we'll go have pizza."

"You're not angry with us for coming here?" Vangie asked cautiously.

"I never was mad at you two." It wasn't a hundred percent accurate, he thought, but it was close enough for government work. "I was annoyed because Lieutenant Petrie called me off the golf course and made me look bad in front of my boss."

Penny nodded sympathetically. "Sergeant Ramsey was annoyed too when he made that sick soldier come to work, but she didn't holler, 'bull-shit,' at him."

Rex focused on the important part of the statement. "Who is sick?" He pulled out his cell phone. "Let me call Ramsey before I check on patients at the base hospital."

"Baxter wasn't sick, sick," Vangie hastily clarified. "He had a lot of dental work, and his cheek was all bruised and swollen. Sergeant Ramsey said since he couldn't talk, he couldn't work. She told the lieutenant she was sending Baxter home to rest because he had a note from the doctor."

"To quarters," Rex said, replacing his phone in his pocket. "Ramsey always takes care of our people first and I'll remind Petrie he should do that tomorrow morning. Now, pizza!"

On the way back to the warehouse, Debbie relaxed her tight grip on the steering wheel, trying to calm down. The situation with the girls brought back too many memories. She glanced at the rings she wore on her left hand. There had been times when she wore them on her right hand and times in combat, when she wore them around her neck on a chain with her dog tags. She took a moment to rub the heart-shaped sapphire. As always, the antique claddagh ring set comforted her. *I'm safe. Nobody will ever hurt me again.*

She'd been devastated when her father turned on her nearly twenty years before, blaming her for what happened on the way home from school one bright, sunny, Montana afternoon. *I was the victim, damn it, not one of the perpetrators, but I was the one he and the Celestial Faith community punished. I won't let Rex Sinclair become a monster in his daughters' nightmares.*

Between the gated community where Major Sinclair lived and the ware-houses on post was Army headquarters. She had a good working relation-ship with the Command Sergeant-Major, the senior ranking noncommissioned officer. Shortly after she arrived at Fort Clark, he'd been accused of sexual harassment after correcting a particularly obnoxious female Army reservist for unprofessional behavior. Debbie had seen the incident and testified on the man's behalf. Her truthful account of the scene had been the catalyst needed to have the charges dropped and ultimately saved the noncom's career.

Debbie signaled for a turn into the parking lot at HQ. Obviously, she'd have to show one egotistical, arrogant officer she meant business. *Whether Sinclair likes it or not, he's going to man up. I'll see to that!*

Streamers of gold, red and orange sunlight lit the dawn sky when she parked in front of the warehouse early the next morning. She climbed out of the Jeep, stretched, and glanced toward Mount Rainier, out today in all its snow-capped glory. Lights shone from the office windows, and she automatically headed for the stairs. Had Major Sinclair already arrived?

Inside, she found Lieutenant Petrie cleaning out his desk and stacking his belongings in a cardboard box. He eyed her and then looked anxiously at the clock above the door again. "Good morning, Master Sergeant."

Debbie nodded a greeting. "Good morning, sir. Is something wrong?"

"Not really. I've been reassigned to the supply unit on the other side of the base. I'm scheduled to report at six a.m., in less than twenty minutes, and I still have to clean out my locker in the break area."

"Go now, sir. I'll arrange to have the rest of your property brought over after PT, sir, and formation this morning. You don't want to start off on the wrong foot with your new commander, sir."

Relief eased some of the tension on the young man's face. "That would be a big help. Thank you, Sergeant Ramsey."

"It's my job, sir." Debbie adopted her gentlest, sweetest tone and tried for what she hoped was her most sincere smile. "Don't worry, sir. I'll keep looking after you while you're still an officer here."

"Thanks again." Carrying the box, he hustled out of the office, brushing by a tall, tanned woman wearing fatigue pants and an olive-drab t-shirt. She was hurriedly braiding her long, mahogany red hair.

"Who was that, Ramsey?" The newcomer continued working on her hair. "So, who did you have to kill to get me reassigned here? If I had to work with Major Ghost one more day, I'd have gone old school and nailed the son-of-a—"

"Why, Gimone Nolan," Debbie interrupted. "How can you say such a heinous thing?" She widened her eyes and opted for her most innocent look. "I'd say your transfer was pure serendipity."

"Pull the other one. I know you too well." Gimone finished the braid, securing it with an elastic band. "What's on the agenda this morning, Master Sergeant Machiavelli?"

Debbie ignored the nickname. "Exercises and a five-mile run." She cast a quick glance at the clock. "Where's Captain Castaneda?"

"Not here yet." Gimone's green eyes narrowed. "Now, I know you've been up to no good. How on earth did you wrest Juana away from Major Ghost? Who do you know with that kind of power, and what kind of blackmail did you use?"

Debbie tried harder to paste on an aura of someone pure of heart and free of malice. She doubted it'd work on her old friend. She and Gimone had survived nearly three horrific years at the Celestial Faith boarding school, and they were closer than most sisters.

Footsteps sounded outside on the tile floor and Rex Sinclair strode into the office, glancing at both of them. "Good morning, Ramsey. Is PT taking place here?"

"No such luck." Debbie smiled and prayed it appeared angelic. "Major, this is Sergeant First Class, Gimone Nolan."

Gimone easily took over the introduction. "Sir, I've been reassigned to your section effective immediately. When I spoke with Master Sergeant Ramsey, she told me to come in time for PT at 0600 hours."

Another long, slow, measured look from the man before he folded his arms and waited by the door. "I didn't know we had any senior noncom slots available, Ramsey. What's going on?"

"One of the things you and I will discuss later, sir." Debbie started toward the exit. "The company will be assembling outside. It's time for PT."

"Wait one second, you little manipulator," Gimone snapped. "If I get stuck with Major Ghost again, I'll be up on charges when I kill the man. What's my job?"

"Come on, Gimone. I haven't even told Major Sinclair yet and you know I'd never screw you."

"Or Juana? What's her job?"

"That's easy." Debbie shrugged and deliberately kept her attention on the taller woman. "She and Lieutenant Petrie received a lateral transfer. He'll be working for Major Bevins and she's coming here as Major Sinclair's executive officer."

"And Sergeant Nolan?" Rex leisurely crossed the room to block the exit. "Does she get Nelson's job? Did you wave a magick wand and get rid of him?"

"Of course not!" Debbie retorted. "I'd never do that, not unless he asked and only if I couldn't talk him out of it." She stopped, trapped by her own tongue.

Rex inclined his head in mocking salute. "All this because I challenged you yesterday, Ramsey?" He gestured toward his office. "Wait there for me. I told you to reenlist, not to throw away your military career."

"What about PT?" Debbie protested.

"I'm sure the two folks you finagled to get here will be able to handle it without us." His deep voice took on an edge. "My office, Ramsey. You have ten minutes to come up with your excuses. I'll be back to hear them after I introduce Sergeant Nolan and Captain Castaneda to the company."

Gimone suddenly looked anxious. "Major, I know Sergeant Ramsey didn't mean any harm."

"It may come as a surprise to you, Sergeant, but I understand Ramsey's motivation perfectly." Rex ushered Gimone out the door. He glanced over his shoulder. "You heard my order, Ramsey. Obey it."

CHAPTER THREE

While she waited, Debbie paced the office, dreading the upcoming scene. Although she fully intended to leave the military, she hadn't anticipated breaking the news to Rex Sinclair in this manner. *It's really not my fault. He forced the issue, not me.* She wished she could have waited until after PT when she'd be wearing a fresh uniform and combat boots, instead of old fatigue pants, a tank-top over her sports bra, and running shoes.

She drew a ragged breath, crossed to the windows. Other than the vehicles, the parking lot was empty. The waiting soldiers had departed under the guidance of Gimone, and Juana. The company wouldn't return from Physical Training, or PT for more than an hour.

"Escape won't work, Ramsey." Rex closed the door behind him. "I know where you live." He remained there, leaning against the doorframe. "Okay, start talking. When did you decide to leave me in the lurch?"

"It's not like that," Debbie protested. "You can get by without me. You had for two years before I was transferred here after my last combat tour. Granted, we video-conferenced, emailed, and called each other when we were apart, but we've never depended on being joined at the hip."

"All right." He nodded. "The Army moved both of us around a lot and I can accept the fact neither of us knew when we'd be stationed together. Why do you think you're getting away with this stunt?"

"No stunt, Major. I was offered an early out. The Army's going to pay me to retire now instead of working for three more years."

"And you suddenly decided to take that option when I refused to let you run my life yesterday?" He arched a dark eyebrow. "Let me tell you what happens next, Ramsey. You call the Retention NCO in charge and tell him you've changed your mind. You'll take a hefty bonus, a guarantee that you'll stay here instead of being transferred or sent overseas, and a promotion.

"Today's Thursday and I want that paperwork signed ASAP or I'll make some calls to be sure you have everything you deserve. I'm going to Fort Sam Houston on Saturday and I'm not leaving my warehouses with a new noncom and XO."

"What if I don't?" Debbie lifted her chin and met his golden-brown gaze. "You can't make me reenlist, not when I'm happy to retire."

"If you're not ready to take charge, Ramsey, I'll put an advertisement in the base newspaper and announce what we did in 2011 thirty days after my divorce was final from Averill. Granted, we don't have a conventional relationship and we've been discreet when we have casual hook-ups. I may get some heat for fraternization, but I can handle it better than you will. There's still a double standard in the military."

"You wouldn't dare." She planted her fists on her hips. "I'll deny it."

"I'm the one who kept the original paperwork. You had a copy." A smile filtered across his face, landed in his eyes. "It was my safety net. With the way you kept in contact with all five of my legal children, who do you think everyone will believe?"

"Not you." She fell back a step when he advanced on her. She knew her voice sounded weak. Damn it. All the care she'd taken of him would add even more evidence against her. "You can't keep me here."

"Sure, I can." His smile broadened. "It's your choice, Ramsey. Do we go public? Or keep our private lives under wraps?"

She glared up at him. "I could file for divorce then. That will work."

"Not if I fight it." His deep tones took on the lazy, southern drawl of his youth. "Face it, Ramsey. You're stuck worse than a cow in quicksand. You're not going anywhere except to the retention office and sticking around a while longer."

"You arrogant son of a—"

"Now, now, Ramsey. Remember how you feel about profanity."

That did it! She cut loose with the foul language she'd learned during seventeen years in the military. She described his appearance, attitude, and mental capacity in terms she knew he'd understand. She was proud of the fact she didn't say "bullshit" once.

When she paused for breath, he grinned down at her. "You didn't learn that kind of language at your momma's knee, Ramsey. We're lucky we're not outside."

"What the hell does that have to do with anything?"

"You'd make it cloud up with those words." He took a step closer and lowered his head, his breath warm on her lips. "Let me add one more thing. If you decide to bring our marriage out in the open, you'll be in my house and bed for good. And I already know how much you like long, slow nights when I take my time with you."

"No way!" She stepped away from him, coming to a stop when he gripped her shoulders. "I wouldn't have you if you were hung with diamonds, Major."

"Then, you'll re-up?"

"Anything other than live with you! How do you plan to keep me from requesting a transfer?"

"I'm the one who has to sign the paperwork, remember?" His gaze narrowed. "How did you get by that requirement with Petrie?"

"The same way I do when I write to your children. I sign your name better than you do, Major."

He chuckled. "You're a spitfire, Ramsey."

"Damn straight!"

He feathered a thumb over her lips, and she shuddered at the light touch. "Don't."

"Fine. We're even, but if you act like my wife, I'll treat you as if you are."

"Thanks for the warning." She refused to let him see that her feelings for him included a strong physical attraction. She'd undoubtedly given away too much on their nights together. "You bastard."

"You know it better than anyone." He brushed his mouth over hers. "Do I have a wife or a noncom in charge of my warehouses?"

"You win." She gritted out the words. "I already said that. What am I supposed to tell Nolan?"

"Let her stay for a month while we get through the reserve units' summer training and our end of the fiscal year inspections. After that, I'll find her a position where she can get an immediate promotion and a decent commander."

"Better than what I've got."

He laughed. "Shrew."

"That's 'Master Sergeant Shrew' to you." Debbie pulled out of his grasp. "What about Penny and Vangie? What happens to them?"

"You look after them until their mother picks them up when she returns from her trip to Hawaii."

"Whatever you say, sir." Debbie stalked toward the door. She'd make him pay for his arrogance. How dare he try to tell her how to live her life or think he'd get away with blackmailing her? Their marriage was pretty much 'in name only' despite their occasional rendezvous, and it wasn't changing because of his whims. And what made him think his daughters were disposable? It was strictly pay-back time, and she was the woman who'd see to it Major Rex Sinclair got what he had coming.

She headed toward the parking lot to collect her uniform from the Jeep. She'd swear Gimone and Juana to secrecy when they had dinner tonight. The military moved people around all the time and most of the enlisted already expected her to be transferred out soon, since she'd only been assigned here for a year. An immediate trip to Texas meant Sinclair would spend most of tomorrow at HQ dealing with the logistics. She'd make her farewells to the company once he'd headed off to his meetings. He'd learn not to mess with her.

Friday night, he'd taken the girls out for dinner and to a movie so they wouldn't notice Ramsey wasn't around, doing the 'least in sight' routine. The drive back to the house provided the opportunity for him to share the plans for their future, that they'd be going back to California with their mother.

Neither girl appeared too surprised by his decision. Penny cried silently in the back seat of the truck the rest of the way home until he parked next to the Jeep Wrangler already in the driveway. When he opened the rear door to the Ford's super cab, she shoved past him, not allowing him to comfort her, running toward the back yard.

Vangie looked him up and down, scorn apparent. "You really are a jerk. No wonder the boys told us it wouldn't do any good to ask you for help, that the Army means more to you than any of us do."

He reached for her. "Now, wait just a moment."

She didn't. She stormed after her sister.

Rex locked the truck and followed the pair. When he arrived in the backyard, he saw Debbie Ramsey sitting on the deck, Shasta pressing close while Penny sobbed in the woman's arms. The puppy whined and tried to lick the little girl's face but couldn't reach it. The noncom had opted for civvies tonight, a purple t-shirt tucked into faded blue jeans. Her long black hair swung loose.

It took a moment and then he recalled she took the half-grown dog to obedience classes on Friday evenings. She usually stuck around afterwards, and they'd discuss the week's events at the warehouse, occasionally over a bottle of wine, but more frequently over cups of strong coffee and her favorite *Bailey's Irish Cream*. Often, those nights ended in bed, but not always.

Debbie continued to stroke Penny's fair hair and murmur soft reassurances before glancing at him. "I'd say you've done enough damage, Major. You'd better go pack for your trip tomorrow morning. I'll clean up this mess, too."

He winced at the contempt in her tone. "Ramsey, I—"

"You don't want to hear any of my other suggestions, sir. They'll start with you should have kept your pants zipped back in the day or invested in a boatload of condoms or—" Her gaze swept over him. "Then again, you could have asked your doctor for a vasectomy."

The icy insults brought laughter from Vangie, who promptly joined the other two females on the steps. She picked up the puppy to cuddle the collie mix who immediately snuggled close. "Ramsey, you're the best."

"I hope you continue to think so." Debbie rocked Penny gently. "You do realize I'll have to become involved in your 'piddly little problems' now."

"The major says he's sending us away to our mother next week," Vangie informed her.

"Really?"

He took a step toward her. "I told you that yesterday morning in the office, Ramsey."

"And I told you to go pack. Leave your daughters to me."

He could say as a commissioned officer, he outranked her, and he was in charge, but he had a feeling it wouldn't go over well when the three of them joined forces against him. He felt oddly grateful she hadn't shared the fact he probably wasn't the girls' biological father, but he certainly wasn't going to admit it. Instead, he went through the glass doors into the open-concept dining room and from there to the hallway that led to the master bedroom.

Two hours later, carrying a bottle of Oregon Pinot Noir and two glasses, he returned to find her sitting alone on the deck in the moonlight. "Where are the girls?"

"I sent them to bed. Penny wanted to sleep with Shasta, and I didn't think it'd hurt her or the dog."

He nodded and poured two glasses of wine. "They're nearly as pissed off at me as you are."

"Well, you're the big man in charge. I'm sure you'll find a way to deal with their heartbreak." She took the glass of red wine, swirled the liquid for a moment and then sipped. "You never did tell me about your new assignment. Do you feel like sharing, or is it top secret?"

"Not from you." He sat down beside her on the wooden steps. "It is from everyone else, but I've always trusted you to have my six."

"That hasn't changed." She lifted the glass to her lips. "It never will. Tell me about it. What are we doing?"

He shifted nearer so their shoulders bumped and lowered his voice. "Two weeks ago, six hostages escaped from South America, all military—"

Early the next afternoon, he frowned at the two girls and the woman who sat silently waiting for him to leave on the Air Force flight to Texas. Vangie and Penny hadn't spoken to him once today, not even on the drive to the airport on base. His daughters wore their favorite jeans and t-shirts while Debbie was back in her ACUs, the camouflage work clothes soldiers wore constantly. Despite their late-night conversation at his house, he knew Master Sergeant Ramsey was still annoyed because he insisted she remain in the Army and finish a twenty-year obligation. She hadn't been happy about meeting them here, but she also hadn't refused to obey a direct order.

"I'll stay in touch with you girls," Rex said.

"Don't bother." Vangie tossed her head. "Next time, Ramsey writes us, she can tell us if you do anything we 'need to know.'"

He grimaced, recognizing the term she must have heard either him or the master sergeant use. He glanced at the noncommissioned officer who didn't look up from the magazine she was reading. "Did you—?"

"Ramsey didn't have to tell us anything." Penny glared at him. "We're not stupid, *Major*. She's the only one who's given a damn about us since we arrived."

"Watch your language, Penny." Debbie kept her gaze on the periodical about decorating houses. "Major Sinclair, your flight has been delayed more than once because of the early morning fog. Do you have some objection if we leave now? I really need to check on the reservists working at the warehouse today."

"Ramsey, things have run smoothly since you arranged for Captain Castaneda and Sergeant Nolan to join our team two days ago. If they need your help, I'm sure they'll text you." He leaned closer so the girls wouldn't overhear. "Let's have brunch. Maybe if they see you setting a good example, then my daughters will remember their manners."

"Whatever you say, sir." Debbie stood. "Come along, ladies. Let's go freshen up. Maybe we'll get lucky, and your father will have left by the time we return."

"Watch it!" His warning was of little use since the three of them quickly walked away leaving him alone.

———

Debbie waited until they were in the restroom. "All right. Enough is enough. All of us are furious with the major, but we won't win by being nasty. He'll think he's justified for being an incredible ass-hat."

"I knew you didn't want us to go to California." Penny grabbed Debbie in a fierce hug. "I knew it when you said last night you were going to get involved. I knew it!"

"So, what are you doing, Ramsey?" Vangie asked. "Are you stealing us?"

"In a way," Debbie admitted, "but it's all—" She paused for a moment to consider how to phrase the news, how to bring them into the loop. "Your dad and I are married."

"What?" Vangie demanded. "When?"

"Almost eight years ago, when your parents' divorce was final."

"Well, then why haven't we been living with you?" A look of fury darkened the brown eyes so much like her father's. "What the hell is going on? Why haven't we heard about this before?"

"You could have told us when we got here," Penny added. The fact that she hadn't reacted before her sister revealed how surprised she was by the news.

"We're combat soldiers and there's still a war going on. Marriage solved big problems for both of us at the time. I know we have a lot to work out, but I've always been good at logistics." Life would be easier for the girls if they believed she and Sinclair had a sincere attachment. "Once your dad leaves for Texas, we're bugging out, too."

Vangie stared at her. "You're a soldier. Won't you be in big trouble?"

"We don't want that," Penny said. "We'll go with our mom and Gary. The major already told her we can't be separated or go to boarding school."

"No problem here." Debbie held up her hand, touched by their willingness to sacrifice themselves to save her even if they were obviously shocked by what she'd shared. "My enlistment ended last night, or rather this morning at midnight. I'd already be gone to my new home if you weren't here, and if your father hadn't tried blackmailing me into reenlisting. There won't be any repercussions from the Army."

"What if Mom says you abducted us?" Vangie asked.

"She can't. I have your father's power of attorney and I contacted the lawyer who handles my business. She's going for full custody and has already started the paperwork."

Vangie and Penny gaped at her, awestruck.

"It's real," Penny whispered. "We're not going back to Mom's."

"No, you're not. Señora Gonzales is sending your belongings as well as your brothers' stuff to my new house. One of my friends is picking up your cat at the airport today. I've tried to take care of everything. What have I missed?"

"Our brothers," Vangie said. "We can call them when we get to your place."

"Okay." Debbie ushered them in the direction of the door. "Now, what do you say? Let's go charm your father with our wit and good manners. Then he'll really miss all of us when we're gone."

Penny giggled and caught Debbie's hand. "Do we have to keep calling you by your last name?"

"No. My first name is Debbie, but nobody's called me that in ages. I may forget to answer."

"Then, we'll remind you." Vangie smiled at her. "We're going to be a family. Can the boys come visit?"

"On school breaks. They can't cut their classes." Debbie led the way across the lounge to where Rex waited.

He eyed them warily. "I'm glad you're back. My flight's just been called."

"Let's wait and see if it's real before we go to the café," Debbie said.

"Good idea." He turned his attention toward the girls. "I'm sorry you didn't get what you wanted, but I have a lot happening right now and I don't have time to take proper care of you two girls."

"It's okay," Vangie told him. "Mom will probably dump Gary before too much longer and her next husband might be a better father."

"Yeah," Penny agreed. With a mischievous glint in her eye, she added, "Of course, if Debbie finds a husband, she might have room for us."

Debbie sighed. Expecting the pair to totally give up sniping at him had probably been too high a goal. She glanced over her shoulder as a young airman approached and gestured to the waiting luggage. "It seems your flight is really leaving. Have a safe trip, sir."

Rex turned toward her. "I'll call you, Ramsey."

"On my cell phone, sir. I'm not sure where I'll be babysitting your daughters." She focused on them. "Kiss your dad goodbye. Heaven knows when you'll see him again. He's not big on communication."

"There's that sharp tongue, Ramsey." He shook his head.

She waited while Vangie kissed his cheek and Penny hugged him. "Enjoy the reprieve, sir."

He nodded and turned away, following the young man with his suitcase and garment bag.

"Wow, we did it." Penny giggled in excitement. "I'm starving, Ramsey. I mean, Debbie. Can we stop to eat before we go to your house?"

Debbie glanced at her watch. "We'll find a drive-through on the way to the motel where I stayed last night. The moving crew will be at your dad's house in two hours, and we've got a lot of work to do."

As they headed for the main doors of the airport lounge, Vangie asked, "Why are movers coming?"

"Because the antiques in the house are mine. I inherited them when my grandfather died three years ago. Your dad said if he could use them, I wouldn't have to pay storage fees and he wouldn't have to keep renting furniture."

"That was decent of him. I don't get it," Vangie said. "Why is he so nice to everyone in the Army when he doesn't have any time for us?"

"We aren't really his kids," Penny answered. "I told you before. So did RC."

"You two always lie. Why would he pay child support for us when all it'd take is DNA tests to prove we're not his? He pays for the boys' tuition and all their stuff at Washington State University in Pullman, too."

"He's a good guy. It's the same reason he told Ramsey to find us presents for our birthdays and the holidays and to have the guys come here to go to college."

They'd obviously figured it out. "He didn't have to make me." Debbie ushered the two girls in the direction of the parking lot. "I wanted to send gifts to you kids, and it made perfect sense to let your brothers use your dad's address to attend W.S.U. Tuition costs less for residents of Washington State."

She took a deep breath. Would her plans for a new life work? Or, once Rex Sinclair learned how she'd tricked him, would he retaliate with a new scheme of his own?

CHAPTER FOUR

As the three of them crossed the parking lot toward the Jeep, Debbie eyed the younger girl. "Who told you that pack of nonsense about you and your sibs, Penny?"

"Mom and Gary. I kept bugging them about living with the major. They said I wasn't even his kid, so he wouldn't take me."

Debbie stopped on the sidewalk, tears stinging. She pulled Penny into her arms, hiding her face in the child's hair. "Did you talk to the major about this?"

"We only arrived on Wednesday, and he had to work Thursday and Friday, so we didn't have time to bring up the really important stuff before he said he was calling our mom," Vangie explained.

"But he did take us out for dinner and to the movies," Penny said, snuggling close to Debbie. "He got us cell phones too because he wanted us to be able to reach him when we called. He told us he was sorry that he didn't actually get our messages before. They were bounced all around the base instead of coming to you or him."

"Did he treat the two of you the same way?" Debbie glanced over her shoulder at Vangie. "Or differently?"

"Pretty much the same, but Mom and Gary said Van isn't his either."

"Yes, she is." Debbie framed Penny's face with her hands. "Didn't you notice their hair is the same color?"

"No, it's not. The major's hair is going gray."

"Yes, but the black part is the same." Debbie felt a smile tremble into life. "Vangie has the same bone structure as your dad. Thank heaven, she has your mom's nose, not your father's."

"That'd be awful," Penny agreed.

"Maybe not," Vangie argued, coming to stand beside them. "Mine wouldn't be broken. How did Dad break his?"

"An ambush in Iraq," Debbie said. "He and his patrol hit an IED on a road on one of his first combat tours." She hugged Penny again, then straightened. "Come on. Let's find lunch."

The girls were quiet while they drove off the Air Force base and onto the freeway. Finally, in the passenger seat, Vangie spoke. "Dad's gone to war a lot, hasn't he? That's really why he hasn't come to visit, isn't it?"

"Yes, you can't have a war for almost twenty years without soldiers going to fight." Debbie concentrated on her driving. "When he came back from Afghanistan in 2011, your mom introduced him to Penny who was six months old. He was so upset your mom hadn't been faithful to him when he was in combat, he filed for divorce right away."

"Do you think he'd have changed his mind if he hadn't married you?" Vangie continued.

"No, but if your mom hadn't fought him on visitation, he'd have spent more time with you when he was stateside. He's a good officer, but he's still lost soldiers in combat, and it makes him afraid to admit when he needs someone."

"He tells you and he doesn't want you to leave the Army."

"Only because I take a lot of grief off his shoulders." Debbie changed lanes and headed for the exit. "At least it's what he claims. He doesn't even tell me what he really feels."

"That's sad." Tears clogged Vangie's voice. "No wonder he wants to send us away. If he got to know us again, he'd realize he still cares about us."

"Exactly." Debbie turned right and headed for the row of fast-food restaurants. "I don't want you girls to have any illusions that he'll come charging after us when he returns and realizes we're gone. It's too big of a risk. He won't be ready to take it for a while."

"We can handle it," Penny said firmly from the back seat. "At least now we know it wasn't our fault he went away. He does love us, or he wouldn't be so scared."

Debbie pulled into a parking lot halfway down the block where they'd be able to choose between different options of quick meals. She knew precisely what the major would say if he'd heard the story she wove for the girls. "Ramsey, you'll go to hell for lying."

It'd torn her apart when her father disowned her. She couldn't believe it when her mother went along with his decision to send her to the Celestial Faith Girls Academy for Troubled Teens near Spokane, Washington. He always claimed to know what was best for everyone, including her, but she'd stopped believing him when he blamed her for being assaulted. *I was fifteen and it wasn't my fault those boys raped me that day or that I ended up pregnant. How did he expect me to stop four of them?*

She wouldn't allow Rex Sinclair to commit the crimes her parents had. Vangie and Penny would be certain their dad loved them even if he was too insecure to show it, too traumatized after six combat tours.

Debbie switched off the Jeep's engine. He wouldn't come after them. He'd view her departure as a betrayal of his trust, and he'd find that an unforgiveable sin.

I'll be thirty-five in September. I can handle his rejection. Vangie and Penny can't. Well, at least I won't let them.

Later that afternoon, Debbie watched the moving truck carrying her belongings leave the gated community and head north. Then she finished loading the Jeep, easing a third suitcase beside the two already secured in the back.

She turned when she saw a small Ford Ranger pull up next to the curb and smiled when she recognized Gimone in the passenger seat and Juana behind the wheel. Waving to her friends, Debbie went to greet them. It was one of the few times she'd worn civvies, jeans, a t-shirt and running shoes while others were in uniform. *It's a brand-new world for me.*

"How's life as a civilian?" Gimone popped out of the truck, then opened the back door to remove a cat carrier. "Here's your roomie. I picked her up when the reservists were at lunch."

"Not mine." Debbie peeked in the crate door and admired a long-haired, seal-point Siamese mix napping on a blanket. "Mocha belongs to Penny, Major Sinclair's youngest daughter."

Juana Castaneda, a petite, dark-haired woman wearing camouflage fatigues and combat boots, came around the back of the truck. "Speaking of which, what's the plan for those girls? They can't stay here by themselves while the major's out of town on temporary duty in Texas. I know you told us about your plans to bring your new riding stable into the 'now', but you never said anything about them."

"They're going with me." Debbie took the carrier from Gimone and headed back to her Jeep. "I've got it covered. Don't worry."

Juana followed her. "Worrying is what I do best, Ramsey. I've been covering your butt since we were kids back in the day. Did the major give you permission to take his daughters with you?"

"Not really." Debbie placed the carrier on the back seat. "I do have his power of attorney."

"Whoa. How did you manage that, Ms. Machiavelli?" Gimone demanded. "You've retired so I can't call you a master sergeant anymore."

"He gave it to me six years ago when he was shipping out to Afghanistan, and he has mine." Debbie hesitated, then decided to share the rest of the story. "Sinclair was always hooked on his ex. Even when counseling didn't work, and she didn't stop cheating on him, he didn't plan to divorce her—"

Gimone frowned. "What changed things?"

"Having the TV reporters show him meeting his infant daughter on the news when he'd been gone eighteen months."

"That'd do it all right," Gimone whistled softly. "What else happened? Why did he give you his power of attorney?"

"Because I started working for him back in 2011, and he was drunk more often than he was sober." Feeling her phone vibrate, Debbie pulled it from her pocket and, without bothering to check the screen, switched it off. "We had the proverbial 'come to Jesus' discussion and he promised to straighten up and fly right if I could guarantee him that he wouldn't return to her."

"What, or who, did he think you were?" Juana demanded. "Gunga-din? Nobody could arrange that."

"I did." Debbie looked at each of her friends in turn. "I married him thirty days after his divorce was final. Do you think I wore these rings for fun? They belonged to his grandmother and his ex-wife never wanted them. She said they were too old-fashioned."

"O.M.G, are you serious, Ramsey?" Juana gaped at her. "Why would you do that?"

"I had my reasons." Debbie drew a deep breath. "My grandparents. When we aged out of Celestial Faith Academy, they were still trying to get my horse away from my family. It took a few years, but they managed it. My dad sold her to them when he was low on cash one spring. Of course, as Grandpa said, they didn't count on the handsome stranger stud next door jumping the fence and getting with Hobby one spring. The colt was the result."

"Your Hobby horse?" Gimone stared at her. "I knew you kept her and her son at different barns on the Army bases where you were stationed. Did Sinclair help with that?"

Debbie nodded. "He went and picked them up for me after Grandpa was diagnosed with terminal pancreatic cancer three years ago. I couldn't go because our unit was shipping out."

"You could have asked for compassionate leave and stayed behind," Juana said, putting an arm around Debbie's shoulders. "I'd have signed off on it for you."

"And then you and Nolan would be in the *sandbox* without me to watch your backs." Debbie shook her head. "No way, Castaneda. We're the *Three Musketeers*, all for one and one for all. Grandma and Grandpa understood. She'd waited for him to come back from 'Nam and, like he told me, he could do chemo without me. They'd let me know when I was needed. I came home for the last month."

"Well, the proverbial apple doesn't fall far from that tree." Gimone stepped up on Debbie's other side. "I'm sorry about your grandpa, but I'm glad you had somebody to help you if we couldn't be there."

"Thanks. Me too. I knew Grandma and Grandpa wouldn't share my new name with anyone from the community in Montana, but I still didn't want to take any chances. So, if I was stateside, I looked after Rex's affairs when he was overseas. When he got back, he looked after mine when I went."

"Did you two ever live together?" Juana narrowed her gaze. "Does anybody know your secret?"

"It's a marriage of convenience. We hook up occasionally, but we're careful, so nobody on base finds out," Debbie said. "The girls know, and now you two do. Other than that, only my lawyer, Bree Hawke does. Sinclair will probably have a fit and fall in it because he says he's too busy to be a dad, but I'm not willing to return the girls to their mother when she didn't even come back early from a four-month Hawaiian honeymoon after they ran away. Plus, they were home alone a lot while she was gone. Their older brothers picked up some of the slack, but they left for college at the beginning of August."

"Makes sense to me," Gimone said. "We're your best friends. We have your six. We'll do whatever you need."

Juana inclined her head in agreement. "You always looked out for us, and the road runs both ways."

Debbie hugged them both. "We wouldn't have made it through the academy without each other."

"Okay, then I have to tell you something else, Ramsey." Gimone glanced past her and at the house for a moment, before lowering her voice. "You changed your name when you left, and Juana began using her mother's when she went off to college. I was so pissed at being stuck there by my mother and her family that I wasn't going to let the bastards take away my father's name or mine."

"That was your choice. What's wrong, Nolan?"

"One of your brothers contacted me last spring. He knew we'd been at the academy together and wanted to know if I had any idea where he could find you. I emailed that I didn't, but I'm not sure he believed me. He may still be looking."

"He can look all he wants. When my grandfather died, my grandmother downsized before she moved into a fancy assisted living place. We arranged for Sinclair to pick up the antiques she wanted to give me. She's the only one who has my cell phone number. If I'm state-side, and she's up for it, we go on a cruise together at Christmas."

"Don't they ask her about you?" Juana eased closer. "You stayed with them after you graduated from high school before you left for boot camp. Isn't your family aware of that?"

Debbie shook her head. "Not after my father disowned me." She lifted her chin. "He gave me three choices if I wanted to come home to Montana when I had the baby. I opted for 'none of the above' and he wasn't happy."

"I knew he offered to help you get an abortion right after you arrived at Celestial Faith." Gimone rested a hand on Debbie's back. "You never shared the rest of the options. What were they?"

"All of them sucked." Debbie blinked hard, refusing to let tears form. "And I couldn't talk about them when I was a kid. The Elders were so anti-abortion. They'd hammered that point in most of their Sunday sermons when I was growing up. I never felt like it was something I could do. My father said I could be one of the bishop's celestial wives and he'd raise the baby as his child. I refused."

"Who wouldn't?" Fury crept across Juana's face. "His son and his buddies raped you."

"Yes. That was a different one of the solutions. One of the bishop's older sons would marry me. I'd be his first wife, a legal one, not a sister-wife and he'd raise my baby as his own."

"Are you kidding me?" Now, Gimone was enraged. "Marry your rapist's brother? Was your father freaking crazy?"

"No, just a staunch member of the Celestial Faith church and polygamist community in Montana. Last of all, someone with good standing there would adopt my child." Debbie shook her head. "I was never going back, and I certainly wouldn't let any of them near my baby even if I was afraid to raise him, scared I'd blame him for who and what his father was. My grandparents helped me arrange an adoption and my son went with his new parents shortly after I had him. It totally pissed off my father who'd promised the bishop he'd bring me and my son back to the fold."

"Another secret your grandma keeps?" Juana frowned, rubbing her chin. "I don't get it, Ramsey. Weren't your grandparents part of Celestial Faith?"

"Nope. They were stunned when my mother joined the community and became one of my father's celestial wives. They weren't hung up on the fact that it wasn't a legal marriage. Grandma told me she and Grandpa shacked up together before they tied the knot. It bothered them that my mother lived with a man who had four other wives and all of them shared the same house with a flock of his children."

"How many brothers and sisters did you have?" Juana asked.

"Three actual brothers and my mom was pregnant and on bed-rest when I left, but if I counted all the kids, there were more than twenty. Not all of them lived with us. Some, like my oldest brother, had already left home."

It was Gimone's turn to seek answers. "Did they all stay in the community?"

"Most of them did. My dad was still totally the boss of the entire family, and my mom wasn't allowed to visit my grandparents more than once a year when she wasn't pregnant. She could only bring one of her kids to see them and it was usually me because my dad wouldn't give my brothers permission to go."

"Sounds horrible." Gimone flicked a glance at the house and gestured toward Penny who was coming toward them, lugging a suitcase. "Well, I'm definitely keeping my mouth shut around your brother if he ever contacts me again."

"Thank you." Debbie looked at her watch, waiting while her friend collected the suitcase and sent the little girl back to the house. "I need to get on the road, or the movers will make the ranch hours before we do. You have my cell number, so call if you need anything. The major will be gone at least a week."

"Won't he have a shit hemorrhage when he discovers you're gone?"

Gimone boosted the suitcase into the back of the Jeep. "Did you tell him where to find you?"

"Not yet. I will when I talk to him. If he has a tantrum, I told you what to do. Get in his face and let him know he's making a fool of himself. He'll back down."

"No worries," Juana said. "We can handle him and the warehouses. You concentrate on having a wonderful adventure. We'll be up to visit."

"Works for me." The front door banged open, and Penny raced toward them. "What's up, kiddo?"

"Daddy's on the phone in the kitchen," Penny reported. "It kept ringing and ringing and ringing. It was making me crazy, so I answered even though Van said I shouldn't."

"It's okay. I'll go talk to him. Meantime, your cat, Mocha, is in the back seat. You should check on her before we're outta here. I'll tell Vangie after I talk to the major." Debbie glanced at her friends. "We've almost finished loading my Jeep. Be right back."

"Anything left to bring out to the rig?" Gimone walked beside her toward the back door. "Put me to work, Ramsey. That's why we're here."

"Okay, then do a quick walk-through. My furniture is already gone. All I want are suitcases, backpacks, Vangie and my dog and cat."

"You got it."

Gimone headed down the hall while Debbie entered the kitchen. She picked up the receiver lying on the counter. "Good afternoon, sir. How was your flight?"

"Penny said you were talking to Nolan and Castaneda. What's wrong and spare me the polite bull—"

"Major! You shouldn't swear on the phone."

"My warehouses? Those damned reservists? What did they foul up?"

"Nothing, sir." Rolling her eyes, Debbie glared at the ceiling. *I'd love to tell him what to do with those damned warehouses.* "Gimone and Juana came to see me. It's not work-related, sir."

"Ramsey, stop 'sir-ing' me. I know you're still pissed because the girls are leaving next week. I won't ignore them the way I have for the last few years. I already told their mother I want more visitation. They're legally my kids and I intend to get to know them."

"Don't do me any favors, sir. It's about time you showed some interest in them. You chose their mother, sir." She clenched her hand on the phone cord. "They didn't."

"Heard and answered, Sarge. I didn't call to fight with you. I wanted to check in with you. We'll discuss the girls when I'm back. Clear?"

"I'll think about it."

"Right." His tone became more authoritative. "Think about it at the warehouses next week."

Debbie pursed her lips and looked at the empty place across the room where her great-grandmother's china hutch had stood. "I don't know, sir. I'm feeling emotionally overloaded. I'm going to ask the Command Sergeant-Major at HQ for two weeks leave starting next week."

"Ramsey, that's bullshit. You damn well get your butt to the office and prep for the upcoming inspections. If you want time off, you can have it when I'm back and not before."

"I'll consider it, sir." She gently replaced the receiver in the middle of explosive obscenities. She'd let the answering service deal with the rest of his calls. For now, she'd do her own last-minute survey and be sure she hadn't forgotten anything.

Shasta came to meet her and trailed her through the house, leash dangling from the pink-camo, heavy-duty nylon harness. Debbie petted the collie-mix's white ruff. "Don't worry, girl. I'm not leaving you behind."

Gimone came toward them, carrying the container with the tuxedo kitten mewing inside. "I think this is it. I sent Vangie out with the last suitcase and her backpack."

"Okay, I'll make one final check and then we'll be ready to hit the highway. Baker City, here we come!"

CHAPTER FIVE

Once on the freeway, Debbie headed north through Seattle. Traffic was fairly light for a Saturday afternoon, and they were halfway to Liberty Valley before Vangie spoke. "We've been so busy today, Ramsey, between getting Dad off to Texas, helping the movers load the furniture and packing up the rest of the house, that you haven't said what your new place is like. Will there really be room for Penny and me?"

"Definitely." Debbie continued driving. "I've been saving money for years. Last spring, I bought Miracle Riding Stable near Baker City in the Cascades. The house is humongous, three stories, eight bedrooms, five bathrooms and that's not counting the mother-in-law suite off the kitchen. The place was designed by the same architect who did the house for the dude ranch next door as well as ones for other early settlers in the area."

"You have horses? Real horses?" Penny demanded from the back seat. "Van loved her riding lessons, but Gary made her quit because he's allergic."

"Not surprising." Debbie focused on the four-lane highway, not sharing the opinion she'd formed of their current stepfather. "Many people who have allergies to cats also have ones to horses. What kind of equitation did you do, Vangie?"

"English. Mostly on the flat. I was just starting to jump when I had to stop. I wanted to train for three-day eventing, but—"

"Well, that may have to wait a while," Debbie said, not mentioning she preferred novice riders to start in western saddles to learn their balance before switching to the more advanced skills required for hunt-seat, jumping and dressage. As the saying went, she also chose the hill she wanted to fight or die on, and battling with a snarky teen wasn't one of her dream events. There would be enough of that later when the three of them discussed her marriage to the major.

"My stable focuses on beginning Western and 4-H. Other than my gelding, Wonder, there aren't any Warmbloods in the barns. Those are primarily the ones used for eventing and he's too old to do that. Mindy MacGillicudy, the previous owner, chose animals that could be trusted with new riders, so she has a mix of smaller, light horses and ponies."

"As long as I can ride, I don't care what style it is," Vangie said. "I used to muck stalls and clean tack to get a discount on my lessons. Sometimes, Penny came with me, but they didn't have any horses she could ride."

Debbie nodded. "It's hard to find safe ones for younger kiddoes, but there are plenty of them at our new place, so we'll teach her."

"Hooray! I can't wait." Penny hesitated. "Ramsey, what does Dad think about horses? Does he like them? Mom didn't say if he rides or not. Does he?"

"Of course. He learned when he was a boy in Texas." The cars slowed around them, so Debbie took advantage of the situation and glanced quickly over her shoulder before changing lanes. "He actually broke Wonder for me when I was in Afghanistan."

"I don't get it," Vangie said. "Why would he train your horse?"

As she continued driving, Debbie explained how their father picked up her horses from her grandparents' home in Eastern Washington when her grandfather was diagnosed with cancer. Rex looked after them while she was away. He'd asked for permission to work with Hobby's green-broke, five-year-old son when he and Debbie *Skyped* and she'd given it. He kept her posted on how the horses were doing, often sending pictures and videos. When she arrived at Fort Clark last year, the two of them visited the post stable together and usually rode at the same time.

Passing the various exits for Liberty Valley, she continued toward the Canadian border. Finally, she turned onto an east-bound highway. It narrowed from four to two lanes after she drove through the town of Lake Maynard. Fields, evergreens, and farms frequently dotted with grazing beef cattle lined the winding road. She slowed down to observe the new speed limit obviously lower because of the rural setting. Occasionally, she glimpsed Cedar Creek through the pastures and trees before the stream vanished from view.

Debbie spotted the turn-off and wondered what it'd take to have her neighbor rent space for a sign on the highway so customers would be able to find the stable more easily. Currently, they had to know exactly where they were going, and she hoped the movers would be able to follow her directions instead of driving into Baker City proper.

"Almost there." She braked, turned right, and headed for the bridge across the creek at the end of the street. Once on the other side, she stopped and allowed the girls to view the rolling fields beside the long gravel driveway. "Welcome to Miracle Riding Stable."

Vangie gazed in the direction of the cluster of buildings a good half-mile away. "Do we have an indoor arena, Ramsey?"

"Definitely. Otherwise, when the rainy season starts in western Washington, we'd be sopping wet." Debbie shifted the Jeep into gear and followed the curving driveway toward the house and outbuildings. "We have three big barns, outdoor arenas, corrals, a round pen, sheds in most of the pastures and, like I said before, the house is gigantic. I stayed in one of the guest rooms when I was here before. It looks like we've arrived before the movers, thank goodness."

She stopped near the huge Victorian-style house, admiring its three stories, towers, balconies, and fancy gingerbread trim. Vehicles were parked in front, including two classic Mustangs, one a candy-apple red and the second a hot pink. "Mindy has company."

"Could it be customers?" Vangie asked.

"Not if they're parked near the house. Parents of the students generally leave their rigs in the lot by the indoor arena and so do the boarders who keep their horses here." Debbie turned off the engine. "Let's go see what's happening and then we'll unload."

"Okay." Penny unfastened her seatbelt before undoing Shasta's. "I'll take her for a walk and keep her with me."

"Sounds good." Debbie opened her door, and climbed out, pausing to tuck the keys into her pocket. She started toward the wrap-around porch. Before she climbed the steps, the front door opened to reveal an elderly white-haired woman who still looked amazing in jeans, a plaid, western shirt with pearl snaps, and lace-up riding boots. "Hey, Mindy. Looks like you're having a going-away party."

"No, that comes later." Mindy laughed. "Right now, I invited a bunch of the neighbors to help get you settled. When you were here teaching camp, you didn't have time to meet them before. It looks like you brought helpers of your own."

"My daughters." Debbie caught Vangie's bewildered look, which rapidly changed to one of pleasure and added an introduction. "This is Vangie, and Penny has doggie duty."

"Fantastic." Mindy beamed. "I'm about to send a load of my things over to Cedar Creek Guest Ranch where I rented a cabin. I'll ask Margo to come by. She and Ann teach school in Baker City. So does Sullivan Murphy."

"Sullivan?" Debbie repeated. "I had an injured reservist with that name helping out at our warehouses last January. It has to be the same woman especially when I see that classic pink sports car. She had one like it. She parked it on the far side of the lot and pitched a fit when anyone drove near it."

"Did Dad like her?" Vangie asked.

"Yes, although she made him crazy sometimes." Debbie smiled at Mindy, then at the teenager. "Sully always put the mission first and wouldn't go on sick call when she was supposed to and the doctors at the clinic frequently contacted your father to rat her out. Plus, he wanted her to park the car closer to the office because she was on crutches."

"Am I hearing my name taken in vain?" A woman called from inside the door, behind Mindy. "Stop until I get there to defend myself."

Laughing when she recognized the voice, Debbie waited. Moments later, a woman with flaming red hair wearing maternity pants and a flowered smock joined them. Debbie looked her up and down. "Wow, Sully. I didn't know you were involved with anybody."

"I didn't plan to be, but there was this hot Army Ranger at Fort Clark." Sully rested a hand on a large baby bump. "And he decided he was really all that when we discovered we were having twins. Tate's saving up his leave for next month when I'm due, so I rounded up his brothers and sisters to help get you settled. Mindy said you were bringing a bunch of antiques to go with the ones she sold you."

"That's right, but we made it here before the movers did." Debbie took a deep breath, then followed the women inside where she was introduced to several strangers waiting in the kitchen. One, a curvy redhead holding a newborn baby was introduced as Cat O'Leary-McTavish. The others treated her with the obvious respect soldiers would give a four-star general.

"Cat came to do a walk-through and make sure the house was ready for you," Mindy explained. "I went through the sales paperwork again and it didn't look like Natasha Hollister, your realtor, told you there could be ghosts here."

Debbie blinked and stared at the older woman. "Didn't you tell me the house was built more than a hundred years ago, around the turn of the last century, in the early 1900s? I'm sure people must have died on the farm."

"Yes, but they didn't stay." Cat rocked her child. "If anyone shows up and weird things occur, we have the guest ranch next door. Call me and either Rob or I will come sort them out."

"Okay." Debbie dragged out the word, glancing around the group of assorted strangers, including two teens about Vangie's age. All of them appeared to accept the words at face value. One of the men, a tall, cowboy type with the typical 'high and tight' military style haircut nodded agreement. She'd apparently moved into the proverbial Twilight Zone.

She ought to have suspected the low price was too good to be true for a two-hundred-acre ranch in the Cascade foothills. However, nothing jumped out at her when she inspected the land on Hobby. Yes, fences needed repairs, overgrown alder, maple, and evergreen trees should be harvested, and outbuildings required new roofs, but nothing appeared that was a deal-breaker. The riding stable was on the market for several years, but Mindy claimed that was because her family was waiting to inherit and didn't want to pay for it.

Debbie wasn't going to say she didn't believe in ghosts or things that went 'bump in the night' not when it appeared to be the price of admission to live in the area. The door banged open behind her, and she glanced over her shoulder. "What is it, Penny?"

"The movers are here." Penny's eyes widened at the sight of the baby. "Wow. What's its name? Can I hold—?"

"Her name is Claire, and she's ten days old." Cat smiled at the nine-year-old. "If you give your puppy's leash to my husband and sit down, I'll show you how to hold her. She's used to her older sisters snuggling her, so the two of you will be fine."

Debbie sat on the porch swing in the moonlight, Shasta snoozing beside her on the wooden seat. Mindy had warned her it was wildfire season but thankfully there wasn't any smoke tonight, just the smells of evergreens, grass, and ripening apples from the orchard in the cooling breeze. She heard Cedar Creek bubble over the rocks, frogs croaking, and coyotes howling or yipping in the night.

Her phone vibrated, and she pulled it out of her jeans. 0200 hours, two in the morning her time, and 0400 his time in Texas. It wasn't a surprise he'd called. They often had one of their 'long, dark tea-time of the soul' conversations late at night or in the wee hours before dawn. She took a deep breath. Okay, she had to protect herself and not give away the truth about where she was or what she'd done.

Time to be on guard, she told herself. "Hello, Major. How's Texas and San Antonio? Made it to the Alamo yet?"

"It's closed for restoration, Ramsey, and you know I don't go there alone. It's a 'hip-pocket' training moment." He chuckled. "Yet, you always ask."

"Well, after your lectures on the subject, it's the least I can do. I don't want you wasting that history degree." She reached over to stroke Shasta's soft fur and the puppy sighed but didn't awaken. "How is your mission?"

"Checked in on the troops and they'll be ready for transport to the Fort Clark base hospital in three or four days. Right now, they're being assessed and fed regular meals. They're in surprisingly good shape."

Debbie listened as he described the returning soldiers and his expectations for the trip to Washington state. When he paused, she interjected open-ended questions that would make him think of other options and possibilities to ensure a smooth transition from one base to another for the injured men.

"So, what's the plan for tomorrow? Are you and the girls going shopping? Save the receipts, and I'll settle up with you when I'm back."

"No worries. I've got it covered."

"And your reenlistment? Is that handled too?"

"I got everything I wanted." Clenching the chain on the swing, Debbie wondered when he'd realize she hadn't answered the question. "I'm going to call it a night. The girls are early risers."

"All right. I'll check in with you tomorrow, Ramsey."

"Sounds good, sir. I can't wait."

She ended the call and woke up the half-grown puppy to take her for one last walk before they headed inside. Thanks to her new neighbors, the house was immaculate. Mindy had arranged for the local cleaning service to scrub everything from top to bottom before the furniture arrived. Sullivan's family had not only moved it into the various rooms, but also made beds, hung curtains, and unpacked dishes. All she and the girls had to do was put away their own clothes.

Debbie locked the front door behind her. With Shasta as an escort, they climbed the stairs to the second floor and the bedrooms. On the way to the master suite, she lingered in the hallway long enough to glance in at the girls. Both were totally zonked. Good, she thought. They had forty horses to feed in the morning and she wanted to hit the barn by 0700. *Wait a second. I'm a civilian now. Time to start thinking like one, so I'll head out for chores at seven a.m.*

She and the girls wouldn't be on their own. Mindy had two barn managers who shared the apartment in the indoor arena, and the women agreed to stay on with Debbie. Between them and the high-school students who worked part-time, the rest of the summer should be easy enough. Once she finished up the last two weeks of day-camp, she could decide what fall programs she wanted to add.

Riding lessons of course, trail rides for her students, some sort of weekend courses for tweens and teens who wanted more horsy time. Still planning the next steps for Miracle Riding Stable, she changed into pajamas and climbed into the king-size, sleigh style bed. She was barely under the covers when Shasta jumped up and snuggled close.

Debbie heaved a sigh. "You ought to sleep on the floor, but why do I think that'd be a new experience? I'll have to speak to the major about the fact that dogs don't belong on hundred-year-old beds."

Moises Pride wandered through the wards of the Army hospital, checking out the various rooms before returning to the one where Sergeant Waco Hawke recovered. This section of the infirmary was on lockdown, not that he had to worry about that. The MPs couldn't see him. Nobody did—

Because I'm dead, dead, dead! A bullet in the back of the head will do it every time.

Moises grimaced when he remembered the details following a foiled escape attempt. Dragged into a room in the *casa* by two cartel *soldados*. Unable to stand on a badly broken leg, the shattered bone sticking out through the skin. Blood draining from a gunshot wound—an AK-47 round through his ribs. Shoved into a chair where he was tied in place. Shot execution style by their *jefe* just to make a point. *Like I wasn't dying anyway—*

He eyed the sleeping man in the bed. *Didn't work, did it Sarge? You still didn't give up the location of the others who escaped with us or where they went.*

Well, there wasn't much going on tonight. Moises glanced at the color TV mounted high on the wall. A cable news channel with a gorgeous blonde in a red dress reading the latest headlines. *Damn, Sergeant Hawke. All she does is blather about politics. Who wants to listen to that shit nonstop? Not me! And I got the power.*

He focused on the remote. It didn't take long to find a baseball game from last spring. *Oh, yeah. That's what I'm talkin' about! If only I could have a beer!*

During the summer, Miracle Riding Stable was open six days a week and closed on Sundays for what Mindy called *family* time. She'd told Debbie that back in the day, she used to open after church, but at her age, it was too exhausting. Only being open Tuesdays through Saturdays from September to the middle of June worked for her.

'Go along to get along,' Debbie decided when she bought the place. She'd intended to change things up once the stable was hers. She didn't do organized religion, not anymore.

Accompanied by the girls, Debbie led the way into the closest barn shortly after oh-seven-hundred hours. "We'll put out the hay and then bring the horses in from the pastures. They enjoy being outside at night when the weather is good. The water tubs should have been filled when these stalls were mucked yesterday. Check them for me, Penny, and make sure the water is clean."

"I'm on it." With Shasta at her side, the little girl took the hand-held screen most people would use for straining pasta and headed down the wide cement aisle. "This is so awesome."

Grateful she'd learned the system when she was here earlier in the spring and summer, Debbie taught Vangie to feed the appropriate amount of hay. This particular barn had fifteen stalls for the ponies. The next stable in the row was for the horses, and the third structure was for the privately owned mounts.

When they reached the second barn, Debbie saw the younger barn manager, Trina Sweeney, a petite redhead in her mid-twenties feeding flakes of alfalfa-grass hay. "Good morning."

"Hi boss." Trina smiled, sky-blue eyes friendly. "Kyra is doing the other barn and we'll be ready to bring in the stock soon."

"Sounds like a plan," Debbie said.

Chores finished a short time later, the five of them started toward the apartment in the indoor arena. Trina looked at her watch. "We'll have to hustle if we want to eat something before church. Do you want to come with us this time, Debbie?"

"I don't do religion."

Vangie's brown eyes widened. "But Naveah and Chantrea Murphy said they'd see us there, and they'd introduce us to everyone. Cat told Penny that she could meet Claire's big sisters who are her age. Does that mean we can't go?"

"If you trust them with us, I have room in my Explorer." A tall, thin woman in her late thirties, Kyra O'Neill ran a hand through her ash-blonde hair. "They could meet you at Pop's Café for lunch because we won't be back until early evening for night chores."

Penny snagged Debbie's hand. "Please, Ramsey. We'd behave appropriately so you and Dad wouldn't be embarrassed."

Debbie ruffled Penny's blonde hair. "Honey, you could never do that. Yes, if it means that much to you two, hurry and get changed. I'll scramble some eggs, then you won't starve until lunch."

Once the younger girl dashed toward the house, Shasta, a tail-wagging escort, Debbie glanced at Vangie. "I haven't been to this particular church yet and I don't know what it's like. I'm trusting you to take care of your little sister. You both have your cell phones, so if something happens that you don't like or makes you uncomfortable, call me. It's okay to get up and walk out of the service if it becomes untenable. You don't have to stay until the end."

"We'll be fine." Vangie stepped up and hugged Debbie. "Don't worry so much. Dad's in Texas, but I'm here. Like he says, I've got your six and Penny's too."

"I know." Tears stung and Debbie blinked hard, holding the teenager. "I won't have you two hurt."

"We'll look after them." Kyra said gently. "I'll bring them to the café to find you and once you know Reverend Tommy and his wife, Virginia, you'll realize why we all go to his services."

"And if we don't get a move on, we'll be late and my grandfather will totally freak," Trina added. "His lectures majorly suck, but my three older sisters' complaints are worse. We'll meet you and Penny in thirty minutes, Vangie."

CHAPTER SIX

An hour later, coffee cup in hand, Debbie sat on the porch swing watching Shasta enjoy a chew stick in the August sunshine. She hadn't been alone in forever. If she didn't have reservists to supervise on the weekends at the warehouse, there were still other duties around the barracks. On her rare days off, she'd go to the post stable and ride Hobby. Today, she had peace and quiet to enjoy her new life and new home.

Early that afternoon, she headed into Baker City. The café was on the opposite side of the street from the church, so Debbie parked nearby. She locked the rig, then went toward the small restaurant. The sign in the window read "Open."

The old-fashioned bell over the door jangled when she walked inside. She glanced around the room, noticing she was one of the few customers. Booths with old-time vinyl seats lined the walls, while the adjacent windows provided views of the town. Tables and chairs took up most of the center. Stools squatted near the long counter dividing the dining area from the kitchen.

A spry, balding man holding a stack of menus came to greet her. "Did you want a table or booth or a seat at the counter?"

"I'd prefer a booth, since my daughters will be here soon," Debbie said. "They went to church, but I didn't expect the services to last this long."

"Oh, Reverend Tommy isn't that long-winded." He smiled, his face crinkling like a crumpled, brown paper sack. "Folks always go for doughnuts and coffee afterwards. It gives them a chance to catch up on the latest gossip. I'm Pop MacGillicudy."

"Any relation to Mindy? I bought her place."

"My cousin." Pop ushered Debbie to a booth. "How many menus?"

"Three and a cup of coffee while I wait. I'm Debbie Ramsey."

"Welcome to Baker City, Debbie."

"Thank you."

She'd barely started to study the menu when the bell over the door chimed again. She looked toward the entry and saw Vangie and Penny, accompanied by Sullivan Murphy and her two sisters-in-law. Debbie waved them over. "Hi there. How was church?"

"Everybody's so nice." Penny hurried toward her. "You've got to come next time."

"I don't think so, but I'm glad you had fun." Debbie patted the seat beside her. "Come, tell me all about it."

It took a few minutes for everyone to get settled. It was little wonder that Vangie felt as if the Murphy foster girls, Naveah Johnson who was African-American and Chantrea Yang, an Asian-American were destined to be her new friends since they were the same age, almost sixteen and going into their sophomore year at Lake Maynard High. All three teens wore fashionably torn jeans, floral, ribbed, shrunken tank tops under their unbuttoned shirts, heavy layers of cosmetics and plenty of earrings in their actual ears. They crowded onto the bench on the other side of the booth.

"We can't stay long." Sully drew up a chair to sit at the end of the table. "We have to be on time for Sunday dinner. Luckily, Virginia, the minister's wife, wanted to talk to Bronwyn, my mother-in-law and Kyra, your barn manager about backpacks for needy kids when they start school in a few weeks. That gave us time to come here."

"I told them I wouldn't need a backpack this year," Penny announced, "because you or Dad would take me shopping for supplies and he already took us to the PX for new clothes."

"Makes sense to me." Debbie glanced at Vangie. "I'm figuring Naveah and Chantrea can give you a heads-up on what's fashionable at the local high school."

"That works. So, Cat O'Leary-McTavish told us that her daughters are coming to horse camp this week along with Devon Barrett-Sweeney." Vangie tilted her head to one side. "Weren't there a couple other kids in your Sunday School class who are coming too, Penny?"

"Yeah, but I don't remember everybody's names." Penny shifted closer to Debbie's side. "Would this be a good week for me to learn about horses?"

"Yes, but I want you to start on one of the larger ponies." Debbie glimpsed the longing on Chantrea's face and added, "If you girls want to come, we have some horses available."

"I wish." Chantrea sighed, narrowing dark, almond-shaped eyes. "My foster mom has horsy issues and she only let us come help yesterday because Quinn and Sully told her that we wouldn't be anywhere near the barns."

"I'm still working on my mother-in-law, Ramsey." Sully rubbed her baby belly. "She lost one of her nephews in a horse-related accident and it's easier to blame the animal than look at the circumstances. You're also going to have my niece, Letty, at camp this week. Tate may say it's nobody's business how we raise the twins, but when they hit the horsy stage, he's the one who will have to deal with his momma."

"O.M.G, Sully." Naveah shook her long black braids and then gaped at her. "When she discovers you're not keeping them away from horses, Mom will majorly lose it. Dad already swore everyone to secrecy about Quinn's daughter taking lessons and Letty is another local going to camp this week."

"Your mom already knows I rode when I was a kid and if she wants to reconnect with Mariah, one of her grown foster kids who is a horseshoer now, Bronwyn will have to re-evaluate the past or Mariah will blow off the Labor Day picnic like she did the Fourth of July one." Sully looked at her watch. "Come on, girls. If we don't get a move on, we'll be on KP forever and I hate dish duty."

When the others left, Debbie gestured to the menus waiting on the table. "Find something good for lunch. I don't know about you two, but I'm thinking a deluxe cheeseburger, fries and an old-fashioned, chocolate milkshake suits me."

———

She'd already taught several sessions of horse camp earlier that summer and developed a system, slightly modifying the one Mindy MacGillicudy used. After morning chores and breakfast, Debbie headed for the farm office to meet the campers and their parents to complete the registration process. Halfway to the indoor arena, her cell phone vibrated. She pulled it out of her pocket and glanced at the screen. "What's up, Gimone?"

"The major's called the warehouse three times today looking for you. Last time, Baxter was away from his desk. That macho, cop reservist, Hollister answered. He told Sinclair you're gone. It was purely out of spite because I jumped his shit for hassling the junior enlisted females and threatened to have Juana write him up for sexual harassment. I haven't been answering when the major calls my cell, but I can't keep avoiding the guy. What do you want me to tell him?"

"The truth. Tell him I retired and that's all you know. He has my cell number. He can call me for details." Debbie glanced at her watch. "Gotta run, Nolan. Day camp starts at 0900. I have to sign in the kids and take their parents' money. Thanks for the heads-up. I'm turning off my cell until the end of camp at 1630. Whoops, I forgot I'm a civilian now. That's four-thirty this afternoon."

Gimone laughed. "Works for me. I'll pass the word to Juana you're incommunicado. Have a horsy good day."

Debbie laughed. "You know it. Oh, and the major already offered to kick Hollister's butt, if need be, so tell Juana not to worry about backup from him."

"Got it."

Debbie took a moment to switch off her phone before replacing it in her pocket. By the time she reached the office, she spotted Kyra coming from the restrooms, cleaning supplies in hand. Trina and one of the teen helpers, Jason, a stocky, blond boy, organized camp t-shirts and rental equestrian helmets for the new students. Carol, the other seventeen-year-old, would be finishing up in the barn, grooming and saddling horses for the advanced campers to go on the first trail ride and for the intermediates to have their first lesson.

A short time later, she'd checked the paperwork for the twenty-four kids ranging in age from seven to fourteen years old. While some of the parents lingered, waiting for the campers to return from the restrooms in their new red t-shirts advertising Miracle Riding Stable, others made their escape. Trina finished fitting the last of the equestrian helmets and labeling them with masking tape. Now, the staff would know everyone's name.

Debbie gestured for the youngsters to create a large circle around her. She'd already introduced herself, but it was time to do it again and incorporate it into what she called the 'name game.' She turned slightly and gestured to the teen beside her. "Hi, I'm the camp director and new owner of Miracle Riding Stable, Debbie, and this is my friend, Jason."

Since he knew the drill from previous weeks, he continued. "Hi, Debbie.

I'm Jason." He gestured to the blonde girl in the bright red shirt standing next to him. "And this is my friend, Letty."

It wasn't her first week in camp, so Letty immediately followed suit, introducing herself and the little dark-haired child beside her. "Hi Jason. I'm Letty, and this is my friend, Devon."

The routine lasted until everyone was introduced to each other. After-wards, Jason led the campers in a series of exercises, explaining they'd do them on the ground and then on their horses once they were assigned. After that, Carol taught them what Debbie called, 'ground school,' how to stop, start and steer before they were in the saddles or even saw the animals, they'd ride all week. The purpose was to teach the campers to move their natural aids or body parts correctly. Then the horses and ponies would respond to the riders' signals.

Kyra and Trina arrived a few minutes later with two ponies. Debbie went through a quick horse safety lecture that culminated in each child learning how to properly lead one of what she called, the 'short horses.' Next, Trina escorted the kids to the restrooms while Jason and Carol put away the two four-legged volunteers, rewarding them with carrots.

Meantime, Debbie, and Kyra went through the roster, assigning the kids into three different riding groups. The youngest beginners were the Appaloosas, the intermediates would be the Morgans and the advanced were now the Mustangs.

"Vangie has ridden English, but this will be her first experience in a Western saddle, so let's have her join the Morgans," Debbie said. "This is a new experience for Penny, so she's an Appy."

"Are you sure about that?" Concern seeped into Kyra's smoky gray eyes. "Penny will be older than the other beginners."

"Tell her she's your helper," Debbie said, her tone calm. "She's with you and the other beginners because she's never been near a horse before. If it becomes an issue, send her to me for the key to the fetlock."

"The what?" Kyra's eyes widened. "Debbie, the fetlock is part of the horse's leg."

"I know that. You know that. She'll learn parts of the horse by Wednesday, but if my stepdaughter is a brat, she'll be in time-out city. I have rules and regulations. She'll adhere to them. The same goes for Vangie."

Kyra whistled softly. "Yes, ma'am."

"That's once." Debbie stiffened at the insult. "Don't ever call me that again!" Remembering she was a civilian now and shouldn't take offense, she added, "Sorry, Kyra. You never call a non-commissioned officer in the Army, ma'am, or sir."

"I didn't know that. Why not?"

"It's considered disrespectful because we've earned our rank through the 'School of Hard Knocks', not by going to college. Guess I haven't been out of my combat boots that long."

"Well, Ms. Debbie, you have a lot to learn and so do I." Kyra smiled. "I never served, but I certainly respect those who did and do."

"Thank you." Debbie returned the smile. "And I appreciate your patience with me as I adjust to civilian life."

The day zoomed by. At sixteen-fifteen hours, four-fifteen civilian time, Debbie rounded up the campers and had them line up according to their riding groups. Carol brought the clipboard and the two of them escorted the kids to their parents who'd parked near the indoor arena. Debbie explained that since she was new and didn't know everyone yet, she expected them to sign out their children before departing.

"That's what Captain Margo, our teacher did at school last spring," Samantha, one of the Hendrickson twins informed Debbie. "Daddy says safety first."

"It's a good rule." Debbie nodded at the tall, dark-haired man, recognizing him as Cat O'Leary-McTavish's husband. He obediently signed his name on the form while he listened to his other daughter chatter about everything they'd done at camp. Devon tugged on his free hand, waiting her turn to tell him about the beginner riding group's activities. "Thanks."

"No worries. We do 'by the numbers' next door too. See you tomorrow." He handed off the clipboard to the next waiting parent. "Let's go, girls. Your ponies at home are waiting for you to clean their stalls."

A short time later, the last car drove away. Debbie passed the clipboard to Carol. The teen headed for the office and then the indoor arena, obviously eager for the next horsy activity before afternoon barn chores.

A silver-haired elderly man strolled toward her, clearly waiting his turn for her attention. He wore a plaid, flannel shirt tucked into faded jeans and battered cowboy boots.

Debbie smiled politely. "Welcome to Miracle Riding Stable. How can I help you?"

"I'm Reverend Tommy Thompson." He approached, holding out his hand to shake hers. "I wanted to stop by and welcome you to Baker City. I had the pleasure of meeting your daughters yesterday."

"Really?" Debbie struggled to control the fear that swept through her. *This is my place and I'm safe. There's nothing he can do to me. He's an old man and I can take him down in a heartbeat.* "That's good to hear."

"I wanted to invite you to visit the church next Sunday." Reverend Tommy stopped, slowly lowering his hand to his side. "Mindy has raved about you."

"How kind of her." Debbie heard footsteps on the gravel and glanced past him to see Penny racing toward them from the barns. "What's happening, honey? Is one of the horses sick?"

"It's Daddy and he sounds mad." Penny held out her cell phone. "He wants to talk to you. I told him Reverend Tommy was here and you were busy, but Daddy says to give the preacher a donation and he'll go away."

With that, Reverend Tommy excused himself. Out of the minister's earshot, Debbie said, "What's going on, Major?"

"Isn't that my question, Ramsey? Where are you? I already know you're not where I expected you to be at Fort Clark, doing what I wanted done at the warehouses."

"That isn't your concern, Major." She felt laughter bubbling up inside. Finally, she had the opportunity to tell him what to do with those damned warehouses. "Let me lay out the situation for you. I took the early out and the money the Army offered for me to retire now instead of in three years. My choice. My decision. I left. It's my responsibility, nobody else's."

"You could have been straight up with me."

"I was. You didn't listen. Now, hear this. My lawyer, Brazos Hawke, will be in touch when you get back from Texas to discuss custody of your daughters."

"I told you their mother would be back to get them on Wednesday."

"If you believed that story, you shouldn't have. She's honeymooning in Hawaii until September, sir. The housekeeper at her home in California has quit. I don't know if the girls told you they'd been alone several nights before they came looking for you. Since nobody else seems to want them, I'm keeping the girls."

"Ramsey, that's bullshit."

"Too bad, too sad." Debbie paused. "I can't think of anything else you need to know. Oh, yes, I do. Juana, Captain Castaneda, may require backup when you return, but you've always been good about taking care of the troops and your officers."

"I can think of a lot of other things for us to discuss now that you're out of the service. Are you sure about leaving the Army for good?"

"Positive."

"You'd better stop calling me, Major. My name is Rex."

"After all this time, I know *your* damned name."

"Then, say it."

"I can't." Her fingers shook as she ended the call.

Rex eyed the cell phone in his hand. Why hadn't he realized there was more to Debbie Ramsey's agenda when they married back in the day? He'd wanted a guarantee his addiction to Averill would end and he'd be safe from her. Instead of 'manning up,' and dealing with his broken marriage, he'd used a young noncom willing to risk her career for him to salve and save his pride.

Collecting Debbie Ramsey's inheritance and looking after two horses while she was away on different combat tours seemed a small price to pay for his renewed independence. He'd assumed her grandparents raised her, but that didn't make sense. She'd told him she'd spent almost three years in a boarding school, and it puzzled him when Vangie said Debbie cut her ties to her family. Why hadn't he followed up? What was he thinking?

They had a lot to talk about, and he'd try to learn some of the answers when he called tonight. At least now he knew why she was avoiding him. Because he'd left his truck in the parking lot at the airport, he didn't have to try to arrange a ride when he returned to Fort Clark on Wednesday. It was time to learn what he could from his daughters about where the three of them were living and what they were doing.

He should wait a while to contact Penny since Debbie had her phone, so he called Vangie. "Hi. Just checking in. What's going on?"

"Kyra's going to teach us how to barrel race," Vangie said. "And I'm trying to put on my horse's bridle, but Copper keeps lifting his head super high like he's a giraffe or brachiosaurus."

"Do you have any treats?"

"Yes, I've got pieces of carrot. Kyra says to give him one before he takes the bit and save the rest for afterwards."

"Okay. This is how I bridled Wonder back in the day because that colt didn't have a clue." Rex talked her through the procedure, describing how to hold the western curb and carrot together before she slid the bit into the horse's mouth. Yes, he had questions about where she and Penny were living with Master Sergeant Debbie Ramsey, but they could wait until Vangie was able to focus on them. It was long past time for him to give something of himself.

"We did it. Thanks, Dad." Vangie paused. "Can we talk later? I don't want to miss out on the gaming class."

"Go have fun, but be careful. Remember, it's patterns first and then speed. When you hit the gaming circuit, the judges disqualify riders who screw up."

"Got it."

"And you're wearing an equestrian helmet, right?"

"Yes. It's a big rule here at Miracle. Ramsey makes everyone wear them even when we're grooming, saddling, and working our horses on the ground not just during lessons or trail rides, which is way different than where I took lessons in California."

"Great. Send me pictures of you and your horse. Tell Penny I want to see hers, too."

"I will."

Smiling, Rex finished the call. There was more than one way to solve a problem, and he was a good investigator. He'd know where the three of them were hanging their proverbial hats before he arrived in Washington State on Wednesday afternoon. Yes, he had his flaws, but at 42 years old, he'd learned to try to control them. At least, that was one of his strengths.

I'm sure Ramsey will lecture me on all my failings, but I don't have to keep my distance anymore except when she initiates a 'knocking boots' good time. I can finally be with her the way I've wanted to for years.

CHAPTER SEVEN

Another warm moonlit summer night and she was free to enjoy it. Everyone else had gone to bed hours ago. At 0200, two in the morning civilian time, she was the only night owl. She and Shasta had the porch swing to themselves. While the puppy snoozed after a busy day on the farm, Debbie sipped a second glass of red Zinfandel. Her phone vibrated and she answered. "Good morning, sir. How's your mission?"

"Coming together nicely. The girls sent me pictures and videos of the horses they've been riding. What kind of barrel racing were they learning today? I've never seen anything like it. Three barrels in a row and no clover-leaf figures like we do in Texas? What's that about?"

"Kyra calls it, 'Speed Barrels', and it's suitable for beginners." Debbie shifted and put her wineglass on the porch rail. "New riders weave up and back through the barrels. It teaches them to steer and ride independently at a walk and trot."

"Interesting. It looked like they were having fun."

"Yes, and then there weren't any complaints when they finished up and had to muck the barns."

"Taking care of horses is part of learning to ride." A momentary silence before he asked. "Did you arrange to see your family now that you're out of the Army?"

"I don't have one of those. It's why I took your kids." Debbie hesitated and decided to add a bit of the truth. "My father disowned me when I was fifteen, Vangie's age. You're not abandoning your daughters the way I was abandoned. I won't have it."

"Understandable. What happened? Why did he disown you?"

"I was a high school sophomore when he took me to Celestial Faith Girls Academy in Spokane. He offered me options that were no options at all. I said, no. When I graduated two and a half years later, I went to live with my grandparents until I left for boot camp."

"I see." His voice softened. "Ramsey, you know everything about me. Can't you trust me a little bit in return?"

"I don't want your pity, Sinclair. The topic's closed." She reached for the wine. "Talk to me about the mission. I need the distraction."

"All right." Another long pause and then he said, "I have something else on my mind first. You made sure all my kids got their black belts, didn't you?"

"Penny doesn't have hers yet. She's a second-level green belt. I'm checking out the local karate school and I'll sign her and Vangie up for classes in September."

"Good. The boys are still studying self-defense, aren't they?"

"Yes. They're taking judo since all three have their black belts in tai-kwon-do, but they continue to practice at the local dojo in Pullman. They know it's a condition for you to pay their expenses until they graduate, since the child support went to college with them."

"How did you manage that, Ramsey?"

"My attorney is a kick-ass lawyer who is a great advocate for women and children. She also has a soft spot for soldiers since her older brother runs the local branch of Nighthawke Security. Bree will teach your ex to suck eggs because neither of us are impressed with a woman who leaves a fifteen-year-old and a nine-year-old home alone while she honeymoons in Hawaii for months."

"I owe you, Ramsey."

"Roger that, Major. Now, what about the mission?"

During the next three days, she taught day-camp and worked on her business plans in the evenings. She found herself looking forward to his late-night calls. She listened to his reports on the status of the wounded former prisoners and shared some of her ideas for riding programs in September. He provided feedback and suggested seasonal bonuses for the staff so the budget wouldn't be over-extended. That made perfect sense.

Thursday after the campers departed, she left Kyra in charge and made a run into Baker City. This town definitely needed a pizza parlor, Debbie thought. Failing that, she picked up fried chicken and various salads at the deli in the mercantile, then swung by the bakery for dessert. She spotted Sullivan Murphy seated at a little table in the corner, happily devouring a thick slab of strawberry cheesecake topped with fresh fruit.

"That looks amazing." Debbie crossed the room to greet her. "How are you doing? I know you had a tough time when you came back from that last tour."

"Losing Raven about killed me. We'd been BFF.s since day-care." Sully waved to the empty chair across from her. "Join me, won't you? Coming to Baker City saved my sanity. I've taken over her job as the 'first shirt' for our reserve unit."

"Didn't she leave big combat boots to fill?" Debbie leaned on the back of the chair but didn't sit down. She wasn't staying long. "What happens if the balloon goes up? You'll be a mom with two little kids."

"Tate only has three more years, but the Army is downsizing, so if they offer him early retirement, he's talking about taking it and then he'll be here with the twins if I have to go. A first sergeant has a lot of responsibilities, and I won't abandon my unit." Sully lowered her voice, glancing in the direction of the kitchen where someone rattled pots and pans. "His father had a heart attack and Tate was home on emergency leave when his Ranger patrol got hit. Twila's husband, Zeke Garvey, was killed, and Tate still has issues about it."

"Shitstorms happen in combat." Debbie straightened when a dark-haired woman about her age wearing an old-fashioned apron over a bright blue t-shirt and black slacks came out of the back. "Hi. I need a dozen slices of cheesecake. Okay to get an assortment?"

"Amazing," Sully said. "I'm going home with you, Ramsey, if you pick up some of the caramel or the turtle one with chocolate, butterscotch, and pecans. Twila, this is Debbie Ramsey who bought Mindy MacGillicudy's place, Miracle Riding Stable. We served together."

"Welcome to Baker City." Twila smiled, professional friendliness changing to a genuine warmth. "I'll put together a box for you. What's the occasion?"

"A staff meeting when I get back. I want to run my new fall riding programs by the instructors, and I thought cheesecake would make my proposed changes acceptable." Debbie eyed Sullivan who looked more pregnant than ever in her smock, bright red hair confined in a neat braid. "Are you coming to the camp show tomorrow? I'll save you a parking place close to the arena, so you won't have to walk too far."

"Wouldn't miss it for the world." Sully returned to her cheesecake. "Letty had an amazing time this week. She loved the way you divided the classes, so she learned to canter. She tried talking her folks into buying her a horse, but I don't think that's going to happen. She complains a lot because the Hendrickson twins already have ponies and so does Devon Sweeney-Barrett who is younger than the rest of them."

"Well, maybe they might consider signing up Letty for the school-year, Saturday riding club. She could spend all day with horses." Debbie pointed to the chocolate variety, holding up two fingers, and Twila cut one piece and then a second. "Once Letty polishes her skills, she could join the bunch going to local shows."

"She'd be in horse heaven. Will you have brochures for that tomorrow?" Sully asked. "I'll mention it to Quinn and her husband."

"Sounds good." Debbie finished selecting various types of cheesecake and then paid the somewhat exorbitant bill. Of course, the fancy three-inch layers were made from scratch with all natural ingredients, she told herself sternly, and she needed to make friends around Baker City, especially since she didn't plan to join the church.

Late Thursday afternoon, Rex parked in front of the main warehouse. He'd have to check the status of the other three large buildings later. For now, he hoped Sergeant Nolan and Captain Castaneda had everything under control and performed up to his high expectations. "Ramsey, this is bullshit. You should have given them more than two days of training."

He headed toward the stairs and the door to his office, automatically checking out the rigs in the parking lot. He didn't recognize the huge four-by-four with Montana plates and wondered who owned that pickup. An eighteen-wheeler was backed into the loading dock, so Rex paused in the warehouse where he spotted Captain Castaneda checking paperwork. "How's it going?"

"Fine, sir. Looks like everything is on the up and up." She gestured to Staff Sergeant Nelson, a tall, broad-shouldered African-American organizing the enlisted to unload the delivery. "We're good to go."

"Then I'll let you handle it." He started toward the offices, then glanced over his shoulder. "Who has that Ford 350 out front? One of the reservists?"

"No, sir. It belongs to a Sergeant-Major Taggart, temporarily assigned to the base. He came to see you."

"Why? We definitely don't have a noncom slot for him and when Nolan is promoted, she'll have the Master Sergeant, E8 one."

"I believe he's working at one of the schools for the college ROTC. students."

"Well, he shouldn't be hunting supplies for them. Master Sergeant Murphy handles that. I'll go see what Taggart wants." Leaving Captain Castaneda to deal with the day-to-day responsibilities, Rex strode toward the east end of the building. In the reception area, he saw Corporal Baxter at the front counter, sorting through paperwork. Sergeant First Class Nolan was at Debbie Ramsey's old desk, checking something on the computer.

A tall, lean, black-haired man in camouflage fatigues stood when Rex entered. "Good afternoon, Major. I'm West Taggart. If you have time, I'd like to speak to you."

"I just got back from a temporary assignment in Texas. I can give you ten minutes, Sergeant-Major." Rex scanned the soldier and decided the man must be in his forties. If he was career military, he'd be accustomed to providing fast reports. "After that, I have three other buildings to inspect. Nolan, be ready to give me a sitrep in fifteen minutes."

"Yes, sir." She kept her attention on the monitor. "I've been dividing my time between them and this building."

"Good job." Rex ushered the senior non-commissioned officer into his office. When he looked more closely at the man's face, he noticed with sudden surprise that Taggart's eyes were the same electric blue as Debbie Ramsey's. What was happening?

Rex closed the door behind them. He went to sit behind the desk and gestured toward the chairs reserved for visitors. Something new had been added, a photograph of Debbie and his daughters. He picked it up, studied the picture, and turned it so he'd be the only one who saw it. He'd pick up the gauntlet she'd thrown at him later.

"What's your business, Taggart?"

"I'm looking for my sister and I figure you know her."

Rex leaned back in his chair. "I've served with a lot of soldiers in the last twenty years, Taggart. Probably you have, too. What's her name?"

"We call her, Sweet. Sarah Wynfreda Esther Eliana Tabitha. And if she's not married, her last name is Taggart. She joined up years ago and—"

"Doesn't ring a bell." Rex glanced at his watch. "You have seven minutes left. Why would I know her?"

West leaned forward in the chair, a muscle twitching in his tight jaw.

"My parents sent her horse to our grandparents. The neighbors told me you picked it up—"

"Really? I don't recall that." Rex shrugged. "Five minutes. When was the last time you saw your sister?"

"Twenty years ago. She was as sweet as her name and only fifteen. I was stationed in Germany and when I came home on leave, she was gone."

"I suggest you talk to your family and ask what happened to her." Rex stood and waved to the door. "I'm out of time."

"Not quite yet." West stood as well, his tone dark and dangerous. "After my grandfather died three years ago, my grandmother sold her house. Where did you take the antiques that should have gone to my mother?"

"I have no idea what you're talking about." Rex rested his hands on the desk. "If you have issues with your relatives, Sergeant-Major, try talking to them. Don't come here and waste my time. Leave my folks alone. They have more important duties than dealing with someone who can't keep track of his kin."

Rex escorted the stranger to the door and then watched as he stormed from the office. "Nolan, we need to talk."

"I have that sitrep for you, sir."

"We'll save it for a few minutes." Rex glanced at the company clerk. "Baxter, pass the word and tell our regulars to collect intel from that Sergeant-Major. Nobody tells him *anything* about our folks, not the ones here or the ones who've left. Keep it on the down-low from the weekend warriors. Got it?"

"Yes, sir!"

In his office, Rex focused on the tall woman in camo fatigues, her mahogany red hair pinned neatly above her collar. All military, all the way. "Okay, Nolan. Spill it. Who the hell is Sweet Taggart? Why does that Sergeant-Major bear such a strong resemblance to Ramsey?"

After the staff meeting, she put the leftover cheesecake in the fridge. Leaving the butler's pantry, her phone vibrated. Debbie glanced at the screen, surprised to see the call was from Mindy MacGillicudy. "Hey, partner. How's it going? Are you enjoying retirement?"

"It's different not going to the barn at the crack of dawn," Mindy admitted. "I was at the new veteran's center yesterday, counseling some of the women and I ran into Ann Barrett, Devon's mother. She's getting married on Saturday and reminded me that I was supposed to give you an invitation. She says your daughters are welcome at the ceremony, too."

"How nice of her, but I don't know how comfortable I'd be at a stranger's wedding."

"She's in Sullivan Murphy's Army Reserve unit. Ann's dad owns the Majestyk Morgan horse farm on the far side of Baker City. He's also the president of the business association here in town. He gets re-elected every year despite his bitching because nobody else wants the responsibility. Like the rest of us, you'll have to stay on his good side, Debbie. Plus, I'm the person who promised to close Miracle for Ann's wedding so everyone could attend the festivities."

Debbie looked at the phone. "You didn't tell me before."

"No, because I'm an old lady who either has dementia after all those years on the farm, or else is a total space cadet. Then again, I could just have been overwhelmed by the adjustment to retirement. It's all my fault, but I need you to bail me out here."

Nothing could be further from the truth. Mindy was one of the sharpest people Debbie ever met. "It doesn't sound like I have much of a choice, but I haven't gone to church since I was a kid. I don't plan on starting now."

"Why not? Is this when I ask what baggage you're packing? Reverend Tommy praises your girls to the skies, but said you brushed him off when he visited. You told him the stable kept you too busy to attend church, and he told me I only missed when I had a sick horse."

Debbie walked into the kitchen. "As the saying goes, not my circus, not my monkeys."

"Definitely lots of baggage. Luckily for you, I'm a former high school psychologist and I'm licensed to provide answers even to unasked questions. If you're not coming to the ceremony, join us for the reception out at Frank Madison's Taj Mahal barn. It may give you some ideas to update Miracle. Frank and his wife, Ginger, will send you a bunch of students because they don't do beginners or children. Ann had to get a pony for her daughter from Cat O'Leary-McTavish."

"Way too much drama for a newcomer to Baker City and again, I don't do church."

But Mindy wasn't to be deterred. "You don't have to attend services. This is a small town, Debbie, and I'm going to keep browbeating you until you agree to come to the reception. Don't make me send Ann or Sully or one of the other female vets to harass you. Because I will."

"All right. You win." Debbie heaved a sigh. "I'll be there. Where is Ann registered so I can get an appropriate gift?"

"Ask Trina. Jassy, her older sister had a fit and fell in it when Ann's ex-husband hosted a garage sale and started selling her things while she was on her last combat tour."

"What the hell was he thinking?"

"He'd filed for divorce and was in 'prick of misery mode' because his wife went off to war without his permission."

"Is that the professional term for it?" Debbie felt a smile tremble into life. "You may turn out to be my kind of headshrinker, Mindy. I might even discuss growing up in a cult with you."

"I'm a good listener, although I've been known to express inappropriate opinions. I did even before I served as a nurse in Vietnam."

"I can deal with that a lot better than I could with some of the Army chaplains who kept preaching 'forgiveness' and 'acceptance' at me."

"Not my style. I'll hold out for Lieutenant Howell M. Forgy, the chaplain aboard the USS New Orleans at Pearl Harbor who said, "Praise the Lord and pass the ammunition." Later, it became a song and rallying cry during World War Two."

"Okay, he sounds like he might have understood, too, so I'll agree with you about him," Debbie said. "Maybe one day I'll share my story."

"Only when you're ready. Meantime, the other women veterans are waiting until after day camp ends and school starts to invite you to join their support group. Margo Endicott started it this summer because she says women have different issues than the guys do, and it helps to talk about them."

"I'm not into sharing sob stories." Debbie headed for the front door. "And now, I'm going to help with horsy chores."

"I'll keep nagging you to participate."

"Don't. It's been a good day so far and I haven't unleashed the flying monkeys yet, but I will."

CHAPTER EIGHT

She contemplated going to bed early since she had a camp horseshow the next day, but after several combat tours, sleep was never much of a priority. Tomorrow afternoon, she'd be doing the horsy version of 'did you want fries or onion rings with that burger?', a question she learned to ask when she worked in a restaurant before she left for boot camp almost eighteen years before.

After she finished printing off brochures for the fall programs, she snagged a bottle of red wine and a glass. She and Shasta headed for the porch swing.

She filled the glass, put the half-full bottle on the porch rail and settled down on the swing to enjoy the wee hours before dawn. A short while later, her phone vibrated, and she drew it out of her jeans pocket. "Good morning, sir."

"Thought you were going to call me by my first name, Ramsey."

"I'm still contemplating that. Did you get your wounded warriors here okay?"

"They're all settled in at the base hospital. When I checked on them after supper, most were sleeping. One was watching the news. How did your first staff meeting go today?"

"Good. Your bonus plan was a hit. Everyone is revved up about selling classes and riding clubs, so we'll see how that goes. I promised Vangie and Penny they could participate too and earn some serious bucks."

"That's fair." Silence for a moment and then Rex said, "You had company here today."

"Really? You already have Gimone and Juana working for you, in addition to the regular folks."

"Not our troops. Sergeant-Major West Taggart."

Debbie gasped and almost dropped the cell phone. "No way. What did he want?"

"I already said it. He's looking for his little sister. Nolan claimed not to know anything about her, but that's you, isn't it? Sweet Taggart? Hell, of a name there, Ramsey. Why did you change it?"

"That isn't important. What did you tell him?"

"To haul ass out of my office. After being in Texas on TDY, I had work to do since you bailed on me and left two people with barely any training in charge."

"Bullshit, Major. Nolan and Castaneda are experts in supply operations. Nobody could ever claim either of them are incompetent."

"Not what Major Bevins says. I ran into him when I was having dinner at the Officer's Club tonight, and he informed me they actually were fantastic at 'spuddle'. They are very ineffective, ineffectual and act extremely busy while achieving absolutely nothing. He wants me to agree to send them back to his neck of the woods."

Angered by the insult to her friends, Debbie's hand clenched on the stem of her wineglass. "And what did you tell him?"

"Spit in the wind and call it a shower. The man's a complete asshat. I trust you, Ramsey. Other than abandoning me in my hour of need, you've always had my six. Since you knew you were leaving, you'd have found the best possible replacements. Plus, the full-time enlisted in all four warehouses are happier with them than I expected."

Relaxing in the porch swing, Debbie sipped her Zinfandel. "All right, then. I'm glad everything is running smoothly."

"And Taggart? What do I do with him if he comes back?"

Debbie shrugged, staring into the moonlit night. "Tell him to go to hell or to the Celestial Faith cult in Montana. They're about the same."

"Already did that." Faint amusement trickled into Rex's voice. "Well, I didn't know about the cult. I suggested he talk to his family about his problems. Was that it? Did you grow up in some sort of religious order?"

"Until I was fifteen." Debbie swirled the wine in her glass. "Have you ever seen those polygamy TV shows? It was a lot like that. Sister-wives, young girls married off to old men, very fundamentalist Christian, highly patriarchal. My mother was my father's fifth spiritual wife."

"I'm amazed they let you leave." Rex paused. "Or was that one of the choices you talked about before?"

"Yes." Debbie finished the wine and refilled her glass. "Like I said, my father told me I could return to Montana at Christmas if I agreed to marry either the bishop, a sanctimonious man older than dirt who beat his wives when they disagreed with him, or one of his grown sons who also didn't believe in 'sparing the rod' on rebellious wives or children or animals."

"And you refused."

"Definitely." Debbie stared into the liquid and debated telling him the rest of the story. She wasn't ready to talk about surviving a rape or her son, so she'd hold off on that. "Like I told you before, I stayed at the academy until I graduated from high school and then moved in with my grandparents for two months. I'd already enlisted and that summer, I went to basic training."

"And West? Did he hurt you?"

"No, he'd left for the Army when I was about five. He was always good to me. He taught me to read and write. Literacy wasn't a big deal for girl children unless they needed it to help cook or do chores around the house and farm. He insisted my father send me to school and made sure I wasn't pulled out after eighth grade like the other girls. West was decent, but I don't want to see him."

"Why not?"

"Because he's connected to the Celestial Faith, and I'm done with them. I was finished when my father blamed me for what happened and sent me —" Her voice trailed off. "Never mind. I can't talk any more about that. Not yet."

"Okay, then we'll wait. What are your plans for the weekend?"

Relief swept through her. Grateful she didn't need to think about the past any longer, she told him about the wedding reception and the tablecloths, placemats, and napkins she'd ordered for the happy couple. "Do you remember Sullivan Barlow? The noncom with the hot pink, classic Mustang?"

"Sure. Is she the bride?"

"No, that's Ann Barrett. The two of them are in the same Army Reserve unit. Sully married Tate Murphy and they have a place up here. They're expecting twins next month, so she's nesting."

Rex chuckled. "Better to do it now before she's a mom. What else have you learned in your new home, Ramsey? Do Hobby and Wonder like living there?"

"You know it. They get more than their share of carrots from the campers, the staff, and the visitors."

Hanging around the hospital and watching his buddies sleep or Waco Hawke stare at the hot, ash-blonde newscaster on TV didn't rank up there as favorite activities so Moises joined the liaison officer when Major Sinclair walked through the ward to check on his compatriots.

Granted, the man couldn't see him, but Moises didn't much care. Anything had to be better than the 'hurry up and wait' routine that bored the hell out of him. When he left the hospital, the officer picked up an order of take-out Chinese and then headed home. He settled into a recliner and turned on a ball game. Definitely Moises' kind of man. Sometime during oh-dark-thirty, he called a woman and they talked for more than an hour, but she didn't come over.

The next day, it was an early morning trip to a warehouse. Moises followed along, careful not to knock anything catty-wumpus as his granny used to say. It turned out the major was in charge of the place. Before lunch, two noncoms showed up with paperwork to collect supplies. One of them, a tall, dark-haired man in camouflage fatigues, seemed to be well-liked not only by the enlisted personnel, but also by their commander. He introduced his companion as a temporary replacement for him.

"So, what's up with that, Murphy?" Amused, Major Sinclair folded his arms and eyed the two men while his X.O. studied the forms. The petite woman in camos gestured for the sergeant-major to join her and they walked away, further into the large building. "Why do you need Taggart to take over for you?"

"My mom called this morning and said my wife has started setting up her classroom for school this year," Tate Murphy explained. "Major Harper gave me leave so I can go to Baker City and put the hammer down."

"I heard you married Sullivan Barlow. Does she let you drive that hot pink Mustang of hers?"

"Not willingly." Tate chuckled. "I did once, and she called the local police chief to report it stolen. We're having twins next month, so I'll go do the heavy lifting and remind her to rest."

"Good luck with that. She was still on crutches when she worked here last Christmas, and it was all Ramsey, and I could do to keep Barlow on desk duty."

"Scuttlebutt is Master Sergeant Ramsey took early retirement and left this man's army," Tate said. "Looks like everything still runs pretty smoothly."

"She saw to it that I had two good folks to replace her before she went," Major Sinclair agreed. "You'll probably run into her up in your neck of the woods. She bought Miracle Riding Stable. I'll look forward to seeing you there." He paused. "Do me a solid and don't share that with the sergeant-major. They have history and Ramsey doesn't want to see him. I promised to run interference."

"You got it." Tate whistled softly. "The guy's a hardass, but I figure Major Harper can handle him. I'm going to be busy doing what Sully calls my 'Doctor Internet' thing, but I'll undoubtedly be over at Miracle sometimes since it's where my niece takes lessons."

Baker City, Moises thought. He remembered Waco Hawke talking about the place. *It's been fun, Major, but I'm headed north with Murphy. Hawke said it was a friendly small town with room for new folks. I want to check it out.*

Friday morning zipped by with grooming, saddling, and practicing for the upcoming camp show. After lunch, the kids tied ribbons on their western saddles and braided more brightly colored decorations into the manes. Once everyone made final trips to the bathrooms, Debbie had them mount up and parade to the large outdoor arena. They were circling the ring when their parents began to arrive.

Through the next two hours, the riding demonstration continued, following the same pattern Mindy MacGillicudy had used successfully for so many years. It began with the kids doing exercises on a variety of different sized horses and ponies followed by basic movements, starting, stopping, backing, and steering before they did more patterns in the arena. They finished with the timed Western games that Kyra taught them. Afterward, the visiting adults toured through the barns while campers took care of their horses.

Debbie pasted on her brightest smile and circulated, talking to the parents about the upcoming fall schedule. She nodded a greeting to Sully Murphy who stood outside the stall where Letty groomed a dainty gray

Arabian-Appaloosa mare. "Hi. How are you doing? Ready for two new recruits?"

"I'm good, and I have almost six weeks to go before my due date. The hard part is telling everyone in the Murphy family that I'm fine and don't need to spend all my days resting on a couch. School starts the first week of September and I'm going to get my students in shape before I go on maternity leave. I don't want them harassing my temporary replacement."

Sully gestured to the tall, curvaceous brunette in faded jeans and a purple sweatshirt feeding the horse a carrot. "This is my sister-in-law, Quinn, Letty's stepmom. I was telling her what you shared with me yesterday about how well Letty is doing even though she's not ready to have Fancy at home yet."

"Tell me more about the Saturday program," Quinn said. "Lyle, my husband, and I were discussing it last night. He's on-board if you include stall mucking, feeding and other horsy chores. He wants Letty to be able to take care of a horse someday."

"That's part of the deal." Debbie handed over a brochure and began discussing the details of the riding club.

With everything done in the barns a little after five pm, the staff met in the office along with Vangie and Penny. Debbie looked around the small room at her help. "We rocked and rolled today. Four kids already registered for the Saturday club starting in September."

Kyra leaned back in her chair. "That doesn't count the ones who signed up for more lessons."

"And those on the waiting list for the last session of camp," Trina added, sitting in the far corner.

"Or those who reserved trail rides for Labor Day weekend," Jason said.

"More big tips. My fave." Carol giggled. "Next year, we should think about training a group to exhibit at the county fair. If they score enough championship ribbons, it'll be good for business."

"Don't forget, the moms who booked birthday parties," Vangie said. "I figure we ought to wait on the bonuses for those, Ramsey. We have deposits, but—"

"Sometimes, people make other arrangements," Penny agreed. "If Gary got pissed at us, he cancelled our sleepovers and parties at the last minute."

"I recommend you don't share that with your father." Debbie rolled a pen in her hand. "I'm pretty sure he's already got a few things to say to your stepdad."

Vangie giggled. "Starting with that's bull—"

"Don't be inappropriate, Evangeline." Debbie reached over to turn on the adding machine. "Let's figure out everyone's paychecks and call it a night. We have a big weekend ahead of us and a wedding to attend."

Although Vangie and Penny went to the wedding with Kyra and Trina, Debbie avoided the ceremony at the church. Instead, she drove to Majestyk Morgan Farm on the other side of Baker City in the early afternoon. White board fences and green pastures lined the first gravel driveway that wound past the huge indoor riding arena and horse barns to a large three-story house.

She parked beside Mindy's small pickup truck and went to find the previous owner of Miracle Riding Stable. Debbie found the older woman putting tablecloths on circular tables and jumped in to help. "Been working here long?"

"Actually, my cousin's daughter and her crew just got here from the church. I hate standing around with my finger in my ear, so I volunteered to give them a hand." Mindy shook out the next white linen cover. "I'll introduce you to Linda later. She has the local housecleaning service, in addition to helping her dad my cousin with the catering end of his restaurant business. I always had her do my house twice a month during the school year and every week in the summer because I didn't know if I was coming or going from the barns."

"Really?" Debbie smoothed out the material on the table. "Maybe she'd be able to fit us in too. Would she also be able to provide healthy meals? I need to stop feeding the girls potpies and other frozen crap before their father shows up. He's into junk food and take-out. A little of that goes a long way."

Mindy laughed. "Considering Linda's dad owns Pop's Café, it should be a no-brainer."

It'd been a good day, Debbie thought, stretching out on the porch swing late that night. Shasta stretched out next to her. The puppy rested her head comfortably on her owner's lap. Everyone had been friendly in town, and she'd done the 'meet and greet' routine with other residents of Baker City. Nobody even questioned why she hadn't shown up at the church for the ceremony. She finished her wine, put the glass on the porch rail and drifted into a light doze.

A short time later, the sound of a truck engine and the crunch of tires on gravel woke her. Her pistol was stowed in the gun safe in the study and she reached for the wine bottle. Almost full, it'd serve as a decent weapon. Shasta yawned, stretched, and then barked before jumping down from the swing. Debbie followed the dog in the direction of the intruder.

She came to a stop when she recognized the man walking into the pool of light as he advanced toward the porch. She wasn't the only one. Shasta raced to meet him, pressing close so he could scratch behind her ears. It felt different to see him in civvies, faded jeans, a red western shirt with white trim and pearl snaps, as well as cowboy boots. "I knew I should have installed gates at the far end of the driveway."

"There's always tomorrow, Ramsey." He strode up the steps. "I didn't feel like talking on the phone tonight, so I thought we'd do it in person. Going to share that wine?"

"I only have one glass." Smiling, she swung around, and headed back to the swing. "Give me a minute and I'll get another one."

"Not needful. We're married, remember? We can share. We've done it before, and it won't be the first time we swapped spit."

CHAPTER NINE

He sat at the other end of the porch swing while Debbie filled the glass half full and then passed it to him. "Is this when I ask how you found us?"

"I saw the t-shirts the girls wore advertising the barn when they sent pictures of what they call, "their" horses. Both Vangie and Penny also mentioned the name of the place when I talked to them on their phones. A little Internet searching, and it didn't take long to locate Miracle Riding Stable." He shrugged and sipped the red wine. "You need to update the website, Ramsey."

"It's on my 'to-do' list. Right now, I'm focused on summer camp. One more week and then I'll switch over to fall programs. I'll have more time for office stuff and promotion once school starts. I'm enrolling Penny in Baker City. Vangie will attend the high school in Lake Maynard."

"When do classes begin?" Rex passed the glass to Debbie. "In a week or so? The Tuesday after Labor Day?"

"No, that first Wednesday, September 4th." It was her turn to drink. "After camp this week, we'll go school shopping on Friday night unless they're too tired or next Sunday or we may hold off until Labor Day."

He nodded, taking the glass from her. "So, you intend for them to be here for the duration. Keep track of what you spend, and I'll reimburse you. Have you heard from their mother? Does she want them back anytime soon?"

"I have no idea. She hasn't contacted my attorney either. Has she called you?"

"Not lately. Guess we should go with the theory, *no news is good news.*"

"Works for me."

He finished the wine. "So, what comes next, Ramsey? It's 0200. How do you feel about breakfast?"

She rose to her feet, picking up the bottle off the porch rail. She took a moment to admire his rough-hewn features, strong cheekbones and the short, salt and pepper hair. "I'm good at bacon and eggs if you want to make the toast."

"Works for me." He chuckled and amusement warmed the golden-brown eyes.

Debbie led the way inside, down the hall and into the country-style kitchen with white, freshly painted walls, wood beams on the ceiling and laminate wood-planked floors, plus natural light from the large windows during the day. Long, wooden counters and cream cupboards matched the walls. A rural tiled backsplash featured chickens, cows, goats, ponies, and sheep. In an attempt to attract a buyer, Mindy MacGillicudy had updated the room with new appliances, thankfully white rather than stainless-steel ones, and a farmhouse sink.

Instead of a contemporary island, there was an old-fashioned dining table, surrounded by comfortable chairs. An antique, working wood stove in the corner would provide not only a place to cook, but heat on the days when they lost electricity. Shasta headed for the rag rug in front of the large woodstove and promptly curled up to sleep.

Debbie went into the pantry and collected the eggs and bacon from the fridge. "I've been buying homegrown meat, fresh fruit, veggies and eggs from Tate Murphy's family."

"It's a small world." Rex opened the bread box on the counter. "He came by the warehouse yesterday and said he was on the way here to look after Sullivan Barlow."

"Murphy," Debbie corrected, laying thick slices of bacon on a cast-iron griddle. "She told me one of the benefits of marrying him was changing her name to his, since she has issues with her relatives who still blame her for that ambush in Afghanistan. Another was gaining his family who she dearly loves, and they certainly adore her. They waited on her, hand, and foot, at the wedding reception today."

Rex removed a knife from the butcher block and sliced the loaf of homemade sourdough. "She say anything about Tate?"

"Considering she spent most of her time clinging to him and referring to him as Master Sergeant Hot Stuff, I think they're good." Debbie cracked each egg into a cup before dumping them into a bowl. Granted, she'd been promised there wouldn't be baby chicks in them, but having grown up on a farm, she wasn't taking any chances. "He still griped a bit about her not letting him behind the wheel of the Mustang."

"He doesn't want to go there." Rex slid pieces of bread into the toaster, waiting to push the lever. "He already told me she called the cops on him once for driving it without permission."

"Not surprised." Debbie added a dash of raw milk to the eggs, then poured the mixture into a skillet. "She and her BFF fixed up the car back in the day. Raven Barlow didn't make it back from the *sandpit* this time, and Sully has a real attachment to their rig."

"You heard more than I did, Ramsey. Where do I find jam for the toast?"

"The fridge in the butler's pantry." She gestured toward the doorway. "I still have issues about not being able to see everything, so leave the sliding door open to the kitchen. The refrigerator has an icemaker and you'll find glasses in the cupboard. Let's drink water with breakfast."

He nodded agreement and followed directions. When he returned with a container of strawberry preserves, he said, "This looks homemade, too."

"It is. Bronwyn Murphy, Tate's mom makes it." Debbie glanced at him and saw the humor build in his gaze. "You didn't think I'd really taken up domesticity, did you, Sinclair?"

"I'm smarter than that." He put the jar of jam and butter dish on the table, then opened cupboards until he found the dishes. He put the plates on the counter next to her, then stepped away. "Where do we go from here, Ramsey? We did fairly well this past year when you supervised the warehouses for me."

"Only because I didn't run around screaming 'bullshit' at the top of my lungs when you pissed me off." She flipped the slices of bacon, then stirred the eggs. "What happens now that I'm a civilian and don't have to cater to your whims?"

"I'm trying to recall when you did that." He tore paper towels off the holder. "My kind of napkins. I think I can handle it if you're angry. I'm worried more about scaring you."

She froze for a moment before she switched off the burners. "Say again, Major."

"Rex." He remained by the table. "Use my name, not my rank. Haven't we always promised each other honesty? What do I have to do to gain your trust, Ramsey?"

The sound of her last name inspired confidence. She glanced at him. Even in civilian clothes, he was the warrior she'd always admired, never admitting defeat and always ready to fight again.

Pasting on the facade of a calm, controlled professional soldier, she dished up the scrambled eggs and slices of bacon. "I'm not afraid of your temper or shouting, but don't ever think of raising a hand to me."

Rex's jaw tightened, and he narrowed his gaze. "Who was he?"

"Take your pick." Debbie carried the plates over to the table. "My father never 'spared the rod,' and most of my brothers used his example as an invitation to abuse us. Our mothers told us not to bother them and they would leave us alone." She paused. "It never worked."

"Mothers? How does that work? I only had one."

"Sister-wives, remember?" Debbie drew out a chair and sat down, waiting while he brought over the toast. "My mom was my dad's fifth wife. He insisted we call all the wives in the house our mothers. By the time I was fifteen, I saw the friction between them. I already knew I didn't want to be one, but I didn't dare say so."

"Makes sense." He passed her a slice of bread. "Let's eat and you can tell me more later."

She smiled. "My turn to say, *works for me*, Sinclair."

Rex had to admit blue jeans suited her. They showed off her curving hips and long legs. The bright blue t-shirt that clung to her breasts matched the electric blue eyes. She'd dug into the food in front of her and he wondered if she'd been eating regular meals. He'd wait to ask those kind of questions. For now, he'd count his proverbial blessings and contemplate how to kick West Taggart's ass around the fort without sharing what he was learning from the man's younger sister.

After they ate, Rex helped clean the kitchen. "Where do I sleep? Got a guest room? Or blankets so I can crash on the couch in the living-room?"

"Are you serious?" She lifted her chin. "Isn't this when you remind me, we're married?"

"We have been for almost eight years."

"I know, and we've slept together before."

He waited. The silence dragged as he tried to come up with the right words. He caught her left hand and squeezed it. "Now that you can't use deployment or an upcoming combat tour to avoid me, how about we re-negotiate our terms?"

"What's your offer?"

"Me."

When she woke Sunday morning, bright sunlight streamed through the windows. Shasta snored next to her, cuddling close in the large sleigh bed. Debbie glanced at the nightstand and froze when she saw the numbers on the radio-clock. Ten-hundred hours? What happened? She always set the alarm for emergencies, but normally woke at five a.m. Country music should have blasted her awake. Why had she slept until ten in the morning?

She checked the switches and realized someone had turned off the alarm. It must have been Sinclair. Only another combat-trained soldier could creep in here and not wake her.

It'd touched her when he insisted on giving her space to consider his suggestion last night or rather very early this morning. She'd almost brought him up to bed with her, but then decided to wait and see how their relationship worked out now that she was a civilian.

Debbie stroked Shasta's soft fur and the young dog yawned, revealing white teeth. "You'd have yipped at Penny or Vangie, but I think the major totally spoiled you. I'll have to remind him he said he'd wait for an invitation."

On the far end of the bed, Bandit stretched into a kitty yoga position, then curled up in a heap on the comforter. Debbie laughed and eased out from under the covers. "Okay, let's go. We have a lot to do today." Gathering clean clothes, she headed for the ensuite and the shower.

Accompanied by the cat and half-grown dog, she went downstairs a short time later. She fed them before she made herself a slice of toast to go with that first cup of coffee.

Pouring a second one, she sauntered out to the wrap-around front porch where she saw Rex sitting in the swing, nursing his own mug of java. He wore civilian clothes again, jeans, a blue-checked western shirt, and his boots. "What did you do with the girls?"

"They taught me how to help with horsy chores. After that, they cleaned up and went off to church with your barn managers. Vangie told me they want to hang out with their new friends. I agreed we'd meet them at the café in town for a late lunch."

"Sounds like we're building a routine." Debbie joined him on the swing. "Shall we take out Hobby and Wonder for a ride? I can give you a tour of the place."

"I'd like that." He looked at her over the edge of his cup. "Captain Castaneda told me she and Sergeant Nolan could handle the warehouses tomorrow morning, so I'll drive back to the base before lunch and get there mid-afternoon."

She nodded, eyeing him warily. He didn't say anything about their conversation in the wee small hours of the morning, and neither did she. After they finished their coffee, she put the cups in the house along with the puppy. It'd take more training for the horses to become accustomed to Shasta accompanying them on rides and today wasn't the time to start.

Debbie led the way to the third barn where the privately owned mounts lived. In addition to her two horses and Mindy's, there were seven other boarders. She unlocked the tackroom and collected a handful of carrots before they walked down the wide aisle to the stalls. Hobby, a solid golden bay mare with black points nickered when she saw them. Her son, Wonder, a bright yellow buckskin with a black mane, tail and legs like his momma's was quick to follow suit. He seemed to recognize Rex who used to ride him at the army base, but then again, it could have been the treats.

While they groomed and saddled the horses in the stalls, Debbie told him about the ranch, describing the two hundred acres. "There's a large wood lot, year-round streams, at least one in each pasture, so I won't have to irrigate. Next spring, I'll restore the hay fields and that will cut down on costs when I raise rather than buy feed."

"Sounds like a good plan." He bridled Wonder. "What was the river I drove across?"

"It's actually called Cedar Creek. Mindy claims when it rises during the winter, it can flood the lower pastures, but I haven't seen that happen yet. I'll have to be careful to keep the stock away from those paddocks during the rainy season."

"You're thinking all the time, Ramsey."

"After all these years, you should know it better than anyone else."

When they rode out, she headed for the trail that wound up the ridge behind the barns. For safety, the campers stuck to the lower levels when they rode on the paths around the arenas, but Debbie wanted to show the territorial views to Rex. At the top of the first hill, she reined Hobby to a stop. A cool breeze brushed her face and she smiled, grateful it hadn't heated up yet. Insects wouldn't irritate the horses. "It's always been my dream to have a place in the country."

He gazed around them at the huge evergreens bordering the track. "You chose well. Now, let's see your spread."

"You've got it." She petted Hobby's brown neck and then squeezed her legs to signal the mare to move forward at a faster walk. When she glanced over her shoulder at him, she saw Cedar Creek shimmering in the distance. Then she focused on what lay ahead.

With three rising terraces, the land spread out around them. Each terraced portion of the farm had its share of barns, storage sheds, and even a cabin or two for the help.

Sooner or later, she'd have to hire ranch-hands to do the maintenance, but that could wait until after day-camp ended and she had time to interview prospective employees. For now, she'd enjoy riding with Rex Sinclair. She flicked a sideways glance at him. He was a hunk and a half in the blue shirt that emphasized his broad shoulders and muscled arms. He made her feel safe for the first time in ages.

When he smiled, her pulses thudded in anticipation. So, perhaps she didn't want that safety after all. Maybe she longed for a little excitement to brighten her days and nights.

While he paid attention to the winding track through the evergreens and the horse he rode, Rex also took time to enjoy the company of the woman riding ahead of him. Her black braid bounced against the back of the blue t-shirt she wore. Her hips shifted in the saddle when she urged Hobby to a slow jog. It wasn't the first time they'd hit the trails together. During the past year, they'd met at the stable at Fort Clark and exercised the horses once a week in the off season.

He allowed Wonder to catch up with her, so the horses were beside each other. "Summers are crazy at the base with the reserve units in for training, so the warehouses kept us busy. When did you bring Hobby and Wonder here?"

"Over July 4th. Fort Clark basically shut down for the holiday and Mindy needed extra help because Miracle closes due to fireworks. It was just her, Kyra O'Neill, Trina Sweeney, and me."

"Explosives and horses don't mix." He reined Wonder closer to his mother. "Are you going to close over Labor Day weekend?"

"I'd planned to be open." Her magnificent blue eyes crinkled in thought. "Maybe we can close early since people shoot off fireworks at night."

"How was it during the Fourth?"

"Awful." She shuddered at the memory, her shoulders shifting. Her hand tightened on the reins and Hobby tossed her head impatiently. Debbie heaved a sigh, obviously forcing herself to relax so the mare would. "It sounded like a warzone all day until midnight for a week straight. Dick O'Connell, the police chief, drove around issuing citations to the out-of-towners who shot off illegal ones."

"Good guy to know." Rex chuckled. "Unless you're Tate Murphy and you're driving Sullivan's hot pink Mustang."

Debbie laughed. "After seeing how particular she was when she parked it at the warehouse, we both know how that went."

Three hours later, they sat in a booth at Pop's Café in Baker City, waiting for the girls to join them. Rex enjoyed the opportunity to look at Debbie. Blue eyes, winged black eyebrows, long black eyelashes and her forehead knit in thought as she studied the menu. A blue shirt advertising Miracle Riding Stable hugged her breasts.

He picked up the cup of black coffee in front of him and sipped. "What's good?"

"I'm in a rut," she admitted. "I study the whole menu and then opt for a deluxe cheeseburger with all the fixings, homemade fries and a chocolate malt."

"Sounds great. I'll have the same thing." He winked at her. "Do those trimmings include grilled onions? I'll have them if you do. I don't want you complaining about my breath when I kiss you. I already told you I want something permanent."

Color rose in her cheeks. "Braggart."

He shifted slightly to avoid the kick she aimed at him under the table. "Not bragging if I know I can do it, Mrs. Sinclair."

"Don't call me that. I'm Debbie Ramsey."

"You bet, and I don't have a problem if you use Sinclair occasionally." He laughed. "Get used to the idea. I already am."

CHAPTER TEN

Families trickled into the town café after church, but the only person Moises Pride recognized was the major. Granted, the man wore civvies, but he still carried himself like a soldier. A dark-haired woman sat across from him in their booth and Moises decided it must be the same one the officer called late at night. She wore an elaborate wedding ring set on her left hand.

Were the two of them having an affair? Before he figured out their business, a teenage girl and her younger sister came in the restaurant, heading toward the adults. Moises drifted closer to listen to the conversation. Okay, so he was poking his nose where his granny would say it didn't belong, but he was insatiably curious.

"You should have come to church with us, Daddy." The smaller girl smiled at the major, waiting for him to stand so she could slide into the booth next to him. "It was fun. Naveah got to sing a solo."

"Who is Naveah?"

"One of the Murphy's foster girls," the woman said, rising to let the teenager into the other side of the booth, opposite her sister. "Tate's parents own an organic farm on the other side of town. You'll meet Naveah Johnson when we take a run out there to buy fresh eggs and veggies. She, Chantrea Yang and Vangie are in the same grade."

"Sounds good." The major passed a menu to the younger girl sitting next to him. "Are you looking forward to school here, Penny?"

"Yes. I already met my teacher. She came to help us move in last week. She's funny and super nice. She's having a baby, but not until Halloween. She says some of the kids call her Captain Endicott while others say, Ms. Endicott, or even Ms. Margo."

"What's up with that, Ramsey?" the major asked.

"It's a blended classroom," the woman explained. "Margo Endicott is a captain in the Army Reserve and now that she's home, she teaches second, third and fourth grades. A brand-new teacher, Lisa Jensen, has kindergarten, first grade and a few second-graders. Ann Barrett and Sullivan Murphy have older kids. I like Baker City School. All of them are reservists."

Moises was waiting for the answer when someone behind him interrupted. "Time to bug out, soldier." He started to turn around, but the woman–a ghost like him, he realized–added, "Let's go!"

He turned. "Who are you?"

The ghostly woman was in camos and combat boots. "First Sergeant Raven Driscoll-Barlow. I outrank you, Corporal. When I say, *jump*, you do it and hope it's high enough." She gestured to a dark doorway on the far side of the restrooms. "Move it!"

He obeyed orders and found himself in an empty cocktail lounge, not what he'd expected. Empty—of living people—but filled with other apparitions.

Some wore various military uniforms going well back before World War Two. He looked around, seeing women in pioneer dresses, a few in flapper attire from the 1920s, and more in what he considered regular civilian clothes. He spotted guys dressed as loggers and miners. There was even one older man in a dark suit who acted as if he were totally in charge.

Wow, Moises thought. *It's like that old movie. I see dead people.* Aloud, he asked, "What's going on here? How did you find me?"

"Those are our questions." This time, a dark-haired man came forward, another Army Ranger. "I'm Zeke Garvey. Died last September in Afghanistan like Barlow, but it was a different ambush."

Moises stared at the two soldiers waiting for him to answer. *Home. I've come home. Why didn't Sergeant Hawke tell me the secret of Baker City? Or didn't he know?*

Smiling, Debbie passed the menu to Vangie and listened while the girls shared what happened at church and the social time afterwards. There were undoubtedly more details that would come up during the week, especially when Penny mentioned Vangie talking to a cute guy. That earned a fierce scowl from the teen and a squeal from the younger one who claimed her older sister kicked her under the table. Rex intervened before Debbie could, telling the girls while he didn't know their mother's rules, his was no dating until they were sixteen.

"Ramsey, tell him that's not fair," Vangie protested. "I've been going out with guys since I was fourteen."

"I've already told the three of you before. Don't involve me in your piddly squabbles." Debbie picked up her coffee cup. "I was in boarding school at your age, and the church insisted we adhere to the community regs. We couldn't date until we were eighteen, or we graduated from their high school. I'm good with that."

"I'm not," Vangie muttered, sulking while she looked through the menu. "Dray was majorly hot, and Naveah says there are even cuter guys at the high school."

"Forget it and him." Debbie sipped her coffee. "Your dad already laid out the rules."

"Glad there's no discussion and we're in agreement, Ramsey."

A few moments later, Pop arrived to take their lunch orders and Debbie introduced him to Rex. After a few pleasantries, the older man departed for the kitchen. As other groups entered the restaurant, the greetings continued. When Cat O'Leary-McTavish arrived, the baby in a snug wrap on her chest and her husband behind her carrying a diaper bag, they paused by the booth.

"I'm glad you're here," Cat said, after the courtesies. "The girls want to come to camp this week, and so does Devon Sweeney-Barrett. She's staying with us while her mom and Harry Colter are gone on their honeymoon. Do you have enough horses?"

"I think so." Debbie frowned thoughtfully, considering the question. "None of the girls are that tall, and I know we still have ponies available. I'll verify it when I get home, but it should work."

"That will make points with the twins." Rob smiled at her. "They told us staying home is boring since we don't go many places with a new baby."

Debbie laughed. Before she could add another comment, the strawberry-blonde twins who were Penny's age and size, joined them. Like her, they wore jeans, t-shirts and running shoes.

Sophie, one of the girls, stepped up beside her mother. "When we came out of the restroom after washing our hands, the mayor saw us. He wants you and Daddy to come talk to new folks 'bout the rules for living here."

"He says, in the lounge," Samantha, her sister continued. "He told us it was grown up business so we *haveta* stay here 'cause some of them are iffy."

"Okay." Cat and Rob exchanged glances and then she gestured to a nearby table. "Wait here for us." She turned to Debbie. "Would you mind keeping an eye on the two of them? If Mayor O'Connell doesn't want the girls, he'll have a good reason. He'll share it with us when we get there."

"No worries," Debbie said. "The twins are always amazing at following directions at the barn."

"And if they want to come to camp this week, they'll remember their manners," Rob said, before he followed his wife across the restaurant.

"Have you met the mayor yet?" Rex asked.

Debbie shook her head. "No. I probably will when the BC Business Association meets next month. I haven't had a great deal of time to socialize because summer is busy at the stable and I'm going from oh-dark-thirty to the end of the duty day and it's not at 1730 like it was on base."

The twins eyed her before Sophie inquired. "Are you like Mommy, Daddy, and us? If you aren't, then you won't *see* the mayor or any of the other folks in the lounge."

"Why wouldn't she?" Rex scanned the pair of nine-year-olds. "What does that mean?"

"Mayor O'Connell's dead." Samantha twirled a strand of red-gold hair around a finger. "He says he died a long time ago when his heart stopped working."

"But it wasn't as long ago as when our first teacher in Baker City died. The school got squashed in a big snowstorm, and they had to build a new one for us." Sophie beamed at Pop as he came toward them, carrying a stack of menus. "Hi. Can we have apple juice while we wait for Mommy and Daddy and Claire?"

"Of course, you may." Pop looked around the dining room. "Where are they?"

"Talking to the mayor 'bout the new folks who've come here," Sophie said. "Not the living ones, but the dead ones."

Pop nodded. "All right, but you girls know most people don't care for those who talk to spirits. You're supposed to keep the O'Leary gift to yourselves."

"Sorry, Pop." It was Samantha's turn. "We forget sometimes because everybody who lives here knows about us."

"That's true." He gave them each a children's menu and put the others on the table for their parents. He lingered to pat their shoulders. "Now, no more sharing your talents and I'll bring your juice."

"Sounds to me like we've moved into the *Twilight Zone*, Ramsey. Is this when I begin humming the theme music?"

Debbie drank more coffee before she focused on Rex. "It's a nice *Twilight Zone*, and now you'll understand why I got such a good price on the stable."

"It doesn't sound like you're too concerned."

"I'm not. Cat informs me I don't have any ghosts living on my place. She did a walk-through to make sure before I moved into the house." Debbie shrugged. "I haven't heard anything go bump in the proverbial night."

"You won't unless you make 'em mad," Sophie told her. "Then, they bang stuff and make lots of noises and leave on the TV like one did at Toney's and Ally Hawke's house."

"Really?" Rex eyed the twins. "Who are they? What happened?"

"Our neighbors and their mom, Captain Heather told our mom she had to come fix it, so she and Daddy did." Samantha glanced warily toward the kitchen, obviously keeping a careful eye out for Pop. "Toney Hawke says it's all better now, but her momma said she didn't like the guy who visited when he was alive and he'd better shut off the TV when he leaves her house, or she'll make our mom kick him out for good. And if he complains 'cause he's not all the way dead yet, Captain Heather says she'll finish the job before she calls in our mom."

"That's what she and Daddy do. It's their job in Baker City," Sophie finished. "They send the ornery ghosts where they don't wanna go. The mayor says it's not the *good* place."

Pop's return with two glasses of apple juice silenced the twins and they focused on the menus in front of them. He glanced at Debbie. "Your order will be up in a few minutes. My daughter and grandson just arrived from church. She's taking over in the kitchen. He's on dishwashing duty, so you'll probably see him bussing tables."

"Thank you." Debbie eyed a slightly amused Rex. "You don't appear too concerned about the place. Aren't you afraid of ghosts?"

It was his turn to shrug. "We've been in enough hot spots over the years, Ramsey. I'm not threatened by any other groups, living or dead. We're a lot alike. I know you can handle most things and I have your six all the time."

"I'm counting on it."

―――――

A lengthy visit to the Murphy farm, followed by a tour of Sully and Tate Murphy's new home on the far side of Baker City took up most of the afternoon. They stopped at the town mercantile to pick up Debbie's mail and visit the deli where she selected fried chicken and cold salads. They returned to the riding stable barely in time for evening chores. After dinner, the girls did the dishes while Rex called the hospital to check the status of the recuperating soldiers. Debbie retreated to her study to organize camp for the next day, assigning horses and ponies to various riders for the last session.

When she finished, she found Rex and the girls setting up for a movie night in the living room. They'd apparently inventoried the assortment of films Mindy MacGillicudy left behind because she'd told Debbie that WiFi was hit and miss in the Baker City environs. Depending on weather and atmospheric conditions, the streaming services close to the Army base didn't always work in the Cascades.

Debbie opted to sit in one of the recliners while Rex nabbed the matching one. After passing out individual bowls of heavily buttered popcorn and glasses of soda, Vangie settled on the couch. Penny plopped onto large cushions on the floor, Shasta next to her with Mocha, the blue-eyed, long-haired Siamese cat lying on the other side of the girl.

"What are we watching?" Debbie lifted up the bowl so her tuxedo kitten, Bandit could curl up on her legs. "Please tell me it isn't one of your favorite dystopian teen flicks. I'm done with the 'odds not being in my favor'."

"It's not." Penny glanced over her shoulder. "And it isn't one of those westerns where you yell at the riders either."

"It isn't my fault they can't sit up straight, yank on the reins, kick the horses non-stop and all of those wanna-be cowboys and cowgirls ride like proverbial sacks of crap," Debbie retorted. "I wouldn't let them in my barns much less in the saddles. And you didn't answer me."

"We let Daddy pick from the DVDs Mindy left because it's his first night here," Penny said. "He says it's an oldie but a goodie."

"Really?" Debbie eyed him narrowly. "What is it?"

Rex raised his glass of soda in mock salute. "It's *We Bought a Zoo*,

Ramsey. I figured it'd be perfect for a woman who purchased a possibly haunted riding stable in the boonies."

"I'd better like it or you're in trouble. And I already told you that we don't have any ghosts here."

"I'm sure you'll love it." He glanced at Penny. "Okay, let's see it. Hit the remote, pumpkin."

The family drama about a widower buying a new home to share with his kids turned out to be a popular choice, one all of them enjoyed. It didn't hurt that it starred Matt Damon. Since morning came early, especially on camp days, the girls headed for bed after the show. While Debbie dumped out the extra kernels of popcorn and put the bowls in the dishwasher, Rex filled two glasses with red wine.

"So, are we going to the swing on the front porch?" He glanced at her and passed her one of the glasses. "Or drinking this in the living-room?"

"Front porch. Then you'll be able to tell me your plans for the warehouses this week." She led the way out of the room toward the front door. "You didn't have a chance to share how the escaped soldiers are doing."

"And you need to tell me your plans for the week. Vangie told me you invited her brothers to come for Labor Day weekend. Are they driving over from Eastern Washington or are you picking them up at one of the local airports and bringing them here?"

"Good questions. I don't know." She sat down next to him on the swing. "I haven't given it much thought."

"Wow, Ramsey." He chuckled. "Never thought I'd hear you admit you weren't prepared for something."

"Oh, I'll prep for it before Friday. Day camp comes first." She eyed him before sipping the wine in her glass. She didn't feel comfortable sharing the rest of the truth, why she always filled her work schedule at the end of August. When she was active-duty, she made a point of volunteering to work Labor Day weekend and let others enjoy popular end of the summer activities.

Her son, wherever he was now, would turn nineteen on August 31st.

For a moment, she remembered holding the sleeping infant with a shock of damp, dark hair. When she was released from the hospital, she returned alone to Celestial Faith boarding school while her grandparents took the baby to a local convent where the nuns proceeded with the adoption.

His new parents offered to send annual letters and photos, but she'd refused contact. Still, every year around his birthday, Debbie always wondered how he was. *Is he happy? Healthy? What kind of life does he have?*

The silence continued while she refilled their glasses. "What about you? Should we expect you for the three-day, holiday weekend?"

"I'll try to come up after we lock down the warehouses on Friday afternoon. It depends on how the soldiers in the hospital are doing." Rex paused. "It's a small world, Ramsey. One of them is named Hawke and I wondered if your lawyer has more than one brother or a missing cousin."

"Interesting question." She leaned back in the swing. "Now that you mention it, I'm curious about the neighbors who have Hawke Horse Heaven on the other side of Cedar Creek Guest Ranch. Maybe they're related to your soldier too. Have you checked out the personnel records yet?"

"I'm still waiting for those to arrive. If you were on base, I'd have you snoop around and see what you could learn, but I can't ask Nolan or Castaneda to do that."

"No, but you could talk to the guy concerned and ask him about his family."

The next morning, Rex jumped in to help not only with horsy chores, but also with grooming and saddling nineteen of the camp horses. That was one of the reasons she admired him. He never stood by and watched everyone else work. The advanced campers headed out for the trail while the beginners learned to groom and saddle their horses and ponies with Kyra.

Meantime, Debbie took the eight intermediates to the indoor arena for their first lesson. By 1100 hours, she had the kids in the saddles and checked their stirrups. She'd reminded them how to hold the reins cowboy style. The campers happily followed along as Jason demonstrated a variety of riding exercises from standing up and sitting down to boot-slaps. When most of them seemed comfortable on their horses, she had them check their balance by dropping the reins and moving their hands from their shoulders to their hips and pointing to their heels.

Situational awareness at full alert, she spotted Rex coming through the small gate at the far end of the arena. He'd obviously showered and changed into his ACUs, camouflage fatigues and combat boots. Leaving Jason in charge of basic riding skill practice, she went to greet Rex, meeting him in the center of the ring.

"Are you hitting the highway?"

"Traffic gets crazy later in the day and I want to give myself enough time to drive to the base. It's bound to take at least two hours, probably closer to three."

"Makes sense." She glanced quickly over her shoulder at the horses and campers. Everything appeared to be proceeding normally, but she wasn't leaving the arena. "Drive safe and call me when you arrive."

His smile warmed the golden-brown eyes. "I will, and I'll talk to you tonight."

"Sounds good." She stepped closer and caught a whiff of his spicy after-shave. As a civilian, the Army regs about sexual harassment didn't apply, so she could follow her heart instead of her brain.

She kissed him. She'd meant it to be a quick soft touch, but it turned into more. Her lips clung to his, her hands gripping his shoulders. Deliberately, she didn't deepen the kiss, not yet. And surprisingly, neither did he.

PART 2

AUGUST 2019

CHAPTER ELEVEN

The sweet, innocent kiss remained on his mind as Rex drove south to the Army base. The audience of kids attending horse camp included his fifteen-year-old daughter, so he couldn't follow Debbie when she stepped away and returned to work. The earliest he'd see her again was Friday night, four days from now.

He was a grown man. He could wait, but when he saw her again, he'd initiate the next move. Of course, how far it went all depended on how she reacted. They both had baggage from the past. Pressuring her or any woman went against his moral code.

Spotting the large pickup with Montana plates in the parking lot at the warehouse irritated Rex. Why was Taggart here? Tate Murphy had already picked up supplies for this week before leaving the base, so there wasn't a good reason for the other noncom to show up. Well, sitting in his own truck didn't provide the necessary answers and Rex pulled into his favorite spot.

Once inside the building, he saw Juana Castaneda and strode toward the petite, dark-haired woman in camos. "Anything new or different?"

"No, Major." She paused and glanced in the direction of the offices. "Sergeant-Major Taggart is waiting for you."

Rex nodded. "I saw his rig. Did he say why?"

"Something about his sister who disappeared after she graduated from a boarding school." Juana paused. "I told him to go on the Internet and research the place, to read the articles and reviews so he'd know what kind of place it was."

"Good advice." For a moment, Rex contemplated doing the same thing, then changed his mind. He'd let Debbie Ramsey share her past rather than allow the Internet to sway his opinions of what had obviously been a heart-breaking, soul-destroying place. Meantime, he'd see what her brother wanted.

In the outer office, Rex saw West Taggart standing near Gimone Nolan's desk and the woman elaborately ignoring him while she typed away at the computer. Nodding to Corporal Baxter, Rex approached the pair. "What's new, Sergeant-Major?"

"Still looking for my sister and I heard Sergeant Nolan was her room-mate at their boarding school back in the day."

"And that means what?" Rex folded his arms as he waited for the answer. "Your sister disappeared years ago. If she wanted to contact you, she would have."

"Makes sense." A faint smile tugged at Gimone's lips, and she narrowed her dark green eyes. "I need to give you a sitrep about the warehouses, sir."

"Then, let's do it in my office." Rex gestured toward the closed door at the far end of the reception area. "I'm sure we'll see you again, Sergeant-Major."

"And my sister?"

"Not our story to tell." Rex lingered long enough to allow the noncom in charge of supply to lead the way to his private sanctum. "Once again, Taggart, go talk to your family. If you ask the right questions, they'll share what they know."

He closed the door behind them and waved to the small radio on top of the file cabinet. She nodded, crossed the room to turn on his favorite classic country station. Music filled the air, an old George Strait song. If Taggart tried to stay and overhear their conversation, he'd fail. Hopefully, Corporal Baxter would encourage him to leave the warehouse.

Concern crept into Gimone's face. "Do you think he'll follow your advice?"

"I doubt it." Rex leaned against the door, lowering his voice. "If he could learn about her from his relatives, he wouldn't be harassing us. I'm consid-ering talking to his temporary C.O., but I don't want this to escalate before Taggart gets orders for his next duty station."

"Those can't come soon enough." Gimone heaved a sigh. "How is she?"

"Fine."

"No, she's not." Shaking her head, Gimone knotted her hands into fists. "I don't care what she tells you. At this time of year, she's the walking wounded. When we were kids, she'd hunker down with two or three bottles of wine in our closet. Juana and I ran interference, so the teachers didn't find her drunk or passed out—"

"She's busy at the stable this year." Rex paused, remembering what Debbie told him about Christmas, her father disowning her, the conditions for returning home to Montana and her insistence his kids be able to protect themselves. Why else would she fall apart eight months later, at the end of the summer? Not eight months, he thought suddenly nauseated as he put two and two together. Nine months after she was sent to boarding school. Someone raped her. Collecting intel was his super-power. He'd use those skills to learn more. "Ramsey didn't drink the first year she was there."

Gimone nodded agreement. "She didn't start boozing it up until the next summer. That first year, she hid her labor pains until the last minute. Juana made sure her grandparents got the word before her dad did, so he couldn't interfere with our plans to save the baby from him. Her grandparents had already arranged an adoption."

"So, by the time he arrived, it was a done deal. The baby was gone." Rex stared at the tall redhead. "The three of you are amazing. You were just kids yourselves. What did you tell him?"

"Nothing. He didn't know about me or Juana. When he visited her in the hospital and asked about the baby, Sweet told him that he'd never see it. If he found it and dragged the two of them back to Montana, she'd kill herself and take the baby with her. First, she'd leave a letter for the Elders, so her father, his wives and all of his other children would be shunned because suicide was a mortal sin in that fundamentalist cult."

"And he decided to cut his losses?" Admiration swept through Rex. "Better to lose one measly girl-child he could disown than to risk his status, his business, and the rest of his family."

"Exactly." Gimone frowned fiercely. "Sergeant-Major Taggart will be watching me so Juana and I can't leave the base. But it's a holiday weekend. You can take care of Debbie for us."

"And I will. Now, let's get back to our business, so I'm free to leave on Friday night."

Shortly before 2100 hours, nine that night, he finished up the last of the paperwork waiting for him. He'd taken a break during the afternoon to visit the hospital and check on the six soldiers. Two of them were being prepped for surgeries the next day, so they didn't need his attention. The other four avoided others in the ward and spent a lot of time catching up on current events by watching television.

Rex stood, walked around the desk, and switched off the lights. On his way out of the warehouse, he considered swinging by the Officer's Club and having a late dinner. Then he changed his mind. He'd stop for something on the way home. He could eat there and have privacy to call Debbie and his daughters.

Once he had the numbers, he'd check in on his sons and see if they'd be able to get themselves to Pullman-Moscow Airport on Friday afternoon. He'd arrange for tickets to be waiting and then he'd pick them up at Sea-Tac, the Seattle-Tacoma Airport. After that, they'd head for Baker City. On Monday, he'd reverse the procedure, so the boys returned in time for classes Tuesday.

At the hospital, Rex parked in an empty slot, grabbed his hat, and strolled across the lot and in a side door. A short walk brought him to the secluded ward and its guard. Rex offered his military identification and waited for it to be checked. "How's it going?"

"Not good, sir. Two of the patients almost escaped after overpowering one of the nurses. We have them in seclusion and more guards posted nearby."

"Why wasn't I informed immediately?"

"Because neither of them were attached to your command, sir."

Rex nodded in apparent acceptance of the answer. He tucked away his ID card, and entered the hall, hearing the snap of the lock behind him. He'd call the commander of the military police in the morning and give the other officer a 'heads-up'. Pausing at the nurses' station, Rex asked, "Where are my people? Asleep?"

"No, Major." The head nurse gestured toward the lounge. "They're watching television."

"Have they requested any visitors?"

"Not yet." The dark-haired, young man glanced down at the files on the counter. "One refused to have his parents contacted. Jackson's wife divorced him and remarried while he was out of the country. Morelli's father died before he left, and his mother passed away while he was gone."

That covered three of the men. "And Wilkins?"

"He said if nobody was coming for his buddies, no one needed to see him either. They're sticking together, Major."

"Do you blame them? It kept them alive, Lieutenant Singh."

The man nodded, narrowing dark eyes. "I know they had something to do with those two privates trying to leave earlier. The doctors wouldn't listen, saying your folks were watching TV all day and will be half the night the same way they've been for the last few days."

"They were." Rex inclined his head, acknowledging that truth. "And checking out the security precautions, too. Just do your best with them and keep me in the loop."

"I will, sir."

The nurse was as professional as he was, Rex thought. If both of them hadn't been, he knew Singh wouldn't have said a word about the situation at the hospital. No surprises, Rex told himself. He'd talk to the doctors in the morning too. He strode down the hall and into the lounge that had been set aside for the new men's use.

Three of them sat in various chairs while the fourth was seated in a dark corner. The local news blared forth, an ash-blonde reporter delivering an editorial about government corruption. While he waited for the woman to finish, he studied four of the men he'd been ordered to supervise during their transition back to military duty. Although they wore newly issued camouflage fatigues, the ACUs were obviously too large for them, but would fit when they gained more weight.

The oldest was Jim Jackson, a tall black man who'd once played college football and earned an Army commission at the university. A warrant officer and pilot, he outranked the others, but he wasn't the leader of the group. Rex deliberately chose an empty chair near the door and sat with his back to the wall. When a stream of commercials began, he glanced at the shadowed figure in the corner. "Learn anything useful?"

"About what?" Sergeant Wilkins was a thin, small man with an anxious gaze that flicked everywhere. He saw everything and never met anyone's gaze. His gravelly voice could have grated on some people's nerves. "Whatcha talking about, Major?"

"Nothing important, Wilkins." Pity stirred within Rex. He had seen Wilkins' scarred wrists and ankles and heard the ragged sound of the man's voice. He didn't need the doctors to tell him that the man had survived years of torture, including being waterboarded several times. "Just chatting."

"Save it for a commercial break, sir." Sergeant Morelli said as the news began again, and the blonde did a final wrap-up of the day's stories.

Rex followed directions and waited until the next segment started, this time with a different newscaster. Jackson had the remote and clicked over to a sports channel. Rex eyed the silent man in the dark corner of the room. "What do you want? Why won't you see your families?"

"We wanta see them, Major. Yes, we do, but nobody's left." Wilkins began to rock back and forth in the chair, only his body moving. "That headshrinker says we're nuts. Yes, we are."

"I'll ask for a different one with more sense." Rex scanned the three men who'd speak to him. "They told me the same thing when I got back from my last tour. I discovered my wife was cheating on me. She showed up at the airport with a new baby when I'd been gone a year and a half. When I said I wanted a divorce, the counselor and unit chaplain told me I was in denial."

"Idiots. They're all dumb asshats," Morelli said. "They won't let us see who we want to see, Major."

"Who do you want to see?" Rex asked.

"Her." Warrant Officer Jackson gestured to the television. "That TV reporter, Tiffany Roberts."

"You couldn't ask for the President?" Rex ran a hand through his graying hair. "Why her, Sergeant Hawke? Do you have any idea how long it's going to take for me to smuggle a reporter in here? The brass will think you want to pass on secret info about what happened to you."

"We'll promise not to tell her anything classified. We'll put it in writing if you want," Jackson said. "You got our word."

"That's a lot of help. Just tell me why."

"Don't want to see my folks." The words were a hissed whisper in the darkness. "My younger sister was a brat, a tattle-tale who lived to make trouble. Broke anything they gave me because I was their favorite."

"You don't have to see her," Rex said. "But your parents—"

"Learned why before I shipped out in '11. My old man was banging her and passing her around to his slimeball friends. My mother knew, didn't stop it. I'm done with them."

Rex stared into the corner of the room, tried to see the scarred features of the man who spoke. "All right. Why the reporter?"

"She was my girl. Dated a few years in high school. She dumped me in '06."

"All right. I can work with that." Rex leaned back in the chair. "Meanwhile, the four of you stay here and concentrate on getting well. No more set-ups. My kids are coming home from college this weekend and it's the only time we'll have to visit before Thanksgiving, so I won't be here to ride herd on you."

"Thought they weren't all yours," Morelli said.

"They're not, but I chose their mother. They didn't and I don't want them blaming themselves for the divorce. I'm the only dad they've ever had." Rex paused. "I want the rest of you to write letters to your families. I'll figure out how to send them next week. Deal?"

"You got it, Major." Hawke spoke for the rest of them. "We'll give you time to get Tiffy here, too."

"Good one. As for the new psychologist—"

"Don't like those doctors. No sir, not me."

"This will be a new one, Wilkins." Rex glanced at the other officer. "I'm going to set up group therapy meetings. Jackson, can you stop any inappropriate questions from the counselor? Will you?"

A new light filtered into the other man's dark gaze. He straightened in his seat. "Yes, Major. Sure, I will."

The brainstorming session lasted another hour. Then Wilkins, Morelli and Jackson wandered off toward their rooms. Rex deliberately didn't switch on any more of the lights but left the room dark so Waco Hawke would be comfortable.

"What happens when you see this reporter?" Rex asked.

"Depends on her. She left for college in California after high school."

"You're not the same person," Rex pointed out gently. "She won't be either."

"I'm a mess and they'll be fixing me up a lot."

"Do you want to see her before or after your surgery?"

"Longer I put it off, the more scared I'll be. How are you planning to do it, Major?"

"Through channels," Rex admitted honestly. "I don't sneak around when I'm in CONUS, Hawke. If that doesn't work, I'll come up with a different scheme. Any idea how to convince her to be discreet?"

"She owes me."

"Whatever debt the two of you had must have been paid long ago, Sergeant."

"No, it wasn't. I saw my old man and her father blathering on the news. They're still scum, and I protected her from them when we were kids. She always did what I wanted."

"For how long?"

"Started when she was a sophomore. Lasted until she graduated, and I enlisted. I didn't make it back from Colombia, but my older brother promised to look out for her if she needed anything. He'd have done it too."

Rex nodded. "Will she listen if I remind her about you?"

"Call her Tiffy, and she will. That was my name for her. Then she'll know it's really me."

"I'll do my best." Rex stood and started for the door. "Are you heading for your room?"

"No, sir. I like this TV better than the one there." The low voice became hoarse and raspy. "I want to see my sister."

"I'll do what I can." Rex paused before he left the lounge. He swung around, stared into the darkness, saw the vague outline of the other man still sitting in the corner. "Everything will be okay, Sergeant Hawke."

"I don't know about that, Major, but I know you'll try."

CHAPTER TWELVE

Debbie opted for a soda rather than a glass of wine while she sat on the porch swing late Monday night. Yes, it was the end of August and definitely not her favorite time of year, but she didn't want to become dependent on alcohol. She was a grown woman, damn near thirty-five years old, and she didn't need wine as a crutch to protect her from overwhelming memories. Then again...

No, she wasn't going into the house and attacking the wine cabinet in the kitchen. She'd leave the glasses and her favorite zinfandel alone tonight.

She leaned over to smooth Shasta's fur and the puppy sighed softly in her sleep. It was wildfire season and Debbie caught the occasional whiff of smoke in the air, but luckily none of the forests around Baker City were ablaze.

Her cell phone vibrated, and she pulled it out of her jeans. Since he knew where she lived, she chose the video option when she answered. She glimpsed the collar of his camo shirt and realized he hadn't changed from his uniform. "Was it a long day? How are your charges? Did you spend the night at the hospital with them?"

"Only a few hours," Rex admitted. "Talked to my oldest boy tonight, and Rory told me they'd meet me at the airport on Friday afternoon. We'll be at the ranch in time for supper. Should I stop for pizza in Lake Maynard?"

"Only if you want to eat at a reasonable hour. I'll call in an order for you to pick up at Petrocelli's Pizza Palace. The locals give them rave reviews." She paused. "I thought your sons used their middle names the way the girls use theirs. Except Rory."

"He didn't share that with me, so I guess I'll find out what they prefer when we meet up. How was your day? Did horse camp go well?"

"It went fine until Wonder threw a shoe. My barn manager, Kyra, told me Mindy used one of her cousin's sons to do the horses and luckily Nick MacGillicudy could fit us into his schedule for an early repair rather than waiting until next week."

"I see that electric-blue glare, Ramsey. He didn't impress you, did he?"

"He tried getting rough with Wonder and I ripped him a new one for it. Told him if he wanted to keep me as a customer, he'd better watch the rodeo cowboy crap or he'd be pushing up daisies."

Rex chuckled. "How'd that go over?"

"Thought he could charm me and when that didn't work, he sulked his way through the remainder of the shoeing. Kyra says he'll be in next Tuesday to do the rest of the stock once the summer season ends, but I'm still not thrilled at the idea. He got pissy when I demanded he use a hoof gauge to check angles and even nastier when I wanted the lengths of the hooves to be the same."

"If the horses can go an extra few days, you'll have time to make calls to find a better farrier. Saw a sign for a horse-trainer on the way to Baker City. You could stop in and get a referral to their shoer."

"Not a bad idea." She saw his barely suppressed smile. "Okay, Major. Why do you want me to make nice with the neighbors? You're up to something. What?"

"You know me too well." He ran a hand through his dark salt and pepper hair. "One of my walking wounded is probably related to them. I need you to find out what the Hawkes in Baker City know about Staff Sergeant Waco Hawke."

Debbie grimaced. "I'm a civilian now, not one of your flunkies."

"Yeah, but I know you miss the action. Come on, Ramsey. It will be fun to keep up your skills. You want to spy for me and interrogate the folks next door, don't you? And I'm still waiting for personnel records to arrive from HQ back east for these guys so I can contact their relatives. Have you checked in with your lawyer yet to see if she's missing a relation?"

Debbie heaved a sigh. Wow, the amusement in his golden-brown eyes made her tingle all over and she'd thought—she'd hoped—she was immune to him. "All right, but only because I fully intended to make friends with the locals."

"As long as you do it, I don't care whose idea you think it was, Ramsey."

She laughed, appreciating the blunt honesty. He didn't hesitate to ask or tell her when he needed help. He had opinions, but he always listened to other people and considered their unique experiences and perspectives. Plus, the fact he was so protective of her horses warmed her heart.

Their conversation continued while he brought her up to speed on activities at the warehouse and she shared more details about horse camp. When they finished talking, she'd relaxed to the point that she could go to bed and grab a few hours of sleep before she fed the livestock.

Halfway through the second lesson the next day, Trina interrupted. "Debbie, Wonder is lame. Who do you want me to take on the trail ride with the intermediates?"

"He got new shoes yesterday. How could that happen?"

"I don't know." Concern filled the younger woman's sky-blue eyes. "Kyra tried reaching Nick on his cell phone, but he didn't answer so she left a message. What do you want me to do? My group is waiting for their trail ride."

"Take Hobby," Debbie said, making an immediate command decision. "I'll check Wonder at lunch time. Maybe he just needs time to adjust to the new shoes."

"Okay, will do." Trina left the arena, hurrying toward the other barn.

Debbie returned to the class in progress. An hour later, she'd finished teaching the beginners to control their horses and ponies at a walk and slow jog. Since it was time for lunch, she helped them put away their mounts, then sent them off to the restrooms to wash up before they ate.

Before she headed to the house to eat her own meal, she paused in the stable where the boarders and her horses lived. She found Trina outside Wonder's stall, accompanied by Penny and the O'Leary-McTavish-Hendrickson twins. All four of them wore what she considered the riding camp uniform of blue jeans, their camp t-shirts, western boots, and equestrian helmets.

"What's going on?" Debbie watched them treat her horse to extra carrots. "It's lunchtime, ladies, and we have a busy afternoon planned."

"Trina wanted us to talk to your horse and see if he'd tell us what's wrong with his foot," Sophie said, tilting her head to one side. "And we told her we'd try."

"Some animals don't do picture-talk with us," Samantha added, "but he does. His foot with the new shoe hurts big-time. Something burns in it and it's worse when he tries to walk, so he wants to hold it up in the air."

"He needs that shoe pulled." Trina hesitated, then lifted her chin. She narrowed her eyes. "This may piss you off, but I don't care if you fire me. A hot nail is one driven into a horse's hoof during shoeing that actually goes into a horse's hoof wall. It's like a sliver that slices into the quick under your fingernail. And Wonder shouldn't have to suffer for days while we wait for Nick MacGillicudy to quit screwing around while he avoids Kyra. So, I called my sister's boyfriend."

"What?" Debbie folded her arms and gave the younger woman a solid onceover. "Who is he? And why did you call him?"

"Because he works with Mr. Zeke who takes care of our ponies' and horses' feet at home," Sophie said. "Mr. Laredo helps, and he is really nice. He always brings treats from the feedstore for Lucky and Stormy."

"And all the other horses, too. He gave us a puppy for our dog to play with when we moved here," Samantha added. "You'll like him. Everybody does."

"We'll see." Debbie patted Trina's shoulder, then gestured toward the door of the barn. "Now, I want all of you to go to lunch. Next time–and there will be one, Trina, because we work with horses and kids–ask me to sign off on your decision first. I need to be in the proverbial loop so I can back you up."

A tear slipped down Trina's face. She blinked hard as a second and third one followed, then she nodded. "Okay, Debbie. I will." She took a deep breath. "Kyra's always had a thing for Nick, so she cuts him way too much slack, but he's a really crappy shoer."

"He didn't impress me yesterday and I intended to find someone else. If this Laredo is as good as you gals think, you may have saved me the trouble. Now, go to lunch!" Debbie waited while they headed for the door, then stepped up to scratch Wonder's bright yellow cheek. She glanced at Penny who lingered nearby. "What's up, honey?"

"Trina was real scared you'd boot her off the place. You're not going to, are you, Ramsey?"

"Of course not." Debbie straightened the buckskin's black forelock. "She put my horse first, ahead of everything else. I'd be majorly stupid if I got rid of someone like that. And I'm not stupid, honey. Now, let's go eat. We'll have to be sure to tidy up the kitchen afterwards because Linda MacGillicudy is coming to clean the house today and we don't want her thinking we're complete slobs."

"Even if we do get busy in the barns." Penny bounced along beside her, a smile filling her face. "Is this when I tell you that Vangie thinks Linda's son is super-hot?"

"Thanks for the sitrep, but I'm still going along with your dad's dictates and saying fifteen is too young to date."

They'd barely finished eating when Trina called. "Laredo's here. Do you want me to bring out Wonder?"

"I've got it covered." Debbie put away her cell phone and stood. "Okay, you two have KP. I have to meet the new horseshoer. Vangie, when you get to the arena, have your class do a dragon walk and ground school with Jason until I get there."

"No worries. We have your six." Vangie rose to her feet and began collecting their plates. "Come on, Penny. My group has a lesson and yours is doing games as soon as we get back to camp."

Debbie headed for the front door, accompanied by Shasta who apparently needed either a puppy walk or was on guard duty. She charged across the porch and ran barking at a wiry, short man in cowboy garb who stood near a brown pickup. He laughed and bent to pet the tri-colored collie. A young boy with the same tawny gold hair climbed out of the truck, obviously eager to make friends with the half-grown puppy.

Smiling, Debbie went to greet them. "Sorry about the attack dog. This is when I walk her before I start camp again. I'm Debbie Ramsey and you've already met Shasta."

"She's awesome," the boy announced as he petted the young dog. He was dressed for the summer in long board shorts, a t-shirt and running shoes. "I'm Luke Roberts and we were on our way to Uncle Laredo's when we got your call. As soon as we finish with the horse, he's taking me to get one of his puppies. My stepmom, Heather, says I don't have to share with my little sisters and they're not much into it, anyway. They keep telling me they have to share with each other, not me."

Laredo chuckled, pushing back a worn leather cowboy hat to reveal amused hazel eyes. "And now you know our family stuff. I'm Laredo Hawke. Trina called and told me to get myself here ASAP or she'd rat me out to her older sis. So, what happened to your horse?"

"He threw a shoe." Debbie gestured in the direction of the third barn where the boarders and her horses lived. "I had him shod by one of the reservists, Mariah Stevens, at Fort Clark before we came here in July. She's incredible, but she's doing her veterinary internship, so she's unavailable."

"Sean Killian, my mentor in Liberty Valley, swears by her when he's not cussing up a storm because she dumped her book on him when her Army unit shipped out for Afghanistan." Laredo smiled. "I can't wait to meet her in person. She grew up in Baker City. I've heard she's supposed to be visiting her foster family this weekend."

"I didn't know that." Debbie started toward the barn, accompanied by Laredo and Luke. "Of course, I haven't been living here that long."

"Oh, you'll get to know everyone sooner or later. It's a small town." Laredo held the gate for her. "So, how did this guy end up with a 'hot nail'?"

"I had one of Mindy MacGillicudy's relatives here yesterday to do his new shoes and it didn't go well."

"Obviously not." Laredo followed her to the stall. His gaze narrowed on the front right foot Wonder held in the air. "Okay, Bubba. Let's see what I can do for you."

He was in with the buckskin a moment later, picking up the hoof to clean it. "Luke, I need that tester, the file, those special nippers, and the stand I showed you. Move it, boy."

"I thought you'd want him by your truck." Debbie watched the boy hustle away, followed by Shasta who apparently considered a foot-race high entertainment. "Don't you need your forge to redo the shoes?"

"Not when he's in pain. Get a bottle of peroxide, the betadine and two small syringes. You'll want to flush the nail hole when I've removed the shoe. He'll need his foot soaked two or three times a day while it heals. I'll come back on Friday and do a reset on the shoes."

Debbie followed directions. Laredo Hawke wouldn't win awards for his bedside–or was it stall-side–manner, but her horse liked the guy. Otherwise, Wonder wouldn't have stood like a rock without so much as a halter or lead-line to control him. When she returned with the medications, she found the buckskin with his hoof on a portable stand while Laredo filed away on the hoof, loosening the nails, humming softly.

Luke was talking on his cell phone. "And Uncle Laredo wants you to come by Miracle Riding Stable with a bottle of antibiotics and a jar of Cat O'Leary-McTavish's homemade applesauce, 'cause she makes it without sugar. He says for you to track down Nick MacGillicudy, too."

Debbie blinked. "Why do you want him, Laredo? He's not coming near my horses again."

"Because I'm going to kick his butt off the planet." Laredo flicked a sideways glance at her and then started filing again. "This guy has two nails driven into the laminae and I haven't even looked at the other three hooves yet. If Nick keeps shoeing like this, more than one person is going to end up with a permanently lamed horse."

Luke finished his conversation and put away the cell phone. "Dad says he'll be here soon with the meds and applesauce, but you're not s'posed to go after Nick again. You'll end up in the hoosegow. Zeke Knight, your boss, will have a major fit because the state fair starts this week, and he needs you to help shoe horses for it. Dad said he'll have Heather handle it. She likes drop-kicking horse abusers into next week and she'll enjoy getting Nick out of the shoeing biz 'cause she has issues with him and his dad. Since she and Mindy are buds, it won't cause problems for you with the MacGillicudys."

"Not fair," Laredo muttered. "I was looking forward to putting the guy in the hospital."

Debbie silently admitted she agreed with Laredo Hawke. He seemed to be doing just fine without anything on Wonder's head, but she didn't want the man flying to the moon when he actually began to remove the nails. Carrots in hand, she entered the stall and proceeded to buckle the halter in place, holding the rope so her horse remained still.

Shasta had flopped down for a doggie nap in the aisleway. That lasted while Laredo eased out the first two nails and began to work on the third, gently easing it loose. Wonder snorted when the puppy jumped up to run toward the gate at the far end of the aisle.

A tall, giant-size version of Laredo sauntered toward them. He had quite a few years on the shoer since she saw silver threads in the tawny gold hair. A light blue denim shirt stretched across his wide chest, tucked into dark blue jeans that ended at steel-toed construction boots.

Laredo pulled the third nail and glanced at the hall. "Glad you're here, Durango. This is Debbie Ramsey, the new owner of Miracle Riding Stable. You can take over and hold the horse. Trina's texted me three times to send her to the arena to teach her class."

"Since Debbie's the owner, shouldn't you and Trina try asking rather than telling her what to do?" Durango inquired, amusement filtering into his rugged features and landing in the dark blue eyes. He winked at Debbie. "I don't know why I bother pointing that out. As my older brother, Bendigo says, when it comes to a horse, it's better to follow their directions rather than argue."

"And Laredo's easier to get along with than Heather," Luke said, leaning on the stall wall. "You never win with her either, Dad."

"Because I'm smart." Durango ruffled the boy's hair so much like his own. "As your grandpa used to tell me, 'When Momma's not happy, nobody is,' and since you'll have another brother or sister to boss you around next spring, we all know to stay on your stepmom's good side."

"Especially since she talked my mom into letting me have one of Laredo's puppies," Luke informed him. "Uncle Laredo, do you have one that looks like Shasta?"

"Definitely." Laredo removed the fourth nail. "You'll see soon enough."

When he entered the stall, Debbie passed the lead-line to Durango Hawke, remaining long enough to stroke Wonder's golden-yellow neck. "There's a feedroom at the far end of the barn."

"My company built this one when Mindy expanded from the other two," Durango said. "I know where to find everything and we'll come down to the arena to find you when Laredo finishes."

"Sounds good." Debbie paused in the aisle. "Laredo, do you have time and room in your shoeing book to take on the stock here? Or should I keep looking for another farrier?"

"I don't share my horses," Laredo informed her. "Trina should have told you that when you agreed to have me come save Wonder's feet."

Debbie blinked and eyed his brother who was shaking his head ruefully. Meantime, Wonder lipped at Laredo's cowboy hat as if it was a new toy. Apparently, she'd just hired a new shoer whether she liked it or not. And frankly, she did. Besides, it'd break Wonder's horsy heart if she didn't keep Laredo and she didn't want to know what Shasta would think.

"Okay, I'll tell Trina when I catch up with her that you're here for the duration," Debbie said. "Meanwhile, can you fit us in next week?"

"My calendar's on my phone. I'll look at it when I finish here and give you a day and time. I'll bring a contract for you to sign too."

"Sounds good." Calling Shasta, Debbie left the barn. She pulled out her phone and texted Rex at the base. He could check in with his soldier and learn if the man had brothers. She wasn't going to interrupt Laredo and Wonder again since the two of them were into horsey and shoer bonding.

When she reached the indoor arena, she ordered Shasta into the viewing stand so the dog wouldn't spook the horses. After that, she entered the ring where she saw Vangie leading Copper into position at the mounting block. The rest of her class were already on their horses and doing balance exercises with Jason. Debbie crossed to the bench to hold the tall Arabian gelding's off stirrup and rein. "How does the kitchen look?"

"We'd barely finished cleaning up when Linda MacGillicudy arrived. I showed her the list you left on the counter, and she said, 'No worries.' She could do everything you wanted, and I asked her to make sure their rooms were ready for my bros."

"Wonderful." Debbie drew a deep breath. "I'm starting to feel like I need to run around the place and repeat the mantra I teach you kids when you're learning to ride."

"Which one is that?" Vangie asked. "Eyes up and heels down?"

"No. I am the boss. I am the boss. I am the boss!"

CHAPTER THIRTEEN

As if she didn't have enough to do, she discovered she was down to less than a week's worth of hay in the boarder barn when she fed Wonder and Hobby that evening after she doctored the young gelding. Luckily, the rest of the horses went out to pasture where they had plenty of grass to eat.

Debbie took a deep breath and went to check the other two barns. She found Kyra in the second feedroom. "Weren't we supposed to get thirty tons of hay last week for the winter?"

"Yes, and Mindy already paid the deposit back in the spring before the sale closed on the stable, but Jones Feed is notorious for running behind."

"Okay, I'll let you finish up. I'm headed for the office to make some calls." Debbie paused. "By the way, I hired Laredo Hawke to shoe the herd. He'll be in next Tuesday and I left a message for Nick MacGillicudy that he is no longer needed here."

"I hope that doesn't come back and bite you in the butt. Laredo's family may be pretty influential in Baker City, but everyone knows he's an addict and an alcoholic. He calls himself a double winner."

"That is such a lie." Furious, Trina stormed out of the tackroom. "You know he's been clean and sober for five years. You're just pissy because he showed up today when Nick didn't and that jerk is still playing hide and seek with you."

"Whoa!" Debbie held up her hand, turning a fierce frown on the pair.

"If Laredo screws up even once, I'll fire his backside, too. I don't do drama, so save it for someone who cares."

She spun around and left the barn. Okay, her new shoer had baggage, but who didn't? He wasn't stoned or drunk when he arrived, and Wonder liked the guy. *I'll keep an eye on Laredo, and we should be fine. If not, I'll have time to find someone else. Once the horses have their hooves done next week, it will be two months before I need the farrier to return.*

In the office, she looked up the number for Jones Feed Store and called. She was bounced from the main sales floor to deliveries and continually received the proverbial run-around for the next thirty minutes. The final story she got was the hay was already in her barns and she was taking advantage of the store.

Debbie repeated numerous times the hay wasn't at the stable and she still wanted her order ASAP. More time passed and eventually, Giselle Jones, in charge of the accounting department answered.

Taking a deep breath, Debbie identified herself and then explained the situation. "Mindy MacGillicudy, the previous owner of Miracle Stable, paid a five-thousand-dollar deposit, but thirty tons of alfalfa-grass hay hasn't arrived. When should I expect it?"

"You need to set up an account with us," Giselle sounded super sweet. "Otherwise, we can't sell to you."

"You already have the order and received a deposit," Debbie said for what felt like the umpteenth time. "The balance is due when the hay is unloaded in my barns. I have a contract."

"Actually, you don't. That contract is with Mindy MacGillicudy. I have no idea who you are."

"You have an account with Miracle Riding Stable. I am the new owner. I'll want the money back since you don't intend to deliver the product we paid for."

"I'm not saying we won't deliver it," Giselle said. "I'm saying you have to set up an account with us. I'll need written notice from Mindy that you have authorization to accept deliveries and handle business at Miracle if you're her new manager and a certified check when the hay arrives."

"I'm the new owner, not the manager. Mindy made a point of sending out letters to her suppliers when I bought Miracle Riding Stable. You got that letter. I have a copy."

"I'll have to check our files and see if I find it, so it'd be easier if you just opened a new account with us and paid a *real* deposit for such a large order."

"When hell freezes over." Debbie ended the call. She debated contacting Mindy, but one look at the clock and she changed her mind. At this hour, Mindy would be counseling the veterans at the local center in Baker City. Instead, Debbie contacted her lawyer. "Bree, I need you to do your magic, kick some butt and take some names."

Brazos Hawke laughed. "Okay, but tell me first that my brothers, the macho jerks didn't irritate you to the max. When they're together, my sister-in-law is always threatening to castrate them in front of Pop's Café and issuing invites for the town to watch."

That made Debbie smile for the first time in more than an hour. "If Laredo hadn't done right by my horse, I'd be holding your sister-in-law's coat while she did her thing, but the guys were great. No, my issue is with Jones Feed in Lake Maynard. They took a deposit from Mindy last spring and haven't delivered my winter hay. I haven't even brought up the order of the baled shavings that I need to bed the stalls. Giselle Jones—."

"She's a major diva. Debbie, it's your business, but if I were you, I'd get my supplies from Summer O'Neill in Baker City. She and Mindy had a few run-ins because Summer drop-kicked Nick MacGillicudy out of her feed-store when he bounced one too many checks on her. And he's her cousin's boy, so Mindy felt she had to side with him."

"Is that going to make trouble because I fired him for laming my horse and hired your bro instead?"

"Oh no. Zeke Knight is older than dirt and he's been shoeing around Baker City forever. Laredo is his apprentice and going to take over for him when Zeke actually retires instead of just talking about it. They shoe for Frank Madison over at Majestyk Morgans, so everyone will think you're trying to get on his good side because he runs the Baker City Business Association."

"I don't give a rat's backside about that," Debbie said. "I've had Wonder from the day he was born, and nobody hurts him. Nick is lucky I'm running a kids' barn, so I couldn't use his behind for target practice."

"You vets are all the same." Brazos laughed again. "When you're ready to hit the gun range, let me know. My little sister and I will take you to our favorite place."

"Sounds good. It's a date." Debbie paused. "So, have I met most of your family now? There's Laredo, Durango, your nephew, Luke, and Mindy mentioned someone named Heather too."

"If you get over to the dude ranch next door, you'll meet my cousins and Durango's half-brothers. They run a branch of Nighthawke Security there and Heather is my sister-in-law. She's always threatening to take stupid people apart to see how they work. She and Durango live close to you on the other side of the dude ranch at Hawke's Horse Heaven. You'll love her."

"Sounds awesome. I'll look forward to meeting her." Debbie decided to bite the proverbial bullet. "My husband mentioned one of the soldiers in his command when he saw their sign. A guy named Waco Hawke. Is he one of your relatives too?"

"My other brother." Brazos sounded tense. "He disappeared on an Army mission eight years ago. Your husband must have known Waco before that."

"That's one of those things I'll have to ask him when he gets here on Friday," Debbie said. "To be honest, I wasn't paying much attention."

"Well, keep me posted on what you find out. Meanwhile, I'll put in a call to Mindy and then I'll deal with Jones Feed. I'm bypassing Giselle and going straight to her dad who owns the place. Call Summer."

"Will do." Debbie replaced the receiver and pulled the small phone book for the town out of the desk drawer. It only took a few minutes to find the number for Summer's Feed and Tack. Luckily, the store hadn't closed yet. A woman answered and Debbie introduced herself. "I bought Miracle Riding Stable, and I need to order alfalfa-grass hay. Do you have it on hand and what's the ton price?"

A long silence and then the woman asked hesitantly, "Is this a joke? I'm not laughing."

"Neither am I." Debbie drummed her fingers on the desk. "I understand you and the MacGillicudys have issues, but I bought the place from Mindy last spring. She ordered the winter hay from Jones' Feed, but that deal fell through and my lawyer, Bree Hawke suggested I call you."

"Heather McElroy is one of my cousins, and she's married to Durango Hawke. She told him if he bought feed in Lake Maynard again instead of from me, he'd be guest of honor at a public flogging in the center of town. I love that woman. I also sell supplies to your other neighbor, Cat O'Leary-McTavish at Cedar Creek. I only keep five ton of hay on hand, but I can get more."

"Sounds good." Debbie wished the landline had video conferencing so she could see Summer's face, but that wasn't do-able. Their conversation continued and she promised to stop in at the store the next day to complete the order of winter supplies for the stable. Summer agreed to waive delivery charges since this would be a large account for her.

When Debbie entered the house a short time later, the scent of baked peaches wafted toward her. She headed toward the kitchen where she saw sparkling counters, shining windows and a gleaming tile floor. She glanced at Vangie who was setting the table. "Wow, something smells wonderful. What did you make?"

"Not me. Linda put a shepherd's pie in the oven before she left. We have peach cobbler and vanilla ice cream for dessert."

Penny carried glasses of ice water to the table. "Wait until you see the rest of the house, Ramsey. It looks amazing and Linda had her people iron the sheets they put on the beds in all the rooms. She'll be back next Wednesday."

"I think I could get used to this." Debbie smiled at the girls. "It reminds me of the days when I had to make sure the troops cleaned the warehouse from top to bottom, so we'd pass your dad's Friday inspections. It's much nicer coming into a clean house after barn duty."

"And not having to do it after we muck the stalls. I'd much rather do those." Vangie placed silverware next to the plates. "How is Wonder feeling?"

"Much better now that his feet don't hurt. He didn't have a fit when I soaked his hoof."

After dinner, they cleaned up the kitchen and pulled out Horse-Opoly, an old board game. They played until bedtime. When they finished, Vangie had the most horses and Penny had the most money, so both girls were happy. Accompanied by Shasta, Debbie poured a glass of wine and headed for the porch swing. She'd intended to hold off on the booze, but she hadn't planned on a drama-filled day, so she deserved a drink.

She'd barely sat down when her phone vibrated. At 2300 hours, eleven at night, it was early for Rex. She switched on the video-chat option. "What's going on, Major?"

"Not a lot." He lifted a bottle of beer in salute. "P.T. tomorrow at 0600 hours, so it won't be too warm when we're running. I thought I'd touch base before the wee hours. What did you find out?"

"Mission accomplished. Your guy has two brothers, two sisters, a sister-in-law, and a few nieces along with one nephew up here in the Baker City—Lake Maynard area."

"Good work. What else is happening in your neck of the woods?" He narrowed his brown-sugar gaze on her. "You're frowning and you have that pissed off look you get when you want me to kick ass, Ramsey. Who's tugging on your Superwoman cape?"

"I handled everything, but it was an experience." Debbie brought him up to speed on the hot nail issue with Wonder, the missing winter hay, and finding a new supplier. "I'd understand if Mindy and I hadn't sent out letters to her vendors when I bought the place, but she also took me around and introduced me to the local ones last spring after the deal closed."

"You know what this is about, Ramsey."

"No, I don't. Are you going to tell me it's a gender-bias issue?"

"Nope, I'm going to tell you that it's a money one. If they keep you jumping through hoops, they'll get to hold onto your deposit for a few more weeks."

"And I'll be out of hay for the horses. That's not happening." Debbie sipped more of her favorite zinfandel. "Okay, I turned my lawyer loose on them and as soon as I get the money, I'll see Summer up in Baker City. Your turn. Tell me about your day."

Wednesday morning, camp started with the kids setting up what Debbie called their stations in the indoor arena to groom and saddle. As usual, she'd forwarded business calls from the landline to her cell phone. While the campers brought their horses into the ring and parked them in a giant circle, she felt the phone vibrate. She pulled it out of her jeans' pocket. "Miracle Riding Stable."

"Good morning, Debbie," Mindy said, cheerfully. "I had a call from Claude Jones, the owner of Jones' Feed. He apologized for the mix-up with the hay and promised to sort things out with his people."

"Really?" Debbie gestured to the next set of students, waving them toward the left-hand wall. "Why didn't he call me?"

"Because he's a horse's patoot. I told him that he needed to do business with you since you're the new owner. I reminded him you bought the place which he already knew. And he sniveled at me about you contacting your lawyer instead of calling him directly."

"His daughter gave me the run-around after I'd already had it from everyone else at his store and I want a total refund."

"Where will you get feed for the horses? You're still boarding my old-timer."

"Yes, and he won't miss a meal. I ordered hay from Summer O'Neill. In case you haven't heard from Nick, I fired him after he lamed my horse. I've replaced him with Laredo Hawke. This is my place now, Mindy, and I'll run it as I see fit. Anybody who doesn't like it can pitch a fit, but I'm not listening and I'm not kissing backsides. I'm protecting my horses."

That earned short, sharp laughter. "Oh, wow. I love it. I'm passing it onto the MacGillicudy clan. You definitely have to join the women's veteran group next week when the kids start school. If you aren't here next Wednesday, we're coming there. You've been warned."

"I thought you'd be pissed because I've made changes."

"Are you kidding? I envy your guts. I never stood up to my family because their love and affection are conditional, and I didn't want to make waves. Herman and the rest of his hangers-on were seriously annoyed when I didn't give them the stable, but sold it to you. Kick tails, partner."

"I will."

During the next two hours, Debbie supervised the grooming and tacking of the thirty horses. It took longer when the kids did it themselves, but it was the only way they'd learn. Meantime, she sent Jason and Carol to inventory the barns, assigning them to count hay bales, bags of grain, supplements, trace-mineral blocks, and baled shavings. She told the students to return their groom kits to Trina and had her check the various brushes to see what needed to be replaced. Kyra was in charge of looking over blankets, pads, and saddles.

When the campers were ready to split into riding groups for lessons, trail rides and games after their morning break, Debbie knew exactly what she needed. She emailed the up-to-date list to Summer O'Neill at the feedstore. While Jason directed her class through the 'dragon walk,' Debbie called her lawyer. "Do you have the refund check from Jones Feed?"

"I'm on my way to Claude's office to pick it up as we speak. He called me a real witch but didn't dare spell it with a 'B' because I'd sue his sorry ass. He tried telling me he was a friend of my father's and that definitely didn't make points. I told him to add on my legal fees. Then I decided we should have broom races and said for him to make out the check to Summer."

"That would be fantastic and save me a trip today. Do you think he will?"

"Hey, I'm the attorney who makes things happen. We'll teach him to suck eggs, as my old 4-H leader used to say. I'll drop the check by Summer's store because I'm meeting Heather and the kids for lunch up at Pop's Café."

"You're amazing. I've already sent her the order for winter supplies."

"She has a hardware section too when you want fencing, gates, and other materials. Then again, I could ask my brother-in-law to stop by and give you a bid on replacement fences."

"Sounds interesting, but he'll need to remember I'm on a tight budget. I haven't won the lottery yet. Guess I better start buying tickets."

"No worries. Your daughter told Luke that her three brothers are coming home from Washington State University this weekend and that's not cheap either. I'll let Jeff know you need a veteran's discount."

Before Debbie could say they were her stepkids, Brazos Hawke ended the call. *Time to go back to work and let people think what they choose. If things work out between Rex and me, they will be mine. Their mother won't care, and I do.*

CHAPTER FOURTEEN

The next two warm, sunny days seemed to fly by. Before Debbie knew it, she was in the barns on Friday after the last camp horseshow of the summer, talking to parents and signing up their kids for school-year programs. When they finished horsy chores, she met the staff in the office to review bonuses so she could write their paychecks Saturday.

The stable would be closed on Sunday and Labor Day Monday, which would provide everyone with a mini-break before autumn classes started. Because they were juniors at Lake Maynard High School, Jason and Carol would only be available on weekends, but Kyra and Trina planned to split the weekdays.

At the end of the staff meeting, Vangie headed to the boarder's barn to groom Wonder before the shoer arrived. Penny was on puppy detail, saying Shasta needed company and a real walk rather than being confined to the backyard. Smiling, Debbie went to meet Laredo when she spotted his brown pickup pulling up near the barn. This time he was accompanied by a slender, petite redhead in faded blue jeans and a western shirt with pearl snaps.

She greeted Debbie with a warm smile and Trina with a quick hug. The junior instructor introduced the other woman as her sister, Jacinth Sweeney. "Everyone calls her Jassy. So, why are you here? Don't you have to work tonight at Pop's?"

"I had the lunch shift," Jacinth said. "Laredo told me if I held Wonder for him, he'd take me to Petrocelli's for dinner and I never can pass up their chicken fettuccine. It's even better than Pop MacGillicudy's."

"Sounds like a great idea," Trina said.

"I made the reservation for the three of us," Laredo said. "We'll be done in about an hour or so and that gives you time to clean up unless you already have a hot date."

"You two are the best." Trina laughed and hugged him quickly. "So glad you remembered I love their lasagna."

Smiling, Debbie watched the younger woman dash off in the direction of her apartment. "That's very kind of you. She's worked really hard at horse camp. She deserves an end-of-summer celebration."

"That's our thought too." The warmth in Jacinth's green eyes faded as she glimpsed Kyra coming toward them. She nodded politely at the older woman. "We stopped by Summer's place and she's on the way here with a load of feed."

"And you're telling me that because—" Kyra's gaze narrowed, and her jaw tightened when she scowled.

"I thought you'd appreciate the heads-up. Everybody in town knows how the O'Neill family feels about Summer buying her father's feedstore when he retired. There wasn't any reason to let Herman MacGillicudy or one of his minions buy it and close it down because we'd all have to go to Lake Maynard for feed and supplies."

Jacinth took a deep breath, then continued. "Summer may be one of you by blood, but none of you listen to Reverend Tommy's lectures about 'throwing stones,' and it's 2019, not 1819. Giving her hell because she never married her kids' dad is so archaic."

"And you always stick your nose in everyone else's business. What about the way you rallied the town to harass Ann Barrett's ex-husband when he tried cleaning up the mess she left at their house?" Kyra shot one more glare at Jacinth before she turned to Debbie. "I don't believe this. Mindy's always bought her feed from the Jones. Did you actually order supplies from my cousin?"

Debbie folded her arms and met the other woman's fierce gray gaze. "I'll tell you the same thing I told Mindy MacGillicudy. This is my place and I'll do as I damned well please. I choose where, how and who I do business with as well." She gestured in the direction of the barn. "Laredo, you know where to find Wonder. I have plans tonight too, so let's get started."

He nodded agreement. "I'm on it. Let's go, Jassy."

One more glare and Kyra stormed toward her car in the parking lot.

Debbie heaved a sigh, shaking her head. If the drama continued, she'd have to consider replacing the senior instructor. Before she did, it might be time to talk to Mindy and ask for advice concerning Kyra. The students liked her, and so did the horses. She was very competent, but she had serious issues about who was in charge, and it wasn't her.

Rex picked up his sons at the airport. They loaded their bags in the back of the pickup, not a hassle on the last Friday in August when western Washington state was in the middle of what had become the usual heatwave. They'd eaten before the flight, so they claimed they weren't hungry and could wait until they reached Baker City. Rex flicked a sideways glance at his oldest boy, Rory, a big, blond, tanned, twenty-two-year-old in a Hawaiian print shirt, long shorts, and flip flops.

Raleigh and Reggie shared the back seat in the super-cab. They'd opted for jeans and WSU t-shirts. Both were tall, and muscular with dark hair, but Reggie wore his in a braid that fell halfway down his back. High cheekbones, heavy black eyebrows, dark brown eyes revealed his Native American heritage. It shocked Rex when all three greeted him with warm hugs and Reggie thanked him again for the hefty graduation check he'd received in mid-June like his older brothers had when they finished high school.

Rex didn't say it was the first he'd heard about it and made a mental note to check in with Debbie regarding the gifts. Undoubtedly, she'd stepped up to do what she thought was right, never bothering to give him a sitrep. Beyond telling him about their classes, his sons barely talked on the journey north and it meant he didn't know much more about them, than he did his daughters. *Time to man up, Sinclair. You can't keep dumping everything on Ramsey.*

The stop in Lake Maynard to pick up the pizza order only took a few minutes, and they were on the road again. Traffic was light on the narrow highway to Baker City. Rory finally spoke. "Vangie says your wife fixed up rooms for us."

"Knowing Ramsey, she probably ordered it done." Rex chuckled. "She prefers the barn to the house, so it shouldn't come as a surprise she insisted on buying a riding stable when she retired from the Army."

"So, we'll know where to find you when you retire, Dad," Raleigh said. "I'm glad we're here for the holiday weekend."

"Much better than hanging out at school like we did last year," Rory agreed.

It made sense they wouldn't have time to get to California for a long weekend. Rex turned off the highway onto the two-lane blacktop that led to the stable and found himself behind a flatbed truck loaded with hay. He followed it across the bridge and up the driveway to the barns.

He saw Debbie standing near another pickup watching someone shoe Wonder. She wore what he'd come to think of as her new uniform, jeans, a Miracle Riding Stable t-shirt, and lace-up boots. She waved and headed toward his rig. He parked, switched off the engine. "Grab your go-bags, my gear and the pizzas," he told the boys.

He didn't wait for an answer. He stuffed the keys into the pocket of his camouflage pants and went to meet her. He reached for her, and she came willingly into his arms. He lowered his head, brushed his lips over hers. "I've missed you."

She smiled up at him. "And you're smart enough to say so. Good job, Sinclair."

He laughed and kissed her again, not quite so quickly this time. "What's going on, Ramsey?"

She glanced over her shoulder. "It's been a day and it's not over yet. Laredo Hawke is here to reset Wonder's shoes since he healed up from those hot nails. It looks like Summer O'Neill just arrived with the feed I ordered and now you and the boys are here too. Somebody better introduce me, and that's you, Sinclair."

"I will." He turned, keeping an arm around her waist. Vangie and Penny had arrived, accompanied by Shasta. Between the chattering cluster of his grown, half-grown, and not yet grown kids, the hugs and the barking pup, there was plenty of action to entertain him. "Give them a few minutes to meet and greet."

A thirty-something, skinny brunette in faded jeans and a red t-shirt popped out of the Chevy pickup and waved a greeting. "Hi, I'm Summer O'Neill. You must be Debbie Ramsey, and—"

"I am and this is my husband, Rex Sinclair. Let's see that hay."

Summer tilted her head, narrowing blue eyes. "We've met before, Major."

Rex nodded. "I've seen you with Maverick Jones at the formal base dinners the past two years. Am I in trouble if I say I'm more comfortable in my ACUs than my dress uniform?"

Summer laughed appreciatively, pulling on a pair of work gloves. "And

I'd much rather wear jeans than an evening gown and heels, and kiss the general's wife's backside, so I'd say we're even."

"It's a small world." Rex followed the two women to the truck where Debbie eyeballed the bales of alfalfa-grass. She pulled out a handful of hay to smell it, then tasted it before she nodded acceptance. He copied her actions before agreeing. "I'll get my boys to help unload."

"Thanks. I hired Jack Madison and a couple of his logger buddies, but they have trouble showing up on time to help with deliveries. I'll text his daddy again and ask if Jack's still busy at the Morgan farm."

"Do you think he is?" Debbie asked.

"Of course not. He's undoubtedly holding down a bar stool at Pop's Café. We don't want him when he's half drunk, but this will get Frank off my back and since he runs the BC Business Association, I don't want him pissed at me. I have enough issues with the O'Neill clan."

"Do I need to know why?" Rex eyed her. She acted tough, but he knew the difference between courage and bravado. "Maverick's covering for me this weekend, and I'll take his duty next week when he has his kids."

"Our kids," Summer corrected, shrugging. "And my family has issues because I won't marry him, but I'm not signing up to be an Army wife. It wasn't my thing when he was in ROTC in college, or when he headed off to combat zones. Told him I wouldn't be following him from one duty station to another and now that he's climbing the officer ranks in CONUS, I still won't."

"It's not easy being a military spouse," Debbie agreed. "Let's unload some feed. I want at least a ton of hay in each barn, and then we'll split up the grain the same way."

"Sounds good. I'll meet you at the first barn."

Rex glanced down at Debbie. She was calm, not upset by the hay-dealer's opinion. "I've never heard you say something so courteous to civilians who criticized the Army before."

"If I was rude, I couldn't ask where she got that shirt. I'm ready to go shopping for one that says, 'My people skills are fine. It's my tolerance for idiots that needs work.'"

"Oh, then you definitely need wine to go with the pizza. Good thing I stopped at the Class VI store to pick up more Zinfandel."

Rory stopped on the porch to wait for his brothers and younger sisters. When he looked across the yard, he saw his father with the dark-haired woman who must be his new wife. During one of their phone calls, Vangie bitched about not being invited to their wedding.

Rory told her there was no way their mother would have allowed it. She always claimed their dad would get over his snit and come home, but it hadn't happened in the last eight years and now it never would. She refused to let any of them visit him even when the man was in CONUS between combat tours in America's longest war.

Scott said it was amazing that Rex welcomed the girls when they arrived, but it didn't shock Rory. He knew who the villain was in their family soap opera. If the annual six-month trips to the condo she'd scored in Hawaii from her third husband over the past four years hadn't been a clue, nothing else would.

He and his sibs hadn't been welcomed at the place their mother shared with her various men and now with their newest stepfather. Penny ranted and raved about the new boarding school and was determined not to go, but Rory hadn't known how to prevent the upcoming disaster. He'd been totally amazed when his younger sisters devised and executed a plan to live with the major rather than waiting for their mother's and stepdad's return from Maui at Christmas.

"He looks happy." Cal joined Rory. "Vangie says the rooms are ours, not guest ones, and our stuff is coming from California. When I asked how Dad pulled that off, she said he didn't. It was Ramsey who pulled the strings."

"Not unless he told her to." Rory eyed his brother. "Dad's used to being in charge. When he called about this weekend, he didn't include a single 'please' or 'thank you'. He said for us to pick up tickets at the airport, not to miss the flight and he'd be at SeaTac to get us."

"You didn't share that before."

"Because I knew Scott would totally freak at taking the old man's orders." Rory heard footsteps and glanced over his shoulder to see their other siblings coming toward them. "Come on. I want to meet Dad's wife."

"Don't call her that or Mrs. Sinclair." Penny advised him. "She prefers Ramsey or Debbie. She always says she doesn't require anger management classes. People better stop pissing her off."

Scott grinned, humor warming his golden-brown eyes. "How does the Major take that?"

"He's the first on the list," Vangie added. "Let's go."

Debbie took a step closer to Rex as his kids approached them. Okay, so they were only legally his children because he wouldn't tell them otherwise. The brawny blond surfer boy must be the oldest, Rory. Next came Raleigh, a lean, wiry dark-haired guy who bore such a strong resemblance to the pictures she'd seen of Rex when he was in college. Did he see it too? His third son was obviously part Native-American. And then there were the girls.

"Breathe, Ramsey. They'll love you."

"I hope you're right."

"I know I am."

Vangie beamed at them. "Ramsey, these are my brothers." She gestured to the blond. "This is Rory. Then, it's Scott—"

"Raleigh," Rex said. "That's what your mom named him."

"I prefer my middle name, Scott." He lounged forward and leaned down to kiss Debbie's cheek. "Thanks for getting the rest of my gear. I took most of it a couple years ago when I moved in with Rory off campus in Pullman."

"All of it isn't here yet," Debbie said, smiling at him. "More will probably arrive next week."

"Great. Then, I'll be able to go skiing over Thanksgiving."

"Only if you take me," Penny told him.

"And only if you ask me. Nobody goes AWOL on my watch," Debbie said. "I might be out of the Army and not take orders anymore, but I never did from junior enlisted."

"And barely from officers," Rex reminded her. "I can't remember how many times you told me that taking charge and seeing to it that what needed doing got done was sergeant's business."

The third boy came forward. "I'm Cal. Nobody calls me Reginald more than once. I don't even know why I got stuck with that stupid name."

"Nothing stupid about it." Rex narrowed his eyes, a muscle twitching in his jaw. "It was my grandfather's name and he helped raise me. That's why your mother chose it."

Debbie felt his arm tighten around her. "Did anyone call him Reginald?"

"My grandmother when she was annoyed. When she bellowed Reginald Calvin, he hit the back door a-running." Rex slowly relaxed. "His poker buddies called him R.C."

"I can go with that," Cal said. "Mom never told me I was his namesake."

"It wasn't a popular choice," Rex admitted, "but she'd named your brothers, so when she said she expected you, I told her what I wanted before I shipped out to Iraq."

"Then, who named me Rebecca?" Vangie asked. "It's not my grandma's name."

"It was my grandmother's name and I always intended to call my first daughter that," Rex said. "Evangeline was my mother's name."

That earned him another long look before Vangie nodded. "Cool. I thought I was named after Grandma E., but Mom never confirmed it. She gets irritated by all the gift cards at the holidays."

"I hope you remember to send 'thank-you' notes." Debbie leaned against Rex. She wouldn't tell him she knew when he needed her support. "It may be old-fashioned, but it's the right thing to do."

"Lupe–Señora Gonzales–our housekeeper insisted on it." Penny glanced up from where she petted Shasta. "Mom never made us do it. We emailed Dad because we didn't always know where the Army sent him."

"He didn't know either until he received his orders."

"Speaking of which, we need to help Summer unload that truck before she hurts herself, and I have to explain to Maverick Jones why I didn't step up and look after her."

Debbie inclined her head and eased away from him. "Sounds fair. Come on, Penny. You and Shasta can help me with the new trace mineral blocks."

"Jason calls them salt licks."

"I prefer a combination of salt and minerals. When you remove the stickers, you can see everything the blocks have in them. The horses need them when it's hot because they lose large amounts of essential minerals when they sweat. If it's not replenished, they may develop an electrolyte imbalance. That leads to low blood pressure or even neurological or cardio-vascular problems."

"Wow." Penny's blue eyes widened. "Ramsey, do you know everything about horses?"

"Not hardly." Debbie laughed. "However, I'm the first to admit it when I don't, and then I do online research on my phone or computer. Let's go, girl. As soon as we finish, there's pizza in our future."

CHAPTER FIFTEEN

Late that night at 0200 hours, two in the morning civilian time, they sat on the porch swing enjoying their wine. Shasta had the far end of the bench style seat, and it meant Debbie needed to sit comfortably close to Rex. The moon floated in the star-studded sky, and she smelled the faint whiff of wildfire smoke on the breeze. Thankfully, the flames were miles away in Liberty Valley and she was on the far side of Cedar Creek, so she didn't have to find a way to evacuate her stable.

Debbie tilted her head so she could see his face. "I like your boys. They were a lot of help today and Summer really appreciated it. How did you teach them to have such strong work ethics?"

"When I wasn't around since the divorce?" He smoothed her hair. "It's okay to talk straight, Ramsey. I inherited my grandmother's house in '05, and the boys helped me fix it up before I sold it."

Debbie mentally calculated their ages. "Sounds more like babysitting to me, Sinclair. Cal would have been four. Scott was six and Rory was only eight."

"They could clean, help carry wood, tear out drywall and the two older ones were good painters by the time we finished. They thought it was fun because we drove to Texas and camped out in the house for almost three weeks. Their mom was far away in California visiting her folks, so we did guy stuff like roasting hot dogs for supper on a bonfire in the backyard. When we sold it, Rory wanted us to buy another one to play with and his brothers agreed. It sounded like a good idea at the time, and I found a different distressed property closer to home."

"What did your ex say about that? Didn't she have a claim on the money too?"

"Not after she and my grandmother fought non-stop while I was in combat. The war started between them when they met, and it escalated after Rory was born."

Debbie grimaced and sipped the red wine. "She knew, didn't she?"

"It was fairly obvious." Rex stared into the distance, steeped in memories. "There never had been any blonds in our family. Averill is a brunette with blue eyes. She told me after he was born that she'd been dating several guys, not just me and wasn't a 100-percent sure, but I was the one she loved."

"And the one who proposed as soon as you heard she was pregnant."

"I loved her desperately and as soon as I held Rory, he was mine. Two years later, we had Raleigh. When he was two, I went for training before I shipped out to Iraq. Averill was amazingly eight weeks pregnant when I came home."

"How long were you gone?"

"Four months. She claimed it was my fault because I left, and she was bored. We had a big fight before I went to the *sandpit* and both of us said unforgiveable things. I loved my boys, and I told her when I got back, I'd file for divorce and take the two of them. It hurt her and she said *if* I came back alive, we'd see."

Debbie covered his hand with one of hers. The two of them sat in silence with the wine for a few moments. She didn't doubt he'd been shocked and cut to the quick. Of course, he'd flung angry words at his ex-wife. After working with him for so long, Debbie knew the argument would have been verbal, not physical. He never would strike a woman.

Finally, Rex said, "We were still at odds when I returned home from Iraq. Then Grandma died. She left a letter saying Averill was a strumpet who went by harlot to save her reputation and she wasn't getting a penny of my grandparents' hard-earned money. Grandma left everything to me, and I didn't tell Averill it was almost a half million dollars, plus all their property in Texas."

"I bet that was an O.M.G. moment. What did you say? It had to be something to avoid any 'community property' issues since married couples are supposed to share their assets in most places."

"Grandma was super smart, and she knew an inheritance was an exception to 'community property' laws in Texas and California." Rex shrugged. "I told her lawyer I'd honor her wishes. It helped when Averill said she didn't want a penny of the old witch's money and the attorney made her put it in writing. We were already having problems because she tended to go on hog-wild spending sprees when I was away. When I got back, we'd be broke."

"What did you do? I know you came up with a plan."

"We'd separated while we were fighting before I left, so I'd set up a different bank account for my Army pay. We already had one strictly for household expenses and I arranged to deposit money in it. I paid Lupe Gonzales to look after the kids and the house. It meant Averill didn't have to worry about that and could work as much as she wanted."

"Makes sense." Debbie refilled their wine glasses. "I wish I realized Señora Gonzales had been with the kids for so long. I'd have offered her a job here. Heaven knows I could use a housekeeper, since we spend so many hours in the barn."

Rex chuckled, taking his glass from her. "Good luck with that, Ramsey. Her family is in California. You can ask, but I don't know that she'd move to the boonies in Washington state."

"Worth a try. I'll drop her an email." Debbie drew a deep breath. "So, you and the boys did male bonding when you were home? It's amazing things didn't change after the divorce, that they still had the moral code you instilled."

"Rory told me if they wanted extras like his surfboard or new clothes or movie tickets or a car to share, they had to earn them. Their mom needed all of the support to pay bills. I didn't tell him the house in Sacramento belonged to me. I used part of my inheritance to pay off the mortgage during the divorce proceedings. Lupe told me when the place needed repairs and she supervised those. I paid the taxes. Averill could live there with the kids until they left home and then it'd revert to me."

"What kind of work did the boys do?"

"Rory mowed lawns until he was old enough to be a lifeguard at the local pool. Scott delivered papers and fried burgers at a fast-food restaurant. They both have part-time jobs in Pullman."

"And Cal?"

"He worked at a horse rescue. He helped with deliveries, mucking, feeding, training. He already has a job looking after the horses on the equestrian team at the college."

"Are you good with that?" Debbie studied the depths of her wine. "Or should we tell them that grades and classes come first?"

"I'm thinking about it. I worked my way through college. No choice since I had a wife and kid to support, but I'm not sure I want that for them."

"Well, I attended the *School of Hard Knocks*. Picked up a few college courses over the years, but never finished a business degree. I can't help you with this conundrum, Sinclair."

"You said your lawyer is making sure the boys have the child support I was paying their mother."

"We arranged for it to revert to them when they turned eighteen or graduated from high school, whichever came first. Between their scholarships, their jobs, and you paying the tuition, they're pretty well set." She paused. "Since we'll have custody of the girls, what's your plan for the California house? Should I tell Bree you want to sell it?"

He considered the question as he sipped his wine. "Would I be a complete wimp if I said I'm not totally comfortable with that yet? Averill is the mother of my five kids, and we were married fifteen years before I was done being made a fool of at every Army base. Granted, she's remarried, all the kids are out of the house and there's no reason for me to support her and the new husband."

He paused, sipped some wine and then continued, "The military is a small world, Ramsey, and even when we moved to a new station, I already knew what was said about me and my wife. I always intended to take possession of the house when Penny was grown and out of there."

"You're not a wimp. You never could be one." Debbie rested a hand on his cheek, feeling the stubble of his growing beard. "Just too honorable for your own good, Sinclair." She paused. He'd be offended if she said what she honestly thought of the way the other woman treated him.

Cheating on him when he was at a military school and then when he was in a war-zone along with emotionally blackmailing him, so he'd raise three kids that definitely weren't his, infuriated Debbie. Telling his teenage sons to work for extras when their dad always paid support and leaving the girls to fend for themselves while his ex-wife honeymooned in Hawaii with her latest toy-boy added to the rage.

He chuckled, put his empty glass on the porch rail and snagged hers, placing it next to his. "Ramsey, why do I have a feeling that you're going to kick tails and take names?"

"Because you're smart?"

"And you're mean."

She sighed when he framed her face with his hands. "What are you thinking?"

"This." His lips brushed hers. "Just this."

She laced her arms around his neck. "You're going to have to do better, Sinclair."

"I will."

He kissed her. This time, it wasn't soft or sweet. His tongue swept into her mouth and the fierce pressure of his lips sent excitement pounding through her. She threaded her fingers in his hair, answering the kiss with a fire of her own. When he finally lifted his head, she struggled to keep her voice steady. "It's about time."

He smiled, outlining her lips with his thumb. "I wanted to wait until you were sure about a lifetime commitment."

She measured the sincerity on his rugged features. "I'm okay. Waiting is vastly overrated."

"I don't think so."

She trembled when the next set of kisses skimmed across her cheek to her ear and his lips trailed down her neck. "We could go upstairs."

"Not yet." He lifted his head, refilled their glasses, and picked up hers. "I want everything, Ramsey, and you're not offering that."

"Close enough." She took the glass from him and saw the amused tenderness in his golden-brown eyes. "You're the only guy I know who'd turn down a roll in the hay. Tomorrow is not going to be a good day for me. It's my son's nineteenth birthday. While I know I did right by him, there's still issues."

She paused and measured Rex slowly. "You already knew about him, didn't you? How? I didn't —."

"There are always issues when it comes to kids, Ramsey." He put an arm around her. "You're dealing with it. And apparently you forgot how good I am at gathering intelligence."

"I know." She enjoyed the comfort he offered. "But I can't do what I've done in the past. I have a business to run, so I'm not getting drunk tonight and hiding until Sunday morning. Sex would be a good substitute."

"Not with me, Ramsey. I'm holding out for real love this time." He picked up his own wine goblet with his free hand. "Your new horseshoer told me he thought Wonder would be ready to go riding this Sunday. Are we sending the boys off to church with Vangie and Penny?"

"Actually, I hoped we'd go to the county fair in Liberty Valley. It's bigger than the one near Lake Maynard, but we want to train some riders to compete next summer. I just need to get on Kyra's good side. She's pissed because I replaced her incompetent boyfriend who lamed Wonder with Laredo Hawke and I'm buying feed from Summer O'Neill instead of being ripped off by a different company in Liberty Valley."

"And you don't want to fire her?"

"Kyra's extremely competent, very safety conscious and the students adore her. I want to keep her, but I don't want to deal with drama. Ideas? Feedback?"

"Piece of cake." He sipped wine. "Tell her that your husband put his foot down and you have to do what I say or we'll have one hell of a fight. Laredo shoes and trims the horses, and you buy feed from Maverick's woman."

"Sounds like I'm back at Fort Clark again and I'm using you for cover."

"Works for us." He winked at her. "And you're the woman who signs my name better than I do. Right?"

"Indubitably." She pressed against him and enjoyed the kiss he dropped on her hair. "Why the hell did you let Maverick Jones near my warehouses when some people refer to him as the general's dog-robber?"

"Hey, they called me that back in the day when it was my job to do whatever was necessary to get the general anything he needed."

"And you still are. Is that what Maverick's doing? Looking after the guys in the hospital this weekend?"

"Yes, because I didn't trust them to behave when I was away from the base."

"Makes sense. Did my new shoer ask about his brother?"

"No, but he did say his oldest brother, Durango, wants me to stop by Nighthawke Security's office at the dude ranch tomorrow so we could have a conversation."

"Are you going to do it?"

"Nope. Told him I need to haul the rest of the hay from the feedstore, so for him to send the man here."

"And then I can watch your six."

"Couldn't do without you, Ramsey."

"Right answer." It was her turn to kiss him.

Another glass of wine and several kisses later, Shasta surprised them when she jumped off the swing to race toward the front door, barking and growling. Debbie felt Rex tense beside her, then relax when Rory stepped outside. He bent to pet the half-grown dog who accepted it as her due before leaving to take care of puppy business in the yard.

Debbie spotted concern on the young man's face. "What's happening? Is something wrong?"

"That's my question." A faint smile slowly replaced the frown. "I heard voices when I opened the window and thought I'd check to see if everything was okay."

"We're fine. We just enjoy being outside at night." Rex finished the last of his wine. "What about your brothers and sisters? Any of them awake?"

"Not at this hour. You still have PTSD, Dad?"

"What makes you think that?"

Rory crossed the porch to draw up a nearby Adirondack chair. "I remember when we flipped houses the guys and I would sack out about ten or eleven at night, and you'd still be working. Sometimes, I'd wake up and hear the saw running or see you framing a wall or tiling a bathroom or painting one of the rooms."

"I bet that made it hard to sleep." Debbie swirled the wine in her glass. "All the noise?"

"No. It made me feel safe because Dad was home."

"There you go." Debbie rested her head on Rex's shoulder. "It's fine. We're fine. Go back to bed."

"In a bit." Rory crossed his ankles. "As long as I'm down here, I can pick your brain about replacing the hot water tank in our house, Dad. We want a bigger one."

"I thought you and Scott lived on campus," Debbie said.

"Too expensive and we do better on our own. Neither of us enjoyed the party scene. I escaped from the dorms in my sophomore year. I bought a three-bedroom disaster a few miles away from the university. It was so bad, I couldn't call it 'distressed' and started working on it when I had time."

"I'm impressed." Rex smiled. "Good choice. Why did you wait to buy a house until you were a sophomore?"

"School rule that freshmen under twenty years old have to live on campus," Rory said. "I remembered what you used to say about knowing the rules and finding the loopholes, so I had a serious talk with Scott and Cal. They started taking community college courses while they were in high school."

"And what did that do?" Debbie drank the remains of her wine. "I don't get it."

"It meant Scott entered W.S.U. as a sophomore and skipped that requirement. He moved in with me right away. Cal had his Associate degree and he enrolled as a junior, so he lives with us too. The plan is to keep flipping houses while we do our undergraduate classes and then we'll have money for post-grad degrees."

"Wow, my turn to be impressed." Debbie elbowed Rex. "Sounds like you were paying attention when I said it was always better to ask forgiveness than permission, Major."

"What does that mean, Ramsey?"

"I'll make a noncom out of you yet. Discovering the loopholes in regs is definitely sergeants' business."

He grinned appreciatively. "Yeah, right. Be careful or you'll get busted to corporal."

"Not hardly, Major. I'm not in your army anymore."

"Want to bet?"

Heat rose in her cheeks when he snagged her chin and his lips brushed hers. "My turn to say, behave yourself."

"And you're still trying to take charge, aren't you, Ramsey?"

"Always!"

CHAPTER SIXTEEN

While Debbie dozed with her head on his shoulder, Rex admired the pictures of the modern farmhouse his sons had updated on Rory's phone. The boys had repaired the foundation, put on a new roof, and repainted the exterior. Now, they focused on the interior.

"It was rented to a bunch of party animals," Rory explained. "They destroyed the place and the owners decided it'd cost too much to restore it especially if they rented it to students again and Pullman is a university town. Once we're done with it, we want to sell it to someone on the faculty, someone with a family who will take care of the place."

Rex skimmed through the series of photographs showing holes in the walls, tears in the linoleum, burns and oil stains on carpet, urine stains on the walls, broken windows, missing screens, water marks from overflowed sinks and bathtubs, burns on countertops, unauthorized painting, and damaged toilets in the two and a half bathrooms.

"Looks like you replaced the toilets, tore out the carpets, installed double-paned windows and put in new vinyl flooring. Good work. What kind of hot water tank are you thinking?"

"We're thinking an eighty-gallon tank so the house will be user-friendly for a larger family."

"Makes sense. What else?"

"Scott is redesigning the kitchen. Like you taught us, it and the bathrooms are the most important rooms when it comes to selling a place. He's suggested remodeling it, so the pantry and laundry are adjacent to it. We want to move the guest bathroom, too."

"Do you have a floor plan of the place?"

"Next two pictures." Rory beamed.

Rex nodded and looked at them. He recognized the limitations of the current house, with a pantry closer to the two-car garage than the kitchen. Most people wouldn't be happy going that far to find staples when they were trying to create a meal. "If the laundry was closer to the porch, parents would be happier because the kids wouldn't be dragging dirt throughout the place."

"I didn't think of that."

"Because you don't have children yet." Rex returned the phone. "Why don't all of us sit down tomorrow night and lay out the perfect model for the house?"

"Sounds like a winner. Scott and Cal told me to ask if you could come to Pullman and do a walk-through."

"I would if I could." The invitation warmed Rex's heart. His sons still wanted him, despite not seeing him for so long. "I'm on special assignment at the base for the next two months. If Ramsey works it out with her staff to look after the horses, we'll come for Thanksgiving, and I'll give you a hand with whatever project is next on the schedule."

Rory glanced at the sleeping woman on the swing. "She's wearing the rings Great-Grandma gave you, the ones that have been in the Sinclair family forever."

"They were too old for your mom, but Ramsey appreciates heirlooms. Most of the furniture here is from her grandparents." Rex shifted on the swing long enough to check his watch. "We should hit the hay. It's 0330. Get the glasses and the empty bottle for me."

He stood, gathering Debbie into his arms, and carried her across the porch. Rory tucked away his smart-phone and followed directions. Shasta followed them inside. When he gestured toward the door, Rory locked it behind them. He headed into the kitchen while Rex climbed the stairs to the suite on the second floor. He lowered Debbie onto the antique sleigh bed, then removed her boots. He drew a blanket over her. Shasta jumped up on the foot of the bed, turned in a couple small circles before lying down in a collie heap.

Smiling, Rex clicked off the lamp on the nightstand and started for the door.

"Don't go."

He glanced over his shoulder, saw her open drowsy blue eyes. "What?"

"Stay with me."

"Even if I won't make love to you?"

"I don't care about that. Just stay."

After visiting with the other ghosts over the last few days, Moises Pride had taken time to explore the town. It included a large structure, the Baker City Mercantile, the café, two bars, the church, a cemetery, and a vintage schoolhouse. More cedar shake buildings of varying sizes lined the roads. His favorite place had to be the large barn on the right-hand side of the main street. A sign painted on the building proclaimed, "Summer's Feed and Tack."

Inside, he'd enjoyed watching people shop. The store had everything from display racks of outdoor clothes, gloves, riding boots, and barn boots to the left. Shelves of gifts and souvenirs, including a few used paperback novels on a spinner took up the front right corner. Pet gear, horse tack, medicine, and farm equipment filled the back-half of the store. Feed was through the back door in the adjacent warehouse.

The owner, Summer O'Neill, a scrawny little brunette, seemed to know everyone in town. Some were friendlier than others, but since it was the only place to get feed for their pets and livestock, she did all right. Her two older kids ran in and out. The youngest, a two-year-old rugrat usually played behind the cash register and frequently threw a stuffed toy dog at him–he was surprised to learn the toddler could see him. If her mother wasn't looking, Moises sent it flying back, which prompted a series of giggles before the kiddo hurled it at him again.

This morning one of the first customers was the major. He wore civvies, jeans, a western shirt, and boots. A young, big blond guy accompanied him, along with a half-grown, tri-colored collie mix wearing a green plaid harness. The trio approached Summer.

"We're here to start hauling hay," Major Sinclair said.

"You're in luck. It just arrived." Summer leaned on the counter. "I talked to my dealer, and he'll bring the rest of it directly to the stable. It doesn't make sense for him to offload twenty-five tons here and then for me to load it on my truck and make eight trips to your place."

"He'll unload and stack it, won't he?" Major Sinclair asked. "My wife has enough to do. I'll be at the base and my boys are only home for the holiday weekend."

"No worries. I've got it covered." Summer glanced behind her, then turned to scoop up the little girl, bouncing the toddler on a hip. "Come on. Let's show the guys where to find hay, Miss Charlie."

"Is it short for Charlotte?" The blond guy, who had to be a college student grinned at the kid. "Hey, girl. I'm Rory Sinclair."

She babbled a response and tugged on her mom's hair. Summer smiled back at him. "No, her dad has always admired Charlie Parkhurst who drove a stagecoach through the Sierra Nevadas back in the olden days. So, we named her after his hero."

"How could a woman do that?"

"By masquerading as a man more than forty years," Major Sinclair said. "Ramsey always points out that Parkhurst managed to successfully vote in presidential elections long before it was legal."

"Amazing," Rory said.

Interesting. Moises decided to trail behind the group when they headed for the warehouse.

The dog stopped, blocking his approach. It barked, then growled. The actions drew the major's attention. He leaned down and petted her. "It's okay, Shasta. We're the only ones here."

"According to you, but we're in Baker City." Summer looked in the same direction.

For a moment, Moises wondered if the store owner actually saw him. Then he decided she probably didn't. Other than the medium and her husband at the café last week, none of the living had.

"Good girl for telling us there's someone else here." Summer reached in a box on a nearby shelf and picked up a treat. "Here you are, girl. Have a reward. As for our guest," she added, straightening, and raising her voice, "remember your manners and don't scare critters or kiddoes. We have rules in Baker City, and you don't want the O'Leary looking for you."

"Hey, I've been on the up and up since I got here." Moises insisted, even though he knew she couldn't hear him. "I like this place and it's not my fault the dog can see me."

"I don't get it," Rory followed the others. "What does visiting Baker City have to do with anything?"

"In Baker City, the ghosts are real," Summer answered. "You'll learn more the longer you stay."

"And this one is going with the major and his kid. Hopefully, the dog will chill when I'm in their rig and I won't have to run behind." He could do it, but it got tiresome in a hurry.

Charlie waved at him. "Bye-bye, sojer."

Moises returned the wave. "Bye-bye, little one. I'll be back to see you."

August sunlight streamed through the windows when she woke. She turned her head and glimpsed the radio-clock. Almost 1000 hours, ten in the morning. She should have been in the barns hours ago. "Damn it, Sinclair."

He was nowhere in sight, so she couldn't kick his very sexy butt to the moon and back. She paused, bemused by the thought. Of course, she'd been attracted to him from day one, but he was married and off limits. Granted, his wife had been far away in California and refused to come to Texas where he was stationed, but Debbie hadn't realized until she tracked him down at a local bar how serious he was about his upcoming divorce. If she'd had more courage, she'd have done a 'happy dance' then and there.

Picking up strangers in NCO clubs for nights of forgettable sex prior to marrying Rex Sinclair didn't count. She'd considered it therapy since she wasn't looking for a relationship but hadn't wanted the past to control her any more than it already had. Rex had offered to give her a pass on consummating their marriage of convenience, but she refused. She'd married him and she wanted a wedding night before she shipped out on another tour to the *sandbox*. After all, she didn't know if she'd make it home and neither did he.

She drew up her knees, wrapped her arms around them, and recalled the night in question. It'd been better than she hoped, and she'd had more than one orgasm. The guy was good back then and he'd been even better when they hooked up several times over the last few years. Sex would be fantastic now since they had a deeper emotional bond.

At the foot of the bed, Bandit stretched out white-tipped paws, then rolled his eight-month-old body in more kitty contortions. He rose and strolled across the comforter so she could pet him. She obliged him for a few minutes.

Finally, she tossed the blanket aside and slid out of the bed to her feet. Shower first, then she dressed and headed downstairs. Bandit was already ahead of her, and she figured he'd gone in search of the cat food dish in the laundry room.

Debbie heard voices in the kitchen. She needed caffeine before going to the barn and went there. She found Penny setting the table while Scott piled homemade muffins into a towel-lined basket.

"Give me a sitrep, Penny. What's going on?"

"Breakfast." Penny beamed at her. "Scott made bacon-cheddar hash. He'll top it with eggs when everyone's here at 1100 hours. We have fresh fruit salad too."

Debbie poured a cup of coffee. "I think we'll be totally spoiled by Monday. Where's everyone else?"

"Outside. By the time Dad and Shasta came downstairs, the guys had helped us with morning chores. Cal said every barn does things differently, so we had to teach them the way we do it here. Daddy told Kyra to take charge of the business until you got there, since she was the ranking supervisor."

"Really?" Debbie eyed the young girl. "Do you want to tell me what that means before I have a fit and fall in it?"

"She and Carol went off to saddle up for pony rides and lessons while she sent Trina and Jason to prep for trail rides. Cal is helping them because he wants to ride along. Daddy called the feedstore and told Summer that he and Rory would be up for the first load of hay ASAP." Penny carefully filled glasses with ice water. "Debbie, what does ASAP mean?"

"It's Army talk for as soon as possible." Debbie glanced across the room to the rug where Shasta normally slept by the woodstove. "Where's my dog?"

"She went with Daddy. He said he missed her almost as much as he missed you at the Army base and she loves road trips."

"I should have known." Debbie murmured into the coffee cup. Anyone who'd let a dog sleep on an antique bed would definitely take her along when he did errands. "Tell me he remembered her harness and leash."

"He didn't think she needed it, but Vangie assured him that Shasta did, or you'd tear his ears off when he got back. The guys laughed."

"Really?" Debbie turned her attention to Scott. "Why?"

"Nobody tells the old man what to do and our mother always back-pedaled from him when he was angry." Scott opened the second oven and slid a stack of plates inside to warm. "She said he'd lose it if anyone argued with him, and we'd get hurt because he'd just returned from combat."

"Bullsh—" Debbie stopped when Penny laughed. "Don't you dare tell your dad I nearly used his favorite word."

"I won't." Penny giggled. "I bet he figures out super quick you cuss better than he does."

"He already knows." Debbie refilled her coffee cup and pulled out her cell phone. It only took a few minutes to check in with Kyra who'd started the first lesson in the indoor arena. When she answered, Trina said the group of trail riders reviewed how to start, stop, and steer the horses in the big corral just like the campers did before they rode out to the woods.

Debbie glanced at the clock. She had fifteen minutes before they ate. It was enough time to go to the stable office, meet the customers, collect the fees, and schedule more lessons. "I'll be back shortly. I don't want to miss out on breakfast."

Halfway across the yard, she spotted Rex's pickup leaving the barn where she kept the majority of the horses she used for trail rides. Rory was behind the wheel, and he drove carefully toward the second stable obviously intending to unload the last ten bales there. She glanced around but didn't see any customers waiting, so she went inside the hay-room. Shasta saw her first and dashed to greet her, still wearing the harness. However, her leash wasn't anywhere in sight.

Smiling, Debbie leaned down to pet the young dog who wagged her tail fervently for a moment before escorting her to where Rex stacked the remaining bales of hay. "Sinclair, we need to talk."

"I've always told you that no good conversations ever started with those words, honey."

She folded her arms and waited while he lodged the next bale of alfalfa-grass into place. "I'm serious."

"So am I." Using hay hooks, he grabbed another bale of hay. "What's bothering you?"

"Not much other than you turning off the alarm and taking charge of my place."

"Just doing my job, Ramsey, and watching your six."

"How do you figure?" She gave up on standing around and jumped in to roll a bale of alfalfa-grass into position, lining it up to begin the next tier on the stack. Then, she went after a second one. "I have a business here."

"Yes, and you need to get more sleep." He snagged the last bale of hay, put it beside the ones she'd set in place. "Do you have nightmares too?"

"Of course." She lifted her chin and met his golden-brown gaze. "Why do you think I sit up until the wee hours? Because I'm waiting for you to call in the middle of the night?"

"I can always hope." He hung the hay hooks on the tool rack. "I call because most nights the memories crowd in on me."

"Sounds about right." She heaved a sigh when he approached and drew her into his arms. She smelled hay, lime aftershave and sweat. She supposed she ought to push him away, but she couldn't. Instead, she laced her arms around his neck, pressing against him. "If I don't go to bed, I don't remember the attacks when I was sending out supplies or having to look for I.E.D.s when I was in charge of delivering them. I don't have to think about the ambushes or the soldiers who died."

"I know."

She shivered when he tipped up her chin, feathered a thumb over her mouth. "I need to be in charge, Sinclair."

"I know," he repeated.

"Then don't try to run my life." She brushed her lips over his. "I can't deal unless I'm the boss."

"I know." His mouth claimed hers in a long kiss.

When he finally lifted his head, she stared up into his eyes. "You have the same problems, don't you? If you're always in control, then it's safe. And if you're not, it isn't."

He chuckled. "You're a smart woman, Ramsey."

"I know." It was her turn to knock his socks off with a prolonged kiss.

CHAPTER SEVENTEEN

Sunday morning, Debbie found Rex sitting on the porch swing drinking coffee. Shasta had curled up beside him, her collie head on his lap. "What did you do with the kids?"

"They went to church. I told them I'd pick them up right after services so we can go to the county fair in Liberty Valley. Since they won't all fit in my truck, I hoped to borrow your Jeep."

"That sounds do-able." She sat next to him, enjoying her morning jolt of caffeine and the September sunshine. "Anything else I need to know?"

"Let's see. Rory and Cal approved of Scott's final kitchen design. He modeled it after the one here, including a woodstove, and added most of the family's suggestions."

Debbie nodded. "He told me cooking here was the most fun he'd had in months. I said he could continue doing it forever, but I'd definitely have to take up running two or three miles a day or I'd gain so much weight, Hobby would refuse to carry me."

Rex chuckled. "Speaking of which, shall we go for a ride before I play taxi-driver?"

"Works for me."

"Before they left, I heard it was Linda MacGillicudy's son's birthday, so I added fifty dollars and signed the card Kyra was passing around. Vangie informed me I was cheap, but I told her since I hadn't met the boy she was infatuated with, it was the best you and I would do."

"I haven't met him either." Debbie sipped black coffee. "Linda tells me that he works part-time at the dude ranch and for his cousin, Heather McElroy, Durango Hawke's wife. He'll be doing construction work for her husband and going to the community college this fall."

"Definitely too old for our girl even if she doesn't think so." Rex finished his coffee and put the mug on the porch rail. "Rory promised to run interference if the situation called for it."

"He's a good big brother."

"I think he's a keeper."

Three hours later, Rex parked in front of the wooden shake building with oversized, carved doors and a large cross on the front peak of the roof. He spotted a cemetery behind it. The historian in him wondered how old it was and if any pioneers were buried there. He'd have to research later. Maybe Debbie would join him for a walk-through the next time they were in town. Visiting the graveyard didn't mean they had to enter the church.

He spotted a silver-haired elderly man talking to two women in their late twenties, one a blonde and the other a brunette. After quick hugs, the pair strolled in the direction of a nearby SUV. The older man approached, nodding a greeting. He didn't wear the traditional dark suit associated with most preachers–and Rex was pretty sure he was one–but a plaid, flannel shirt tucked into faded jeans and cowboy boots. "Hi there. I'm Reverend Tommy. Welcome to Baker City."

"Rex Sinclair. I'm here to collect my kids."

The introduction earned him an amused look. "So, you're the guy who tells Debbie Ramsey to give me a donation and I'll go away."

"Has it worked? After escaping from a cult when she was a kid, Ramsey isn't much for organized religion."

"Then I'll take the donation for our food bank and bring my wife with me when I visit." Reverend Tommy gestured toward the door on the far side of the building. "Everyone is in the fellowship hall for coffee and doughnuts. I'll take you to meet them. Where is Debbie?"

"Feeding horse lunch. She sent me here instead of letting me help."

"Sounds reasonable." Reverend Tommy held the door open and ushered Rex inside a large room filled with people sitting at an assortment of tables. "Looks like your family is with the Murphy clan. I'll introduce you."

"Not necessary. I met them when we visited their farm."

Penny glimpsed them and jumped to her feet, rushing to greet him. "Daddy, you made it in time for snacks. Virginia, Reverend Tommy's wife, says I can take home a maple bar for Ramsey. She told me that they're her fave."

"Sounds like a winner." Rex hugged the little girl. "Maybe one day we'll convince her to come with you and Vangie to church."

"I don't think so, but in his sermon today, Reverend Tommy told us it's better to honor God in your heart than in front of your neighbors."

Rex nodded agreement, eying the preacher. "Did more folks need to hear that?"

"Yup. Baker City isn't that big, and we have a few hard-nosed people who should be practicing what I preach rather than taking the proverbial 'better than you' road. I have faith one of these days, they'll learn to listen and treat their fellows with compassion."

"Good luck with that." Rex followed Penny toward the cluster of people sitting around one of the tables. Besides his sons, he saw an older couple, two teen girls next to Vangie and a dark-haired, younger version of the noncom who always came to the warehouse for supplies. In addition, there was a tall, curvaceous brunette who bore an even stronger resemblance to Tate Murphy.

Rex remembered hearing that Tate had a twin. Introductions ensued and he learned she was Quinn Murphy-Chapman. She was accompanied by her husband, Lyle, a local business executive who wore a dark suit, and her three children, blonde stair-steps who'd opted for more formal attire than their peers, dresses, and heels for the girls who looked like they were between Penny and Vangie's ages, slacks, a collared shirt, and a tie for the boy. Quinn wore jeans, lace-up boots, and a red W.S.U. T-shirt which definitely made her popular with Rory and his brothers.

Rex rested a hand on his younger daughter's shoulder, glancing at Tate Murphy who sat next to his extremely pregnant wife, Sullivan. "I didn't see the Mustang, so I wasn't sure you were here."

"Master Sergeant Hot Stuff drove," Sully said. "Warn Ramsey that some of the women vets are showing up on Thursday to visit her. I won't be there because I'll be teaching school."

"I'll pass the word." Rex suppressed a smile. She didn't seem too concerned about being so close to her due date. "Did you find a substitute teacher for your class while you're out on maternity leave?"

"Art McElroy said he'd enjoy being back in the classroom for a few months. He used to lecture at the University of Washington and he's on the school board, so he'll be fine. It's not easy finding a teacher for a small-town school. There's four of us and we're looking for a sub for Margo Endicott when she has her baby at Halloween."

"Don't you have a teaching certificate, Dad?" Scott asked. "Rory said you had a history degree, too."

"Yes, but I discovered I preferred the Army. I figured when I retired, it'd be soon enough to teach school."

"When will that happen?" Tate grinned at him. "Aren't you up for Lieutenant Colonel?"

"At the next promotion board in November," Rex agreed. "And with three boys in college, I figure I'll stay in the military a while longer."

Sully tilted her head to one side, studying the younger Sinclair males. "So, what's the plan for you guys? Are any of you following in your dad's footsteps?"

"I'm going to law school," Rory said. "Scott's torn between being a head chef and a restaurant manager. And Cal wants to be a large animal veterinarian, specializing in horses."

"Wow, that's impressive and expensive," Sully said. "The two supply sergeants in my reserve unit are doing their internships at an equine practice. They enlisted for college benefits."

"Which is why we're flipping houses," Rory added. "Law school isn't cheap, and neither is veterinary medicine."

"Now, I'm impressed," Joe Murphy, the patriarch of the family, said. "I'll bet you're proud of your boys, Rex."

"And my girls," Rex said, smiling at Penny and Vangie. "We'd better hit the road since my wife wants to go to the county fair in Liberty Valley. She asked me to tell you she'd stop by tomorrow for fresh produce after the boys and I leave for the airport, if that's okay. They're flying back to Pullman in time for classes on Tuesday."

"It's fine." This time Bronwyn Murphy, a silver-haired, plump woman who didn't look old enough to have several children and grandchildren spoke. "She can meet the entire family because they'll be visiting on the holiday."

"I pulled some strings to get Mariah Stevens here," Sully added. "I'll have her email you, Cal. The two of you can meet when she and her sister are in Pullman, and they'll tell you what hoops you have to jump through for vet school. Ramsey can talk to her about shoeing your stock, Major."

"I don't know about that," Rex said. "She's arranged for Laredo Hawke to do them for now, but we'll see what happens."

Halfway to the door, he spotted Kyra O'Neill, the senior instructor at Miracle Riding Stable. He paused and reminded her that Debbie was doing a research trip in Liberty Valley, and they wouldn't be back in time for evening chores. Kyra promised she and Trina would handle them.

———

It took slightly over an hour to reach the fairgrounds outside of Monroe in Liberty Valley. It wasn't cheap entertainment, Debbie thought, after Rex paid for parking, then for their admission and handed out spending money to all five of the kids. When Rory protested he had enough of his own, Rex told him to save it for the return to college the next day.

"We're going to the horse arenas to watch the kids compete for the championships," Debbie said. "What do the rest of you want to see?"

"I'll start with horses," Cal said. "How about the rest of you?"

"Horses first and then I want to check out the commercial booths. They should have 'Watkins' products in one of the buildings." Scott must have seen the curiosity on Vangie's face because he added, "They sell organic spices, flavorings, and extracts. I can always tell the difference between their vanilla and the store-bought stuff when I bake."

"Do we get to show our horses here next summer, Ramsey?" Penny asked.

"No, this is for the kids who live in Liberty Valley. If you're the champion in your division at the Lake Maynard fair, you'll compete against them in Puyallup at the state competitions. And if you win there, then you go to the national contests."

"So, why are we here?" Vangie inquired. "It doesn't make a lot of sense."

"The equestrian judge here is coming to Lake Maynard next July and I want to see Clancy Dawson in action," Debbie explained. "Some judges are pro-money, rather than riding skill. If that's her style, then there isn't any point in grooming our students to compete."

"It's all research," Rory said. "And Penny claims that's your strength. Okay, N.M., let's go kick some butt."

"N.M.?" Debbie raised an eyebrow. "What does that mean?"

"New Mom. You and Dad aren't the only ones who use acronyms."

Debbie gaped at him, then elbowed Rex when he laughed. "Did you put him up to that?"

"No, but I already told you that he's a keeper."

The seats framing the arena weren't full and they easily found a row where the seven of them could sit near each other. Penny claimed the place next to Debbie to ask questions. The twenty riders were teens about Vangie's age. It was a western stock seat class, and they rode a variety of horses, paints, palominos, bays, sorrels, and chestnuts.

A statuesque redhead in cowgirl attire stood in the center of the ring obviously assessing their performances as they walked around the ring. She spoke to the woman accompanying her who signaled the announcer on a reviewing stand at the far end of the arena and the man called for a western trot or jog.

Most of the riders held their horses to a slow shuffle and didn't bounce in the saddles. A few posted and Debbie wondered what the judge thought of that since it wasn't traditional in western equitation. There wasn't any way to know until the class ended. The next gait was a walk again before the riders transitioned to a show-ring lope.

Once they finished riding on the left track, it was time to reverse onto the right one, with the horses leading off on their right front feet. Walk, trot, walk and lope before lining up in the center of the ring. The judge walked down the line, calling out a few of the riders to complete individual patterns. Then she had everyone take turns backing their horses and returning to their places in line. After that, she had them dismount and remount.

"Why is she doing that?" Penny murmured. "She isn't letting them use a mounting block like we do at home."

"She wants to see if they can get off correctly and then get on without one," Debbie said. "It's old-fashioned or traditional horsemanship."

"Are you going to teach us how to do it?" Vangie leaned around Cal. "I don't know if I could jump up on Copper like that."

"I'll teach you, but it takes practice." Debbie glanced at Rex and saw the amusement on his rugged features. "I cheat with the campers because I don't want them stressing the horses. I haven't found an equine chiropractor in Baker City yet."

"I bet you know what I'll say about that." He chuckled and put an arm around her shoulders. "Ask the neighbors."

"I will."

A short time later, the ring steward left the judge to carry a sheet of paper over to the announcer. In a few moments, the man began to call out numbers and placings. Onlookers applauded as riders left the arena picking up their ribbons at the gate. The last four would be advancing to state fair competition the following week.

"Now, what happens, Ramsey?" Penny asked.

"Another class with a different division of riders, probably younger ones who will compete in stock seat equitation. According to the schedule I printed off, there will be western pleasure and patterns after that. Tomorrow, they'll have the English competitions."

"We're not coming back for that, are we?" Vangie tugged on a dark braid. "No offense, but this could get majorly boring."

Debbie laughed. "No, this is a one-day excursion. You and the guys can go check out the rest of the fair if you want. We'll find you in the commercial buildings or the carnival."

"We'll go after the next class," Scott said. "I'll bet Dad won't want the girls wandering around the fairgrounds by themselves."

"You got that right," Rex agreed.

Debbie saw more people filtering in from the far end of the building. They must be coming from the horse barns. Amazement filtered through her when she recognized Laredo Hawke strolling beside another guy, a lean, dark-haired man in western clothes. Laredo spotted her too and waved a greeting.

"Hi there." Laredo gestured to the other man. "Debbie, this is Sean Killian, the first shoer I apprenticed with when I graduated. Sean, this is Debbie Ramsey, the new owner of Miracle Riding Stable in my neck of the woods. I just added her stock to my book."

"It's a pleasure." Smiling, Sean adjusted his cowboy hat to reveal warm gray eyes. "My daughter is showing today, and I invited Laredo to come cheer her on with the rest of us."

"That's odd. The judge is leaving the ring," Rex said. "Isn't she doing this class?"

"Conflict of interest," Sean held out his hand to shake Rex's. "She and my older brother are involved. Even if Clancy can be totally impartial, some folks will have issues especially since she teaches lessons at my wife's stable and Lynn, my daughter is one of their students."

"Makes sense." Debbie introduced the family, not surprised when Sean and Laredo chose nearby seats. A few minutes later, Clancy Dawson sauntered down the wide aisle accompanied by a petite, dark-haired woman, and a young boy a few years older than Penny. More introductions followed as they met Sean's family.

Cal winked at Debbie. "This is one of those 'be careful what you wish for' moments, isn't it, Mom?"

"Be nice or you'll be mucking forty stalls when we get home," Debbie told him. She glanced at Clancy. "I wanted to watch you work because you'll be at the Lake Maynard Fair next summer and I'm hoping to have some students there to compete."

"Awesome." Clancy grinned at Cal and then at her, mischief lighting the violet eyes. She dug in her pocket and pulled out a business card. "Call me when they're ready to have a show at your barn and I'll come judge it."

"Seriously?" Debbie gaped at her for a moment. "Baker City is quite a distance from Liberty Valley."

"I know, but it gives me an opportunity to hang out with Darla Connors, the owner of Painted Pony Park. We've been friends forever and we hardly get to do 'girl chat' when she's showing her purebred stock and I just adore her, Ben, and their kids. I'm their godmother. I can stay over with her and then I won't charge you mileage."

CHAPTER EIGHTEEN

An hour later, Clancy Dawson returned to the arena to judge the first junior riding class. By the time it finished, Penny and Vangie were ready to tour the rest of the fair with Rory and Scott. Cal stayed to watch horsemanship competitions with Debbie and Rex. Western pleasure began after stock seat equitation, and they observed two of those classes. Afterward, they toured several of the horse barns where Debbie admired the signs and banners created by the students in 4-H. Vangie and Rory caught up with them halfway through the last stable.

"Where's Penny?" Debbie asked. "Is she with Scott?"

"They're at the carnival and we need your help," Vangie said. "Penny saw this bear in a purple princess dress with sparkly tulle, screen-printed stars, and lacing. She has a wand and tiara, too."

"Sounds beautiful. What's the problem?" Debbie paused to read the next sign about the gaits of horses. "Does she need more money to buy it?"

"It's at one of the carnival booths. She spent all her money shooting at the targets to win it and now she's broke," Rory said. "We tried to explain that these games are a total rip-off, but she started crying. She says it would be the perfect girlfriend for her Army Ranger bear and she's mad because we won't give her more money."

"It's a waste," Vangie agreed. "None of us shoot well enough to win it, and the guy at the booth isn't any help. He keeps telling her she could win it if she hits the target twenty more times."

"He gave her a little toy dog," Rory said, "and she's going to give it to Shasta when she gets home."

"Not unless it's doggie-safe. I don't want her swallowing buttons or stuffing when she tears it apart." Debbie sighed. "Well, come on. Let's go save the day for your youngest, Major. You'll have to take the boys to the range, and I'll take the girls. Next year, Penny will be able to kick butts."

"I wouldn't be the least bit surprised." Rex put an arm around her waist.

Debbie didn't tell him how much she enjoyed his touch. Instead, they strolled through the barn and bypassed the large indoor arena, cutting past the other ring where riders competed in an obstacle course. They found Scott trying to convince Penny to leave a booth while the man behind the counter did the opposite.

"Enough." Debbie stepped up and handed Penny a tissue. "Talk to me, kiddo. What's the problem?"

"I want that bear." Penny pointed to a twenty-inch, golden bear dressed as a fairy princess. "I spent all fifty dollars Daddy gave me." She sniffed again, showing a tiny stuffed toy too small to fit in Debbie's fist. "And all I got was this itty-bitty dog."

"You gotta win it," the operator informed them. "She did okay, but it takes twenty-five shots to win the grand prize."

"And how much was the dog?" Rex asked.

"Five. She only made three shots, but I'm a nice guy."

"You bet you are." Debbie looked the scrawny, long-haired fellow up and down. "You took fifty bucks from my kid and only gave her a crappy dog that isn't even the same size as one of those purse puppies. She's done."

"Gotta play to win." He seemed unperturbed by her assessment. "Two dollars a shot. Her dad can have a try."

"Oh, I don't think so." Rex reached in his pocket. "Ramsey's the one pissed about all this."

"Seriously?" Debbie scowled at him. "You're not?"

"It won't do any good if I play with these toys. Someone needs to learn a lesson." He handed the operator forty bucks. "I figure you should teach it until Penny goes to the range and learns how to do it herself."

Penny wiped away the last of the tears, staring up at him. "Are you going to teach me to shoot, Daddy?"

"No, sweetness. I'm going to delegate that."

"I'm not laughing, Major."

"Hey, like you always tell me, it's sergeant's business to train lower-ranking enlisted and junior officers. We'll add civilians to that list."

Hoist with my own petard, Debbie thought, trying to hide her amusement. She glowered at him before she turned back to the booth operator who definitely hadn't been listening to Rex's advice. "Right. Talk to me."

"Okay, little lady. This game has eighteen quick shot targets, with flying cans, falling cards, moving ducks and a bonus wheel with spinning targets."

"Sounds fun." Debbie picked up the light air rifle. "Let's get started."

Fifteen minutes later, they walked away. Penny happily carried the princess bear while Vangie tucked the small toy dog into the pocket of her jeans. Penny beamed at Debbie. "This was the best time ever. Thanks, Ramsey."

"No worries." Debbie ruffled the little girl's blonde hair. "Honey, these games are total scams. Unless your dad or I are with you, skip them. Okay?"

"That's the same thing we told her," Scott said. "She wasn't listening."

"It's hard to compete with a fancy teddy bear to hear what your older brothers and sister are saying. I always ignored my stepdad's lectures." Rex pointed out. "What's next? Shall we go find some food? It won't be as good as Scott's, but I'm starving."

"That's another rip-off," Scott said. "We'd do better eating at a restaurant on the way home."

"Spoilsport," Debbie teased. "The best part about coming to a fair is having all the junk food."

"Definitely." Vangie giggled. "I want a super-stuffed spud and a Belgian waffle for dessert even though Scott makes better ones."

When they arrived home shortly after eight that night, Debbie took time to walk through the barns. Everything looked perfect, no surprise. Kyra seemed to be enjoying the chance to be the woman in charge. As long as she didn't start an argument with the rest of the staff, Debbie was good with it. Once she returned to the house, she found everyone in the kitchen helping Scott make cookies.

Debbie poured a cup of coffee and settled down at the old-fashioned table in the middle of the room to watch Rex cream butter and sugar together. Only a *real* man would allow his son to be recreational director and not take offense at his directions.

The first batch of chocolate chip cookies was in the oven when Shasta stood and stretched, abandoning her new toy before she pelted toward the front door, barking.

"Sounds like the doggie alarm is going off." Debbie followed the young dog. "I'll be back. Save me a test cookie."

When she opened the front door, she recognized the tall, tawny-haired man standing outside. "You're Laredo's brother, right?"

"Durango Hawke." He nodded. "Is your husband here? I want to talk to him."

Debbie stepped back. "Come inside. He's in the kitchen with the kids."

"This is a private conversation."

"All right." Debbie swept him with a steady gaze. Six foot six or so, broad-shouldered, narrow-hipped, he carried himself like the soldier he must have been before he became an independent contractor at Nighthawke Security. He wore blue jeans, boots, and a faded, sleeveless chambray shirt. "Wait here. I'll be right back."

"It's between the two of us."

"We'll see." Debbie gently closed the door on him and returned to the kitchen, accompanied by the dog. "Major, we have company."

***

It was a case of 'hurry up and wait,' Durango thought as he stood on the wrap-around porch. Most people would be concerned about a stranger showing up without an invitation, but Debbie Ramsey didn't appear worried. Even when he'd visited while Laredo was shoeing her horse, she'd radiated pure sweetness and charm. She hadn't been upset by his younger brother's brusque behavior, and tonight she was perfectly polite.

How did her husband stand the cloying, sugary behavior? Or was that why she was here, and he was at the Army base more than three hours away?

What was putting him in such an uncharitable mood? Durango shook his head. She'd been more than decent, so why was he angry because she didn't act more like Heather? His wife was the queen of his heart, mind, and soul. She didn't ask for his love. She demanded it as her due and of course, he worshipped her and their girls.

The door opened, and he saw Debbie Ramsey, followed by a lean, wiry man in civvies. He wasn't big, only four inches taller than her five feet, six inches, but he carried himself as if he were ten feet tall and bulletproof.

He held out his hand. "Rex Sinclair."

"Durango Hawke." He eyed the fellow who only had a few years on him. He wasn't sure what he expected Debbie Ramsey's husband to be, but this guy wasn't a paper pusher. One warrior always recognized another.

"You don't look much like your brother," Rex said.

"Laredo?" Durango stiffened. "He's the short one of the bunch."

Rex glanced at his wife who stood beside him, then rested a hand on her shoulder. "He did a good job on Wonder and we're expecting him this week to do the rest of the herd. But he's not your only brother, is he?"

"No." Durango met the man's gold gaze. "You know Waco."

"That's right."

"What do you have to say about him?" Durango glimpsed the wary glance Debbie gave her husband. "Tell me."

"Major, you can't." Debbie's voice broke the rising tension. "It's not—"

"Sure, I can." Rex smiled at her. "You're not at the base to save my sorry ass, Ramsey, but the General has my six."

"He won't like this," Debbie warned.

"Damn it! Tell me what you know about my brother."

The rising anger in Sinclair's fierce, bronze gaze would have stopped a lesser man, but Durango wasn't intimidated.

"I need your help with him." Rex's tone remained detached and utterly calm. "He escaped with five other men. They're willing to work with us and reconnect with their relatives. He isn't. He only wants one visitor."

"Why are you telling me this?" Durango demanded. "Aren't you afraid I won't raise a stink?"

"You won't." Debbie didn't raise her voice. Instead, she dropped it to barely above a menacing whisper. "Say one word of this conversation and I'll swear you made up the whole thing. You're just a crazed vet whose brother never returned from a covert mission. You blamed my husband and went after him."

"My father runs Nighthawke Security. He'll listen to me."

"Not when you're dead." The lack of emotion on her face and in the narrowed blue eyes made the threat even more dangerous. "Whatever the major wants, he gets."

Durango stared at her. He'd discounted her as being a woman and now he recognized the truth. She was more deadly than her husband. When had he seen that kind of ferocity before? It hadn't been from a female or in combat. So, where? And who?

"My brother? Is he all right?"

"He will be." Rex hesitated. "He wants to see Tiffany Roberts, the television reporter. Even with the general authorizing it, we can't arrange it without raising a ruckus."

"I can," Durango said. "But I won't. Before he left, he—"

Sinclair measured him with a slow gaze but didn't speak.

Debbie asked, "What did he do?"

Durango met the other man's eyes and ignored the question. "Tell Waco I don't share my women."

———

Moises watched Sergeant Hawke's older brother stride away, heading toward a classic Chevy pickup. They had different colored hair and eyes, but he saw the resemblance in their bone structure, and the way they stood and walked. "Looks like the Hawke family has some serious issues, and I bet it's going to take a while to talk them out," he murmured to himself.

The major and his woman obviously weren't ready to go back into the house. They headed for the porch swing. She reached for his hand, holding it. "What's the next plan?"

"We leave it for now. After he thinks about it, Durango may decide he wants to see Waco, and I can facilitate that."

"Makes sense to me."

Moises left the two of them snuggling on the porch and sauntered through the door into the hall. He heard voices in the kitchen and followed the sound. One of the boys lifted fresh baked cookies onto a plate while another slid a different sheet of chocolate chip dough into a double oven. The girls were stirring up a batch of what looked like snickerdoodles.

"This is so fun," the young blonde girl announced. "We haven't made cookies since Gary told Lupe we couldn't hang out in the kitchen with her. Thanks for thinking of it, Scott."

"He's a dirtbag, Penny," a tall, dark-haired boy answered. "Averill collects them. I wish she'd have let Dad have custody years ago."

"That wasn't about to happen." This time, it was the oldest blond guy. "She kept saying he'd be back. Have any of you told Dad she doesn't like us calling her 'Mom' in front of the latest flavor of the week? Before Gary, she didn't even bother marrying most of them unless they had money to spend on her."

"That was weird." The older girl finished mixing the ingredients together. "I think it was because she realized when you guys left, your support went with you. We talked to Ramsey's lawyer, but we haven't heard anything from Averill or Gary."

"And I don't think you will. We didn't say anything about her going to Hawaii for six months every year." A pony-tailed, Native American loaded the dishwasher. "Has anyone else?"

"No," Penny shook her head. "We thought it was better not to tell Dad yet."

"Good decision," the oldest boy said. "Keep it to yourselves." He paused. "Lupe told me since you two were going to boarding school, Gary had said her services were no longer required."

Moises crossed to the rocker near the woodstove and sat down to enjoy the rest of the conversation. The tri-colored collie mix lifted her head and eyed him suspiciously, then evidently decided she'd just remain on her rug and guard the younger members of the family. He wished he could tell the major what they said, but that didn't seem do-able for now. Maybe time would provide the confidence these youngsters needed, and they'd share more of their history with their father and stepmother.

Moises grimaced. If he'd ever dared to call his momma by her first name, she'd have skinned him alive. It'd have been a case of *'I brought you into this world, boy, and I can take you out of it.' Sorry, Momma. The soldados and their jefe did that before I came home.*

Rex drew Debbie closer. "It's been a wonderful weekend."

"It could get better." She smiled, ran a finger along his jaw. "Kiss me."

"Are you sure?"

"I've never been surer. Kiss me."

He chuckled and then followed the order. A sleeveless western blouse revealed her arms, clung to her breasts. His mouth went dry. "You're lovely tonight."

She tipped her head back, smiled up at him. "Kiss me."

He framed her face with his hands, stroked her cheekbones with his thumbs before brushing her lips with his. "You're so special."

"You talk too much. Kiss me." She slid her fingers through his hair.

He kissed her. The first kiss led to a second, a third. Finally, he lifted his lips from hers. He trailed slow kisses over her cheeks, to her nose, up to her eyelashes, her brows. His lips explored the column of her throat. He unsnapped the first two pearl buttons of her blouse. She moaned when he kissed the top of her breast. He slid one hand inside her bra, found her nipple, and coaxed it to life.

She wriggled closer. "Are you taking me to bed tonight?"

"Maybe, Ramsey. I'm not sure if we're ready yet or need to wait a while longer."

CHAPTER NINETEEN

Debbie heaved a sigh. She'd spent the evening being a good stepmother. She'd raved over the cookies, played several hands of Skip-Bo, and listened to the stories the boys told about their university adventures. At 2300 hundred hours, eleven at night civilian time, Vangie and Penny headed off to bed, escorted by Shasta and the two cats. The guys hung out with Rex, discussing more modifications to the house they were flipping, and she'd abandoned them for solitude.

Now, she sat on the porch swing enjoying a glass of wine and some alone time. She glanced at the front door when it opened, and Rex came to join her. "So, what's the plan for tomorrow?"

"The boys are flying out at 1400 hours, so we need to be at the airport two hours before that and it's a three-hour drive from here."

"It means you should leave right after breakfast." Debbie swirled the red zinfandel in the glass. "I guess if I plan to jump your bones, we'd better make an early night of it."

"How serious are you about that?" He sat next to her and reached for the glass. "My turn. It's been almost eight years since our wedding night. I told you then we didn't have to consummate the marriage for it to be legal. We've had what you called a few casual hook-ups after that, but you've avoided anything serious."

"I know." She waited for him to return the glass and sipped more wine, before handing it back to him. "I wanted to have you before I went to

Afghanistan on those tours in case it was a one-way trip. I definitely needed those nights with you before you shipped out and the others when I wanted someone to hold me."

"You never told me that."

"You never asked."

"Of course not. I'm a guy. You're a beautiful woman. Why would I say, 'no'?"

She laughed. "You're good for my ego."

"As the saying goes, turnabout is fair play and you're usually great for mine." He finished the wine, stood, and held out his hand. "So, let's call it a night, Mrs. Sinclair."

"I'm ready."

Upstairs, a few minutes later, she watched him close the bedroom door. It'd been one thing to talk about having sex. It was another to do it. She caught her breath when he crossed to her. "Now, what?"

"This." He drew her against him, brushed his lips over hers. "We have what's left of the night. Relax, darling."

She smiled, laced her arms around his neck. "I can do that."

Several kisses later, she stepped back and peeled off her t-shirt, dropping it on the carpet. "Your turn. Lose the shirt."

He chuckled, then followed directions. "Now, what?"

"This." She slowly ran her hands over the mat of hair on his wide chest until she teased the hard buttons of his nipples.

"I told you earlier. Turnabout is fair." He unhooked the front clasp of her bra, and it landed on the floor.

She caught her breath when he explored her breast with his mouth. "Now, you're teasing me."

"You're right." He drew on her nipple, sucked gently, then harder.

She gasped when he cupped the other breast and tormented the nipple with his thumb. She kissed the side of his neck, nipped his ear. "Don't stop."

"I won't." He guided her in the direction of the king-size bed. "I've barely started."

Between kisses, they shed the rest of their clothes and she pulled the covers away from the sheets. When he reached for her again, she went into his arms. She turned her head and their mouths met, clung. Her tongue enticed his into a passionate duel. Slowly, he shifted, so they lay side by side. They kissed, one long kiss fading into the next.

She shuddered when his hand covered the curls between her legs. One finger slipped inside her, followed by a second. She gasped when his thumb found the small nubbin, moaned when he rubbed it gently and he kissed her, swallowing her cries as he pleasured her. His hand moved against her, skilled fingers starting a new pattern as they slid in and out of her. She pressed ever closer, nails digging into his shoulders.

"Kiss me, Ramsey."

Why was he so calm when she caught fire at his touch? He continued the rhythm with his hand, and her excitement built. She moaned before catching his lips with hers.

He smiled, his lips trailing toward her breast. "Wait until I have my mouth on you."

"Are you serious?"

"Definitely. I remember how wild you are when I do that."

She nibbled his ear. "It's so amazing. Nobody had ever done it before I was with you."

"I know." He kissed the hollow of her throat. "And I'll do it again tonight."

He shifted and started the pattern with his hand again, sliding his fingers in and out of her while his thumb rocked into the small bud. He covered her breasts with long, slow kisses. She arched upward as he sucked on one nipple and then the other. Her hips ground back and forth against his hand while he moved his fingers. She heard herself moaning, gasping, crying out his name as he continued tormenting her on a journey to the stars, becoming part of the universe until she exploded in a million pieces.

When she returned to sanity, she found him lying beside her waiting. He kissed her forehead, her eyebrows and then their lips met in a long, slow kiss. She nibbled her way down his neck, nipped at his ears, and he groaned. Kisses interspersed with soft touches as she caressed his chest, their legs tangling together.

"My turn." He slid down in the bed. He cupped her bottom and brushed his lips up one thigh, then the other.

She wasn't sure when he got her legs over his shoulders, but she gasped when his mouth claimed her. His tongue delved deep, two, or was it three strokes? His lips sought a certain spot, and he tugged on the nub of flesh. He lapped at her with his tongue before he settled in earnest on her. She bucked against him, pushing up into the kiss and his mouth. Her hips writhed and she matched the pattern he set. How could she resist him? She exploded in delight.

"Let's finish this." She gaped at him when he shook his head. "No? Why not?"

"I want to kiss you again." He lowered his head and licked the small bit of flesh.

She moaned as his mouth found her. His tongue drove into her. She found herself rising, falling, meeting each movement of his tongue. When she returned from the whirlpool of madness, she looked at him, staring into his face. He was still between her legs.

She struggled to breathe normally. "Not again."

His smile widened. "Yes. I haven't had enough of you yet."

She arched against his mouth as he started again. Thought fled as he licked, sucked, and finally took her with his tongue. When she opened her eyes a lifetime later, he lay next to her, his hand stroking her hair. She let her fingers stray over his broad chest, teasing the hard buttons of his nipples, seeing the concern on his face. "What's wrong?"

"Since I finally know what happened in the past, I'm concerned about what we do next." He kissed her. "I never want to hurt you."

She rolled on top of him. "You can't. You won't. And if you don't have me, I'll have you." She leaned forward and nibbled her way down his neck, nipped at his ears, and he groaned. Kisses interspersed with soft touches as she explored his chest. When she turned and picked up the condom from the nightstand, he took it to sheathe himself.

He parted her legs with one hard thigh. "Are you ready?"

"Yes." She felt him probe with his body this time, and he eased slowly inside her.

He shifted, pushed deeper, gripping her hips. "Shall we start now?"

"You know it." She rose, fell against him. "Which of us is in charge?"

"I am." He moved under her, guiding her through a series of long, leisurely strokes. He kissed her as they moved together. Soon, he changed the pattern of his thrusts. His pace increased and so did hers until she reached the heights. He was still hard, buried inside her. He began to move again. She met him, motion for motion.

They ascended, higher and higher. Each thrust took them further and further. She could only go with him. He smiled, drawing her closer, and his lips claimed hers. His tongue plunged into her mouth as he drove her past the stars. Their hips met, clashed, and they achieved fulfillment in an explosive moment.

She lay on top of him, meeting his golden-brown gaze. She gazed at his rough-hewn features, edging the strong cheekbones and once upon a time, the broken nose. She brushed her lips over his. "How long do we wait before we do it again?"

He grinned up at her. "Give me a few minutes, sugar."

After they made love a second time, she fell asleep in his arms. He was gone when she woke a few hours later. She showered, dressed, and went downstairs to find Scott making breakfast. He gave her the proverbial sitrep, telling her the rest of the family was out in the barns finishing horsy chores while he enjoyed being alone in the kitchen.

"Better you than me," Debbie teased. "Household stuff never appealed to me when I was a kid."

"Not to me either," Scott admitted. "Cooking is different."

"As long as you're having fun." She left him to it and went outside. Shasta was the first to spot her and raced to greet her, tail at full wag.

Debbie leaned over to pet the half-grown, collie mix. When she entered the first barn, she found the horses eating. The same went for the ones who had stalls adjacent to the indoor arena. She found Rex and the other four kids in the boarder barn where he was communing with Wonder, a bright yellow buckskin with a black mane, tail, and legs like his momma's. Penny shared carrots between the pair.

Hobby, a solid golden bay mare with black points, nickered when she saw Debbie. Appreciating the sound of affection, Debbie stepped up to pet the older horse and straighten out the black forelock. "We should head for the house. Scott will have food on the table soon."

Vangie took two more carrots and went off to feed the last of the privately owned horses. "We're ready. Kyra and Trina will be back for night chores, but they're headed to the town picnic at the Madison place. Chantrea Yang texted me and invited us to come there, too."

"After Sully Barlow-Murphy told me that she'd pulled strings to have one of the reservists in her unit show up, I told Bronwyn Murphy you'd stop in today for meat, eggs and vegetables, Ramsey."

"Who was that?" Debbie scratched the side of Hobby's cheek. "I don't know everyone in her unit."

"I guess it was one of the supply sergeants who also shoes horses, the one who's studying to be a veterinarian."

"She's going to call me when she gets back to Pullman," Cal added.

"It must be Mariah Stevens." When Rex offered his hand, Debbie took it. "I wonder if her twin sister is coming too."

"You'll have to tell me when I call tonight."

"Definitely!"

They arrived at the Seattle-Tacoma airport two hours before the flight to Pullman, Washington. Rex glimpsed the amusement on his oldest son's face as they headed for the departure gates. Back in the day, Rory used to tease him about always scheduling everything and then adhering to that 'set in stone' itinerary. "Did you have a good weekend?"

"A great one, Dad." Rory bumped his arm. "I really like Debbie. You two fit."

"What does that mean?" Rex eyed the trio, noting the way the other two nodded. "Clarify it."

"You act like you're on the same page most of the time." Scott ran a hand through dark hair, narrowing brown eyes. "There isn't any tension between you."

"She's not the type to have raging fits, scream accusations and storm out in a huff for days," Cal finished. "We like her, and the girls feel safe with her. She was awesome when she won the bear for Penny yesterday. Averill never would have done that in a hundred years."

"She'd have bitched nonstop about Penny wasting her money and dragged the kid away from the carnival," Rory added. "And if you insisted on getting it for her, the thing would have ended up in the trash."

Rex folded his arms, hoping he appeared in control. "Why are you calling your mother by her first name?"

"Her choice," Rory said. "Gary is five years younger than she is and she doesn't want anyone knowing she's older than him."

"It wasn't just Gary. She never liked us calling her 'Mom' in front of any of the other guys she dated or the two men she married." Scott glanced toward various ticket counters. "Guess we better check-in since we still have to get through security."

"Sounds like a plan," Rex said.

They weren't youngsters, so Rex didn't ask for a gate pass to accompany them to the departure lounge. Instead, he hugged them goodbye and watched them successfully leave. Rory had promised to call when they arrived home and told him they'd be in touch with Debbie's attorney, providing input about where their sisters should live.

Still considering what he'd heard and contemplating his options, Rex sauntered toward the parking lot and his pickup. He frowned when he recognized a large four-by-four with Montana plates in a nearby slot. What was West Taggart doing here? As if the silent question conjured him up, Rex spotted the tall, lean noncom coming toward him, towing a large suitcase.

For once, the man wore civvies, jeans, an ironed western shirt, and boots. He was accompanied by a scowling, teenage girl in fashionably torn denim shorts, a skimpy t-shirt, and flip-flops, a backpack strap slung over one shoulder. Long curly, black hair fell halfway down her back, framing a lovely tawny face with brilliant blue eyes.

Rex paused and nodded a greeting. "Taggart."

"Major." West stopped, measuring him with a cool, steady gaze. "Coming or going?"

"Dropping off my sons. They were home for the weekend." Rex glanced at the girl. "Hello. I'm Major Sinclair."

"Araceli Taggart." She tilted her head to one side. "How old are your sons?"

"Twenty-two, twenty and eighteen. They attend Washington State University in Pullman. Your turn. How about you?"

"Almost fourteen and I don't care what he says." Araceli jerked her head at her father. "I'm not staying in Montana or getting married to one of his yucky friends or relatives."

"I don't blame you." Rex swept a slow gaze over the other man, seeing annoyance build on West's face. "I suggested you talk to your family about what happened to your sister. I didn't advocate child marriage or trafficking."

"I had a weekend pass." A muscle twitched in West's tightening jaw. "I have to decide where Celi will stay when I ship out in three weeks. She may not like my family's religious beliefs—"

"Who would?" Araceli tossed her head. "Not happening. I'll run away again."

Rex smiled at her. "Worked for your aunt. You're a chip off that particular block."

"Really?" The girl lifted her chin. "You know what happened to her?"

"Sure. She graduated from the boarding school she attended and joined the Army." Rex turned his attention to the other man. "You should have been straight up with me, Taggart, and told me exactly why you wanted to find her."

"Would it have changed anything?" West demanded.

"Of course." Rex gestured toward the other man's truck. "Go wait for your father over there while I give him a sitrep, Araceli."

"If you're going to tell him what dirtbags they are, I want to stay."

"No, you can't. I won't even tell my sons what they did to your aunt and you're a helluva lot younger than they are."

West frowned, narrowing blue eyes. "Your sons know Sweet?"

"Yes." Rex waited for the teenager to stomp away. When she was out of earshot, he lowered his voice. "Why would you choose to leave her in a polygamous cult?"

"I don't have much choice. Her mother passed away. Cancer. Her grandparents have health issues and can't look after Celi. She only has one aunt whose husband was transferred to Japan. I told my parents to cut the crap and my father agreed not to push her to join their church."

"And you trust them?"

"Hell, no! All they say about Sweet is she chose banishment over them and she's living in sin somewhere."

"She wouldn't call it that." Rex ran a hand over his hair. "All right. I'll contact her and see if she's willing to look after Araceli. There will be conditions, but none of them will include trafficking your daughter."

CHAPTER TWENTY

After having Rex around all weekend, Debbie missed his company at the Murphys' festivities. Vangie hung out with her friends, Naveah and Chantrea. Penny played with several of the kids she'd met at horse camp, including Samantha and Sophie, the twins from the dude ranch. Meantime, Debbie enjoyed visiting with a very pregnant Sully and her husband, Tate, along with the rest of the Murphy clan. Tate explained his parents began taking in foster kids after their youngest son enlisted in the Marines.

Although most were adults now and had successful lives, they often visited on holidays when Bronwyn Murphy, the family matriarch hosted reunions. Halfway through the afternoon, two slender redheads, mirror images, both dressed in similar cowgirl attire, approached. They greeted Sully with warm hugs, then turned toward Debbie. Even though they weren't in camouflage fatigues, she recognized them as soldiers she'd provided with supplies not only in Afghanistan, but also at Fort Clark. In addition, Mariah Stevens had shod Wonder and Hobby last spring.

Debbie smiled at the duo. "Wow, this is a surprise. I hadn't realized you were Baker City natives."

"Not often anymore," Mariah said. "Sasha isn't, but I dragged her along with me. Between the university, the Army Reserve and Life 101, we don't know if we're coming or going. What are you doing in this neck of the woods, Ramsey?"

"I bought Miracle Riding Stable on the other side of town." Debbie sipped an icy soda. "You'll have to stop in when you have time and see the horses. I hired Laredo Hawke to shoe them."

"I've heard good things about him," Mariah said.

"We stayed over with Sean Killian and his family last night." It was Sasha's turn to furnish details. "Sean told Mariah all about his former apprentice and said we might run into him up here."

"If you do, I'll introduce you." Debbie saw mounting concern on Sully's face. "What's going on?"

"Laredo will probably stay next door at the Madison's fancy Taj-Mahal barn unless his sister-in-law Heather or his brother Durango shows up here. My mother-in-law isn't real thrilled about horse-shoers."

"Which is why we're only here for a token visit because you pulled all sorts of strings, Top. If you weren't the head noncom of our reserve unit and we didn't want to piss *you* off, we'd have blown off today like we did the Fourth of July." Mariah glanced toward the house and grimaced when the back door opened and a short, silver-haired woman in jeans and a flowered top hurried across the porch toward them. "Don't say anything about horses, Sasha or the internship at the equine practice."

"Already got the 411 on the trip here." Sasha pasted on a professional smile that didn't touch bright blue eyes. "I was listening."

Hours later, after horsy chores, dinner, and a movie with the girls, Debbie sat on the porch swing enjoying a glass of her favorite wine. Shasta snoozed on the far end. "We have one more day before school starts. Then we'll have the lonely cobble-wobbles without the girls."

Shasta's plumed tail dusted the swing, but she didn't open her dark brown eyes. Debbie laughed softly and reached for her phone when it vibrated in her pocket. She pulled it out of her jeans, turning on the video-chat feature. "Hey there. Did the boys catch their flight?"

"No worries. We made it in plenty of time and Rory hardly laughed at me for being so time conscious. How was your day?"

Debbie brought him up to speed on the two picnics, the first at the Murphy farm and the second next door at Majestyk Morgans. "The girls had a great time. We're going to run into Lake Maynard and hit the office supply store, so they'll have everything they need for school on Wednesday."

"Keep track of what I owe you."

"You got it." She saw the frown wrinkling his forehead and uneasiness in the golden-brown eyes. He rubbed his jaw. "What's wrong? Did Maverick Jones blow the babysitting detail this weekend?"

"No. I stopped in at the hospital this afternoon and the guys are fine." Rex took a deep breath. "I ran into your brother at the airport today."

"Please tell me he was shipping out."

"Not yet, but he's returning to his unit in Afghanistan before the end of September. I found out why he's been trying to find you."

"Share the news, Major."

"It's not good, Ramsey."

She felt dread build inside her. "Is he hurt or sick?"

"No, he's fine. It's his daughter. She's thirteen—"

"And?"

"No family other than your brother, mother's passed away and she runs off when he tries to leave her with your relatives in Montana. Her grandfather found her at a shelter in Missoula last spring. He took her back to the family home and she split again as soon as she could."

"Smart kid." Debbie swirled the wine in the glass. "Does he have half a clue about what they intend to do to her?"

"He says they've promised not to make her join their church. He claims he doesn't believe them, but—"

"How did you manage to interrogate them?"

"I met them for dinner and got more info from Araceli. She says they're setting up a marriage for her. Because she's Hispanic, she can only be a celestial wife, not a first or legal one. They expect her to start popping out babies in the next year or two. When she told her dad about what they were doing, he seemed to be skeptical and said she was exaggerating. Meanwhile, she has a college fund from her mom and Celi wants to use it for school, not a dowry. Since your brother won't be around, he can't put the kibosh on those plans."

"He wouldn't anyway. It'd cause a permanent breech between him and the family. He's not ready for that yet or he wouldn't insist on taking his daughter there." Debbie swallowed more wine. "What do you want me to do? Take her for the duration?"

"It's your decision, Ramsey. I'll back you 100 percent."

"I can't leave her to be abused." Debbie stared into the night for a moment. "I won't see him or provide any contact info. I don't know how you'll arrange the logistics, but that's your strength. Consider this one of your covert missions."

"Okay. I'm on it. Do you want to meet us at my house?"

"It's too close to the base. I'll meet you in Liberty Valley near the freeway. You, or your surrogate, and my niece. Not him. Not ever."

"Sounds good. I'll call with details when I have them." His tone softened and his gaze warmed. "I'm proud of you, honey."

"You're only saying that because you don't want to sleep alone next time you're here."

He chuckled. "Is that likely to happen?"

"No. I'm making a list and planning to totally jump your bones in a couple of weeks."

"I can't wait. Tell me more."

After lunch on Tuesday, Rex arranged a conference with Gimone Nolan and Juana Castaneda. It didn't take long to provide a sit-rep about West Taggart to the two soldiers and why he really wanted to contact his younger sister. "Ramsey says she'll take on the girl but isn't seeing him because he's still actively involved with their family and doesn't 'need to know' anything personal about her."

"Makes sense." Gimone leaned back in one of the visitor chairs. "So, what's the plan, sir?"

"I called and told him we could meet for dinner. I let him think Ramsey will be there, but she won't. I want one of you to take the girl and her things to my house."

Juana and Gimone shared a look, before the junior officer spoke. "Gimone will do that. You should arrange for Ramsey's niece to have a new cell phone."

"Why?"

"Because if she's in the habit of running away, Taggart has probably activated the GPS on her cell. Since we don't want him to know how to find Ramsey, the girl's phone needs to go," Juana said. "How are you going to get her to Debbie?"

"I'm going to be here all day tomorrow in case Taggart comes by, so I'll need one of you to take her to meet Ramsey in Liberty Valley."

"That's me." Juana crossed her legs. "I'll enjoy seeing her. I'll call and set it up with her. If I pick up the kid before oh dark-thirty, I can be back by lunch. We'll let everyone think I have a doctor's appointment."

Rex nodded agreement. "I appreciate this. We're keeping the plan on the down-low."

"You don't have to worry about that." No emotion leaked into Gimone's face. "We learned security long before we joined the Army."

After a visit to the hospital, Rex headed for one of his favorite diners off post. He spotted West Taggart's large pickup and parked next to it. Inside, he found the noncom and his daughter already seated in a booth.

Rex joined them, sitting next to the teenager and taking the menu the girl offered. "Hello. Are you ready to stay with your aunt, Araceli?"

"As long as she's not a freak, no problem."

Rex chuckled. "That's the last thing I'd call her."

"And you better not be rude to her." West glanced at the entry. "When will she be here?"

"Dinner first, and we'll discuss it." Rex ignored the long look the other man gave him and read through the list of specials.

An hour later, they'd finished eating. Rex sipped coffee and waited for the teenager to scrape up the last of her hot fudge sundae.

"Where's Sweet?" West finally asked. "She's not coming here, is she?"

"No. That was one of her conditions. She'll take Araceli, but she's not interested in seeing you." Rex held up his hand before there were any interruptions. "Taggart, you're going to have to choose whether you continue a relationship with your family or her. She's already chosen."

"I don't understand."

"Did your father share the options he gave her to return home from the boarding school in Spokane?"

"I know." The spoon clattered in the tall glass dish and Araceli glanced at Rex, then at her father. "I overheard Grandfather talking to the bishop and his son about it. She could be one of the bishop's celestial wives or marry one of his sons and be his first wife, a legal one, not a sister-wife or have a different husband from one of the other families in their community."

"That's ridiculous." Fury filled West's face and he glared at Rex. "Sweet was only fifteen when she went to that school. You can't be serious."

"If they're seeking a husband for your thirteen-year-old daughter, what makes you think it didn't happen to your sister first?" Rex spotted Gimone Nolan coming toward them. "Araceli, give your father your cell phone."

"What? Why? I need to be able to contact her, and she needs to be able to call me."

"I'll provide her with one." Rex slid out of the booth and gestured to the teenager. "This is Sergeant Nolan. She'll start you on the journey, but one of the conditions is that you don't tell anyone where your aunt lives."

"No worries. If I don't want to be around them, I won't rat out anybody else." Araceli laid a smart phone on the table. "Are you going to get my stuff from Dad, Major?"

"Yes. When he's back from Afghanistan and ready for you to live with him, I'll furnish transportation from your aunt's home to him at the base."

Gimone must have heard the last comment because she added, "You'll also need her transcripts so she can go to school, her birth certificate, a power of attorney and a medical release in case she needs to see a doctor, sir."

"I'll handle it, Sergeant." Rex waited while the girl hugged West and then eagerly walked away with Gimone chattering about the new adventure. "How long was she in Montana?"

"Two years. Everything was fine until last spring. On a video-chat, she told me either I came to get her, or she was leaving." West shook his head. "When I talked to my mom, she said girls got hormonal when they reached puberty and Celi would be fine. I started looking for Sweet because I thought it might be an option, but—"

"And then Araceli wouldn't wait any longer. She ran away." Rex's flat tone didn't make it a question.

West inclined his head in agreement. "The first two times, my dad found her and took her home, but the next time she disappeared, the Red Cross contacted me, and I arranged for emergency leave last month. I hoped to get some straight answers when we visited this past weekend, but I kept hearing she needed more discipline."

"I believe in that, too. So does your sister." Rex topped his coffee from the carafe at the far end of the table. "Did your father tell you why he sent her to that boarding school?"

"Just that she was a kid in trouble."

"People used to say those kinds of things about girls when I was growing up." Rex held West's gaze. "Haven't you heard them, too? There's still a double standard in this world."

"Are you saying she was pregnant? It's why he rejected her?" West shook his head. "I don't believe it. She was barely fifteen. In her letters, she told me more about the yearling filly she was training than any boy."

"She wasn't any more willing than your daughter is, but she didn't have the courage to run away." Rex drained the last of his coffee. "She's a brave woman. She'd have to be to survive five tours in the *sandbox*, but it will take time before she sees you. And she'll never see them again."

The silence mounted between them as they paid the bill and left the restaurant. In the parking lot, West unloaded three suitcases and two old military duffels. "Do you know who assaulted her?"

"She hasn't given me the names yet." Rex put the bags in the back seat of his super-cab. "I'll share them with you when she does. Take my word for it. I'd never let my daughters anywhere near those people and I won't let yours either."

West froze, tension riding his shoulders as he stiffened. A greenish tinge formed around his mouth. "Who? Any idea?"

"Not yet." Rex leaned against the side of his Ford truck. "Do you want to bet she wasn't the only victim? If I were you, I'd cut my ties with that cult, Taggart."

Rex didn't wait for an answer. He put the last two boxes in his truck and then left. In the rearview mirror, he saw West Taggart pulling out a cell phone. Who was he calling? The family in Montana? It might take a while for him to realize he wouldn't get the truth from them, but at least he had a certain amount of information now.

Araceli focused on the tall, red-haired soldier in the driver's seat, barely paying any attention to the traffic around them on the freeway. "How long have you known my aunt?"

"We were roommates at Celestial Faith Boarding School."

"For a long time?"

"Until we graduated from their high school. Then we enlisted."

"Wow. That's something. My mom was in the Army. It's how she and my dad met. I miss her. She'd never let me stay with my dad's family during the school year. I could only visit in the summer."

"Interesting." Sergeant Nolan flicked a sideways glance at her, then focused on the road again. "Why?"

"Because girls can't have real classes after sixth grade. I tried telling my dad I wanted to go to the public middle school, and he kept telling me not to make waves while he was gone. He's an okay guy, but he didn't get it." Araceli heaved a sigh. "All that cooking and sewing crap at the church school bored the hell out of me. Seventh grade was a total waste of time. I hope my Aunt Sweet gets it."

"She will, but first things first."

"What does that mean?"

"She changed her name. It's why your dad couldn't find her."

"No way! That's so awesome! I bet she won't want me calling her, "Sweet", will she?"

The comment earned a warm smile. "And it's another thing you can't tell your dad. She won't want the cult to know her new name or where she is or anything about her."

PART 3

SEPTEMBER 2019

CHAPTER TWENTY-ONE

Wednesday morning, Debbie helped with horse chores. Kyra had a few lessons to teach after school, but said she'd do trail rides with Trina during the day. Vangie caught the bus to the high school in Lake Maynard and Penny rode to the Baker City elementary-middle with the O'Leary-McTavish twins.

Debbie debated leaving Shasta home, then decided against it since Linda MacGillicudy would be coming with her crew to clean the house and the half-grown dog had started barking at odd times and places. The last thing Debbie wanted was to offend the woman who took so much responsibility off her shoulders and made her life so much easier.

Once she'd organized everything, she left on the road trip to meet Juana Castaneda in south Liberty Valley. Shasta happily sat in the passenger seat, occasionally barking when a semi-truck was too close to the Jeep. The collie co-pilot's antics amused Debbie but didn't slow their trip and they arrived at the restaurant just before lunch. She carefully parked at the further end of the lot, leaving a space for Juana's toy pickup. There was even time to walk Shasta in the pet area and then return to the Jeep.

Debbie spotted the little red Ranger a few minutes later. Juana pulled in beside the Jeep and switched off the engine. She wore camo fatigues and combat boots, her dark hair pinned up in a neat bun beneath her cap.

She climbed out of the rig and greeted Debbie with a warm hug. "Civilian life becomes you."

"You're only saying that because you wish you could wear blue jeans all the time."

"You've got me." Juana gestured toward the passenger seat. "Come meet Araceli."

Debbie eyed the slender teenager in jeans and a snug tank top climbing out of the pickup. Long curly black hair around a lovely golden face, high cheekbones, big electric blue eyes framed by long dark lashes. "She looks like—"

"You on the first day I met you." Juana's smile warmed her face and dark brown eyes. "Although you were wearing what Gimone called a frontier girl's dress."

"Ick!" Araceli wrinkled her nose in disgust. "I left that crap back at my grandparents in Montana. I'm not into old-timer stuff."

Debbie laughed and slipped an arm around Juana's waist for a quick hug. "How long did it take you and Gimone to get me into what you called 'real' clothes? Two weeks?"

"We had to convince you that you wouldn't go to hell for dressing like a person instead of a cultist." Juana beckoned for Araceli to approach. "This one already knows to be true to herself."

After she hugged her friend once more, Debbie went to greet the girl. "No wonder you impressed Major Sinclair enough to call me."

"He's okay for an old guy. He listened to what I said, and he believed me." Araceli took a step closer. "Sergeant Nolan said you changed your name. What do you want me to call you? Aunt—"

"Debbie or Ramsey. It's what my stepdaughters call me. Their brothers tease me and say I'm their new mom."

"So, not Sweet?"

"I haven't been Sweet Taggart for almost eighteen years."

"Awesome." Tears filled Araceli's eyes and one slipped down her cheek. "Thank you."

"For what?" Debbie drew the girl into her arms, rocked her close. "What's wrong, honey?"

"I've been scared for so long. Nobody believed anything I said, and I thought—" Araceli gulped back a sob. "The bishop came. He stared at me like I was a horse he was gonna buy and his son who was almost as old as my father asked what size bra I wore— I told Dad, but he— I told him I wanted my momma. She'd have understood."

"I know." Debbie smoothed the thick black curls. "I can't bring back your mom. I can keep you safe from them. Did Bishop Levitt or his son, Jabez or any of the grandsons put their hands on you?"

The girl pulled back slightly, widening shocked eyes. "How did you know?"

"Because as the saying goes, 'leopards don't change their spots' and they did that to me."

Debbie held the girl tighter. "I'm signing you up for karate with my girls, Penny and Vangie, so you learn to kick butt. They're excited about meeting you, but today was the first day of school."

"And I have questions about them." Juana patted Debbie's back. "Let's eat because I have to be back at the base by 1400 hours."

"What's that?" Araceli asked.

"Two o'clock, civilian time." Debbie adjusted the passenger window for Shasta and locked the Jeep. "Food is in our future, ladies."

After they were seated in a booth, they had glasses of strawberry lemonade all around and ordered their meals. Araceli headed off to the restroom. Debbie leaned back in the booth. "Can I say my older brother is a monster jerk?"

"How many guys do you know that actually listen to women, much less girls?" Juana stirred the ice in her glass with a straw. "Didn't the major have issues when he understood you were keeping his daughters?"

"Once he realized it was not negotiable, he was fine." Debbie sucked up some of her drink. "We're building a relationship."

"Is that what you call it?" Juana lowered her voice to barely above a whisper. "Gimone wanted me to find out if you've knocked boots yet."

Heat filled Debbie's face. "Whiskey tango foxtrot! What is it with you two?"

"We're celibate for the moment because the reservists are hitting the warehouses for training, and you know what those guys are like. They're one-night wonders. Now, how about your bedroom rodeo? The major looks like he knows what to do and how to do it. Does he send you screaming to the rafters?"

Debbie kicked her friend under the table. "Yes, he does. He always has. Since we're married, it's perfectly legal. And that's all I'm going to say."

"Okay, then tell me about the girls. What's the story with them?"

"My lawyer's on the case and we're keeping them in the state. Rory, Rex's oldest boy, took my attorney's number. He and his brothers are contacting her this week to provide their statements. They want the girls safe, and the boys say Sinclair's ex, their mother sleeps around. Her latest husband is a slut-puppy extraordinaire, too. They tell the boys they have an 'open' marriage."

"In the words of your niece, 'Ick'. I'm so not into that."

"Me either." Debbie smiled at Araceli when she rejoined them. She'd apparently taken time to wash her face and repair her makeup. "You timed it right. Here comes the food."

Moises Pride enjoyed hanging out at the riding stable. There was always something happening here. The college boys had left Monday with the major, but the house still rocked and rolled between the two cats who took turns sharing a recliner with him and the dog who growled whenever he was near. The two girls and the major's wife didn't seem to notice they had company, but Moises was good with it.

He usually hung out on the porch with the woman, Debbie Ramsey, until the major called and then left the two of them to talk alone. Apparently, they expected more company. Debbie had left to pick up her niece when the two girls went off to school. *I might not know the particulars yet, but I'll find out sooner or later.*

A few happy mommies and daddies showed up to go trail riding, obviously thrilled at the start of school. The horses had grown accustomed to Moises' presence and ignored him in favor of the carrots the visitors brought. Once he'd watched the first group ride off in the direction of the woodlot, he floated back to the house in time to see the cleaning service arrive. The woman in charge read through the list left by Debbie, then divided up her troops as well as any Army sergeant.

Moises followed a lanky, dark-haired young man hauling a vacuum and bucket of cleaning supplies to the third floor. He started in the furthest bedroom, stripping the bed before he washed windows and mirrors, dusted furniture, and vacced the carpet. One of the women showed up with clean, ironed sheets for the double bed and the guy moved onto the next room.

This time, it was the supervisor who arrived with fresh linens. "How are you doing, Dray? When do you have to be at Nighthawke Construction to do your paperwork for your new job?"

"It's fine, Mom. I texted Heather and she told Jeff that I'd come after lunch. This is a big house, and I don't want you doing everything by yourself when you have the night shift at the café with Grandpa."

"I'm not by myself. I have help."

"Yeah, but you were already short-handed before two of your workers left for college." Dray pulled back the blankets to strip off the sheets. "Have you talked to Dominique about hiring a couple of her part-time real estate agents or to Reverend Tommy about the folks who show up at the food bank? Some of them are looking for work."

"And more of them are looking out for it."

The two of them quickly cleaned while they talked, dusting, vacuuming, and washing windows and the large mirror above the bureau.

The woman wiped down the dresser. "I have to say Ramsey's sons are tidier than you are. All their clothes are put away and even if we're changing sheets, the beds are already made. Just had to clear away the dust."

Dray laughed. "Right, Mom. I met them at church, and they were only here for a couple days. Rory, the oldest, told me they'd be back for Christmas and then they'd stay longer."

"What about Thanksgiving?"

"They flip houses, and their folks are going to Pullman to see the latest project. Rory showed me pictures of the place."

"Wow. Debbie and her husband should write books about how to raise self-sufficient kids. The rest of us could take lessons."

Another laugh before Dray threw a pillowcase at her. She picked it up and flung it in the direction of the pile of linens at the door. Then, it was her turn. She grabbed the next pillow and whacked him with it.

Smiling, Moises left the room. He drifted downstairs where he found another woman cleaning the living-room and a man scrubbing the bathroom. *There's too much traffic in here for me.* When he sailed through the door to the front porch, he discovered he wasn't the only one who felt overwhelmed. Mocha, the long-haired Siamese, sat on the rail washing her paws while Bandit, the tuxedo cat curled up for a nap on the swing. Grinning, Moises joined them.

He had a busy day at the warehouses. When he walked out to the parking lot, Rex spotted West Taggart standing by his truck. Rex returned the man's salute before greeting him. "Did Araceli call you?"

"Yes. She said my sister was driving and couldn't talk to me. That wasn't completely true, was it?"

"Close enough for government work." Rex shrugged. "I told you already. She's done with your family."

"Celi said Sweet was pissed at me because I let my father and his wives get rid of the dolls, stuffed animals, and most of the books her mom and I gave her. I didn't know they'd do that on her thirteenth birthday."

"Not a surprise." Rex unlocked his pickup. "If she's old enough to be a wife and mother, Celi doesn't need a bunch of childish toys. Will you be able to get any of them back?"

"I don't know. I've called and told my mother I want back those keepsakes, but I'm not sure I'll get them. I'm going online to try to replace the ones I can. I need an address to ship them to her."

"Use mine. It's the same one I already gave you." Rex glanced at his watch. "Discussion's over. I have an appointment. Stop by the warehouse before you ship out." He didn't wait. Instead, he climbed in the Ford and drove away.

It didn't take long to reach the hospital. He parked in an empty slot, grabbed his hat, and strolled across the lot and in a side door. A short walk brought him to the secluded ward and its guard. Rex offered his military identification and waited for it to be checked. As usual, the guys were watching Tiffany Roberts read off the latest news. Rex waited for a stream of commercials.

When they started, he glanced at the men. "Okay, what about those letters to your families?"

"I collected them," Warrant Officer Jackson said. "Got them in my room. What did you find out about the reporter?"

"I haven't talked to her yet, but I touched base with your older brother, Hawke. He has issues with you."

"Not surprised." Waco rocked in his chair. "What did he say?"

"To tell you he doesn't share his women."

"Crap." Jim Jackson glared at Waco. "What did you do, asshat?"

"Tried jumping his fiancée one night when he was doing sniper duty for a Nighthawke mission. Turned out she'd made friends with a Ranger officer in Iraq on her first combat tour. He thought it was fun to teach her dirty tricks, and she kicked my ass."

"Would have been helpful if you shared that before I tracked down your brother and asked for his assistance," Rex said drily.

"Are you still working on it, Major?" Sergeant Wilkins twisted his hands. "Or giving up?"

"It's like what my grandpa used to say, Wilkins." Rex glanced at the shattered noncom. "Never give up on a go-ahead show. You guys do your part and I'll do mine. But from now on, no more secrets, Hawke."

"Yes, sir!"

***

After a trip into Baker City to register her niece for school, Debbie headed straight to the riding stable. When she parked near the house, Shasta was ready to jump out for a quick potty trip. Accompanied by Araceli, Debbie headed toward the front porch. Before she reached it, Kyra came out of the barn.

"What's happening? Are the horses okay?" Debbie asked, concern mounting. "Do we need a vet?"

"They're fine. You got a big delivery from California today." Kyra smiled at Araceli. "Hi, I'm Kyra O'Neill."

"She's my senior instructor." Debbie rested a hand on Araceli's thin shoulder. "This is my niece, Celi, and she'll be joining your classes tomorrow after school. As for the delivery, it must be the kids' belongings."

"It's what we thought. All the boxes were labeled so Linda MacGillicudy had her crew put them in the different bedrooms. We figured the kids could unpack them."

"Works for me." Debbie waved at her Jeep. "Will you and Trina help us unload Celi's things? She will have the room next to Penny's."

"I'll get her. Linda told me to tell you she put mac and cheese in the slow cooker. There's a green salad in the fridge and one of Twila Garvey's cheesecakes for dessert."

"Wow, I love housekeeping days especially when dinner's already prepared." Debbie opened the back of the Jeep and pulled out an old canvas duffel. "Let's get you settled, Celi."

"Is it my turn to say, 'Works for me'?"

Despite Debbie's unspoken qualms, the introductions between the three girls went smoothly when Vangie and Penny arrived home from school an hour later. They seemed to hit it off right away. They helped each other unpack their belongings amid a storm of giggles, laughter, and occasional shouts from one room to the other. Shasta trotted back and forth between the three bedrooms, keeping a doggie eye on the trio.

Debbie left them to it and went to the barns to help with afternoon chores. She'd much rather muck stalls than do housework. By the time she arrived in the boarder barn, the ten horses were already grazing in the various pastures. She stretched out the hose and topped water tubs, dumping the dirty ones. Wonder seemed to think he needed to rinse out his mouth after grazing in his paddock and his fifteen-gallon, heavy plastic red tub had a half-inch of dirt in the bottom. Everyone loved a comedian.

Her phone vibrated and she pulled it out of her jeans. She hit the video-chat feature and saw Rex's smiling face. "What's up, Major? It's early for you."

"Wanted to check in and make sure everything went okay when you got Araceli. She called her dad already."

"That jerk. He totally bailed on his kid. It's lucky she didn't end up married and pregnant." Debbie turned the shut-off switch on the hose and leaned against the stall wall. "Tell me you already did me a solid and kicked his ass all over the base."

CHAPTER TWENTY-TWO

Thursday morning, the three girls went happily off to school and Debbie sauntered toward the boarder barn with Shasta at her heels, ready to help with trail rides. Kyra was already saddling up for lessons. Business slowed with most of their customer base back in school, but Mindy MacGillicudy had catered to parents who educated their youngsters at home, so it meant they'd be in to ride on weekdays. In addition, more adults who preferred to ride together sans children, joined Trina's trail clubs.

Debbie groomed and tacked Hobby and Wonder before she headed off toward the other barn to help with the rest of the horses. Luckily, Trina incorporated prepping their mounts into the program and the riders happily socialized while they worked. Afterwards, everyone led their horses out to the large corral where they followed the same routine the campers had during the summer. However, neither Debbie nor Trina mentioned that.

While Trina started the warm-up lesson, Debbie took Shasta back to the house. The young dog growled and barked at the living-room door before sulking off to the kitchen and her rug in front of the antique wood-stove. Debbie sighed. As soon as she had time, she'd teach her mare to accept the pup and the three of them would roam the ranch. Meantime, Shasta would just have to get over herself.

The riders finished up before lunch and Debbie took them to the office to collect their fees. Trina fed the horses before going to her apartment to have her own meal. Debbie started toward the house and stopped when a convey of vehicles, pickup trucks and SUVs pulled into the front yard. Wondering what was happening, she strolled toward the one in the lead, pausing when she recognized Mindy MacGillicudy.

The elderly white-haired woman who still looked amazing in jeans, a cowgirl shirt, and lace-up riding boots waved a greeting as she popped out of her rig. "We decided to bring the veteran's group to you this week. Next time you have to join us in town."

"Say again!" Debbie eyed her. "Didn't I tell you I was too busy?"

"And I told you if you didn't come to us, we'd come to you." Mindy turned to a tall, curvaceous redhead in her thirties. "This is Heather McElroy, your neighbor on the other side of the dude ranch. She was a nurse in the *sandbox*."

Heather smiled, pointing to the brunette about her age climbing out of the passenger side of the brand-new green pickup. "My best friend, Kate Flanagan. She served with me."

Debbie spotted Cat O'Leary-McTavish lingering to take the baby out of the back seat of her car. Twila Garvey helped her toddler from a red Subaru. "I don't believe this."

"You should," Heather said. "When Mindy told us we were coming here, I cheered and left my twins with their father. It's a kid-free day for me and Kate."

"I have riding clubs today," Debbie protested.

"Jacinth Sweeney will be along to ride with her sister. They're both experts with novice riders. Virginia Thompson is coming to babysit so we can talk because Cat and Twila didn't want to take their young-uns to day care." Mindy reached back into her truck and removed a box of doughnuts. "Come on, Debbie. You're in charge of making tea and coffee."

Shaking her head in bewilderment, Debbie led the way to the house. "Well, I'm warning you now that my dog is having issues and I don't know how friendly she will be, so let me put her in the pantry."

"No worries." Kate crossed to take the toddler from Twila. "We have dogs at home so we know they can be on guard-duty whether we approve or not. Twila brought cheesecake."

"Okay, then I'm ready to be sociable." Laughing, Debbie gave up the battle and ushered her guests up the steps to the front porch. "So, how does your meeting start?"

"With food first, and then Mindy does her ice-breaking routine,"

Heather said. "Her cousin Linda left sandwiches, quiche and chips yesterday."

"Why do I think this was a Baker City conspiracy?" Debbie followed the rest of the women behind Mindy to the kitchen. "Good thing Linda also made us supper, so we didn't touch anything else."

"She's the brains of the family." Mindy put her box on the table and pointed toward one of the cabinets. "If Debbie hasn't reorganized the place, there should be mugs in that cupboard, Heather."

"I haven't gotten to the house yet," Debbie retorted. "I'm still working on the barns."

Laughter and female voices attracted Moises' attention and he drifted into the other room. The collie mix rose from the rug in front of the woodstove and advanced on him, growling. The sound drew the attention of a redhead in a flowered top and blue slacks holding a baby. The new momma walked toward him. "Who are you, and why are you here?"

Moises blinked, slowly starting to recognize the medium he'd seen once in town. "It's not a joke? You can really see me?"

"Yes, and I'm talking to you. Were you invited here, or did you come on your own?"

"What's happening, Cat?" It was the oldest woman who asked and came toward them. "Is everything okay?"

"That's what I'm trying to learn." Cat joggled the sleeping baby. "Debbie, did you know you have company?"

"What kind of company?" This time, it was the dark-haired owner of the house. "The kind that *you* see?"

"Yes, and now I'm waiting for answers."

Cat focused on Moises again and dread swept through him. "I'm Corporal Moises Pride. I came with the major. This is an entertaining place and I like it better than hanging out at the hospital waiting for Sergeant Hawke and the rest of the guys to decompress."

"Sergeant Hawke?" Cat repeated. "Who is that?"

"If it's Waco, then he's my worthless bro-in-law who has the morality of a tomcat on the prowl." Heather continued putting plates on the large kitchen table. "When Kate agrees, we're going to neuter him without anesthetic as soon as he makes it to our place."

The comment earned more laughter and Moises began to relax.

"Sounds like they know Sarge better than I do. He always bragged about the Ranger groupies he bagged. The rest of us on the team used to tell him if he could actually do it, he didn't need to talk about it."

Cat swept another gaze over him before turning to her hostess. "Debbie, it's up to you. Can he stay, or do you want him to go?"

"I need to know more about him," Debbie answered. "I wouldn't send anybody to the hospital ward where Rex's men are assigned. He says they're griping about the food, the activities and the head-shrinkers there. I still have rules here. Number one is behaving around my girls. Is he the reason why my dog's upset?"

"Yes, but I haven't done anything to her," Moises said quickly, "and I only went upstairs to see what the cleaners were doing yesterday. I never go near the bedrooms when the family is home."

Cat smiled approvingly at him. "Seems like you heard the rules my husband and I laid out a few weeks ago even if we didn't actually introduce ourselves. We'll do that later today when you, Debbie and I have a *real* conversation, what I call a ghostly intervention."

Debbie sat on the porch swing three hours later. To her amazement, she enjoyed the opportunity to discuss combat experiences with the other women. Granted, Twila Garvey hadn't actually served, but she'd been system support for her career military husband who'd died in an ambush a year ago. Cat O'Leary-McTavish was a special case, accepted by the other women because she talked to the ghosts who haunted Baker City. Moises Pride wasn't the only dead soldier who called the place home.

The discussion between Debbie, Cat and Moises resulted in an agreement about what the former Army Ranger could and couldn't do on the farm. Cat had also given him advice on how to travel from one place to another, so he'd be able to return to town. He didn't have to wait until someone was driving somewhere to hitch a ride.

He'd be able to move around by using what she called 'thought' transport. Cat said for him to think of where he wanted to be, and he'd go there. He'd apparently popped out to visit the café in town, then returned to tell them it worked before he left again to see new ghostly friends.

The front door opened, and Debbie spotted Heather McElroy coming to join her. She was one of those gorgeous women who would be easy to hate. Even if she wore faded blue-jean cut-offs, flip-flops, and a loose tank top, she looked like a model. Vibrant red hair cascaded to her waist. With high cheekbones, a pointed chin, and huge green eyes, she carried herself like a warrior queen.

"Are we ready to start up again?" Debbie asked. "I needed a break after Cat's 'come to Jesus' meeting with Moises especially after hearing how he died. It totally freaked me out. Did she tell you they made your brother-in-law watch his execution?"

Heather shook her head and sipped strawberry lemonade from the glass she carried. "No, and you're not even from Baker City like most of us. I bet that was tough to hear. We know the O'Leary has special gifts, but I wouldn't want them."

"Me either." Debbie shuddered and drained her coffee. "So, who is us?"

"Okay." Heather drew up an Adirondack chair. "Why do I think Mindy didn't tell you the story of Baker City or its people?"

"Because she didn't. Our focus was on the stable and me buying it."

"All right. Then, it's time for a history lesson. In February 1910, it snowed until there were drifts more than ten feet deep. Clouds couldn't get over Mount Carmody. A foot of snow fell each hour and it continued day after day, night after night. Valentine's Day, it suddenly warmed up, and the snow changed to rain. Then, the avalanches started."

Debbie's eyes widened and she gaped at the other woman. "How many?"

"Five in total. Two big ones hit the town, wiping out the train station, the hotel, the school, three shops, and five homes. Sixty people died. It took months to dig out all the bodies. The last funeral was for Mrs. Doireann O'Sullivan, the schoolteacher who'd come from Ireland. After her husband died in a farming accident, she'd returned to teaching and remained at the school until her death."

"Is that the school my kids attend?"

"The only one in town," Heather said. "The one Twila and I attended. It was rebuilt afterward. Cat and her daughters say Mrs. O'Sullivan is still there, but she only teaches during the haunted town festival."

"The what?"

"In October, everybody gets together for a fundraiser. We set up a haunted town and take money from the tourists. In Baker City, the ghosts are real, and they're related to the old-timers."

"Do I want to know who the old-timers are?"

Heather laughed. "The founding families. You've already met some of us. Baker City was established by the O'Learys, the McElroys, the

Sweeneys, the O'Connells, the Garveys, the O'Neills, and the O'Sullivans. Seven Irish boys met on a ship bound for America. The Murphys, came after World War One so they're somewhat respected, not total newbies like the MacGillicudys who are Scots-Irish and didn't get here until the 1940s. Mindy would be the first to tell you they don't count for much to many of the folks who live here."

"And the O'Learys are the town mediums."

"Always have been." Heather swirled her glass, so the ice tinkled merrily. "Cat has only been here for a year and she's a great addition. I used to tell Durango I wished we had an O'Leary when he wanted to know what happened to his brother."

"But Waco Hawke isn't dead."

"No, not yet. Like I said before, if he keeps pissing me off, I'd be happy to change that."

Debbie silently debated the conundrum. Should she share what she knew? If she didn't, how could she help Rex arrange for Waco to reconnect with his family? "He wants to see his brothers and sisters in addition to Tiffany Roberts."

"I know, and Durango's being a complete asshat about it, not that I totally blame him." Heather frowned thoughtfully, staring off into the yard. "I can say it because I'm married to the jarhead. You can't. Tiffany's bringing Luke up for his birthday in a couple weeks. It's a touchy subject, but I should be able to broach it if we get some privacy. If not, it will have to wait."

"All right." Debbie glimpsed the new, small, bright yellow school bus in the driveway coming toward the house. "I'll check in with the major and see if he can make it here, then. If she agrees, we could arrange for them to meet."

Heather nodded. "And if it doesn't, we wait. Durango has a lot of baggage after cleaning up several of Waco's messes over the years before he disappeared on that covert mission. There's no way my husband will let his bro hurt Tiffany or her son again."

It didn't take a rocket scientist to put two and two together. Debbie blinked. "I met Luke when he helped Laredo with Wonder's foot the first time. You mean Luke is—"

"Exactly." Heather rose to her feet as the bus came to a stop in front of the house. "Most people think the obvious since Luke has such a strong resemblance to Durango, but you and your husband need to know the truth. Waco is scum. Always has been, always will be. Watch your six around him and be ready to kick his ass to the curb. He doesn't respect boundaries and he'll jump you—"

"He may try." Debbie stood, preparing to greet Penny and Araceli. "If he does, you won't have to castrate him. But I will need help burying the body."

"You've got it." Heather high-fived her. "Just call and I'll bring over my bulldozer. I call her Frou-Frou. She has a six-way blade and I'll teach you how we dispose of trash in Baker City. We'll push up a young tree, create a hole, put him in it and then let the tree return to its natural place. Nobody will ever find him. Of course, we'll have to hope Cat understands and doesn't rat us out when he shows up and whines at her."

Debbie laughed. "Like the saying goes, 'winner, winner, chicken dinner!'"

Her new school and her teacher, Ms. Barrett, were perfect, Araceli thought. Instead of cooking, sewing and lots of faith-based lectures filled with Bible verses about obedience and knowing her place, there'd been math, science, reading, writing, history, and a baseball game during P.E. Best school day ever!

Araceli followed her new cousin, Penny, off the bus. Aunt Debbie stood waiting on the porch for them, talking to another woman. "Who is that?"

"Captain Heather. I know her from church. She lives two doors away at Hawke's Horse Heaven." Penny headed toward the house. "You'll meet lots of folks there on Sunday."

"I'm not doing that."

"Doing what?

"Going to church." Araceli bit her lip. "If it's a have-to, then it's a deal-breaker."

"Ramsey doesn't go either." Penny heaved a dramatic sigh. "You can stay home with her, but you'll be sorry. Everybody is really nice. Reverend Tommy says they have to 'walk the talk,' not be hypocrites."

"Yeah, like that's going to happen."

Her cousin sighed again and hustled forward to hug Debbie. "School was great today. What did you do?"

"Entertained the women veterans' group. Come on inside and I'll introduce you before your riding lesson with Kyra. Twila Garvey brought extra cookies for you kiddoes from the bakery. Remember to save some for Vangie."

That night, Araceli lay in bed missing her mom, missing the stuffed, plush bear made from one of her baby blankets, missing the vintage rag doll she used to snuggle every night. She wished she could cry, but she'd learned better in Montana.

Tears brought more whippings, not less. She shuddered, remembering the way her grandfather called her out to stand in front of the rest of the family, all his wives and kids after supper, at night. He'd slowly remove his belt, then unfasten the buckle, setting it aside, telling her to 'bend over and grab her ankles,' before the thick leather strap struck her rear end, again and again.

Mom and Dad never hit her, but after she died, he didn't believe Araceli anymore. He told her to stop making up lies about his parents who were totally weird and mean. It bothered her then, bothered her when she lived with them, and it bothered her even more tonight.

Araceli eased out of bed, pulled on her robe, and tied the belt snugly around her waist. Next came her slippers, and she headed into the hall.

Her aunt slept in the huge bedroom at the far end of the hall, but when she looked, the room was empty. Maybe, Aunt Debbie was still downstairs and would have time to talk. She'd grown up in Montana. She'd know what it was like to be called an adult and have everything she cherished taken away on her thirteenth birthday. *To be given a wedding dress and told that someone was going to marry you this summer whether you wanted it or not!*

Araceli drifted through the rooms but didn't see her aunt. She tiptoed to the front door and tried the knob. It wasn't locked. When she opened it, she saw her aunt sitting on the porch swing, a glass of wine in one hand. Shasta slept on the far end, but at the sound of footsteps, she lifted her head and yipped at Araceli.

Debbie glanced at her. "What's up, sweetheart? Bad dreams?"

"Kind of." Araceli breathed in the night air. "I miss my mom."

"Come join me and tell me all about her." Debbie sipped more wine and shifted on the swing to make room so Araceli could sit beside her. "I never met her, but she must have been awesome to have a daughter like you."

CHAPTER TWENTY-THREE

Friday morning on the way to the barn, Debbie pulled out her cell phone and called Mindy MacGillicudy. The older woman had said she was still an early riser, so Debbie didn't bother to feel guilty. "Hey, Mindy. Got a question for you."

"Go ahead. I owe you after being so hospitable yesterday. Now that you know the other vets don't bite, maybe you'll join us next Thursday afternoon at the veteran's center in town."

"I already have it on my calendar and Kyra O'Neill said she'd look after the girls and run the place until I return." Debbie took a deep breath. "I remember you told me that you were a school psychologist and helped troubled kids."

"That's in my skill set," the older woman responded. "Do you want to talk about your past?"

"Not ready yet, but I do want you to counsel Araceli. She needs more help than I can give."

"You said she was your niece."

"My oldest brother's girl. He's getting ready to go back to Afghanistan and rejoin his Army unit. After her mother died two years ago, he took her to our parents in Montana before he shipped out."

Mindy whistled softly. "Aren't they part of some cult?"

"Yes. Sister-wives, barely teenaged girls married off to old men, very fundamentalist Christian, highly patriarchal. My mother is my father's fifth spiritual wife. Since Araceli reached puberty, they were planning to get her a husband. There was a big rite of passage on her thirteenth birthday so the marriageable men could look her over."

"What was that like? I take it she trusted you enough to describe the event to you."

"She did. She was given a wedding dress to wear to the community party. There was a big bonfire, and they burned the books her parents had given her. They took away the toys, including a hand-crafted teddy bear her mom made her out of an old baby blanket. If Araceli behaved appropriately, her new husband might dole them out to her for their children."

"But she didn't behave."

"No, she had more courage than I did. She ran away numerous times. My brother was told it happened three times, but last night she admitted it was more like a half dozen. When she went to the police, they returned her to the family ranch."

The boarder barn was empty except for the horses. Debbie snagged a handful of carrots and went to commune with Hobby. While she carried on the conversation, she fed treats. "Araceli was physically, psychologically, and emotionally abused. My father made beating her with a belt a family spectacle and his various wives–including my mother–were complicit in the abuse. Araceli says they often 'ratted her out' to him so she was whipped more often."

"That's horrible, Debbie. Did it happen to you too?"

Of course, it had, but Debbie didn't feel like admitting that truth, although the audience when she was a girl wasn't as large. It'd taken a lot of years and support from her best friends to recover from being the family scapegoat.

Instead, Debbie said, "I don't think Celi would be comfortable in a formal setting, but perhaps you'd join us for dinner and talk to her."

"Sounds like a winner to me. I could also chat with your stepdaughters, and it might make it easier for Araceli to be part of a group session sometimes. Vangie told me she and Penny ran away to you and your husband when their mom went off to Hawaii with what Vangie called 'her new toy-boy' and you're trying to get full custody. My report would provide support for that."

Tears burned and Debbie blinked hard. "Come early so you can ride with Trina and me today. Then you'll be here when the girls arrive home from school, and it will look perfectly natural."

"Okay. Now, I want you to do something else for me."

"What?"

"Call Bronwyn Murphy and ask if she'll make a new teddy bear for your niece. She'll probably love the idea because then it will give her the perfect excuse to make a couple for Sully and Tate's twins. It won't be the same for Araceli, but it will provide some comfort."

"I'll do it right now. I already asked Celi to make a list of her favorite books so I could order them online for her."

Late that night, Debbie sat on the porch swing with her constant companion. With Shasta at her heels, she'd checked on the girls before she came outside and discovered all of them sleeping soundly. It meant she was alone when her phone vibrated. Switching it onto video-chat, she answered. "Hello there. How was your day?"

"Good. I got your texts last night that Araceli was venting. How is she now?"

"I lined her up with a therapist. Figured Mindy could help her more than I can." Debbie heaved a sigh. "Things have escalated since I left the cult. Now, they prep the girls for their weddings on their thirteenth birthdays. The actual marriages for first wives don't take place before they turn sixteen, which is the legal age of consent in Montana, but celestial marriages can take place as soon as the girls reach puberty."

Rex grimaced. "That's disgusting. Got more details, Ramsey?"

She nodded. "Yeah. My father explained to Araceli that she'd be visiting various families around the community so they could check her out and see if she'd fit into their homes. When she wanted to attend school, this fall, he told her it wasn't needful. She would learn more about housekeeping, cooking, sewing and child-care by 'guesting' with prospective in-laws."

"What else?" A muscle ticked in Rex's tightening jaw. "I'm sure she told you more."

"Oh yeah. If she didn't behave appropriately, he'd already given permission for her hosts to punish her. She said it'd be more public beatings." Debbie drew a ragged breath. "My stupid brother didn't tell them not to hit his kid. Have you talked to him lately?"

"Not for two days. He's ordered replacements of some of her stuff and if it arrives in time, I'll bring it with me next weekend."

"Sounds good. I talked to Bronwyn Murphy. She's totally into crafts, so she's making a new teddy bear for Araceli. We went online and picked out a blanket that looked like the one she had when she was little-bitty and had it sent to Bronwyn. It won't be a hundred-percent the same, but Celi says if she snuggles it enough, it will come close."

"Then we have a plan. Has she talked to her dad lately?"

"No, she told the therapist how mad she was at him. Mindy said that's healthy and Celi can wait on it. I suggested she touch base with her mom's family and give them your address so they can write to her. She did that tonight."

Confusion spread across Rex's face, wrinkling his forehead and landing in the golden-brown eyes. "Why didn't she use your address?"

"She explained to them I was avoiding West and his relatives after being abused by them when I was a girl. Surprisingly, they understood and promised to keep any pictures on the down-low, so she said she'd send them photos of the horses she rides."

"Which one has she chosen?"

"She's still riding around the lesson barn. I think she'll opt for Sagedust, a little gray Arabian mare, but we'll see." Debbie reached for her wine glass. "I heard from my grandmother this afternoon. She wanted to know if I'd arranged to leave the ranch so we could go on a cruise over the holidays."

"What did you tell her?" Rex leaned back in his recliner and picked up a can of beer. "I hoped we'd visit the boys at Thanksgiving."

"I remembered you suggested it. I brought it up with her and she agreed to join us in Pullman. Then, she'll come back and visit here for a month until New Year's. I described the mother-in-law suite and asked if she'd consider moving in with me."

"What did she say?"

"She puddled up and said she'd love it, but she wants me to take more time to think about it." Debbie swirled the wine in her glass, then sipped. "I introduced her to the girls and told her that she might be the one who wants to think, because this place can be a real madhouse when all the kiddoes are here. I said I could use her help especially during the busy seasons, but I didn't want to overwhelm her."

Rex chuckled. "If she's anything like you, it won't take long for her to organize everything and everyone at Miracle."

"Where do you think I learned it?" Debbie smiled at him. "I also contacted your former housekeeper, Señora Gonzales. I offered her a job here. She didn't turn me down yet. She said she'll be talking to you."

"I suppose if I don't give you a glowing reference, you'll kick my butt back to Texas."

"Wow, you're getting smarter and smarter, Major. She didn't cut me any slack when I told her I was your wife. She said I screwed up when I let you decide we should keep our marriage a secret."

"How the hell did she get that idea?"

Debbie shrugged. "Well, if I wanted her to work for me, I needed to throw someone under the bus, and it wasn't going to be me."

Another low, sexy laugh. "Fine. Just remember payback's hell and vengeance will be mine next Friday night."

"Promises, promises." Heat rose in her cheeks, and she hoped he didn't see the blush. By the knowing look, she tended to doubt it. "Tell me more."

On Saturday evening, when he pulled through the security gates at the housing development where he lived, the guard waved Rex to a stop. He opened the window and waited. "What's going on?"

"Got a delivery for you, sir." The guard brought over two medium sized boxes. "Not sure what they are, but judging by the return address, I'm guessing books."

"Makes sense. There was a fire where my niece lived, and she lost a bunch of them." Rex opened the driver's door, slid out and took the cartons, sliding them across to the passenger seat. "Be prepared for more."

The older, silver-haired man smiled. "Gotta love a kid who reads."

"Exactly. I hope it rubs off on my daughters."

Between visits to the hospital, checking in on the reservists working at the warehouses, filling in for Maverick Jones with the general and late-night conversations with Debbie, the weekend flew by. Monday morning started with P.T. at 0600 hours followed by a full day at the warehouse. Mid-afternoon, he was working through a stack of paperwork when Corporal Baxter came to the door.

"Sir, you have a call."

Rex eyed him. "Who is it?"

"A woman and she won't give a name. It's not Master Sergeant Ramsey."

"Thanks. Shut the door and then put it through. Track the location of the caller."

"Yes, sir."

When the phone buzzed, Rex picked up the receiver. "Sinclair."

"Where are my daughters?"

Rex straightened in the chair. They'd barely spoken in the last seven years, but he'd always remember the high-pitched, shrill soprano voice that grated on his last nerve now. Why had he ever considered it and the 'baby-days' act super sexy when he met her? He'd been stupid back then. "Hello, Averill. Where are you? Home? Or still in Hawaii?"

"That's not what I want to know. Where are they? The schools called and said they didn't show up for class. What have you done to them?"

"They're not going to boarding school. Are you home in Sacramento? Ask Lupe where they are." He didn't know if his ex-wife would pass the test or not, but it was worth a try. "Are you there? Is she?"

"I let her go. I didn't need her since the girls are going to school back East. I'll see them when I'm ho–. They're home for Christmas."

"Really?" Rex paused. "Is your plan to leave the house completely empty for months?"

"Of course not. I arranged for a property manager to handle short-term rentals for travelers who need somewhere to stay for a few days or weeks. They do the maintenance between guests so there's no need for me to pay Lupe and her husband."

"Slight problem there, Averill. *I* was the one who paid them. How did you intend to bypass the direct deposits?"

He let the silence continue for a long moment before he said, "Just a moment. Someone's here." He put the call on hold, then pressed the intercom button. "Baxter, have you got her twenty?"

"Almost, sir."

Rex picked up the call again. "You didn't say where you were, Averill."

She heaved a dramatic sigh. "There's no reason for me to hurry back from Maui since the kids are all supposed to be in school, Rex. Now, stop messing around and tell me where the girls are."

"Probably getting home from school unless Vangie has cross-country tryouts."

"I can't believe you signed her up for that. She has to take care of Penny after school."

"Not her job. Vangie is a kid, not a parent. I expect her to have a life." The door opened and Corporal Baxter nodded at Rex. "Fair enough. You're in Maui. Until Christmas, right?"

Another sigh. "Stop acting so put-upon. Yes, I'm here and the girls have my number, even if they're not calling me. They learned that trick from their brothers who play incommunicado when I leave in June."

"I see." He wouldn't yell at her, give her the satisfaction of knowing he was furious. "My lawyer will be in touch, and the girls are staying with me."

Rex replaced the receiver and eyed the warehouse clerk when Corporal Baxter tapped, and then opened the door. "What did you learn?"

"I got the cell phone location for you, sir. She's in Lahaina, Hawaii. Do you want me to call her back?"

"No. I'm calling my sons. I need privacy for that."

"Yes, sir." Baxter gently shut the door before walking away.

He wanted answers and yelling at Rory wouldn't provide a decent sitrep, Rex thought. His good intentions faded when his oldest son answered. "I just talked to your mom. What the hell is the matter with you? Why didn't you call me? How long has this crapfest been happening?"

"Which crapfest?" Rory asked. "Call me confused."

"Don't bullshit me, boy. She's been in Hawaii since June. Apparently, she's not planning on returning until Christmas. It's damn near the middle of September. When were you planning to give me a sitrep?"

"How were we supposed to know you'd give a rats' ass, sir? You've been least in sight for eight years. Yeah, you were in combat a lot, but other soldiers *Skype* with their kids. You never did. If you had, I'd have told you that she's hightailed it to Hawaii with her boy-toys for the last four years. She said it was legal for me to look after the other kids because I was eighteen."

"That's bullshit. You should have emailed me—"

"Oh, you bet I could when she and her flavors of the month or week censored all our Internet communications and cut us off during the summer. Why didn't you call us?"

"Because I was in a damned warzone most of the time."

"Yeah, right! And now, you're blaming me because she dumped on Scott and Cal too. This isn't my fault. I freaking did my best with the rest of the family and I'm only twenty-two. If it's not good enough for you, then you can just go to hell!"

"That's bull—" Silence and Rex knew his son ended the call. "This is bullshit."

Only one person would have his back even if she labeled him an asshat, so he called her. "It's me, Ramsey."

"What's going on, Major? I'm about to hit the trails with Mindy and Trina."

"Isn't Mindy the therapist?"

"That's right. Did you need to talk to a shrink or a chaplain? I already know you won't share problems with your chain of command after the soap opera with your ex."

"True enough. Tell the therapist she needs to interrogate the girls. Their mother is in Hawaii until Christmas."

"Say again, sir. I didn't get that."

"Yes, you did. You heard me, Ramsey. Apparently, the crap has been going on for years. She's made it a regular thing for the kids to fend for themselves six months out of every year. Rory already yelled at me for not asking, so you don't need to rip into me about this shitshow."

"Oh, I will anyway. I can't skip an 'I told you so,' moment. Right now, just embrace the suck, Rex. Contact the other boys and see what you get out of them. I'll talk to the girls and brief you later tonight."

He glowered across the room. "Can't believe you still have my six when I'm an utter jackass."

"I've always had it, Sinclair, and I always will." Her voice softened. "Remember, the road runs both ways. I count on you to look after me, and you always do." She paused. "The girls have been with us for almost a month, and this is the first time we've heard from their mother. I'm touching base with Bree Hawke and checking on custody status."

"All right. I'll talk to Scott and Cal. Tell the attorney to go forward with selling my house in California. Averill intended to rent it out and keep the money. That's not happening."

CHAPTER TWENTY-FOUR

Evening horse chores didn't take long with everyone helping, and afterward, they headed inside for dinner. Debbie waited until after they ate and the girls cleaned up the kitchen, loading the dishwasher, sweeping the floor, wiping down the surfaces. Normally, she'd have left them to have a confidential group session with Mindy, but that wasn't the plan tonight.

Instead, Debbie arranged a variety of cookies from the town bakery on a plate while the counselor filled three glasses with milk and two cups with coffee.

"Everybody find a seat." Debbie gestured to the table. "We're going to talk."

"I have homework," Araceli protested.

"And I don't care." Debbie pointed to the chairs. "It can wait until Mindy's done with you. Sit. Eat. Listen. You're not the only one with issues."

"We're fine, Ramsey," Vangie said. "No issues here."

"Not what I heard." Debbie folded her arms and waited until petite, blonde Penny hastily sat next to Mindy. "Your dad called. He talked to your mom."

"Oops," Penny said. "What did she want?"

"Don't worry about her." Debbie turned her attention on Vangie. The teen had changed from the fashionable jeans and tank top she'd worn to school to riding clothes. She'd secured her black hair in a low ponytail so it wouldn't interfere with an equestrian helmet. "Worry about me. The two of you inferred you'd been home alone nights after your brothers left for college."

"That's true." Penny reached for a large chocolate chip cookie. "It's why we came to you and Dad. Lupe had to go home at six 'cause Mom cut her hours."

"And you told me your mother was in Hawaii with your stepdad."

"Also true." Vangie pulled out a chair and sat down across from her sister.

"Do you want to tell me what you left out of the story?"

The two girls shared a look and then Vangie said cautiously. "We told you she was on her honeymoon until—"

"When would she return?" Debbie lowered her voice to the one she used when she expected answers from a recalcitrant junior enlisted. "What day would she be back?"

Penny winced. "I bet you know."

"Say it." Debbie rapped out the order.

Vangie took a deep breath. "She usually comes back around the middle of December."

"Whoa!" Araceli stared at the other two girls. "Usually? When did she leave?"

"The middle of June. Cal was pissed because she wasn't there when he graduated from high school." Penny took a bite of the cookie, chewed, and swallowed. "We couldn't tell you, Ramsey."

"Really?" Debbie advanced on the table. "What had I done to scare you? What did your dad do?"

"Nothing!" Vangie jumped to her feet and hustled across the room. She flung her arms around Debbie. "You were so upset about us being alone for a few lousy weeks. We figured we'd better do that discretion thing Dad talks about and not tell you it was going to be a lot longer than a couple of days."

"What discretion thing?" Araceli snagged a peanut butter cookie. "I never heard it before."

"It's a quote from Shakespeare and it's frequently misused. Some people say, 'discretion is the better part of valor.'" Mindy told her. "I don't think Debbie or Vangie's and Penny's dad would mistake caution for courage. So, how often does your mom go to Hawaii, Penny?"

"Ever since she got the condo from her third husband, Seth, four years ago. She's gone from June to December. Van and I decided to find Dad when Cal was leaving with Rory and Scott for college, and Mom signed us up for boarding school."

Debbie hugged Vangie and then guided her back to the table. "Okay, I don't know if you two realize this or not, but your dad and I can use this pattern to ensure we have custody, and he won't feel guilty for selling the house in Sacramento."

"Mom's house?" Vangie stared at her. "How could he do that? Don't they have to split the money when they sell it?"

"No, she doesn't have a share in it because it came from what he inherited after his grandparents died. He owns it. I told you he was a good guy. He always wanted a roof over your heads, so he paid for everything he could. The house, the boys' college tuition, your school stuff, Lupe's salary." Debbie drew out a chair and sat down with the rest of them.

"Our brothers don't know," Vangie said. "If they did, they'd have shared it."

"Well, now you can tell them," Mindy said. "Debbie, are you contacting your lawyer tonight?"

"In one snickerdoodle and my coffee," Debbie agreed. "We'll visit her tomorrow after school."

Late that night, she sat on the porch swing watching the stars in the ebony sky while she waited for Rex to call. She'd tried him earlier, but he didn't answer, so she texted him a few times, leaving the ball in his proverbial court. Headlights appeared in the distance, crossing the bridge over the creek, and she watched a truck cruise up the driveway to the house.

Well, that's interesting, she thought. After he got off duty, he was on the road, so no wonder he didn't answer. Before she stood up, Shasta jumped off the swing. Debbie rose and the two of them went to meet him. "What's happening? Don't you have work tomorrow?"

Rex reached for her. "I reshuffled things to take the morning off. I needed to see you."

"I'm here." She stepped into his arms and hugged him. "Did the other boys rip you a new one?"

He nodded. "I'm such an asshat, Ramsey. I was so pissed about my ex not being faithful to me when I was in combat, I never thought she'd bail on the kids. I assumed she loved them, and we both know what 'assume' means."

"Then I won't tell you." She held him. "Did you eat dinner, or shall we make breakfast before we go to bed?"

"I ate."

"Let's call it a night." She stepped back enough to put an arm around his waist, and they walked toward the house. "I have an appointment with the lawyer tomorrow after school. I'll call her and see if she can set up a time for us to meet with her in the morning."

"Sounds good. I talked to Lupe today and she said she was interested in the job here, but her husband needs to find local employment. He sent his resume to Hawke Construction. He also does grounds-keeping and maintenance, so I said we might have work for him here."

"Could be. What kind of maintenance?" She listened while Rex described the other man's skill set. Obviously, Rex needed to talk and feel as if his contributions mattered. He wasn't ordering her around and she'd be supportive, not as a wife, but as a person. It was 'sergeant's business' after all.

Morning came early. He shut off the alarm and left Debbie sleeping with the dog and cat for company. He hit the shower and shaved under the spray. Once he dressed in clean camo pants and a t-shirt, he pulled on his boots before going downstairs to the kitchen. The girls would be heading for school, and he'd make breakfast, pancakes all around.

He was on his first cup of coffee when he heard footsteps. He turned and saw Vangie in fashionably torn jeans and a snug-fitting tee that covered the ring in her belly button. She obviously didn't plan on going to the barn, since she wore flip-flops. She'd already done her hair and makeup. "Hello there."

"Hey." She walked across the room and hugged him. "I'm sorry, Dad."

"For what?" He wrapped an arm around her shoulders. "It's no wonder you and your brothers are pissed at me. I'm the one who screwed up big time, sweetness."

"Not just you. We should have shared what was happening. Mindy said if we'd told you or emailed you, then you'd have had an opportunity to make things right. We took those chances away from you."

"Yeah, but all of you are kids. Mindy may have a point, but were those reasonable expectations? I'm the grownup and I ought to have acted like one." He kissed her forehead. "What if we both agree to do better?"

"That works." Vangie hugged him again. "Now, I'm gonna set the table. I have to catch the bus in forty minutes."

"Sounds like a winner." He refilled his cup and returned to stirring the batter.

Penny was the next arrival, followed closely by Araceli, both girls also dressed for school in jeans and T-shirts. "Hi, Dad. Do you have to go to work?"

"After lunch. Ramsey and I have a meeting this morning." He glanced over his shoulder at the slender, dark-haired teen who shadowed Penny, worry on the other girl's face. "What's on your mind, Celi?"

"Are you really their father?"

"Yes." He ladled out a spoonful of batter on the griddle, followed it with a second and then a third. "It's how I knew you'd be safe here."

"And you didn't come to take me away?"

"Of course not." Debbie entered the kitchen. She wore a bright blue fleece robe that matched her eyes. "Granted, if he keeps turning off my alarm, I'll be hiding his body, not sending him back to the base on time for work."

"Promises, promises, Mrs. Sinclair. Have some coffee and it will cheer you up."

She still smiled at him, apparently amused by him this morning. "I told you not to call me that."

"I wasn't listening."

"Why aren't I surprised?" However, she crossed to the counter, snagged a mug, and filled it, topping off his as well. "Penny, get the orange juice out of the fridge. Celi, grab the butter, syrup, and napkins. Major, tell me you put bacon in the oven to go with breakfast."

"Only if you don't call me that at home." He winked at her. "I have better things to do than hide your body."

She elbowed him. "Not in front of this audience. Behave yourself."

The comment earned laughter from Vangie before she went to open the back door for Shasta who trotted inside and headed for the comfy rag rug in front of the woodstove. "Oh, wait till I tell the boys that you're giving Dad orders, Ramsey. They'll love it."

Moises Pride sat in the rocking chair near the antique woodstove in the kitchen, watching the family interact over breakfast. The dog slept at his feet. She'd grown accustomed to him and so had the cats. It almost felt like home. He'd popped in and out of town often enough that he'd started to make friends with some of the other ghosts. Zeke Garvey, another ghostly Army Ranger in town, provided more advice about how to travel to different places than the medium, Cat O'Leary-McTavish had.

After the girls left for school, the major and his woman cleaned up the kitchen, then vanished upstairs. Moises didn't follow. Like he'd said before, those rooms were off-limits when the folks were home. Two hours later, he heard someone knock on the front door and drifted into the hallway to see who'd come to visit. It wasn't the instructor or trail guide coming to ask the boss questions about the stable and its operations. Instead, a tall, twenty-something, blonde in a sky-blue suit, matching stiletto heels and carrying a fancy briefcase followed Debbie Ramsey into the kitchen.

The woman shook hands with the major. "Bree Hawke. I'm Debbie's lawyer and since she has your power of attorney, that means I represent your interests, too. She said we need to talk about the custody of your minor children."

Major Sinclair nodded. "I just found out my ex has been going to Hawaii from June to December and leaving the kids behind for the past four years. We need to change things up."

Bree nodded. "Sounds like a winner." She lifted her briefcase onto the table and opened it, removing the paperwork. She passed several pages to Debbie and to Rex. "This is what I've completed. Go through it and make some notes. I visited my sister-in-law last weekend, and she told me you know my older brother, Waco."

"Yes." The major gave her a solid onceover, then added, "He'd like to see you when you're comfortable visiting."

"Seriously?" The blonde returned the stare. "I hardly saw him after he enlisted thirteen years ago. He barely visited the family. Why would he ask?"

The major rested his hands on the table. "He blames himself for not doing more to protect you when you were a kid. He told me your dad kicked him out of the house more than once."

"Now that is weird. He was my folks' favorite son."

"Not after he promised to take your dad out if he messed with you again."

"Whoa." Bree Hawke tapped a pen on the table. "Okay, now I do want to see him. If he'll do a deposition, it'll help with the case I'm building against my dad and his perverted friends. They think they're above the law because of their status in Washington, D.C., and their high-powered friends."

Moises whistled softly. She'd need protection if she was going after the ring of child molesters Sergeant Hawke had told him about. "All right, I'm visiting the medium and asking for help," he said, even though none of them could hear him. "I'll be back. Don't let her leave without me."

When the girls arrived home from school on Wednesday afternoon, Penny led the way toward the front door. "It looks like Linda MacGillicudy is still here with her helpers," she said, spotting the woman's vehicle. "She comes to clean the house every week and that means we'll have something good for supper. She cooks at the café in Baker City, too."

Araceli adjusted her backpack. "It's kind of strange Aunt Debbie doesn't cook at all. She must have learned how when she was growing up. It's a big deal at my grandparents' ranch. The grandmas, aunts and other wives and girls take turns cooking, but they also do all the cleaning, gardening, looking after the chickens and livestock near the big house. The guys ride out to take care of the cattle, build fences and do farm stuff."

Penny's blue eyes widened. "What are you talking about, Celi? How many grandmas do you have? We only have two, my dad's mom and my biological mother's."

"My grandpa has seven wives and all of them live in the same humongous house in Montana," Araceli said matter-of-factly. "Mindy told me it was okay if I shared stuff about my dad's weird relatives. I didn't have to keep them a secret."

Penny climbed the stairs and crossed the porch. "Well, I'm glad you're sharing, but I don't get it. If they have such a big family, why did Ramsey end up at a boarding school?"

"I guess because she threw a big fit when they tried to find her a husband. She told me I was really brave when I ran away lots of times since they were doing that to me."

"But you're only thirteen."

"They said I was old enough to get married this summer, but I didn't wanna." Araceli opened the door and led the way inside. She heard the vacuum roaring in the living room and paused to look inside. She'd never seen her aunt cleaning the house, but there was always a first time.

However, it wasn't today. Instead, a dark-haired guy in faded jeans and a blue t-shirt vacced the carpet. Even if he was barely an adult, he was an obvious expert because he left perfect rows on the rug and no footprints from his running shoes. He waved a greeting and kept working.

Penny flashed a smile in his direction. "Hi, Dray. We didn't try to mess things up, but we spend more time cleaning the barns, so we're glad your mom is here."

He hit the power button, turning off the machine. "Yeah, well she brought cookies and cheesecake to go with the spaghetti and meatballs in the slow cooker, so you'll be doubly grateful. She said your mom doesn't live in the kitchen."

"As far from it as she can get," Penny agreed. "Dray, this is my cousin, Araceli Taggart, who just came to live with us a week ago. Araceli, this is Dray MacGillicudy and I already told you about his mom, Linda, who has the cleaning service."

Araceli studied him as he approached. Black hair curled down to his shoulders, but she still spotted the square-shaped ears, rare for most people, but common in the Taggart family. He had distinctive angled eyebrows that almost matched hers and the same color of electric blue eyes. High cheekbones, and his lean, wiry build reminded her of her father, his younger half-brothers, and their sons.

Dray smiled. "Welcome to Baker City. Where are you from, Araceli?"

She shrugged. "Now, it's here. Why? Are you always so snoopy?"

He laughed, reaching into his jeans, and pulling out a wallet. He opened it and revealed an old photograph of a young teenage girl, hair in long black braids, with brilliant blue eyes. She held a newborn, dark-haired baby in a tight embrace. "This is my mom and me."

"It doesn't look much like her," Penny commented. "Does Linda dye her hair brown? Or wear contacts?"

"I'm adopted." Dray removed the picture. On the back in faded ink were the letters, SWEET followed by the words, 'Taggart and son' and numbers, 8/31/2000. "She was from Montana. Taggart isn't a common name around here, and you look so much like her. Are you related to her?"

Araceli slowly shook her head. Before she ended up living in the community with her dad's family last year, she'd always told the truth. Her mom, aunt and grandparents hated what they called fabrications, but things had changed for her in Montana.

Lying was a survival skill and she'd grown skilled at it. "Nope. Never heard of her. Come on, Penny. We have to change and get to the barn for our lesson. We don't want to be late for Kyra's class or she'll make us spend the afternoon scooping horsy poo."

CHAPTER TWENTY-FIVE

After dinner and dishes, the girls settled at the kitchen table to complete their homework. They had a plate of assorted cookies from the town bakery because Vangie claimed they needed sugar to help them think. Debbie laughed and grabbed a couple of snickerdoodles to go with her tea before heading to her office to plan the upcoming October horseshow. She and Clancy Dawson had chosen the second Saturday in the month because the schools in Lake Maynard and Baker City would be out for a three-day weekend.

Halfway through designing the poster advertising the show, Debbie glanced away from the computer monitor and saw her niece standing in the doorway. "What's up? Do you need help with an assignment?"

"I'm okay." Araceli hesitated for a moment, then entered the room. "I need to talk to you. Is now a good time?"

"Sure." Debbie hit 'save' on the desktop and waved the young teen to a chair. "Is this private? Do you want to close the door?"

"Pretty private." Araceli closed the door and settled in the seat. "Do you know Dray MacGillicudy?"

Debbie shook her head. "Not really. I don't think I've met him in person yet, but I've heard about him. Linda told me her son was helping out because some of her workers went back to college. Isn't that the boy Vangie likes?"

Araceli nodded. "He was cleaning the living-room when we got home today. He showed me a picture."

"Really?" Debbie clenched her fists. What had the boy done to her niece? What did the girl feel she needed to share? "Appropriate or inappropriate?"

"It wasn't gross or anything." Araceli took a deep breath. "It was an old photograph of what looked like you holding a baby but a long time ago."

"What?" Her stomach felt like it twisted, and Debbie gasped for air. "How did he get it?"

"He's adopted. He really looks like my Taggart cousins in Montana. Your name—not the one you have now, but your first one—Sweet Taggart is on the back of the photo along with a date, August 31st, 2000. Was that—"

"His birthday." Debbie eyed the girl. "What did you tell him?"

"Nothing. I lied when he asked if I knew you. I figured you should be the one to tell him." Araceli narrowed her Taggart blue eyes. "That's why they sent you away, isn't it? Because you were going to have a baby and you didn't want to get married?"

"That's right." Debbie leaned back in the chair. "I was only a little older than you are now. My father kept nagging me about quitting ninth grade and accepting one of the bishop's sons as my future husband, but I never liked Jabez Levitt. He was a nasty bully."

"Wow." Araceli's eyes widened and she sat up straighter. "How did you get into high school?"

"Your dad insisted I have an education. One day, the bus dropped me off at the end of the driveway and I was walking the rest of the way home when —" Debbie's voice trailed away. She couldn't tell a young girl she was gang-raped by four boys while her older half-brother held her down for them. "Afterward—"

"My mom was a MP." Araceli stood, came around the desk and wrapped her arms around Debbie in a warm hug. "She taught me how to be careful and said sometimes bad stuff happens to girls and women. Is that why you were having a baby?"

Debbie clutched the girl tight. "Yes. It's also why my father gave me certain choices if I wanted to go back to his house, but I wasn't taking a baby there."

"Or marrying the bishop or one of his sons or somebody else or letting them have your kid. Major Rex says I'm brave, but you are, too."

Tears burned but Debbie struggled to hold them back. "Let's make a pact, Araceli. I won't lie to you, and I need you to promise to always tell me the truth. Deal?"

"You've got a deal." Araceli heaved a sigh of relief. "I'm glad I shared. Now, I need to do my homework. What are you going to do?"

"I'm not sure, but I'll tell you when I figure it out."

Late that night, she allowed herself the comfort of her favorite wine while she cuddled with Shasta on the porch swing. When her phone vibrated, she pulled it out of her pocket and answered, but didn't turn on the video chat option. "Hey, Sinclair. How are you?"

"Fine, but obviously you're not. What's wrong?"

"How do you know?"

"You're avoiding me. Not letting me see you. Tell me what's happening."

She took a deep breath. "It's been almost twenty years and I've talked to my share of chaplains, support groups and counselors, but I never told them everything."

"What did you share?"

"Only that I was raped." She took a hefty swallow of red wine. "I didn't even say how many there were, or—"

Silence and then he asked quietly, too quietly. "How many, Ramsey?"

"Four." Another gulp of wine. "Five if I count my half-brother who held me down for his B.F.F., the bishop's son, and gagged me when I screamed, but Kenan insisted he didn't participate when my father confronted him. Kenan claimed he wasn't responsible because I acted like I was better than everybody else in the family and he didn't take either of his turns—"

Rex swore before he asked, "What brought this up?"

"My son lives here." She drained the glass and refilled it. "He has a photo of me holding him right after he was born. He showed it to Araceli. She looks so much like I did back then. And—"

"And what?"

"She lied. She told him she didn't know me."

"Then, she told you. What are you going to do?"

"I don't know."

"Yes, you do, Ramsey. First choice. Are you selling your place? Are we moving on, running away from him?"

"Never!"

"Okay. Second choice—"

"I have to see him. Talk to him."

"There you go. There's my sergeant. I'll join you Friday."

"Why? He's nineteen. I can handle this."

"I have your six. Wait for me."

"Don't be stupid." She switched to video-chat and glared into Rex's face on the smart phone. "I've handled a shitload of kids his age for damn near twenty years. I kept them alive in the greatest shit-show on earth. I've got this. I don't need you."

He smiled. "That's my woman. Kick ass, Ramsey."

When he finished talking to her, Rex texted West Taggart and ordered the senior noncom to meet him at the warehouse at 0600 hours. Time for a real sitrep and it wasn't something to be shared on the phone, but only in person.

He arrived before the other man. Drinking coffee, Rex waited in his pickup until he saw West's rig pull in beside his. He opened the door and climbed out, returning Taggart's salute. Rex handed him a large paper cup. "I don't know about you, but I needed caffeine. High octane Americano from the stand near my place."

"Thanks." West frowned. "What's going on, Major?"

"Your sister and I talked last night."

"And you got names?"

"One and a clue to another."

West peeled back the lid, chugged coffee. "I'm going to Montana to pick up as many of Celi's belongings as possible this weekend. Had a 'come to Jesus' confab with the elders. They finally agreed to act like they believe the crap they preach. They'll intervene because my father taking away the gifts a deceased veteran gave her child was misguided, and tasteless and they don't want me going to the media."

"Do you have someone to watch your six?"

"Not necessary." West's attention appeared to be on the cup. "You were an Army Ranger. Didn't you learn in training, 'two people can keep a secret—?'"

"If one of them is dead," Rex finished the quote. "Let me know if you need an alibi or money for bail."

"Works for me." West held out his hand. "I'll call when I'm back so you can take Celi's things to her. Who am I looking for?"

Rex told him.

———

Mindy MacGillicudy had said the women's veterans group met at the new center in Baker City on Thursday afternoons. Debbie stopped at the town café first. Pop turned from where he refilled coffee cups for the various people sitting in the booths and at the tables during an early lunch rush.

Debbie nodded. "I'm looking for Linda."

"Cooking. Thursdays, we do a burger special. Do you mind talking to her in the kitchen so she can get up these orders?"

"No worries." Debbie walked around the end of the counter and into the old-style area with its row of deep-fat fryers, stainless steel refrigerators, and a giant walk-in cooler. Classic country music poured from a radio on one of the counters. She spotted the older woman slapping burgers on the grill. "This is like the days when I was a fry cook before I went to boot camp."

Linda's smile reached soft brown eyes. She laid buns to toast on the other side of the grill. "Sounds like a winner. Grab a hairnet from the box and I'll put you to work running the fryers. My so-called sous-chef bailed on the showing up for work thing. You'll need another bag of onion rings from the freezer."

Debbie eyed the brown-haired, sturdy woman in jeans and a flowered shirt under her bib-style, white apron. Then she jumped in to help. "I came to talk to you about your son."

"I didn't know you had a chance to meet him."

"Yeah." Debbie dropped French fries in the basket and lowered it into the hot grease. "Not lately. I haven't seen him in nineteen years."

"What?" Linda whirled away from the grill. "What are you saying?"

"Your son showed my niece a photo yesterday and asked if she knew me." Debbie loaded several more baskets with potatoes, hanging them on the stainless-steel rack before she switched to the ones with battered onion rings.

"I changed my name as soon as I could. It was Sweet Taggart once, but not anymore. I've been Debbie Ramsey since I graduated from high school. Picked the name out of a phone book because my grandmother suggested that strategy. We didn't want anyone to find me or my son, so I didn't take one from the family bible." Debbie gestured to the burgers. "Better flip those before they're dead."

"Oh my God." Linda turned her attention to the hamburger patties. "I didn't know."

"Why would you?" Debbie pulled a pair of plastic gloves from the carton and began layering lettuce and tomatoes on a series of plates. "My grandparents arranged the adoption."

"They said you didn't know the father's name so it was listed as unknown on the birth certificate. My ex-husband thought you'd probably—"

"Been a typical teen girl who was experimenting and got caught. My grandpa wanted to protect me and the baby after I escaped from a polygamous, fundamentalist religious cult in Montana." Debbie flicked a glance toward Linda. "I'll talk to your son, but I'm not telling him his biological father raped me when I was fifteen, or where the bastard lives."

"Thank you." Linda drew a deep, ragged breath. "Dray's a good boy. He won seven scholarships to go to a university, but he's taking a gap year or two. He'll attend community college and work to save up money. If I'd known where to find you, I'd have stayed in contact. I always wanted an open relationship with my boy's biological mother."

"I couldn't handle that when I was a kid." The timer buzzed and Debbie headed for the fryers. "Part of it was because the cult would have come after me and him. The rest was because I had a lot of growing up and healing to do."

She knew she sounded totally calm and matter-of-fact, but it wasn't real. If she hadn't been dumping, salting, and serving up fries and onion rings, her hands would have been shaking. Her stomach felt tied up in knots. She'd almost gagged on her coffee this morning and she'd set out cold cereal, milk, and juice for the girls because she couldn't face a cooked breakfast today.

She'd learned to compartmentalize her emotions while she was in the Army, Debbie thought. The military trained her to stay alive and five combat tours during America's longest war had provided more survival lessons. She'd learned to master her emotions, not allow them to control or touch her.

"Thank you," Linda repeated. "I want you to come to my house when you're ready. I have photo albums to share with you. I always made one for each of us while he was growing up."

It was Debbie's turn to say, "Thank you," before she focused on fry cook duties in the diner.

Two hours later, she left the diner and drove to the veteran's center.

Grateful for the help, Pop had offered a free lunch, but Debbie told him she'd eat later because her girls would have a fit if they didn't get to come to the café for his awesome burgers and milkshakes. Linda had intervened, saying Mindy freaked out when people were late for the group therapy sessions.

I can't eat. Not yet. Not when Linda said Dray worked as a receptionist at the veteran's center on Thursdays. I nearly bailed on the meeting, but I can handle this. Nobody is shooting at me.

A few minutes later, she parked in front of a blue and white, two-story house. As she crossed the parking lot, Debbie glimpsed a small cardboard sign taped in one of the downstairs windows. It read, Welcome Home, Brothers and Sisters! She climbed the steps to the front porch and saw the U.S. flag along with the distinctive black and white POW/MIA one. A plywood sign, this one in red and white, hung by the door, proclaiming this was the Ward O'Neill Veterans' Center.

Inside, she found a table in the entry covered with brochures describing different forms of mental health resources available for veterans. Deciding to look at them later, she glanced around. A staircase led to the second floor and a door to the right opened onto what would have been a living room in a private home.

She took a deep breath and walked inside where she saw a young man sitting behind a desk, his attention on the appointment book in front of him while he talked to someone on the landline phone. She stopped and stared at him. Even sitting down, he was tall, and she thought he probably topped six feet. He had shoulder-length, curly black hair. He had the same distinctive angled eyebrows she did and her square-shaped ears. Poor kid.

He hung up the receiver, then glanced at her, narrowing bright blue eyes. "Welcome. How can I help you?"

"I think it's more the other way around." Debbie approached the desk. "I understand you've been looking for me. Once upon a time, I was Sweet Taggart."

His jaw dropped and it was his turn to stare. "Who are you now?"

"Debbie Ramsey. I changed my name as soon as I graduated from high school." She strolled further forward, hoping she appeared cool and collected, not as if she was shaking inside. She sat down in the chair facing him. "I didn't know you or your parents lived here when I bought your cousin, Mindy MacGillicudy's place. That wasn't your mother's name back in the day."

"She returned to her maiden name when my dad left us. We moved back here after the divorce. He didn't want a kid who wasn't his. I haven't seen him since. He doesn't call or write or even send birthday cards."

"I'm sorry. Someone should have told him when he signed the adoption papers, you were his kid from that point on. It might not have done any good though."

"No, it didn't." Dray frowned. "You're younger than I expected."

"I'll be thirty-five next week." She saw his frown intensify and his forehead wrinkled as he obviously did mental calculations. "I was almost sixteen when you were born. I had to grow up fast and make adult decisions. Other than your dad being an asshat, do you have a good life? Are you happy?"

That earned a nod, and he kept staring at her. "You have other kids. Why did you give me away?"

"Whoa, boy! Don't go there." Debbie held up her hand. "I told you. I was fifteen, not old enough to be a decent mother. I'd just escaped from a polygamous cult. They still wanted me and you."

"No way!"

"That's what I decided. One of my first grownup decisions. No way they were getting you. And you're my only biological child. The others are mine by marriage."

"What about Araceli Taggart? How is she related to you? Your daughter?"

"She's my niece." Debbie shrugged, hoping she still looked calm and collected, a professional soldier. She wouldn't reveal her emotions. She couldn't. "Her mother's dead and her dad's headed back to the *sandbox*. He doesn't want the cult to have her, so she's with me for the duration."

"They're still around?"

"Oh yeah. And still doing evil things." Debbie looked at her watch. "I have to go."

"Where? I just met you. I have a ton of questions."

"Save them." Debbie stood. "Where do I find the women vets? If I'm late to the meeting, your cousin, Mindy, will have serious issues."

Dray managed a smile. "Upstairs in the conference room. I'll show you. Can we talk afterwards? Please?"

CHAPTER TWENTY-SIX

Debbie was the first to arrive in the conference room for the meeting. Dray said the rest of the women were undoubtedly hanging out in the kitchen near the coffeepot and fresh pastries from the bakery. She told him she'd wait for them upstairs and declined his offer to bring refreshments.

Alone at last, she closed the door before she sank into one of the comfy office chairs. She shuddered. She'd dreaded the two meetings today, but they'd gone better than she expected.

Linda MacGillicudy was surprisingly understanding and kind. *And Dray, her son—not mine—was so courteous. She raised him to be a decent, empathetic human being. I didn't expect that. Maybe I should have, but how could I?*

The door opened and Mindy entered, carrying a tray with two cups of coffee and a small plate with four doughnuts covered in granulated sugar. She bumped the door with her hip, closing it behind her. "Dray said I should come talk to you and learn more about your past."

Debbie glared in the direction of the door and then focused on the older woman. She didn't look much like a psychologist in her usual attire of jeans, a cowgirl shirt, and lace-up riding boots. "I didn't say I wanted to share it."

"Dray always reminds me of what my mother used to say about some people having old souls." Mindy put a china cup in front of Debbie. "Cream, sugar and a doughnut will help cure what ails you."

"Really?" Debbie picked up the cup. Tears stung and she blinked hard. "I doubt it."

"I don't. Talk to me. That will do more than you think." Mindy sat across from her. "I told the others we'd start the meeting in twenty minutes. They'll respect our privacy since I've had confidential sessions with them over the summer when they've shared their deepest secrets. Spill your guts, Sarge."

Debbie heaved a sigh. "What if I refuse?"

"I'll keep harassing you until I get the info I want. You have choices. Either you talk or I go interrogate your kid. He's at the front desk so he won't be hard to find."

"Bitch."

"You say it like it's a bad thing." Mindy sipped her coffee. "I'm waiting and I never was the patient sort, not before I was a nurse in Vietnam and definitely not after."

"If I tell you I was assaulted?"

"Remember, I told you I was in the Army before you were born. I worked in high schools for beaucoup years until I retired. There's nothing new under the sun, Debbie— nothing I haven't heard before. You can try to shock me, but it won't work. Have a doughnut and save me from those calories crawling onto my hips. My horse, Sonora, will thank you the next time I come to the barn to ride."

"You win. You know some of it already, but I'll share the rest." Debbie snagged a sugar encrusted doughnut, bit into it, chewed and swallowed, sweetness melting on her tongue. "I already told you I was born into a cult. That particular day, the school bus dropped me at the end of the driveway to my father's ranch. Generally, he or one of my mothers met me when the weather was bad and drove me the rest of the way to the house. It was cold and clear. November in Montana, right before Thanksgiving. Sunny, no fresh snow. They weren't there so I started walking—"

"Mothers?" Mindy reached for a doughnut. "After talking to Araceli, I understand your family is fully engaged in a polygamous, fundamentalist cult that encourages misogyny."

"I wouldn't say 'encouraged'. They rule with it." Debbie shook her head, then managed a weak laugh. "When I was a kid, my father had five wives. Celi says he's up to seven now. He wasn't real thrilled when my mom had me because he preferred boys. He let her name me though— Sarah, after my great-grandmother. His other four wives informed her that as his fifth wife, she didn't have sufficient status to choose my name. To my father's first wife, the senior ranking woman or mother in the household, I was Wynfreda. The second one called me Esther. The third said I was Eliana. And the fourth claimed my name was Tabitha."

"Good lord," Mindy said. "It's a wonder you didn't grow up with sixteen different personalities like that gal, Sybil."

Debbie laughed again, more genuinely this time. "West, my oldest brother started calling me 'Sweet'. It was an acronym for the five names. By the time he enlisted in the Army and left for boot camp when I was five years old, everyone else did, too."

"So, what happened that day, Debbie? You got off the school bus and started walking home. Tell me about it."

"Only if it remains confidential. I don't want Dray to know my sad story."

"I don't share what my clients tell me. It's a basic tenet in the "shrink-patient" relationship. Remember last week when we told you the same rule applies to group therapy? This is a safe place to share."

When Debbie arrived home after the meeting, she needed a mental health break. She told the girls she was taking Shasta for training while they played horse games with Kyra's class. She saddled up Hobby and took the trail that wound up the ridge behind the barns. For safety, Trina led her riders on the lower paths around the arenas like she had the campers, but Debbie required solitude. At the top of the first hill, she reined the twenty-two-year-old Quarter-horse mare to a stop and let her breathe.

Shasta dashed back and forth on the track, not running too far away, obviously thrilled at this new adventure. A cool September breeze brushed Debbie's face. She petted Hobby's brown neck and then squeezed her legs to signal the mare to move forward.

She focused on what lay ahead. With three rising terraces, the land spread out around them. This main trail wound through the upper reaches of the farm, circling the property, and it'd eventually end back in front of her house.

Her phone vibrated and Debbie paused to pull it out of her pocket and read the text from Rex. He wanted to know how the meeting with her son went, and she wasn't ready to share the details. She sent a response she was riding the ranch. Safety first. She wouldn't turn off the phone in the event of an emergency, but that didn't mean she'd use it. *I'll touch base with him later. For now, I'm making this ride a top priority.*

Hobby snorted at Shasta but didn't spook at the pup's doggie races under the huge evergreens bordering the trail or her return to escort them on the trail. Debbie kept the horse at a steady walk. It took almost two hours to circumnavigate the ranch and by the time she rode through the last gate, she felt at peace.

She frowned when she spotted a visitor waiting near the house. The tall, brown-haired man wore a dark three-piece suit, a white shirt, black tie, and highly polished dress shoes. In his right hand, he held a thickly carved wooden cane. The pickup parked behind him had a sign on the door, Hawke Construction.

"Waiting for me?" Debbie rode closer. "I'm Debbie Ramsey. What can I do for you?"

"Bree Hawke sent me." The man turned slightly and picked up a black fedora off the hood of the truck. "I'm Jeff Ransom, the manager of Hawke Construction. She said I needed to come give you a bid on the other three boundary fences. We already did the one between your place and the guest ranch next door."

"Doesn't her older brother own the company?" Debbie petted Hobby's neck. "Won't he have concerns if you offer to do work here?"

"He's the one who has to deal with his sisters and his wife. Since I'm married to Durango's youngest sister, Amie, one might call this a family affair and she's already laid down the law." Shasta trotted forward to sniff at him, and Ransom bent to pet the half-grown dog. "I do what the women tell me. It goes along with 'if momma ain't happy, nobody is' and there's enough drama at the company and Nighthawke Security. I don't need more."

"Who does?" Debbie felt a smile trickle into life and surrendered to her amusement. She laughed. "Do you have a map of the acreage? Or shall we drive around the place?"

"No reason not to do both."

Araceli came out of the third barn and headed in their direction. Debbie swung out of the saddle and handed the reins to her niece. "Will you look after Hobby for me, please? I have a business meeting with Mr. Ransom."

"Works for us. Vangie put chicken potpies in the oven for dinner. We can eat when you finish."

"And that definitely works for me." Debbie hugged the teen. "I appreciate you girls picking up the slack."

"Mindy texted me and suggested it because she's determined to make you show up every week for the veterans' group. She said today was heavy-duty and you'd need us to do for you what you do for us, 'cause good relationships should be reciprocal."

"That woman." Debbie gestured toward the house. "My computer's in the den, Ransom. Let's go look at some pictures of the ranch."

"I'll grab the maps from the truck."

By late Thursday afternoon, he'd talked to the realtor in California, Bree Hawke recommended. They'd agreed on a price for the five bedroom, three-bath colonial-style house in Sacramento. Rex had filled out the paperwork, and then returned the agreements to the real estate office as well as sending copies to Bree in Lake Maynard. He'd also contacted Lupe Gonzales and brought her up to speed. She'd agreed to put Averill's belongings in storage.

Anything worth shipping to Washington State would be sent to Miracle Riding Stable or to the boys in Pullman. Everything else would be donated to charity. In addition, Lupe would have a cleaning service take care of the inside of the large house while her husband, Pedro looked after the lawns and garage. Once everything was squared away for Rex, they'd organize their belongings and move to Baker City. Pedro had been hired by Hawke Construction. Lupe said the wages and benefits were better than those of his previous employer.

Rex called Rory and apologized again, then told him to expect the household goods from California. His oldest son promised to touch base with Lupe and let her know what he and his brothers wanted, so the communication lines were open once more. All in all, it'd been a productive day, Rex thought as he drove to the hospital.

It only took a few minutes to clear security and then head for the lounge the recuperating soldiers preferred. Waco Hawke sat in his favorite chair, attention on the large-screen television and Tiffany Roberts reciting the afternoon news. The other five men gathered around a table playing poker with Bree Hawke who appeared to be winning, judging by the large pile of corn chips in front of her.

Rex glanced at Waco. "When did she get here?"

"Two hours ago. Said something about her partner having a real-estate dinner to attend, so Bree opted to come harass us."

"Have you had a chance to talk to her?"

Waco shook his head. "Nope, but Jackson said he'd haul everybody off for dinner at 1800 hours and then she's all mine. Bree said it worked for her."

"Sounds good." Rex glanced across the room and met the attorney's eyes. "I'll wait my turn."

Bree Hawke grinned at him. "This morning when I filed it at the courthouse in Lake Maynard, I also sent off copies of that paperwork to the lawyer in Texas who handled your divorce. Now he's aware of the upcoming change in custody of your daughters, Major Sinclair. Your ex-wife will be served in Hawaii. Then I was free to come take all these guys' snacks."

"Let me know if I need to hit the vending machines to get you more ammo," Rex said. Laughing, he sauntered toward a vacant recliner.

As usual, Debbie headed for the porch swing after the girls called it a night. The weather hadn't changed from summer to the fall rainy season yet. She still caught the occasional whiff of wildfire smoke in the air. Shasta sighed and stretched out next to her, and Debbie petted the young dog. It'd been a busy day. The reasonable bid Jeff provided for the new fences was do-able and she'd paid a deposit so he could have Nighthawke Construction start soon.

He'd agreed to add highway gates at the entrance of the farm. In addition, he'd promised to return and inspect the house provided for the new ranch-hand. Debbie said it needed to be ready for occupation by the middle of October when the Gonzales family arrived from California.

Pedro would only be working part-time for her since he had a full-time job at Hawke Construction. After she finished the conversation with Jeff Ransom, she headed inside to remove the potpies from the oven before they were ruined.

Over dinner, the girls told her all about school and their plans for the weekend. Vangie wanted to attend the Friday night high school football game if she gave permission. Vangie explained she could go with Naveah and Chantrea. Their parents would provide transportation to and from the game. Meantime, Penny had been invited to spend the night with Sophie and Samantha, the twins who lived at the dude ranch. Their mother would call the next day to make final arrangements. Araceli wanted to go to dinner and a movie with a classmate who turned out to be the younger sister of Trina, the trail instructor.

Debbie agreed to all of the plans, which earned a big hug from Penny who promptly shared that she hardly ever attended sleepovers in California and Vangie was only able to go to high school activities if one of her older brothers was available to babysit. That didn't come as much of a surprise, and Debbie decided to share the info with Rex the next time they talked.

When it was her turn to choose a subject, she shared the truth about her original name and the fact Dray MacGillicudy was her biological son. Once again, she kept his father a secret. By the expression on her face, Araceli obviously suspected there was more to the story, but she didn't reveal her thoughts at the supper table.

Penny asked where Debbie found her new name and Vangie wanted to know if her father had been trusted with the secret. She looked relieved when Debbie admitted he knew all about her past. It was why he wanted them to rescue Araceli from the cult in Montana. The vibration of the phone in her pocket interrupted Debbie's musings. She switched it to the video-chat option and smiled at Rex. "How are you tonight?"

"Muddling through. Bree Hawke came to see her brother today and it opened the door for the rest of the guys to agree to invite their families to visit."

"Awesome." Debbie reached for the glass of wine on the porch rail. "I met my son today."

"How did that go?"

"Good. He's decent and more than I expected." She described the meeting at the veteran's center. "I want to introduce you to him and his mother this weekend."

"I know his mother."

"No, you don't. You know me, but I didn't raise him. Linda MacGillicudy did. He's a credit to her. Pop, the guy who owns the town café is Dray's grandfather. He stepped up after Linda's ex-husband walked away."

"Did Dray ask about his biological father or your family?"

"Sort of, but I finessed the situation by telling him I escaped from a cult, and I wanted to protect him from them. That's the story he hears for the duration."

"Sounds fair." Rex narrowed his golden-brown eyes. "You don't look as stressed as you did last night. I'm glad."

"Me too."

While the conversation continued, she brought him up to speed on the new fences, plans for the update to the house for Lupe's family, and what the girls intended to do Friday night.

"Sounds like we could have a grown-up date, Ramsey. Do you want to meet me in Lake Maynard? We'll do dinner and dancing."

"Let's save that for Saturday night and we'll celebrate my birthday a couple days early. Instead, I'll call in an order to Petrocelli's and you can pick up some pasta on the way here tomorrow afternoon. We'll have a romantic dinner and privacy so I can jump your bones."

He laughed. "I'm up for that."

"I knew you would be."

CHAPTER TWENTY-SEVEN

Friday morning, Debbie held her usual staff meeting with Trina and Kyra where they discussed the upcoming horseshow as well as ongoing business concerns and what they expected to do at the stable over the next week.

Kyra would announce details of the show to her regular students so they could sign up for the event, and Trina would share the news with the weekday riders. If they paid at registration, they'd receive a discount on their class fees. If they opted to pay the week before the show, it'd cost more. Because they intended to limit the number of participants, it meant some people might miss out on the event.

Trina was a certified 4-H judge, which meant she'd be able to judge the obstacle course and western games. It'd not only bring in more money but would be a popular attraction for riders who preferred those contests to equitation competitions.

"I think this event will be a winner." Debbie glanced at the other two women. "Okay, if we're going to open on Sundays and Mondays, we'll need two part-time instructors. Do you know anyone who might be interested?"

"That will be too hard on the horses." A frown creased Kyra's forehead and she narrowed her gray eyes. "We switch things up in the summer when we're open six days a week."

"We give the older, more dependable horses Saturday off if they've done camp sessions from June to August," Trina agreed. "Can't we just do what Miracle Riding Stable has always done? Close on Sundays and Mondays? I agree it'd be good to have someone part-time who could do the feeding, watering and mucking chores and it'd be easier to hire a barn manager than another instructor. It'd give us two full days off and I'd love that."

Kyra nodded. "We've always stressed safety over high-speed riding. It prevents accidents and broken bones for the riders as well as injuries to the horses. That not only saves on vet bills but limits the number of times we need the massage therapist and equine chiropractor, plus we don't have the liability insurance claims. It's too high a standard for many instructors."

Debbie leaned back in her chair. She tapped a pen on the desk thoughtfully. "Jason asked me for more hours last Saturday. Do you think he'd be willing to come in to do chores on Sunday and Monday afternoons? He can't do mornings because he's in school. He knows how we do things and it'd give you two some much needed time off."

"That could work." Kyra looked at Trina. "What about your sister? Jassy was saying she needed another job since she isn't getting that many hours over at the dude ranch. Cat and Rob won't open for guests until next spring. Maybe—"

"I'll call and check her availability. She's only at Pop's Café on Friday and Saturday nights right now because his business slows down in the fall. She might like two mornings a week."

Their discussion continued for another half-hour until the first students arrived for Kyra's "Mommy or Daddy or Grandma or Grandpa and Me", classes. She went off with a contingent of munchkins who were excited about brushing and saddling their ponies prior to riding them.

The older instructor always insisted on parents or grandparents being ready and willing to help the children with everything from feeding carrots to cleaning hooves to eventually assisting the kiddoes with independent riding and amazingly it didn't diminish how many customers signed up for the classes.

Trina met her group of college riders and took them off to the barns. They'd prep the horses and have a warm-up lesson in the outdoor arena before they headed for the trails. Debbie told Trina she'd exercise the dog and then meet them in the ring after she saddled up Hobby. She tried to tell herself it was work, but the opportunity to ride her beloved mare with like-minded people who loved horses as much as she did was pure enjoyment. Plus, she got to wear her cowgirl boots rather than her combat ones.

The rest of the day flew by and before she knew it, the small, bright yellow school bus from Baker City was pulling up in front of the house.

Penny and Araceli waved, and Debbie went to meet them. "What's the plan, ladies?"

"I'm going to ride Sagedust in the gaming class before I help with chores," Araceli said. "After that, Trina and I are cleaning up and going to get her sister."

"Sounds like a good plan. See me to get money for dinner and the movie." Debbie turned her attention to Penny. "What about you? I talked to Cat O'Leary-McTavish today and she told me either she or her husband, Rob, will pick you up in an hour."

"I need to get ready." Penny dashed toward the house.

Araceli and Debbie followed her. "What do you think? Is this place working for you, Celi?"

"Definitely!" Araceli hugged Debbie. "Best home ever since I lost my mom. Mindy asked if Dad missed her too and that made me remember how he and my aunt cried at the funeral."

"It sounds like he was devastated by her loss." Debbie wrapped an arm around the young girl's shoulders. "I know you were too."

"Yeah, Dad got so mad when my grandfather and his wives kept introducing women from the church to him. He told me none of them were like my mom and he wasn't taking second-best. I understood, but the rest of the Taggarts didn't."

"No surprise there," Debbie said. "Saucers have more depth."

An hour later, she started back to the barn to unsaddle horses and help with evening chores. She paused in the front yard when Cat arrived. The redhead popped out of a classic Mustang with a friendly wave. Debbie smiled at her. "Hey, where's the kiddoes?"

"I escaped while Claire was napping, and the twins decided if they did barn chores with Jassy before she left, they could play with Penny when she arrived. Rob promised to 'daddy up' and mind our kids and the ranch, so I'd have a few minutes of 'me' time."

"Sounds like you have a wonderful husband."

"He claims he's the lucky one." Cat strolled toward her. "Gotta love a guy who knows how to make me feel like I'm special. So, how are you and Moises doing?" She nodded toward the porch and then grinned mischievously. "Has he been behaving himself and following the Baker City rules for haunts?"

Debbie blinked, remembering the woman's previous visit when she announced there was a ghost in the house. "Considering I forget he's supposedly here most of the time, I'd say we're fine. He doesn't bang around the place or leave the t.v. on like Heather said her haunt did or—"

"Or turn the lights on and off in the house at all hours of the day or night, turn the stereo on full blast, slam doors, interrupt when you're working horses, take them out for rides, or add items to the shopping list you're sending to Summer at the feedstore?"

"That's somebody who doesn't have much fetching up," Moises informed the women, even though only Cat O'Leary saw and heard him. "I haven't seen my momma or gramma around here, but they'd smack me upside the head if I embarrassed them like that."

"I'll let you tell Rob about his manners next time you come to the dude ranch." Cat laughed. "He did all that and more when he was in your combat boots," she told Moises.

"I don't get it." Moises blinked. "He's alive."

"Now," Cat said, glancing at Debbie. "Sorry. When the dead start talking to me, I sometimes forget to include the living in the conversation. I've only been an active medium for a year."

"How is that possible?" Debbie stared at the other woman. "Wouldn't you have that talent all the time unless something traumatic caused it to appear?"

"My parents encouraged me to block my talent when I was a kid. My dad threatened me whenever I talked to people, he couldn't see. I didn't *recall* I had the *O'Leary Gift* until I won Cedar Creek Guest Ranch in a contest and moved to Baker City last fall. Rob was already here and dealing with his hijinks brought us together. I remembered who and what I was."

"But your daughters act like having these psychic talents is perfectly normal."

"For them it is." Cat's attention returned to Moises. "I gave your message to Heather McElroy, and she passed on the 411 to her husband. He's arranged protection for his sister so she can go forward with building that case you were worried about."

"What case?" Debbie asked. "She's helping my husband have full custody of his daughters. Is it that one?"

"No. She's forwarding evidence of a ring of child molesters to the county prosecutors. Ben Griffin is working with her. He's not afraid of the high-powered muckety-mucks who think they're above the law and have the right to molest children."

The slamming of the front door drew Debbie's attention, and she spotted Penny racing toward them. "Okay, I'll keep my husband in the loop, too. I know he'll want Bree Hawke to remain safe especially since she is also helping him with some soldiers assigned to him."

"I'm going to check in on them tonight," Moises said. "I haven't had the guts to travel that far before."

"You're an Army Ranger," Cat told him. "Rob tells me there's nothing Rangers can't handle. He should know. He was one back in the day. Try it and see. Use the 'thought travel' I taught you and if you need help, just call my name. I'll get the message."

"Sergeant Hawke blamed himself when the *jefe* of the cartel killed me, but it wasn't his fault," Moises said. "He should have left me to die in the jungle when they shot me, but he wouldn't."

"Rob tells me Army Rangers don't leave their comrades behind," Cat said gently.

The conversation ceased as Penny joined them and Debbie promised either she or Rex would pick up the little girl the next morning. One more hug and the chattering nine-year-old left with Cat O'Leary-McTavish. By seven that night, Debbie was alone in the house. Well, not really, she thought, as she fed the dog and cats. She simply didn't have any human company yet.

Kyra had left for a date in Baker City, ostensibly with Nick MacGillicudy. Debbie hoped her former horse-shoer showed up and acted decently. The last thing she wanted was drama on a busy Saturday when she needed her senior instructor doing her best with the kids, tweens and teens prepping for the show in October.

Shasta yipped and raced toward the front door. Debbie followed. She opened the door in time to see Rex climbing the steps. "Hey, handsome."

"I'll bet you say that to all your husbands." He chuckled and came closer. "Are the kids gone?"

"Everybody is." She kissed him. "Come inside."

He did, carrying the take-out bag toward the kitchen. "So, we're alone at last."

"Yes." She took the food from him, put it in one of the double ovens, so she didn't have to trust Shasta to leave it alone. Grasping Rex's hand, Debbie pulled him in the direction of the stairs. "Let's go. We'll have company by 2300 hours."

He grinned. "I can take orders as well as give them."

"I'll keep that in mind when we reach the bedroom."

"Fair enough, Ramsey. Fair enough."

When they reached the bedroom, he closed the door. She trembled when he crossed to her, laced her arms around his neck. "I've missed you."

"These last three days felt like forever." He lowered his head and their lips met.

Several kisses later, she peeled off her T-shirt, dropping it on the carpet. "Your turn. Lose the uniform, Major."

He chuckled and followed directions. "You got it, Sarge."

She slowly ran her hands over the mat of hair on his wide chest and teased the hard buttons of his nipples.

He unhooked the front clasp of her bra, and it landed on the floor.

She caught her breath when he explored her breast with his mouth. He drew on her nipple, sucked gently, then harder. She gasped when he cupped the other breast and tormented the nipple with his thumb. She kissed the side of his neck, nipped his ear. "Keep going."

"I will." He guided her in the direction of the king-size bed. "I've barely started."

Between kisses, they lost the rest of their clothes, tumbling onto the bed. He reached for her again and she pressed close to him. She turned her head and their mouths met, clung. Her tongue enticed his into a passionate duel. One long kiss faded into the next.

She shuddered when his hand covered the curls between her legs. One finger slipped inside her, followed by a second. She gasped when his thumb found the small nubbin, moaned when he rubbed it gently and he kissed her, swallowing her cries as he pleasured her.

His hand moved against her, skilled fingers starting a new pattern as they slid in and out of her. She pressed ever closer, nails digging into his shoulders. Why was he so calm when she caught fire at his touch? He continued the rhythm with his hand, and her excitement built. She moaned before catching his lips with hers. "Please, Rex. Please."

He smiled, his lips trailing toward her breast. "I can't wait until I have my mouth on you."

"Neither can I."

He shifted and started the pattern with his hand again, sliding his fingers in and out of her while his thumb rocked into the small bud. He covered her breasts with long, slow kisses. She arched upward as he sucked on one nipple and then the other. Her hips ground back and forth against his hand while he moved his fingers. She heard herself moaning, gasping, crying out his name as he continued tormenting her on a journey to the stars, becoming part of the universe until she exploded in a million pieces.

When she returned to sanity, she found him lying beside her waiting. He kissed her forehead, her eyebrows and then their lips met in a long, slow kiss. She nibbled her way down his neck, nipped at his ears, and he groaned. Kisses interspersed with soft touches as she caressed his chest, their legs tangling together.

"My turn." He slid down in the bed. He cupped her bottom and brushed his lips up one thigh, then the other.

She wasn't sure when he got her legs over his shoulders, but she gasped when his mouth claimed her. His tongue delved deep, two, or was it three strokes? His lips sought a certain spot, and he tugged on the nub of flesh. He lapped at her with his tongue before he settled in. She bucked against him, pushing up into the kiss and his mouth. Her hips writhed and she matched the pattern he set. How could she resist him? She exploded in delight.

"Let's finish this." She gaped at him when he shook his head. "No? Why not?"

"I want to kiss you again." He lowered his head and licked the small bit of flesh.

She moaned as his mouth found her. His tongue drove into her. She found herself rising, falling, meeting each movement of his tongue. When she returned from the whirlpool of madness, she looked at him, staring into his face. He was still between her legs.

She struggled to breathe normally. "Not again."

His smile widened. "Yes. I haven't had enough of you yet."

She arched against his mouth as he started again. Thought fled as he licked, sucked, and finally took her with his tongue. When she opened her eyes a lifetime later, he lay next to her, stroking her hair. She let her fingers stray over his broad chest, teasing the hard buttons of his nipples.

She leaned forward and nibbled her way down his neck, nipped at his ears and he groaned. Kisses interspersed with soft touches as she explored his chest. When she turned and picked up the condom from the night-stand, he took it to sheathe himself.

He parted her legs with one hard thigh.

She felt him probe with his body this time, and he eased slowly inside her. He shifted, pushed deeper, gripping her hips. She rose, fell against him.

He moved under her, guiding her through a series of long, leisurely strokes. He kissed her as they moved together. Soon, he changed the pattern of his thrusts. His pace increased and so did hers until she reached the heights. He was still hard, buried inside her. He began to move again. She met him, motion for motion.

They ascended, higher and higher. Each thrust took them further and further. She could only go with him. He smiled, drawing her closer, and his lips claimed hers. His tongue plunged into her mouth as he drove her past the stars. Their hips met, clashed, and they achieved fulfillment in an explosive moment.

She lay on top of him, meeting his golden-brown gaze. She gazed at his rough-hewn features, edging the strong cheekbones and once upon a time, the broken nose. She brushed her lips over his. "Do we have time to do it again?"

"Definitely." He kissed her. "Then we'll hit the shower and I'll have you again, Mrs. Sinclair."

"Promises. Promises."

CHAPTER TWENTY-EIGHT

Still wearing camouflage fatigues and combat boots, he drove up the long, curving driveway to the huge lodge style house on Saturday morning. With seven wives and twenty plus children all living together, it was little wonder his father needed a place with thirty bedrooms and a dozen bathrooms, West thought. He eyed the county sheriff's rigs parked alongside several others, ranging from cars to SUVs to pickups that belonged to the family. Interesting, he decided. He stopped nearby, careful not to block any of the other vehicles with his truck.

He'd no sooner exited the rig and locked it than a solid-looking older man in a dark uniform approached. "I'm the newly appointed interim sheriff. Hank Sanders."

West waited. "Good morning. What's happening?"

"Bad news, I'm afraid." Sanders eyed him. "Are you a member of the family?"

West nodded. "I'm West Taggart, one of Elder Taggart's sons. Is my father okay? My mother? The other wives? The kids?"

"Which one of his wives is your mother?"

"Rhododendron. She's number five." West folded his arms and waited a moment. "Is she all right?"

"She's fine. So is your dad."

West heaved a deep breath. "And the kids? The rest of the moms?"

"Okay. Your brother, Kenan and his friends went hunting—."

"Really?" West rested a hand on his truck. "Is that what they call it?"

"What would you?"

"After twenty-plus years in the Army, I don't drink and shoot." West shrugged. "If I recall, most Friday nights, Kenan and his buddies always load up on booze and head for the hunting cabin on the other end of the ranch. Dad doesn't allow alcohol in his house. It's against his religion."

"Good to know." Sanders nodded. "So, you're home on leave?"

"No, I'm here to meet Elder Barnabas who said he'd help me collect my daughter's things. I had to get special permission from my CO to travel this far from Washington State. I have to be back at the base by 0600 hours Monday."

"Some of the other law enforcement officers are talking to the kids. Which one is yours? I'll have them move her up the list."

"She's not here." West folded his arms. "She's safe from the cult's machinations."

"What cult?"

"The one here." West met the other man's gaze. "Since the old men pass the girls around as soon as they reach puberty, my kid ran away. She had the Red Cross contact me in Afghanistan."

Sheriff Sanders stiffened. "This is news to me."

"Shouldn't be. Araceli said she went to the cops and neighbors begging for help. They returned her to my dad several times, and he beat her for going to the law." West glanced toward the house and saw the door opening. A woman in a long dress, silver hair piled in a bun, peered out from the porch and he recognized his father's first wife. Before she joined them, he added. "If I'd known they'd lay hands on my daughter, I wouldn't have sent Celi here after her mother died. When I was growing up, they never hit us. At least, not the boys."

"Things change." The words made a mark on the law enforcement officer's face as he obviously compartmentalized his feelings. All expression faded when the man asked, "Will your daughter make a statement?"

"No, her counselor and I won't let her. We're having a hard enough time regaining her trust. Read the reports your deputies filed if they didn't just throw them out." West nodded to the woman as she neared. "Aspen, Sheriff Sanders told me there was a problem. He didn't say what."

"It's a tragedy, not a problem, West." She glared at the officer. "Kenan and his friends were at the cabin last night. They heard a ruckus and two of them went outside to see what bothered the cattle. They shot each other. Both of them died."

"What?" West stared at her. "I'm sorry. That's terrible. Who else was involved?"

Aspen Taggart looked at the truck before she answered. "Didn't you bring Araceli with you?"

"Of course not. She's safe."

"We expected you last night." Aspen narrowed her brown eyes. "Did you have car trouble?"

"Pulled off and slept in a rest stop. I've told you, and Father, and the other wives before. Sending a woman or one of my half-sisters who is barely legal to climb into my bed is totally inappropriate."

That earned him one of her fierce glares before she snapped. "Nobody sent them."

"You'll go to your hell for lying." West recognized an ancient pickup coming up the drive. He walked away, ready to meet the driver. Behind him, he heard the sheriff start to interrogate Aspen Taggart and suppressed a smile.

His grandmother had always chided him for what she referred to as 'stirring the pot to make it boil', but as the saying went, 'revenge was a dish best served cold' and after what the people here did to his sister and attempted to do to his daughter, he had a lot of debts to repay. He'd started the previous night and that wasn't a story he planned to share with anyone, not even Rex Sinclair who'd set the plot in motion.

Elder Barnabas, a gray-haired, wiry farmer in overalls and boots climbed out of the battered Ford. He held out his hand to shake West's. "Good to see you, son. Sorry about the circumstances."

"I barely know anything," West lied. "Do you?"

"Only what your father shared before he called the sheriff and his folks. The crime scene experts are still at the cabin. I ran into one of their road-blocks. Did you come the other way from town?"

"Left the base at oh-dark-thirty yesterday morning and I'm heading out ASAP. I can't be late to report on Monday."

"Makes sense. Let's see what we can do."

It took much longer to collect the three boxes taken away from Araceli than West had anticipated. The cops needed to go through them and ask questions about what he knew of his half-brother and the other man's companions.

West played the part of the prodigal, law-abiding son who had nothing to hide. It made the situation worse for his father because the new sheriff wasn't thrilled about having to deal with a polygamous community enmeshed in a tragic accident and now a forthcoming scandal.

It made fewer points with the Taggart clan when Sanders insisted on bringing in social workers to interview the minor children. When the officer asked why Elder Barnabas was there, West reluctantly admitted he'd sought assistance from the bishop and elders because 'family was family' and he didn't want to expose his relatives to the media if it wasn't necessary. That created even more of a stir.

It roused Kenan Taggart's anger and the dark-haired, rangy man in cowboy garb stormed after West when he carried the last box to the truck. "Can't you just keep your mouth shut?"

"I don't have anything to hide." West put the carton on the hood of his rig and turned to look at the man who was three years younger. At nearly forty, Kenan Taggart shared much of their father's physical characteristics, including the bright blue eyes. "Do you, Kenan?"

"Like what?"

"Our sister, Sweet. What really happened to her?"

"The little snot was your sister, not mine." Kenan sneered. "Not really. Rhodi is just another of our father's sluts. My mother is his only legal wife."

West throttled down the rage that rose inside him. "If you have issues with our dad, raise them with him. My mother has stood by him forty-two years. She deserves respect."

"Not from me."

Curling his hands into fists, West counted silently to ten. "And my little sister? Where is Sweet?"

"Who knows? Who cares? Jabez Levitt was the one who wanted her, and she spit in his face. He was the one who took her and then gave her to his other friends."

"Bishop Levitt's son? Your best buddy for more than thirty years?" West glanced at the house. "Is he coming today?"

"No, but we'll meet you at the tavern in town tonight unless you plan to bring your media pals or the cops." One last sneer before Kenan stomped away. "If you have the guts—"

"I'll be there," West called, "but I don't promise to keep my mouth shut."

"Well, we'll close it for you then."

You and your friends can try, West thought, *but don't count on it.*

Late that night, he lay prone in the rocks, waiting and watching. He knew what his brother was driving. He'd left the three men, Kenan, Jabez

Levitt and Micah Vermont drinking in the bar. Half drunk, the two of them admitted they'd raped his little sister while Kenan held her down.

West hadn't finished one bottle of beer barely managing to control his nausea. He'd claimed he had a long drive ahead. He did, but it'd wait until he finished his business.

Out in the dark parking lot, he'd slashed the brake line on Kenan's truck, not quite all the way through, but close enough for government work. The bar closed at midnight, a half hour ago, so the three of them should be headed home soon.

Headlights dipped, then rose again as a truck approached. West picked up his rifle, peered through the scope. He recognized his half-brother's rig. He saw shapes of three men inside. Almost time.

Kenan drove well above the speed limit, fishtailing into both lanes as he navigated the 'S' curves of the highway. He hit the brakes right before the sharpest one. The truck skidded and slammed into the guardrail. The heavy pickup broke through the rails. It rolled, tumbling over the rocks and down the steep cliffside.

West adjusted the rifle, aimed for the gas tank, and fired. A regular bullet wouldn't affect the reinforced steel, but the two tracer rounds he used were made for this. The first one hit the target. The second was for insurance. The truck exploded into a huge fireball. Nobody escaped.

"Better than Hollywood." West crawled back from his position and checked to be sure he left nothing to show any sign he'd been there. He stood, slung the rifle strap over one shoulder, and headed across country to where he'd hidden his own pickup.

Time to rock and roll. He had a long drive ahead of him. He'd make up time on the road, so if anyone asked, he'd be where he was supposed to be when he was scheduled to be there.

As usual, Saturday was busy at Miracle Riding Stable with trail rides, lessons, riding clubs and pony rides. It didn't surprise Debbie when Rex jumped in to help wherever help was needed, the same way he had when they worked together on the army base. He saddled horses, walked ponies, helped with barn tours and with chores at the end of the day. It meant she wasn't exhausted when she headed upstairs to shower and change for their date.

After almost eighteen years in the military, she didn't have a lot of civilian clothes to choose from, so she opted for an electric blue, sheath midi-dress that matched her eyes. It featured three-quarter sleeves, a V-neckline, and a wrap-style design at the front. She finished off the outfit with thigh-high stockings and blue spike heels. She was the first one downstairs while he finished getting ready.

Debbie discovered Vangie and the younger girls putting a meal together. The three of them still wore the jeans and T-shirts they had all day but had washed up before they started cooking. "Are you sure you're okay staying home alone?"

"That depends." Penny continued setting the kitchen table. "Are you guys going to Hawaii until Christmas?"

"No way." Debbie smiled. "Okay, you win. We'll probably be back before midnight. You have our cell phone numbers and if you need us, call."

"Trina and Kyra are in their apartment at the indoor arena." Araceli carried over individual salad bowls. "We can call them on their cell phones and if they don't answer, one of us can run over and get them if we have an emergency."

"We have a plan." Vangie opened the oven and removed a cheese-covered chicken, rice, and broccoli casserole. "We're good, Ramsey, and now we can watch one of our teen 'angst' movies without you whining."

"I resemble that remark." Debbie laughed, then turned when she heard footsteps on the stairs. Rex wore a nice pair of brown pants with a matching blazer, paired with a long-sleeved white shirt and leather belt. He'd always looked amazing in his dress uniform, but she silently admitted he was still a hunk in civvies. "Wow, I'm impressed."

"Me too."

She felt warmth rising in her face when his gaze swept over her. "Shall we hit the road, Sinclair?"

"If we must." He cupped her elbow, guided her in the direction of the front door, and whispered, "If we didn't have an audience, I'd take you back upstairs and see how long it took me to get you out of that dress."

"Later." Debbie murmured. "Right now, I want that birthday steak dinner you promised."

On Sunday, Rex helped with chores and cooked breakfast while Debbie slept late. Last night or rather early this morning, she'd told him that dinner, dancing and jumping his bones made it one of the best birthdays she'd ever had. He certainly agreed. When they finished eating, Araceli volunteered to clean up the kitchen while Penny and Vangie changed from their barn clothes for church.

"Aren't you joining them?" Rex eyed the dark-haired teen who looked so much like her aunt. "I've got this under control."

"I don't do church anymore." Araceli rinsed glasses and continued loading the dishwasher. "I stay home with Aunt Debbie, and we meet Vangie and Penny at the café for lunch."

"Sounds like a winner." Rex glanced toward the staircase at the sound of puppy feet and then footsteps. He collected a mug from the cupboard and filled it with coffee, smiling at Debbie when she entered the room.

"Thanks." She took the cup and followed Shasta to the back door, letting the half-grown dog into the yard to do a morning potty run. "So, what's the plan for today?"

"Major Sinclair made French toast for breakfast. There's more batter. I can make some for you. Vangie and Penny are going to church with Kyra and Trina." Araceli tucked silverware into the basket in the dishwasher. "After you eat, let's go riding before we head into Baker City."

"Works for me." Debbie went into the pantry and came back with Shasta's dish. "Let me feed her while you wait on me. I'm loving it. Is this one of those birthdays that's going to last a week?"

Araceli giggled. "Definitely."

Cruising the trails on horseback took the rest of the morning. When they arrived in Baker City, Rex dropped Debbie and Araceli at the café, claiming he needed to find a parking space. That earned him a suspicious gaze from the teenager, but Debbie accepted the words at face value.

Luckily, the town bakery was open for business so he could order her favorite old-fashioned carrot cake with cream cheese frosting. Twila Garvey promised to have Linda MacGillicudy deliver it on Wednesday, which was Debbie's actual 35th birthday.

He arrived at the café before Vangie and Penny did and slid into the booth across from Debbie so he could enjoy gazing at her. Electric blue eyes, winged black eyebrows, long black eyelashes and her forehead knit in thought as she studied the menu. A blue shirt advertising Miracle Riding Stable hugged her breasts. Yes, she looked the same each time they came here, but it never grew old.

A brown-haired, sturdy woman in jeans and a flowered shirt paused by their booth as she tied the strings on a bib-style apron. "Hi, Debbie. I think this is getting to be a Sunday tradition."

"And so are your wonderful burgers." Debbie gestured toward Rex. "Linda, I don't think you've met my husband, Rex Sinclair. Rex, this is Linda MacGillicudy, Dray's mother. Araceli met him last time you were cleaning the house, but I don't know if you two were introduced."

"No, we weren't." Araceli flashed a charming smile. "Penny and I had to get to the barn so we wouldn't be late for our lesson and have to muck stalls instead of riding."

"That makes perfect sense." Linda narrowed brown eyes, her gaze sweeping over the girl in jeans and a bright blue shirt that matched her aunt's. "Dray's right. You do look a lot like Debbie when she was your age."

CHAPTER TWENTY-NINE

As they enjoyed old-fashioned milkshakes and waited for their burgers at the café, Debbie noticed Dray MacGillicudy bussing tables and chatting with different customers who'd come to the restaurant after church. When he drew close to their booth, she took a deep breath. *Time to embrace the suck*, she told herself sternly. "Dray, do you have a minute? This is my husband, Major Rex Sinclair, Vangie and Penny's father. Rex, this is my son, Dray MacGillicudy. You already know the girls, Dray."

Dray put the tub holding dirty dishes and silverware on a nearby table, a slow smile sliding across his handsome, youthful features and landing in the bright blue eyes. "It's good to meet you, sir."

Rex stood and shook hands with the younger man. "Likewise. Ramsey is looking forward to getting to know you after all this time."

Debbie glared at the take-charge officer. "I didn't say that."

"We've been together too long for me not to understand your hopes and dreams." Rex gripped Dray's hand a moment longer. "We'll want to see you at the ranch whenever you have time. My daughter thinks you're super-hot, but she's fifteen. Jailbait. Got it?"

Ensconced in the corner of the booth beside her sister, Vangie flushed. Her cheeks burned brilliant red, and she wailed, "Dad!"

Debbie flashed her a sympathetic look. "Your father is being a stereotypical, macho jerk from Texas, honey. Get used to it. He's not going to change, but I'll help you hide the body. Okay?"

"No wonder we love you best, Ramsey," Penny said. "Celi and I will get the shovels as soon as we're home, Vangie."

Dray chuckled, stepped back, and grabbed the tub of used tableware. "Nice to meet you, Major and good luck. You'll need it now that you've pissed off all these women." Still laughing, he headed for the swinging door to the kitchen.

Rex returned to the booth and his seat beside Penny. "Don't even think about kicking me under the table, Ramsey. Things may change when they both grow up, but your boy is too old for my girl right now."

"I hate you, Dad!"

"And you've obviously mistaken me for someone who cares," Rex said, his tone low and even. "I laid out the rules before. No dating until you're sixteen and only with boys your age and only if your stepmother and I approve of them."

"You really are acting like a macho asshat." Debbie kept her voice low, glancing around at the people in the café, hoping they wouldn't talk about what they'd seen. Baker City was a small town and gossip had to be a mainstay, but so far, she'd been lucky enough not to draw attention. She tensed as Linda and Pop approached, the woman's arms and hands laden with platters of burgers, and fries. The food smelled delicious, but Debbie wasn't sure if she'd be able to eat.

Linda paused. "Okay, I've got three cheeseburgers, one chicken sandwich and a double-decker with bacon. Who gets what?"

Pop put the two baskets of onion rings in the middle of the table and refilled Debbie's and Rex's coffee cups while Linda passed around the food. His worn face wrinkled with the memory of past smiles, he grinned at her. "Linda tells me your birthday is next week. Family eats free on those days, so I want to see all of you here for dinner."

A lump rose in Debbie's throat, and she gulped back a sob. "Are you serious?"

"Of course, I am." Pop patted her shoulder. "I need another daughter and more grandchildren." He winked at Vangie. "And don't bury me beside your daddy, but I agree with him. Wait a few years before you settle for my grandson. As the old song goes, 'you better shop around'."

"I didn't say that," Rex protested.

"I know, so I am." Coffeepot in hand, Pop began to make the rounds of the restaurant, talking to the rest of his customers.

"Dad's right." Linda nodded, pulling a bottle of ketchup out of her apron. "Girls date and he hated it when I did. Used to threaten to poison my boyfriends." She paused. "Should have let him do it to my ex-husband."

Araceli giggled. "They're so nice." She passed her phone to Vangie. "Here, I found that song he was talking about. Aunt Debbie, can we really come here Thursday night?"

"I don't think it's an offer we dare refuse." Debbie reached for the ketchup. "We'll be here after horsy chores even if the major is stuck at the base."

"I'm up for it," Araceli said.

"Me too." Penny waited for her turn with the ketchup. "And we can deal with Dad being fussy about our friends. Right, Van?"

"Yeah, I guess." Vangie returned Araceli's phone. "It's different, but it's okay."

Before Rex opened his mouth and inserted the proverbial combat boot, Debbie shook her head and pointed to the huge bacon burger and side of crisp fries in front of him. "Choose a different hill, Major."

A trip to the Murphy farm to pick up fresh vegetables, cheese and meat always followed lunch. When she pulled off the highway, Debbie frowned because the gates were closed. An auburn-haired woman in jeans and a T-shirt popped out of a waiting car. Debbie recognized her as Ann Barrett, the bride from a few weeks before, who was also a noncom in Sully Murphy's Army reserve unit and Araceli's teacher.

Debbie hit the button to open her window. "What's happening? Where are the Murphys?"

"At the hospital in Lake Maynard." Ann's wide smile brightened her spring-green eyes. "Sully thought it was false labor again, but her mother-in-law, Bronwyn, decided it was probably the 'real thing' and insisted Tate take her there ASAP. I promised to hang out here and give everyone their food orders. Of course, I didn't tell Granny Murphy I was activating the phone tree."

Debbie laughed. "That makes good sense."

"What's a phone tree?" Penny asked.

"Our reserve unit uses it for contact purposes," Ann explained. "We're supposed to wait until the balloon goes up and we're headed back to combat, but after the ambush last time, I figured people would want to know about the babies. Sully promised to name one of them after our former top sergeant, Raven Barlow."

"What ambush, Ms. Barrett?" Araceli stared at her teacher. "Did you get hurt over there?"

"Not me, but Sully Murphy did, and her best friend died along with some of our other folks." Ann approached the Jeep and reached through the rear passenger window to rest a comforting hand on Araceli's shoulder. "You said your dad is headed back to Afghanistan again to catch up with his unit. You may want to visit him before he goes."

A tear slid down Araceli's face. "I'll talk to Aunt Debbie about it."

"Winner, winner, chicken dinner!" Ann gestured to Rex. "Come on, Major. After I give you this order, I can head to the hospital. Move it."

Rex opened his door. "One of these days, I'll manage to convince you and Ramsey that officers are supposed to give orders and enlisted are supposed to follow them."

"Don't hold your breath. We're experts in 'sergeants' business' and we already know who runs things," Debbie told him. "It's not you."

They weren't the first to arrive at Miracle Riding Stable. A late-model, bright green pickup was parked near the house and Debbie recognized Heather McElroy leaning against it. She chatted with a younger woman who wore similar clothes, jeans and a purple-print, western blouse, ash-blonde hair in a loose bun. Both of them turned to face the Jeep as Debbie drove closer.

Rex whistled softly. "Remind me never to question your abilities again. You do miracles, Ramsey."

"Come on, Major." Debbie smiled. "Durango Hawke's wife is part of my veterans' group, and she will introduce you to Tiffany Roberts. I wasn't sure if Heather would be able to pull this off and neither was she, so we wanted to wait until it was a *fait accompli*."

Debbie glanced over her shoulder at the girls. "Make yourselves useful and put away the food before you head to the barns to help Kyra and Trina with horsy chores. Penny, remember to walk Shasta. Don't take her with you to the stable because it's not safe for her or the humans when the horses are going to pasture."

"We're on it." Vangie was the first one out of the rig. She grabbed a carton of vegetables out of the rear compartment and headed for the house, followed by her sister and Araceli.

Heather wore faded blue-jean cut-offs, flip-flops, and a white tank top under a man's blue plaid shirt. Vibrant red hair cascaded to her waist. She carried herself like a warrior queen. She nodded at Debbie and Rex as they approached. "Tiffany and I talked. She opted to visit now instead of waiting until later. Durango has the kids and doesn't know where we are. He thinks we're headed to the hospital to see Sully and the babies."

"Has she had them?" Debbie asked.

"Not yet. We'll bring him up to speed when we get back. He'll have a freaking fit, so just know it's him, not a volcano."

"Are you concerned about that?" Rex focused on Heather first, then glanced at Tiffany Roberts. "Waco Hawke really wants to see you."

"So, I heard." Tiffany tilted her head to one side. Expertly applied cosmetics accentuated the blue-violet eyes. Despite the apparently casual clothes, she could have stepped into a television studio to report the news at any moment. "Is this an off-the-record appointment or is my camera operator allowed to accompany me?"

"Not yet." Debbie felt more than saw Rex's tension. "You'd need to go incognito and keep this on the down-low until the military is ready to announce his return."

"Really?" Tiffany sighed dramatically. "You're telling me that my old high-school boyfriend has delusions of an undying romance, and I can't share what could be a terrific 'breaking news' moment. This really bites."

"Afraid it's reality as we know it," Rex admitted. "Are you interested in seeing him or not?"

"I'm interested if I get an exclusive story out of it later."

The conversation continued with Tiffany pushing for a news story and Rex holding the line on media exposure. Nothing had been agreed to when the women left, and he eyed Debbie, obviously frustrated. "What the hell am I supposed to tell Waco Hawke? His former girlfriend will only see him if she gets to put him up for display on news at 2300 hours."

"You could always say what goes around, comes around." Debbie shrugged. "He should have stepped up when she wanted a commitment instead of running for the hills or volunteering for one covert mission after another."

"Women." Rex glared down the driveway. "This is payback because he was a jerk when he was young. For God's sake, Ramsey. It's a scientific fact his brain hadn't finished developing eight years ago. Is she still pissed about that?"

"Oh, I think she's got more emotional ammo than him being a stupid asshat." Debbie debated sharing what Heather McElroy had told her and decided against it. If Rex knew Waco had a son, the truth might slip out the next time he was on base. For now, she'd keep that particular secret. "Cat O'Leary has been visiting and talking to Moises Pride. You should ask Waco about him."

"Who is he?"

"A ghost. He says Waco was a witness when the cartel executed him."

"Wait a minute." Rex held up his hand. "I thought you insisted there weren't any dead people here. When did that change?"

"When Moises came to visit. He likes it here better than in town because it's more entertaining." Debbie shrugged again. "He doesn't do any of the things Cat talks about, turning lights on and off, or making a mess in the barns or slamming doors or leaving on the television. Apparently, Waco was able to do some dream walking before the escape. Heather says he astral projected himself into her house and didn't behave himself when he was there. You might bring that up too."

"Maybe I should be taking notes. It sounds like I haven't been getting straight intel from the fellow."

"He's a guy. What did you expect?"

"The truth." Rex frowned, concern filling his face. "Should I be worried about your dead houseguest and the girls or you?"

Debbie shook her head. "No, he's not a problem. It's like what Cat O'Leary says— we don't have to worry about dead men—it's the 'live ones' we need to watch out for!"

Debbie headed off to the boarder barn to help finish mucking stalls. Rex started to follow, but his cell phone interrupted. He pulled it out and eyed the screen recognizing West Taggart's name and number. "What's up, Sergeant-Major?"

"I'm back from Montana and I needed to know where to drop Celi's things. Not comfortable leaving them with the security folks at your place when you're not due home until tomorrow night."

"Head to the restaurant where I met you and Araceli a few weeks ago. I'll have Sergeant Nolan swing by and collect Araceli's belongings. Anything else I need to know?"

"Not at the moment." West paused. "I'm headed back to my unit in ten days. I'd like to see her before I go."

"I'll see what I can do. Having her stuff will help make amends."

"Works for me. Thanks, Major."

Rex ended the call and then contacted Gimone Nolan. She agreed to go to the nearby restaurant and meet West Taggart. That done, Rex strolled in the direction of the barns ready to jump in and muck stalls with the rest of the family.

It didn't take long to drive to the major's favorite diner off post. Gimone spotted West Taggart's large pickup with the Montana plates and parked next to it. She inspected the gleaming truck. It'd obviously been detailed outside and undoubtedly inside, scrubbed, and polished within an inch of its vehicular life. Now, why would a guy do that immediately after a lengthy road trip?

Letting the question linger in her mind, she entered the restaurant. She spotted West Taggart sitting in a booth. He stood when he saw her. She glanced over his immaculate civvies, ironed jeans and a plaid western shirt, polished boots. He'd showered and shaved before he came. Did he think this was a date?

No, he couldn't be that stupid. She crossed to the booth and sat down across from him. "What's the story, Sergeant-Major?"

Faint amusement slipped across his handsome face, landing in the brilliant blue eyes so much like her best friend's. "Why do you think there's a story, Nolan?"

"Gimone." She reached in her pocket, pulled out her smart-phone and clicked onto the Internet. She passed it to him, so he'd see the news of a horrible highway accident in Montana immediately following a tragic hunting one.

She smiled sweetly as the server arrived, armed with menus and glasses of ice water, playing to their audience. "And next time you're late, *darling*, you'd better bring my favorite flowers."

"I'll remember that." Grinning appreciatively, he handed back the phone. "It's long-stemmed red roses, right?"

"Nice try. Too clichéd. I'm the one who prefers tulips but since they bloom in April and it's September, I'll let you off with sunflowers or zinnias."

"I'll keep that in mind. Will you settle for a steak dinner instead?"

"Definitely." She accepted the menu, ordered a glass of red wine to start, and perused the selections. When they were alone, she asked, "Were you able to retrieve Celi's teddy-bear and favorite vintage rag doll?"

He nodded. "Along with everything else I could get. Did she tell you about them?"

"No, your sister did after she comforted Celi one night." Gimone saw the words make their mark on his face. He closed his eyes for a moment, but she'd seen the glimmer of quickly suppressed tears. "Come on,

Taggart. You already knew we were in contact even if I never told you about her."

Celibacy was vastly overrated, and she wouldn't tell him that she intended to get lucky after dinner, take him home with her and jump his bones. The major hadn't told her to keep her pants zipped and what he didn't know wouldn't bother him.

He reached across the table and snagged her hand. She squeezed his. "What's on your mind?"

"I'm just glad my sister has you and the major in her life to watch her six when she won't let me."

"Oh, she'll change her mind someday, and it may be sooner than either of us think if she watches the news."

CHAPTER THIRTY

Late Sunday night, they sat on the porch swing enjoying each other's company before Rex left for the army base. He'd already loaded his gear in the pickup. Like her, he preferred driving long distances when the highways were clear of most traffic. He'd opted for coffee since he'd head south soon, but she'd chosen a glass of her favorite wine.

"So, what's the plan for this week?" Rex rested an arm around her shoulders. "A wild celebration of your birthday on Wednesday?"

Debbie laughed. "No, I think we've already done pretty much everything I wanted this weekend. I'm good."

"Can't argue with that." He finished the last of the coffee and put the mug on the porch rail. "Your brother is shipping out in ten days. Is Celi going to see him before he goes?"

"I'll talk to her and Mindy about it." Debbie swirled the wine in her glass. "She should say goodbye, so she'll have fewer issues if he doesn't make it back. When does the advance party for his unit return?"

"In January." His lips brushed her cheek. "He called earlier today. He picked up the rest of Celi's things from Montana. I had Nolan meet him and take them to her place. I'll bring them up in two weeks. Are you going to see him?"

She shook her head. "Not yet." She shifted and their lips met in a quick kiss. "Maybe when he gets back. He doesn't know why I chose the Army after I graduated."

"He knows what Celi shared," Rex said, his tone low and even. "She overheard your father and the bishop discussing the choices you were offered. It shocked him, but I didn't cut the guy any slack. I told him if they were willing to marry off his daughter, why didn't he understand it happened to you first?"

Debbie tensed, shifted slightly away so she could turn to face him. "You didn't tell me that before."

"I was caught up with the logistics of getting Araceli here and then making sure your older brother understood he'd failed his kid, not the other way around. She didn't do anything wrong by running off when he was in combat and asking the Red Cross for help."

"Would you have been so understanding if it happened before your daughters turned up here? What if they'd contacted the Red Cross rather than just finding us?"

"I hope I'd have acted better than your brother, but I don't know. It really shocked me when they arrived in August. Worse was finding out my ex frequently abandoned them during the last four years. This past month has been a learning experience, Ramsey."

"For both of us." She drank the rest of her wine and put the glass next to his on the rail. "What are your plans for the week?"

"Well, I'm obviously going to have the proverbial 'come to Jesus' meeting with Waco Hawke and let him know his former girlfriend is only interested in a news story, not him. Then, I'll ask about your ghost. I want to know how to find Moises Pride's family. They deserve to know what happened to him. Once I have more details, I'll bring Maverick Jones up to speed."

Debbie nodded. "That sounds good."

The comfortable silence between them lasted a little longer. Finally, he stood and offered his hand. "Walk me to the truck?"

"Okay." She rose to her feet. "Keep me posted on what you learn about Moises. I'll pass it onto Cat O'Leary, and she can share it with him." Debbie paused. "West doesn't need to know *why* I went to boarding school—"

She stopped when Rex didn't speak, an unwelcome suspicion tormenting her mind. "You told him, didn't you?"

"He had to know, Ramsey. He could have taken Celi back or sent her there at some point."

"Damn it!" She slipped out of his light hold. "It was my choice, Sinclair, not yours! He still has a relationship with those people. He hasn't cut them out of his life, but I cut them out of mine nineteen years ago when my son was born." She glared at Rex. "Hit the road. I'm done."

He reached for her. "Ramsey, think about it. He won't tell them how to find you."

"The hell he won't. You may trust him. I don't. He left. I wrote to him when I was at boarding school. He never came. He abandoned me twenty years ago just like he abandoned his own kid."

"How do you know he got those letters? He claims the last one was about Hobby, the filly you were training."

She drew a ragged breath, stunned by the betrayal. Why wasn't he putting her first instead of supporting her worthless, older brother? Didn't she matter at all? "He's like you. The US Army comes first. And I don't want him around me or my son. I won't have any of the other Taggarts in my life either."

"Okay." He took a step closer, rested his hands on her shoulders. "That makes sense."

She wrenched free, stepped back. "Go back to the army, Sinclair. It's always been what you love best."

She stalked away, climbed the steps to the porch. When she glanced over her shoulder, she saw him standing by the truck for a few moments. Then, he climbed in the pickup and drove away. It wasn't the first time she'd watched him leave her, but it was the last.

With that thought, she collected the glass and coffee cup off the rail. She carried them inside, lingering to lock the door before she went to the kitchen.

Upstairs, a few minutes later, she headed for the shower. Under the spray, she allowed herself to cry. Dreams died hard. She'd learned that lesson years ago. Why had she ever forgotten it?

Just because he'd made a strategic withdrawal didn't mean he'd surrendered, Rex told himself as he drove through Lake Maynard, heading south toward the highway. At forty-two, he'd been up the mountain and faced more than one dragon. It'd take time for her anger and hurt to fade. She didn't bear grudges. Once she had a few days to think about it and calm down, she'd realize he always had her six. She definitely had his.

She kept my kids. She never even threatened to send the girls with me. Of course, she did tell me before she didn't think Averill and I deserved them. On the freeway, he signaled for a lane change and stepped on the accelerator. He had a long drive ahead of him. Suddenly, he remembered what his grand-mother told him when he and Averill separated, that he'd find the right person someday. "It may be more romantic to be the first love, but it's better to be the last," she'd said.

He hadn't quite believed that particular life lesson before he met Debbie Ramsey. Of course, he also hadn't been in love with her when he married her. He wanted a guarantee he wouldn't crawl back to his first wife. A lot of men wouldn't have bothered to be faithful to a stranger, but he wasn't like that. Once he gave his word, he kept it.

She was his wife, for better or worse, for good. At the moment, their situation might be a bit fraught, but she'd eventually talk to him. She always did.

When he finally parked in front of his house and switched off the ignition, he took time to text her and let her know he'd arrived safely. She didn't respond, but he hadn't expected immediate forgiveness. For now, he'd follow his grandfather's advice and be quick to try to mend fences or wounded hearts.

Monday morning started with P.T. at oh-six-hundred hours followed by a full day of work. Mid-afternoon, he was reading a stack of efficiency reports about the warehouse personnel Captain Castenanda had prepared for him. Corporal Baxter tapped on the office door. "Sir, that woman who called before is on the phone."

"Master Sergeant Ramsey?"

"No, sir. She always gives her name, but this is the one in Hawaii and she doesn't." The stocky, young man in camos waited. "Do you want me to take a message?"

Rex shook his head. "It could be about my kids. I've got it." When the phone buzzed, he picked up the receiver. "Sinclair."

"How could you?" Fury laced the high-pitched soprano voice. "How dare you sell my house?"

"It isn't yours, Averill. It's mine. You know I used my inheritance to pay off the mortgage and that is an exception to the community property laws. You had occupancy until the last child left home. Granted, it was supposed to be when Roberta graduated from high school, but you abandoned her long before that."

"And that's another thing. Why did you have your lawyer file custody papers calling me an unfit mother?"

"A woman who leaves her minor children to go to Hawaii for six months, for the last four years is unfit." Rex paused. "And refusing to allow me to see my kids when I was stateside and entitled to visitation only added more fuel to my lawyer's case."

"I never refused," Averill squawked. "You could have come to California anytime."

"Not when I was stationed elsewhere in CONUS, and you wouldn't let the kids fly to my duty stations."

Rex silently admitted it was a bit of a stretch because he hadn't forced the issue and demanded to see his children after the divorce was final, but this was the story Debbie and Bree Hawke developed. It was a good one, and he'd chosen to go along with it.

"After knowing you twenty-three years, did you think I wouldn't realize all you wanted was money? Your chickens are coming home to roost, Averill. Find another deep pocket."

"I want the girls back in California."

"As we say in the Army, 'Want in one hand, crap in the other and see which fills up first.' They're my daughters too, and they're where they choose to be."

"You haven't heard the last of this or of me."

"I better have." Rex gently replaced the receiver. He reached for his wallet, dug out the card from Bree Hawke, and called to give her a sitrep. When they spoke, the attorney said she hadn't heard from the girls' mother or her counsel. If or when Bree did, she'd be in touch.

That settled, Rex sent a quick text to Debbie. She didn't answer, but she also hadn't blocked his number, so he decided to count his blessings.

Next, he called Rory, Scott, and Cal to give them a heads-up on Ramsey's birthday. Rory told him that they'd ordered flowers, chocolate, and a huge teddy bear in camos to be delivered by Wednesday. Rex stared at the receiver in his hand. "How do you know she wants a toy like that?"

"Lupe always says people often give others what they'd love to have themselves. We checked it out with the girls. They said Ramsey doesn't have any keepsakes from her childhood. Celi told us her parents probably took them away on her thirteenth birthday. No wonder Ramsey cut them off as soon as she could."

"I'm proud of you, son. Thanks for being smarter than your old man."

Rory chuckled. "So, what are you giving her?"

"I ordered a cake and, of course, I'm sending flowers too. I'll talk to her friends and see what else she'd like, but I already have a few ideas for my rancher wife."

"Good thinking."

They talked a while longer about the classes the boys were taking and the remodeling of the house they were flipping. When he ended the call, Rex glanced at the clock. It was late enough to touch base with Vangie and learn what his daughters were doing for their stepmother's special day.

Vangie told him they were going to the hospital to see Sully and Tate Murphy's babies that night. "They have twin girls. Ramsey says Sully named one after her best friend, Raven and Tate named the other one, Reveille. We're stopping for flowers and gifts on the way. We won't be staying long since Sully isn't ready for visitors. I told Naveah and Chantrea that I'd go with them to Tate and Sully's house tomorrow to help prep for when they bring home the babies. Their brother, Lock is looking after Sully's dogs."

"Sounds fun." Rex jotted a note to call the florist in Lake Maynard again. Maybe—who knew?—there would be a vase shaped like a classic Mustang. At the end of the duty day, he walked out to the parking lot with Gimone Nolan. She opened the trunk of her Chevy Malibu so he could remove the boxes. "Any ideas what I should give Ramsey for her birthday?"

"What have you done so far?" Gimone asked. "Juana and I usually take her out for dinner. We want to visit her next weekend, but we need you to sign off so we can go to Baker City, since it's so far from the base."

"No worries. I ordered a cake and flowers. My kids are stepping up to make the day special and I called Linda MacGillicudy too."

"Who is she?"

"The woman who adopted Ramsey's son." Rex studied the tall redhead. "Did she tell you that she reconnected with him?"

"She texted us, but she's always super busy on the weekend with the stable so we haven't had time to get all the details." Gimone lifted out the next box. "We're looking forward to seeing him again."

"I didn't know you ever had."

"Debbie's grandparents pulled some strings and took us to the hospital to visit the two of them right after he was born." Gimone followed him to his pickup. "I didn't share any of that with West Taggart. Figured he didn't have a need to know."

"Then we're on the same page." Rex took the box from her and put it on the rear seat in the super-cab. "She's pissed because I told him about the attack."

"I knew you must have because Juana and I didn't." Faint amusement trickled into Gimone's face, sliding into the green eyes. "I think he remembers what his granny said."

"What's that?"

"When we were girls, she told us that some women talk too much to the guys who share their beds, and we shouldn't."

Rex stiffened. "I didn't think he'd overstep the bounds, Nolan."

"Oh, he didn't start anything inappropriate, Major. I did. I always wanted a hero and he's the first unattached one I've had." Gimone paused. "I saw the shit-storm that happened in Montana on the Internet. West didn't share any details, but I'm not stupid. Sooner or later, it's going to be on the TV news."

Rex loaded the last box. "Sergeant-Major Taggart is headed for Afghanistan soon."

"I know. This is temporary, but it doesn't mean I'm not enjoying myself." Gimone glanced at her watch. "Juana and I are meeting him for dinner tonight. He's grilling the steaks. You're welcome if you want to join us."

"Wish I could." Rex chuckled. "I have another meeting. Take care." He returned her salute and watched her walk away.

For a moment, he wondered if anyone else would analyze the occurrences in Montana over the weekend and come up with the correct answer. Then he decided the cops undoubtedly wouldn't have a clue. Like West Taggart said, 'two people could keep a secret—'" While neither of them were dead, again neither of them were talking, much less admitting the truth of what happened.

At the hospital, he parked in an empty slot, grabbed his hat, and strolled across the lot and in the side door. A short walk brought him to the secluded ward and its guard. Even though the military policemen knew him, Rex still offered his identification and waited for it to be checked. When he reached the lounge, he found the guys watching Tiffany Roberts read off the latest news.

Waco muted the sales pitches once the commercials started. "What did you learn, sir?"

"I met your high-school sweetie yesterday," Rex said. "She is only interested in a news story, not you. When I told her she couldn't bring a photojournalist along, she told me she wasn't wasting her time here. She demands a 'breaking news' feature."

"Well, that's an *embrace the suck* moment." Warrant Officer Jackson shook his head, pity on his dark features. "What do you want us to do about it, Hawke?"

Waco grinned. "Not much to do when Tiffy's got her tailfeathers in a knot. At least now she knows I'm back."

Sergeant Wilkins rocked back and forth in the chair, only his body moving. His gravelly voice trembled. "Could change her mind if you ask again, sir. Yes, she could."

"Maybe." Rex paused, eyeing the group of damaged men. "I have another question. Does anyone know someone named Moises Pride? An Army Ranger who didn't make it home with you?"

Silence fell as they looked at him and then each other. Finally, Waco said, "He's dead, Major."

"I know." Rex scanned the rest of the men who still appeared baffled. "My wife has a place in Baker City, Hawke, and the local medium says there's company in that house. Tell me about Pride. Do I need to be concerned about him?"

"Crap." Waco didn't move from his seat in the dark corner of the lounge. "If the O'Leary's involved, then my sister-in-law will be too, and she never cuts me any slack."

"Is that the woman who kicked your ass, Hawke?" Jackson asked.

Waco nodded. "Yeah. Pride was a good man. He won't raise a stink like I did."

"Tell me about him," Rex said. "We need to find his family and let them know he's not coming home."

"Could let Tiffany Roberts do a story about him, sir," Sergeant Wilkins said. "Yes, she could." He swayed forward and back, his body shaking. "Be 'breaking news' and then she'd have to visit Hawke to learn more. Yes, she would."

The comment drew everyone's attention. Rex smiled at the tormented survivor. "Brilliant idea, Wilkins. I'm glad you're here to help us brainstorm."

PART 4

AUTUMN 2019

CHAPTER THIRTY-ONE

Monday night after the girls went to bed, Debbie enjoyed her usual habit of sitting on the porch swing with Shasta as her companion. The dog lay on the deck chewing a homemade doggie cookie, courtesy of Summer O'Neill who'd dropped off a bag of them when she brought in the grain order. The moon glowed overhead, and stars twinkled in the ebony sky. Debbie caught the occasional scent of wildfire smoke on a cool breeze. Autumn rains would start in the next few weeks, a definite sign of the change in seasons.

Her phone vibrated and she pulled it out of her pocket to see Rex's number. She didn't answer. She'd read the texts he'd sent but she wasn't ready to respond. He could just hurry up and wait. When she'd been at the hospital earlier in the evening, Tate Murphy had shown her a photo of the flowers Rex ordered. He must have paid extra to have the bouquet placed in a pink Barbie Mustang toy car.

A text popped up. "Signed off for Nolan and Castenada to visit this coming weekend to celebrate your birthday. Prep a place for them."

Did he think she was stupid? She'd already planned to have Linda's crew refresh the guestroom on the third floor. What would it take for him to realize they were through? He'd crossed the line when he shared private info with her brother. She debated sending a text telling him to "F off and die," then decided against it. She wouldn't give him the satisfaction of knowing she'd lost her temper. This was justifiable anger, damn it!

Another text, this one included a picture of Sully's flowers in the bright pink car.

He'd gone the extra mile for the other sergeant and Debbie wondered if he'd seen pics of the newborn twins. She didn't have to talk to him. Not yet anyway. Maybe not ever. Taking a deep breath, she sent off photos of the sleeping infants in the hospital nursery. Tate had proudly pointed out their dark red hair, telling her that his mom, new grandma, claimed they got it from her as well as their mother.

Tate had said that between the Murphy clan, the soldiers in Sully's Army Reserve unit and her students at Baker City School, there were enough flowers to furnish a garden. They'd also provided a variety of presents for the babies and Sully. "Captain Endicott says she's collecting dinners for us to freeze on nights we don't want to cook."

"I'll sign up for that," Debbie told him, earning amused looks from Vangie, Penny and Araceli. "Okay, so I never cook when I can get out of it, but that doesn't mean I can't. I'll put a hamburger and potato puff casserole together for you. It reheats perfectly."

"It sounds good." Araceli had smiled at both of them. "If I help, will you make one for us, too?"

Debbie had shrugged and agreed. They'd admired the babies a bit longer, but she'd taken the girls and made a strategic withdrawal when Tate's in-laws arrived. Sully's mother pitched a fit because her daughter was sleeping, and the nurse refused to wake her. Tate didn't make any points when he'd said his wife had given birth early that morning and entertaining company was the last thing she needed or wanted. The only people she'd asked to stay when he went to the nursery were his parents and twin sister.

Penny waited until they were in the hospital parking lot before she asked why Mrs. Murphy was avoiding her mother. Debbie silently debated for a moment before sharing Sully's family had issues with her because of an ambush that killed several of the soldiers in her unit during her last combat tour. "Her best friend died there. So, Sully really doesn't want to see them at this time."

"That doesn't make sense," Vangie said. "It's not like she caused it, and you told us she was hurt, too. She had a broken leg when she worked for you and Dad at the warehouse."

"No, but grief hits people in different ways." Debbie waited until the girls piled into her Jeep before she suggested they stop at Petrocelli's for pizza on the way home. It provided a sufficient distraction.

Focusing on the current moment, Debbie glanced at her phone again and the steady stream of texts updating her on his day. She grimaced when she glimpsed the note describing the call from his ex-wife. What would it take to convince the other woman to leave them alone? It wasn't as if she truly wanted the girls to return. If she had, she'd have been on the first plane from Hawaii when they ran away. *They were expendable, like I've always been.*

Determined not to respond to him, she turned off her phone and called the dog. "Let's hit the sack. We have to be up in five hours."

On Tuesday, she headed for the barn after the girls left for school. She'd promised to wait and make the casserole when Araceli was home. Meantime, Debbie called Twila Garvey at the bakery and ordered a gift basket with a variety of cookies to be delivered to the house when Sully arrived home.

Twila suggested including a slice of Sully's favorite New York style cheesecake as well. Since it was baked for more than two hours, it wouldn't hurt her or the babies when she was breastfeeding. Debbie agreed, promising to stop in and pay for the order when she picked up the girls at school.

Her phone vibrated while she groomed Hobby for the morning trail ride. It was instinctive to pull it out and answer since it could be Trina or Kyra with a horsy emergency or one of the teachers from the school. "Hello. It's Debbie Ramsey."

"About time. Are you still pissed at me?"

"What do you think? Or is that question too tough for you?"

"Yup, you're still miffed."

"I'm a hell of a lot more than miffed, Major. You had no business going behind my back and sharing confidential information."

"I told you when I chewed out the guy early on, Ramsey. I haven't shared where to find you, and I won't. You didn't say to keep the names of your assailants on the down-low."

She caught her breath. "I didn't think I needed to spell out chapter and verse for you. What's wrong with you, Sinclair? I never thought you were stupid. Do you honestly believe I wanted to be humiliated in front of him?"

"Okay, slow down, Ramsey. I don't get it. What humiliation? You were the victim, not the perpetrator of a heinous act."

"Who the hell do you think you're talking to? I'm no victim! I'll be thirty-five years old tomorrow. I did five tours in the *sandbox,* and I damn well take care of myself."

"I'm not disagreeing. I get it. You're pissed off and you know it's safe to fight with me because I won't abandon or reject you. Talk to your counselor. She'll tell you the facts you don't want to hear from me. You were victimized when you were barely a teenager—"

"I'm not one now and nobody's ever putting me in that situation again. You and my brother can both rot in hell!" She ended the call and powered off the phone before Rex called back. She didn't know where they were going after this argument. It wasn't the first one they'd had, but it seemed like the most serious.

Rex grimaced and put away his cell phone. He'd count his blessings and be grateful she was talking, or rather yelling at him. It didn't mean they were back on track again and he couldn't leave the base for a week and a half. He glanced at the office doorway where Juana Castenada lingered in the opening. "What is it?"

"You wanted to go over the evaluation reports for the warehouse personnel this morning, sir. Is now still a good time, or shall I come back later?"

"Now works." He wouldn't send away a subordinate who was on time for their meeting. Avoiding his responsibilities would make him look like the asshat he sometimes felt he was. "Close the door. We ought to discuss these reports in private. Is there a reason you held off on the one for Sergeant Nolan?"

"I wasn't sure if you'd trust me to be impartial about her since we've known each other for years."

"Will it stop you from providing an unbiased opinion of her capabilities?"

Juana narrowed her dark eyes as she contemplated the question. Then she shook her head. "No, if anything, I might err the other way and be a harsher critic of her failings."

"That's fair." Rex picked up the first form. "I'd like to send her file to the next promotion board. She has enough time in grade and excellent work experience to be considered for advancement."

"She's only been here a month, and Major Bevins supervised her before. He really didn't approve of her job performance." Juana asked. "Won't that affect the outcome?"

"His emails asking to have the two of you returned to his bailiwick offsets any criticism. So will my endorsement of your evaluation. Let's move on, Captain."

Moises Pride sat in one of the Adirondack chairs on the porch that evening, watching Debbie Ramsey and the dog on the porch swing. The two cats had gone upstairs with the girls, and he missed having them cuddle on his lap. They'd undoubtedly choose his company the next day when the girls were at school, so he'd settle for that.

Debbie's phone buzzed and she pulled it out of her pocket to look at the screen. She didn't answer the incoming call. Instead, she replaced the cell phone in her pocket. He winced, feeling a sudden pity for the major. The guy was on duty. He couldn't leave the base and resolve the issue with his woman. *He must have talked when he should have listened, but ignoring him isn't going to solve your problem, Sarge.*

Not for the first time, Moises wished more than one person in Baker City had the medium's talents. Of course, he wouldn't approach her in the middle of the night, but there was always the morning. He'd go to the dude ranch then and talk to her. She'd know who to contact to help Sergeant Ramsey.

The phone hummed again. A second call went unanswered, then a third. Debbie finished her wine and stood. "Come on, Shasta. Let's call it a night."

When the pair headed into the house, Moises considered the issue. Maybe he couldn't visit the medium right now, but there wasn't a reason to keep him from going to the cocktail lounge at Pop's Café in Baker City and talking to the ghostly inhabitants. Perhaps one of the other residents would provide advice on how to help in this situation.

The next morning when Debbie went downstairs, she found Vangie making French toast while Araceli packed lunches and Penny set the table. "What's this? Usually we make breakfast together."

"It's your birthday." Vangie glanced over her shoulder, then focused on flipping the egg-soaked bread on the griddle. "How much are you going to pay us not to sing 'Happy Birthday' to you?"

"Umm, I'm not sure about that."

"Wrong answer, Ramsey," Penny said, pouring orange juice into glasses. She launched into an off-key version of the traditional song. Araceli and Vangie promptly joined in, and Shasta howled accompaniment.

Laughing, Debbie ushered the half-grown dog to the back door. Her cell phone buzzed, and she pulled it out to check the screen. When she answered, Trina wished her a happy birthday and told her the horsy chores had been completed without her.

Debbie no sooner ended that call than she had one from the three Sinclair boys at W.S.U. More good wishes, promises of presents on the way and another resounding chorus of the 'Happy Birthday' tune before they left for their classes.

Tears stung her eyes when she took a cup of coffee from Araceli. "This is rapidly becoming the best birthday ever."

"It's hardly started," Penny pointed out, looking confused. "Haven't you always celebrated it?"

"Your dad sends flowers and gift cards or presents," Debbie said. "Juana and Gimone take me out to dinner, but my family—"

"They don't do stuff for the girls because they'll be leaving to join other families in the cult as wives and mothers," Araceli explained. "Boys are treated differently because they get to stay home if they want even when they're adults for the women and girls to cater to them."

"That sucks." Vangie carried a platter over to the table. "So, now we know why you and Dad always sent us special stuff for our birthdays and we'll make sure we do the same for you. Is now a good time to tell you I want a car for my sixteenth birthday?"

"You betcha." Debbie sipped the black coffee. "Here are the rules. First, you need to complete driver's education classes. Luckily, they start in October at your high school, and we've already registered you for that. Then, you'd better talk to your dad about the kind of car you want. Better hope it won't turn out to be like Sully Murphy's."

"What does that mean?" Araceli pulled out her chair. "I don't get it."

"Naveah and Chantrea told me that Sully and her best friend got their Mustang from a junkyard and then had to totally rebuild it from scratch." Vangie passed around the French toast. "I don't know anything about engines or transmissions."

"Neither did they," Debbie said, "but they learned."

While they ate, the girls discussed cars, upcoming football games, and even the haunted town celebrations in Baker City for Halloween. It was the first Debbie had heard of the activities.

Penny explained everyone got together to create a spooky festival. "Sophie and Samantha told me all about it. Tons of people come for it even from Liberty Valley and the town uses it as a fundraiser to save money for a memorial."

"What kind of memorial?" Debbie asked.

"It's a monument to remember the people who died in the avalanches a long time ago," Araceli said. "Mrs. Barrett says when we have enough money, it will list everyone's names. We're going to start practicing our part today."

"What's your part?" Vangie finished off her orange juice. "I know everybody at Lake Maynard High is talking about it even if our school isn't totally ancient like yours."

"It will be similar to the program they did last year." Penny began to clear the table. "Samantha told me they sang the ABC and multiplication songs like little kids do. And the older girls and boys had to recite poems and speeches in front of the whole class."

"That doesn't sound too scary to me." Debbie stood and went after more coffee. "What's the big deal?"

"Some of the older kids are ghosts and so is Mrs. O'Sullivan, the teacher in charge." Araceli loaded her plate in the dishwasher. "It's going to be awesome and really creepy. Wait until you see us."

Debbie eyed the three girls. They seemed more excited than scared or concerned, so she decided to bide her time and talk to Kyra and Trina about the Halloween festivities. "What are you doing for this event, Vangie?"

"Naveah and Chantrea told me we could either sell tickets and refreshments or we could dress up as ghouls or zombies. We'd hang out with some actual ghostly loggers and a few volunteer firefighters who are still alive. We get to chase the tourists out of the graveyard, but Cat O'Leary always makes us promise not to give them heart attacks."

"So, she's involved in this activity, too?"

"She has to be, Ramsey," Vangie said. "Who else would talk to the ghosts in Baker City and arrange for them to do their parts?"

"Okay, good to know." Debbie glanced at the clock. "Whoops, time to hit the road, girls. I'll wait to hear more about this endeavor later."

CHAPTER THIRTY-TWO

By mid-morning, the florist arrived with three bouquets of fresh fall flowers, one from Rex, another from the three boys at Washington State University and a third from Juana and Gimone. The college students had also sent gourmet chocolate and a huge teddy bear in Army Ranger camo fatigues, including jump boots and beret.

Debbie blinked away tears when she unwrapped the gift. Why did a stuffed animal make her want to cry? Her few toys had been taken away on her thirteenth birthday and passed out to the younger children. It was a normal occurrence in her father's house, so she hadn't grieved them, well at least not much. It would have been a different story if he'd repossessed Hobby, the filly he'd given her, but he didn't.

Even when she was at the boarding school in Spokane, he'd said the horse was waiting for her to come home. Granted, he'd changed his mind once she put her son up for adoption and left the fundamentalist community for good. It'd taken six years for him to sell the mare to her grandparents. Debbie didn't doubt that if hard times hadn't been knocking on his door, she never would have gotten back her horse.

She'd barely finished lunch, a grilled cheese sandwich, a cup of chicken noodle soup and coffee when Shasta yipped. The collie mix headed for the front door to greet Linda MacGillicudy and the cleaning crew. Debbie followed the dog. She smiled at the other woman waiting on the porch. "Hello there."

"Happy birthday." Carrying a large cake box, Linda entered the house. "Twila called and let me know the cake your husband wanted was ready, so I picked it up along with the presents he ordered from Summer. Those are still in my truck."

"Wow, this is a surprise." Debbie led the way back to the kitchen. "I think it's rapidly becoming the best birthday I've had in years and if you tell me that's an old-fashioned carrot cake with cream cheese frosting, I'll know for sure."

"It is." Linda grinned, her smile warming the soft brown eyes. "I told Dray to buy ice-cream when he gets off work in Lake Maynard. He wants to pop in and wish you a happy birthday. I thought you might let him have a piece of your cake."

"We'll have it later when the girls are home, too." Debbie nodded a greeting to the rest of the workers as they entered with cleaning equipment. "I need the guestroom on the third floor prepped for my best friends who are coming to spend the weekend."

"Anything else?" Linda asked. "Or shall we just do the usual?"

"The usual, please," Debbie said, grateful for the older woman's expertise and professionalism. Linda knew what to do. She didn't have to be told to clean the entire house, scrub floors, windows, and appliances, change the sheets in the bedrooms on the second floor, prep meals. "I'm going to leave you folks to it and take Shasta for a training session. She's learning to go trail riding with me."

"Sounds like a winner. We'll see you when the kids get home from school, and everybody can have cake."

"Works for me." Accompanied by the dog, Debbie escaped to the barn. Back in the day, she'd have spent hours with the other women and girls scrubbing her father's house from top to bottom. Not anymore, she thought. Thankfully, Miracle Stable made enough money to pay Linda to do the heavy cleaning.

I'm thirty-five years old, a grown-up and I can do what I want to do. She laughed softly. *Hey, I always have ever since I graduated from high school even if the U.S. Army did think it was in charge for almost eighteen years.*

On her way to the barn to get Hobby, she texted Trina and Kyra to invite them to the festivities in a few hours. Since they had helpers today, Debbie asked them to bring Jacinth and Jason as well. Then, it was time to hit the trails. Shasta seemed to remember their last excursion and happily trotted beside the horse until they'd climbed the first ridge. Then it was time for doggie races under the evergreens. The dog dashed back and forth on the track, not running too far away, obviously thrilled at this new adventure.

Debbie petted Hobby's brown neck and squeezed her legs to signal the mare to move along the main trail. It took almost two hours to circumnavigate the ranch and by the time she rode through the last gate, she felt ready to celebrate her birthday. It was a strange experience to have so many people making a big deal of what she'd always privately considered a trivial matter, but she could handle it.

When they reached the front yard, Shasta raced toward an older blue pickup parked in the yard. She leaped and barked at the inhabitant in the cab, a young brown and black puppy who returned the favor. Dray came across the porch, accompanied by his mother. By the tension in Linda's body and her fierce frown, the two were obviously in the middle of an argument.

Debbie reined Hobby to a stop and eyed the pair. "What's going on?"

"I came to wish you a happy birthday." Dray stalked in the direction of the truck, fury mingling with disappointment on his face. "There's flowers and ice-cream in the house for you."

"And a new dog in the truck." Debbie called Shasta back away from the rig so she could ride closer. "I can't believe you brought me a puppy. What kind is it?"

"It's a heeler mix." Linda froze in her tracks. "Are you serious, Debbie? You want it?"

"Why wouldn't I?" Debbie frowned as she glimpsed mud and grass stains on the puppy's legs, paws, and the top of its head. "Where did you find it?"

"I was on my way here and the jerk in front of me threw him out of the passenger's window at a traffic stop. Luckily, the dog landed in the ditch. I hadn't started rolling forward yet, or I'd have hit him. I'm taking him to my uncle's place for a vet check and Mom says I can't keep him."

"Dray, for the love of God, will you just think? You have four dogs and ten cats already, plus all those chickens, turkeys, ducks, and rabbits in the garage. If you bring home one more critter, there won't be room for us in the house. We'll have to move in with your grandpa."

"He's not that big," Dray protested. "He can't be more than ten or twelve weeks old. He can sleep in my bed."

"Not when you already have the other dogs and a half dozen cats sharing it. We're not keeping him, Drafus Tillicum MacGillicudy."

"That's perfect," Debbie said. "After he sees the vet, bring him back here. Shasta will love having a doggie buddy and you can visit him here, Dray."

"And that's another thing." Linda planted her fists on her sturdy hips. "Uncle Mike isn't a vet. He's a medical doctor. What are people going to say when you bring a puppy into his clinic?"

"Not much. He'll have his grand-daughter Robin help. *She's* a veterinarian. And they saved Cat O'Leary's dog when Herman poisoned it last year."

"And you'll have them call me so I can pay for it." Debbie swung out of the saddle, dropping the reins on the ground so Hobby would stand and wait for her.

She headed for the truck, opened the door, and examined the puppy. Dray and Linda were right about the breed. He had the distinctive short, straight coat with different shades of mingled black, and gray hairs mixed into white fur with an even shorter undercoat. His fur was relatively rough to her touch, but that was perfectly normal for an Australian Cattle Dog too. So, were the pointed brown ears with black fur around the bottom of them.

Wagging his tail, he greeted her with doggie kisses when she lifted him gently into her arms. He couldn't weigh more than eight or nine pounds. The universe must have been watching out for him, or being thrown out of a car near a highway could have killed him. He had a mask of darker fur over both brown eyes, a brown muzzle, chin, and chest with more brown hair on all four upper legs.

"He's adorable." She pulled out her phone to text Trina and Jason to look after Hobby. "Let's go clean him up first, Dray. It will give us an idea of what to tell the vet about him."

"Okay. Thanks, Debbie." He followed her toward the house. "Can I start bringing more animals here?"

"Only if you call and ask me first." Shasta danced alongside them, obviously thrilled and interested in the new addition. "What's his name?"

"I haven't thought of one yet."

"Well, we're not calling him, 'Hey you' so start thinking."

Behind them, Linda heaved a sigh. "All I can say is what my dad would. The apple doesn't fall far from the tree. Dray, maybe you should ask your bio-mom if she has room for cats in the barns. They could live in the feed-rooms and hunt mice and rats. Same goes for the chickens. Maybe she wants her own flock and eggs."

"Now, those are very good ideas." Debbie led the way into the kitchen to the farmhouse sink. "Bath-time for you, doggie. Dray, get some clean towels out of the laundry."

The puppy was surprisingly docile while they bathed him. The injuries seemed to be mostly cuts and scrapes. Debbie didn't like the look of the bump on his head or the swollen left front leg, but as her son said, the puppy was lucky to be alive. Despite her refusal to let Dray keep it, Linda had called her niece and arranged for the younger woman to examine the puppy.

When she arrived home from school, Vangie begged to ride along to the clinic, offering to hold the little heeler. "Please, Ramsey. Shasta hangs out with Celi most of the time and Penny has both cats. Bonzer should be mine too, not just yours."

"Bonzer?" Debbie arched an eyebrow. "What does that mean?"

"I looked it up on my phone." Vangie cuddled the sleeping pup, snuggling him tightly in her arms. "It's Australian slang for "most excellent, cool, great." It's what they say instead of "awesome" and since he lived through a horrendous incident, I think it's a perfect name for him."

Debbie shared a glance with Dray. "Works for me. What about you?"

"I like it. He's your birthday present, *Other Mom*, but you could share him with Vangie."

"I will." Debbie gestured toward the door. "Go and hurry back so we can have cake and ice-cream."

"And more presents for you." Vangie jerked her head in the direction of the hall. "Let's go." She paused. "Rory says Dray is Dad's stepson, like we're your stepkids. It means we're like stepbrother and sister, so it'd just be gross if I still thought he was hot. So he isn't, not anymore."

The new assessment amused Debbie especially when she saw the stunned shock on her son's face. "Now, that's sad. I always thought it'd be nice to have another son the girls thought was hot."

Vangie shrugged. "Oh, he can be hot to other girls, Ramsey, just not to his sisters or Celi. Okay?" She paused. "Will you explain that to Dad, so he doesn't lose it when he hears Dray's taking us to the vet?"

"He shouldn't since all you care about is the dog and this isn't a date because we have a blended family with lots of kids."

Debbie watched the two teens depart. She hadn't shared the fact she and Rex weren't really speaking at the moment. Her stepdaughters didn't need to know and apparently, he hadn't told them either. At some point she'd figure out how to wreak vengeance for betraying her confidences about her assailants. Until then, she'd keep her distance.

Best birthday ever, she thought as she sat on the porch swing that night. Shasta slept on the far corner of the swing. When they went inside, the collie mix would head into Araceli's room for a while to guard her from bad dreams. Meantime, Bonzer was fast asleep on the new doggie bed in Vangie's bedroom—well, that was what the older girl claimed. Debbie bet when she checked, she'd find the heeler curled up with the teenager.

The veterinarian reported he had bumps, bruises, a cracked rib, and sprained leg, but luckily no broken bones. She prescribed pain relievers, antibiotics and recommended plenty of rest. Debbie leaned over to pet Shasta. "You'll have to take it easy with your new friend, but the doctor says he'll be able to play with you in a few weeks."

Her cell phone vibrated, and she pulled it out of her jeans. She recognized the caller as Gimone. "Hey girlfriend. What's up? Don't tell me you and Juana aren't coming. Linda, the super house-cleaner has the guest-room totally revved up for you two."

"We'll be there. I'm just calling to wish you a happy birthday. How was it?"

"Wonderful. Rex's daughters and Celi made me breakfast this morning. His sons sent flowers, chocolate, and a regulation teddy bear."

"What did the major give you?"

"More flowers, a bottle of my favorite wine, gourmet chocolate and that's not all."

"Keep talking, Ramsey. What else?"

"He ordered a blue Carhartt jacket for me at the feedstore. Summer O'Neill stocks up on all sorts of farmer clothes. She has more than the town mercantile. Linda MacGillicudy picked it up along with a matching vest and an assortment of gloves."

"Doesn't sound very romantic to me."

"Okay, but it will come in handy this winter when the rainy season starts. The jacket's fully lined and has a hood. Dray gave me a puppy."

"Last time we talked, you told me all about your son. Sounds like you're getting along well if he brought you a dog. What kind?"

"A little heeler. The vet says he's eight weeks old. Vangie and I are squabbling over him. He's her dog after school and mine all day when she's gone." Debbie laughed. "It works out really well. I called Summer and authorized Vangie to use my account. She bought a shitload of supplies at the feedstore, a bed, a crate, a harness and leashes, toys, plus his own dishes and food."

"Where did Dray find him? Is there a breeder near you?"

"There is, but it was a rescue." Debbie recounted the day's events and what Linda MacGillicudy said about their son being the proverbial chip off the Ramsey block. "He also got the license number from the car and turned that over to the police chief in Baker City. Dick O'Connell is accustomed to Dray saving critters and either finding them homes or keeping them, so Bonzer is safe with us."

Gimone laughed. "I can't wait to meet him. How does your other dog feel about having company?"

"She's loving it and the cats couldn't decide which one should bathe him more. My menagerie is doing well. What about you? What's new at the base?"

"Not much. The last of the reserve units are finishing their training this week because the fiscal year ends in three days and the new one starts the first of October. Juana says I have to tell you the dirty deeds I've been doing before we visit."

"What deeds are those?"

Silence for a moment and then Gimone heaved a long sigh. "You're not much of a TV viewer, so I'm pretty sure you haven't been watching the news."

"True. We have a lot of outdoor activities around the barn, so I'm riding horses, doing trail rides, helping Kyra with lessons, attending a veteran's support group every week and supervising homework each night, all before the paperwork that goes along with being self-employed. What's the dirty deed?"

Another sigh. "I jumped your big brother."

"What! Are you serious? Why would you?"

"Because he's big in more than one way and he knows how to rock my world, Ramsey."

"I still don't get it. Why on earth did you do that?"

"Multiple orgasms, girlfriend. I told you Juana said I had to confess my dirty deeds."

"Well, you have, and I still think you're disgusting. He's my brother for Gawd's sake."

"Yeah, but I always wanted to nail a hero and I had to do it before he leaves for Afghanistan next week." A pause before Gimone continued. "He knows that I know where you are. He's also grateful you're looking after Celi, but he hasn't asked where you two live and I haven't shared. Neither has Juana."

"What makes him a hero? I think he's a jerk. I wrote him a ton of letters back in the day and he never came to the school."

"Wake up and smell the coffee, Ramsey. The guy didn't get them. I'm not sure if your old man put the kibosh on outgoing mail or if it was a school policy. My family didn't stay in contact and neither did Juana's when we wrote to them. We were lucky to have your grandparents in the picture."

Debbie scowled and reached for her glass of wine. sitting on the porch rail. "I just assumed West bailed on me. That's the cult's way."

"Well, we've been in the Army long enough to know what 'assume' means. Now, do you want to know why he's a hero?"

"Um, I thought it was because he was a career soldier who has more tours in the *sandbox* than we do."

"You really need to watch the news. It's over, Debbie. Let it go."

"What's over?" Dread swept through her, and she hastily sipped her wine. "Did the major say something about me being pissed at him?"

"Yeah, but only once. He said he told your bro about the attack. It's a done deal. Let it go."

"I don't understand."

"I know. Watch the news. I could send you a link from the Internet stories about a shitstorm in Montana, but I won't. Check it out on your phone, computer, or TV."

Debbie froze for a moment, utterly shocked. "Oh, my Gawd! They didn't."

"Check it out," Gimone repeated. "And as Juana would say, '*Que sera, sera!*' What will be, will be!"

CHAPTER THIRTY-THREE

Debbie ended the call. Carrying her empty wineglass and followed by Shasta, they went inside. While she dropped off the glass in the kitchen, the dog headed upstairs to Araceli's room.

Debbie went into the living room. She moved the new teddy bear in the recliner and sat down, holding the camo-clad stuffed animal on her lap. She reached for the remote, turning on the cable news. Tiffany Roberts sat behind a desk reciting the day's headlines. Partway through the show, a feature started about a fundamentalist cult in Montana. She asked the male reporter to recap the story that prompted so much attention to the patriarchal, religious group.

He mentioned two deadly accidents that occurred the previous weekend. Two drunken hunters had shot each other and the following night three of their friends subsequently died in a horrific accident when their pickup truck crashed through a guardrail, rolled down a cliff and burst into flame. They'd apparently been drinking at a local watering hole and were well under the influence when the bar closed.

Next came more information about the upcoming funerals on Saturday and the ongoing investigation into polygamist activities and child trafficking. Debbie clutched the bear tightly and listened to the names of the dead men. Tears rolled down her cheeks. All of them were gone. Like Gimone had said, it was over. *Time to let it go! And now I can!*

At breakfast, she told the girls she needed to visit Rex at the army base, and she'd be back late that night or early the next morning. Once they knew he and Araceli's father, were perfectly safe, they were fine with the news. After they left for school, Debbie called Mindy MacGillicudy and told her something had come up at the army base, so she'd miss the veteran's meeting that afternoon. "I have to see my husband and discuss the matter in person. Will you be able to stay overnight with the girls?"

"Sure. Is this something we'll talk about later?"

"Maybe someday, but not now." After a few more pleasantries, Debbie ended the call and contacted Linda to arrange for a birthday dinner at Pop's Café on Friday night, giving her the same story. Next on the agenda was bringing Kyra and Trina up to speed. They promised to look after the horses, dogs and cats as well as the girls until Mindy arrived. Once everything was settled, Debbie changed clothes, packed an overnight bag, and hit the road.

On the long drive, she contemplated what to say to him. *I was so angry and humiliated when he admitted he'd told my brother about the attack. I never thought of what their reactions might be once Rex knew the name of one of my assailants.* She'd argued with him instead of asking about his plans when he learned about her past.

She'd been a noncommissioned Army officer for years. When she was in the military, she'd always looked at all the possible solutions to problems, but she'd failed to do that in this case. If it'd been a mission, soldiers could have died because she failed to consider the consequences of her actions. So, why was she surprised her attackers paid the ultimate price for what they'd done?

I should have realized two combat vets wouldn't adhere to politically acceptable norms. They're alpha males determined to obtain what they perceived as justice especially since there was no point looking for help from the law. The statute of limitations expired years ago.

She knew that much since she'd investigated the possibility of going to the police, first when she was at the boarding school and then later as a teen and finally as a young woman, a soldier in the military. However, she wasn't the only one who'd be at risk.

The bishop would have manufactured a case against her as a promiscuous girl and he could have rounded up plenty of witnesses. Her own family wouldn't have hesitated to testify against her, plus Dray's safety would be jeopardized too. No, she'd made the best decision she could at the time.

If she'd gone to the authorities when she was twenty-eight, before the statute of limitations for gang rape expired, her father and Bishop Levitt might still try to gain custody of her son who'd barely be a teenager. *And they'd blacken my reputation in the process. Victims are still judged more harshly than their assailants. I don't know if I could have endured a trial, but I should have realized Rex and West would stand up for me when they knew the truth at this late date.*

She remembered the way her older brother always corrected other boys and men in the church. He'd even stood up to their father and insisted she be allowed to attend high school, not a normal activity for girls in their community. West was a lot like Rex Sinclair. Both men had moral compasses that weren't swayed by whims or external factors.

Justice first, she thought. Rex insisted on standing up for all five kids he and his ex-wife had. He knew they weren't his, but he was the only father they'd known, and he wouldn't turn his back on them. He was a good man, a decent one and she was lucky to have him.

She reached the house in the gated community shortly after lunch. He wasn't home yet. That didn't come as a surprise. She didn't want to face him at the warehouse, so she'd wait for him here. She parked in the driveway. Before she headed inside, she called Juana and asked her friend to make sure Rex left on time, rather than spending the evening at work.

"Do you want me to tell him that he has a visitor?" Juana teased. "Or is that a secret?"

"It's confidential for now," Debbie admitted. "I'm going to check out the house and see if he has any 'real' food or if I need to hit the commissary. He tends to opt for junk food and take-out most of the time."

"He's not the only one," Juana pointed out. "We know what you're like. You and Gimone binge on chocolate cupcakes when you think nobody's watching."

"Stuff it." Laughing, Debbie headed inside.

———

Rex parked next to the Jeep Wrangler already in the driveway, his hopes rising. She was here. He walked around the house to the backyard. He saw Debbie Ramsey sitting on the stairs to the deck, with a bottle of her favorite cola. She wasn't dressed for riding stable success in her usual jeans and a blue T-shirt. She'd opted for a western style, blue denim dress with pearl buttons and a turquoise, concho chain belt. No boots either. Long, tanned legs ended in low-heeled sandals. Her black hair swung loose and free.

He grinned. "Wow, what a surprise. Why do I deserve this honor when you've been ignoring my calls?"

"Stop being a smart ass." She gestured to the step beside her. "Come tell me what rotten things you've been doing, Major."

He chuckled and followed orders. Sitting next to her, he slung an arm around her shoulders and took the bottle from her. "I was out of your favorite imported sodas from Mexico. Somebody went grocery shopping."

"Only because you never have anything healthy in your fridge." She sighed and rested her head on his shoulder. "Don't ever do that again."

"Do what, Ramsey? Avoid the crowds in the grocery? Neither of us like them." He kissed the top of her head before taking a swallow of soda. "Spill it. What's on your mind, Sarge?"

"Montana." She trailed a finger down his cheek. "I saw the news. When it comes to logistics, you're a genius. You set it up."

He handed back the icy bottle. "If I say I don't know what you're talking about—"

"I'd tell you not to lie to me." She kissed him. "Don't do it again."

"Do what?"

"Arrange for bad actors to meet their justifiable demises."

"I can't promise that." He cuddled her close to him. "If someone hurts you or my girls, he's going down."

"Don't be gender biased. What about the boys?"

"Okay, you win." He smiled at her, appreciating the humor in the bright blue eyes. "I'll dust them too unless you get to them first."

"Deal." She heaved a sigh. "I don't know what I was thinking. You've always had my six. I didn't expect the fallout, but nobody else needs to know that."

"Fair enough." He watched her finish the cola. "So, what happens now?"

She looked at her watch. "Well, I'd say you take me to bed, and we have make-up sex."

"I'm good with that."

"Except we're having company for dinner in two hours."

He stood, caught her hand, and pulled her up to stand beside him. "Then I guess we'd better stop talking."

"Is that the best you can do?"

"You've never complained before." He swung her up into his arms and carried her toward his bedroom. "Don't start now."

"I'm not." She nipped his ear. "I told Gimone to bring her latest hero."

"Who is he?"

"My brother."

"Are you serious, Ramsey?" Rex stopped and stared down into her face. "Are you really ready to see him?"

"Well, considering the two of you were in cahoots when he went to Montana, it's time for me to step up like you did." She laced her arms around his neck. "Keep walking. I want to jump a hero too."

"You've got it. And you've got me too."

"Only if you realize it's forever."

He lowered his head, kissed her quickly. "I knew that eight years ago when you accepted my grandmother's rings."

"And I knew it when you went the extra mile to collect my horses and inheritance from my grandparents, long before my grandma told me you were a keeper. I told her so even if I kept that news from you."

"Good to know it wasn't a marriage in name only for you either."

While he carried her down the hall, Debbie traced the fierce line of his jaw with her lips. At the same time, she unbuttoned his shirt. "It's been ages since I had you."

"Only four days." He carried her into the bedroom.

"I thought we were done."

"Not while you're alive and I am, too."

"Good to know," she mocked, clinging to his wide shoulders. When he lowered his head, she eagerly met his kiss. It felt as if she dissolved into pure wanting when his hand cupped her breast, his thumb finding her nipple through her dress. The world spun. She turned her face into his shoulder when he put her on the king-size bed and followed her down. His mouth recaptured hers.

She threaded her fingers into his hair. Then she started a new path with her hands trailing over his features. She stroked one finger down his cheek, feeling the faint stubble of an evening beard. When he lifted his head, she feathered a line of kisses down the strong column of his neck. She pushed off his camouflage shirt. His t-shirt followed and she enjoyed the sight and feel of his muscles.

"I missed you," she whispered the words against his skin.

"Good. Now, tell me you love me." He unfastened the first pearl button on the western placket of her dress, then the second.

"What if I make you wait?"

"Oh, you'll surrender." He undid the third button, parting the material to reveal her skin. "It's just a case of how much I make you want me." He unfastened the front clasp of her bra.

She shuddered when he flicked his tongue over her nipple and tangled her fingers in his hair. She drew him closer. "Don't stop."

He lifted his head and smiled. "You haven't said what I want to hear." He pulled out of her embrace and rolled off the bed to unbuckle his belt and undo the top button of his pants.

She didn't plan to wait. She sat up, unfastened her sandals, and kicked them off. She rose to her feet and removed the concho chain belt. She finished unbuttoning her dress. She skimmed out of it and hung it neatly over a chair in the corner of the bedroom.

He was close enough to touch her, caress her, kiss her. She felt the excitement build in her veins. She knew it was the same for him. She could tell by the shudders when she tormented him with her hands, her mouth, and her body.

She stroked the shoulders that fascinated her so much. She explored his broad chest. Each lingering movement of his hands on her breasts, of his mouth as he feasted on her nipples, burned fire into her body. He lifted his head, then picked her up and carried her to the bed, following her down.

She arched eagerly against him, but he was in no hurry. Instead, his fingers continued to tease her. She shook with wanting as his lips traced warm patterns on her stomach, then on her thighs. How much more did he expect her to bear? She groaned as his mouth found her. His tongue drove into her. She found herself rising, falling, meeting each movement of his tongue. When she returned from the whirlpool of madness, she looked at him, staring into his face.

He was still between her legs. She arched against his mouth as he started again. Thought fled as he licked, sucked, and finally took her with his tongue. When she opened her eyes a lifetime later, he lay next to her, stroking her hair. She let her fingers stray over his broad chest, teasing the hard buttons of his nipples. She couldn't wait any longer.

She rolled on top of him. She pressed him back into the sheets, against the pillows. He chuckled. His hands clasped her waist. He pulled her astride his narrow hips. She gasped as he claimed her. Despite her position on top of him, he was in control and set their pace. All she could do was respond to his demands and she did. She followed the rhythm he set. His passion filled her senses. All she could think of was him.

She cried out his name as the world exploded, shattering into a million glowing stars. He followed her over the edge of the universe. She collapsed on top of him. She pressed her lips against his neck and tasted the warm salt of his skin. "I love you."

He held her tight. "I love you, too."

An hour later, she was in the kitchen setting up the center island with plates, glasses, and silverware. Large potatoes baked in one oven while the foil-wrapped loaf of garlic bread she'd brought from Baker City warmed in the other. The assortment of cheesecake slices waited in the giant refrigerator for dessert. Whenever Debbie glanced through the glass doors and saw Rex preparing to grill steaks, she had to smile. He pulled out his phone and studied the screen for a moment.

Laughing, he came inside to show her a picture of Vangie fitting a harness on Bonzer. "Talk to me, Ramsey. How and when did she get a puppy?"

"Actually, he's my birthday present. We decided to share him, so I'll have him days and she'll have him after school. Dray brought him to us yesterday after some asshat threw him out of a car window at a traffic stop." Debbie held up her hand before Rex spoke. "And the cops are on the hunt for the guy since Dray gave them his license plate. You're not exercising your brand of justice."

"Wow, you're tough."

"You should know." The doorbell rang and she went to greet their visitors. They'd come in Gimone's Malibu.

Debbie looked through the window at the driveway. She hesitated for a moment when she saw the tall, dark-haired man open the passenger door. Although the duty day had ended, he still wore fatigues and combat boots.

She felt the comforting touch of Rex's hand on her shoulder. "I'm okay."

"I'm here. If you change your mind, I'll send him away."

"No, I can handle it." She took a deep breath and opened the door. "Good to see you. Hope you remembered the salad."

"I've got it." Juana reached in the back seat and removed two bags. "We stopped at the deli, and I got three different kinds. I forgot to ask if you brought the girls."

"No, it was a school day. You'll have to wait until the weekend to see them." Debbie glanced at her older brother again. He reeled against the car fender, his gaze locked on her. "What? Did you think I dropped off the face of the planet, Westley Taggart? You should know better. You sent me your kid."

He slowly straightened. "You're really here? Sweet, you're really alive."

"And you're really stating the obvious." She started across the porch. By the time she hit the driveway, she was running. She ran toward him, and he met her halfway, pulling her into his arms.

He hugged her tight. "So good to see you."

"Likewise." She tiptoed up to kiss his cheek. "And I'll tell you the same thing I told Sinclair. No more waxing bad actors when you're in CONUS. Try it again and I'll kick your tail from here to the moon. Got it?"

CHAPTER THIRTY-FOUR

West watched the three women standing near the center island in the kitchen. Two of the women still wore camo fatigues, but his younger sister was in jeans and a t-shirt, flip-flops on bare feet. His parents would have freaked out if they saw the bright blue polish on her fingernails and toenails and the long black braid that bounced against her hips, but the sight amused him. He still saw the girl she'd been in the thirty-five-year-old woman who talked with her friends while Gimone poured wine into glasses and Juana scooped deli salads into serving bowls.

He'd known his sister was alive and well when she took on his daughter. Seeing Sweet—no she'd said she'd changed her name to Debbie—and holding her made it real. She passed her phone to Gimone. "I told you about him, but you haven't seen Bonzer, the puppy I'm sharing with Vangie, the major's oldest girl yet."

While she and Juana studied pictures on the cell phone, Debbie opened the giant fridge and pulled out a bottle of beer. She passed it to West, then followed it with a glass of red wine. "You probably want to socialize with Rex out on the deck while he grills the steaks instead of listening to us catch up."

"Won't he want a beer too?"

"Not when I'm here. He knows I don't like the taste or smell of it. He drinks it when he's home alone." Debbie glanced over her shoulder. "You haven't said anything, Castenada, but I can read your mind after all these years. What's on your mind?"

"Where did you get the puppy?" Juana asked, amusement on her face, lighting up the brown eyes. "Do they have a shelter near you?"

"If they do, I haven't found it yet. Actually, he's my birthday present. We decided to share him, so I'll have him most days and Vangie will have him after school. Dray brought him to us yesterday after some asshat threw him out of a car window at a traffic stop."

"Dray?" West asked. "Who's that? Your significant other?"

"Her son," Gimone said. "He brought her flowers for her birthday and the puppy was along for the ride. Got any pics of Dray, Debbie? We haven't seen him in forever."

"Scroll back and you'll find them." Debbie turned and headed back toward her friends. "He looks like a teen version of West."

"Your son?" West carefully put the bottle and glass on the counter. "Celi didn't mention him when she talked to me. She told me about the Major's daughters and the horse she's been riding. How old is your son? How can he be a teenager? Isn't he only seven or eight?"

"He just turned nineteen." Debbie took the phone, light reflecting off the vintage sapphire and diamond claddagh ring on her left hand, as she apparently sorted through the gallery on it. "He's working at Hawke Construction this year and taking night classes at the community college. He helps out relatives of the family that adopted him and volunteers at the vet center. I'm very proud of him. Here you go, Gimone."

"Nineteen?" West stared at his younger sister, his mind racing. "I don't get it."

When she turned a brilliant, blue stare on him, nausea rose inside him, and his gut clenched. "You were pregnant when—"

"Wow, a rocket scientist," Debbie mocked. "Didn't either of our parents share why they actually sent me to Celestial Faith Girls Academy for Troubled Teens? They blamed me for being a soon-to-be teen mama after the bishop's son and his friends attacked me. Sinclair and I had good reasons to step up for your kid. I was really pissed off when you didn't come see me at the boarding school after I wrote so many letters, but—"

Baffled, he gaped at her for a moment. "I never got a single one, Sweet. I mean, Debbie. If I knew you needed me, I'd have been there."

"That's what we figured out at this late date." Gimone told him, narrowing her green eyes. "It just took us a while because writing to family members was a weekly class assignment. We'd do it or be sent to spend hours in the chapel with the preacher railing at us about being sinners. Juana used to tell us not to put anything important in those letters, so they couldn't be used against us by the staff. Now, take that wine out to Sinclair and we'll do girly stuff without boring you."

"I'm not bored," West protested. "Besides, I don't want to leave Sweet—I mean Debbie—now that I've found her."

"I'm not going anywhere, and you'll be able to see me through the glass doors. Go help Sinclair."

West collected the icy beer bottle and glass of wine, then slowly paced toward the French doors. He glanced over his shoulder and saw her standing by the granite-topped island. She waved him forward, and he reluctantly obeyed. How was he going to make more amends to the damaged woman who thought he'd deliberately abandoned her? No answer came to mind, at least not yet.

Rex nodded at his brother-in-law as he approached before turning the steaks on the grill. "Dinner is close, but you don't look ready to eat."

"You didn't tell me Sweet—I mean Debbie—was pregnant after the attack."

"No, I didn't." Rex reached for the glass of wine. "Figured if I did, you might have second thoughts about waxing them and I'm on special assignment at the base. I couldn't get leave to take care of business in Montana, so I depended on you."

"They needed to die." West leaned against the porch rail and drank some of his beer. "I have no regrets about that. What's her son going to think about what we did?"

"He doesn't have a need to know." Rex sipped the red wine and watched the two T-bones sizzle beside the three smaller tenderloins. "Debbie put him up for adoption right after he was born. When she ran into the woman who raised him, they decided the boy shouldn't know he was a child of rape. He's a good kid. I like him better now that my daughter has decided he's another brother, not a super-hot guy she met at church."

"Makes sense." West reflected for a moment. "What's going on with you and my sister? I offered to bring you a beer, but she refused. That case in the fridge must belong to you since she doesn't care for it."

"Playing detective?" Rex chuckled and shook his head. "I couldn't tell you before. We got married almost eight years ago when my divorce was final. We kept it on the down-low while she was active duty."

The sliding door opened, and Debbie came out on the deck. "Ready for plates yet?"

"Soon." Rex handed her the empty wine glass when she approached, admiring the way her jeans and T-shirt clung in all the right places. "Our bad. We should have told your brother about us."

"If you'd shared more than you did, Sinclair, I'd have had a bigger fit and fallen in it." She glanced at West, then her gaze returned to him. "You can't catch up on twenty years in less than an hour, West. If you weren't headed to the *sandbox* in a few days, I'd invite you to my ranch."

"Breaking news. I'm not. My unit was supposed to be back in CONUS shortly after New Years, but our tour was cut short. They'll be home in time for Thanksgiving, so I've been reassigned to the advance party. We're setting up facilities and transportation for training here during the next six weeks."

"Sounds like the Army." Debbie flashed a quick smile. "So, what's your plan for Celi?"

"I'll be doing some traveling back and forth to California. She's settled and happy with you. Would it be okay for her to stay longer?"

"It's fine." Out of the corner of his eye, Rex glimpsed Debbie's nod of agreement. "Looks like the steaks are ready. Grab the plates, please."

Conversation ebbed and flowed as they gathered around the dining room table to eat dinner. West shared some of the team-building activities he'd suggested for his unit members while they decompressed. Juana and Gimone talked about the reservists who'd finished up their training in the warehouses.

Because Rex couldn't reveal his efforts with the escaped soldiers, Debbie picked up the slack. She discussed the upcoming horseshow as well as the new riding clubs, in addition to the Halloween celebrations in Baker City. She encouraged Rex to describe the house his sons were remodeling in Eastern Washington.

While they were cleaning up after the meal, the telephone rang in the kitchen. Rex answered. He listened for a moment, then said, "That makes no sense. My wife is here, and she cleared our guests with security tonight."

Debbie glanced at him when he was quiet again. She saw temper rising on his rugged, rawboned features and landing in the golden-brown eyes. She walked across the room and rested a hand on his arm. "Whatever it is, we've got this."

He nodded, then spoke into the receiver. "Keep my ex-wife at the gate. I'll be there in a few minutes to deal with her."

He'd barely hung up when West sauntered toward them. "Want me to take care of this business too?"

"No," Debbie told him. "I already told the pair of you the rules. Now, let's go kick some butt and take some names. What's non-negotiable is where the girls are and where they're staying. The boys are safe in Pullman at the university."

"Whatever you say." Rex took her hand. "We'll be back in a few minutes. Make yourselves at home."

"We're coming along," Juana informed him. "We can't miss the drama."

Debbie laughed. "Okay, the more the merrier. After this, there's coffee and cheesecake for dessert."

When they arrived at the security gate a few moments later, Debbie and Rex led the way to the white brick guardhouse. She saw a new black SUV parked in a slot close to the door. Even though it'd been years, she still recognized the tall, brunette woman standing toe-to-toe arguing with the uniformed, gray-haired sentry. A handsome blond guy in his early thirties waited near the rig. He wore khakis and a Hawaiian shirt.

"That must be the current husband." Debbie gave him a slow appraisal. He was what she privately considered a 'pretty boy' and definitely not her type. He frowned when he saw them and stepped closer to the vehicle, obviously threatened by the group of soldiers.

"Why are you here, Averill?" Rex stopped a few feet away from his former wife. "You didn't say you intended to visit."

"I came for my daughters." The woman turned to face him, her gaze narrowing on Debbie. "Who is she? Your latest girlfriend?"

"Debbie Ramsey-Sinclair." Deliberately, Debbie lifted her hand, so the antique wedding ring set glittered in the evening sunlight. "And the girls ran away to us almost two months ago. We're keeping them for the duration."

"What does that mean?" Averill shot a hazel-eyed glare at Rex. "They're mine, not yours."

"I'm listed as their father on all five birth certificates. According to the custody agreement, each of the kids were supposed to visit us two week-ends a month during the school year and every summer as soon as they finished school." Rex put an arm around Debbie's waist. "You kept them away from us."

"How could I send them when you were always in combat?"

"Not always," Debbie said super-sweetly. "We alternated tours. They could have been with me when the major was overseas. We heard all about the shenanigans at your house and the way you kept them incommunicado in addition to being gone six months each year."

Averill planted her hands on her hips. "That only happened a few times."

"For the last four years," Rex said. "It's over. Your belongings are in stor-age. The girls are with me, and the boys are adults. They can choose how often they want to see you."

Silence ensued for a long moment while she stared at him. Then she said, "The court may let Vangie choose, but Penny is only nine and I have a say about where she lives. You already have the house up for sale and I won't see any of the proceeds. What can I have if I walk away and don't fight for custody of her?"

"Your life." Rex said, his tone even and emotionless.

Debbie elbowed him in the ribs. "You don't want to be bothered with the kids. Go enjoy your life with your new husband. Leave the responsi-bility to those of us who can handle it."

"Does she always speak for you?"

"She has my six," Rex agreed. "Always has. Always will." He turned his attention to the waiting security guard. "They're leaving now. See to it."

"Yes, sir."

On the walk back to the house, West said. "If you change your mind, let me know."

"I'm not amused," Debbie told him. "We're working on the 'let it go' principle. I'm pretty sure she'll leave, since she's not getting what she wants."

"What's that?" Juana asked.

"Sinclair's money." Debbie tucked her hand into the crook of his arm. "And you're not paying her one more cent. She's had enough out of you. Got it?"

He chuckled. "Got it, Sarge. Like my grandpa used to say, 'if your wife isn't happy, nobody is.' And it's my job to make sure you're happy."

"That road runs two ways." She smiled at him. "And I'm good with it."

"We both are."

"Now, that's what I like to see," Moises Pride said, sauntering alongside them. "A happy ending, or maybe it's a happy beginning."

EPILOGUE
OCTOBER 2019

Ten days later, life at Miracle Stable was insanely busy and Debbie didn't know if she was coming or going during the week before her first local horseshow. On Wednesday morning, Vangie surprised her with the news her older brothers would be home for the three-day weekend. They'd arrive Friday afternoon and drive back to Pullman in eastern Washington on Monday. Grateful, she'd heard about it early enough to share the news with Linda MacGillicudy who would be coming to clean the house that day, Debbie approved the plan and then headed for the barn.

As Kyra pointed out the students wouldn't know how to prepare their lesson horses for the event. That meant Debbie and her crew, Kyra, Trina, Jason, Carol, and Trina's older sister, Jassy had approximately thirty animals to bathe, and clip prior to the show. In addition, they had tack to clean. Linda had promised her father would bring his new food truck and sell refreshments on Saturday, so that was one less hassle.

Debbie shared the daily update during the late-night call with Rex and he told her that he'd come early enough to help on Saturday. She reminded him that he didn't have much of a choice because Vangie, Penny and Celi would be showing their favorite horses for the first time. He needed to pull whatever strings were necessary to have West Taggart receive a weekend pass to travel to Baker City, so her brother could do the appropriate 'daddy cheer squad' thing for his daughter too.

"No worries, darlin'. I have your six." Rex chuckled. "What else is happening up in your neck of the woods."

Debbie leaned back on the porch swing. "Clancy Dawson is coming to do a walk-through Friday to check out the arenas. Jeff Ransom is sending along some of his guys and gals to help Dray and Trina with the trail course in the outdoor ring. Cat O'Leary talked to Heather McElroy who rounded up Hawke Construction because their daughters ride with Jeff's and all their girls along with Ann Barrett's are coming to show their ponies."

Rex grinned appreciatively. "So, what does Durango Hawke think of that?"

"Not sure. I'll undoubtedly hear about it tomorrow afternoon when I meet Heather at the veteran's group."

"Well, keep me posted."

"You know it." Debbie smiled, wishing he was there in person, not just on the phone screen. "What else is on your agenda?"

"Making love to my wife all night long once the show is over, so rest up this week."

She giggled. "Tell me more."

The next two days zoomed by and before she knew it, Friday arrived. She'd finished walking Clancy and her best friend, Darla Connors through the facilities at Miracle Stable. Darla said her daughter would be showing her Paint gelding in the classes judged by Kyra and Trina, but not Clancy's since they didn't want any drama.

"Drama?" Debbie asked. "I don't get it."

"Bayleigh is Clancy's goddaughter," Darla explained. "And I know Clancy won't cut her any slack, but you don't want to listen to complaining parents at your first outside show. Narcissists are the bane of small businesses and their owners."

Debbie nodded, remembering what Sean Killian had said about avoiding controversy between outsiders when his daughter showed her horse at the fair last month. "Thanks for watching my back. I appreciate it."

"Well, it's reciprocal," Clancy told her. "When you come to a show at Darla's barn, you'll cover hers."

"Definitely." The two women had barely left the grounds when a mid-size Subaru pulled in the drive. Instead of going toward the indoor arena, the vehicle headed in the direction of the house. Debbie went to meet the visitors and was thrilled to see her stepsons in the SUV, Rory behind the wheel. The three of them greeted her with warm hugs before grabbing duffel bags and backpacks. She explained the girls weren't home from school yet but would be along soon.

"Sounds good," Rory said. "It will give us a chance to bond with Vangie's dog before she gets here."

"He and Shasta are my dogs too." Debbie laughed. "I bet you're hungry after that long drive. Let's go raid the kitchen."

"Sounds like a winner," Scott told her. "I've missed my 'real' kitchen."

"It's certainly missed you and so have we." Debbie slipped her arm around Cal's waist. "Are you willing to act as a ring steward tomorrow? We need another horsey guy to help."

"Count on me," he promptly replied.

"I will," Debbie agreed.

Thanks to everyone's assistance, the horseshow ran super smoothly. Debbie received compliments not only from the attendees, but also from the audience, parents, visitors, and other supporters. Despite Rex's vow to make love to her all night long, they didn't. Instead, she slept soundly in his arms. Once again, he'd turned off the alarm when he went downstairs the next morning, allowing her the opportunity to sleep late.

When she reached the kitchen, she discovered Scott and Vangie setting up a buffet. Debbie eyed the pair. "That doesn't look much like breakfast."

"It's not." Vangie flashed a bright smile. "You were so busy with the show yesterday you forgot something else."

"What?" Debbie eyed the dark-haired teenager who looked so much like her father. "Is there a reason you're skipping one of your favorite Sunday activities, church in Baker City?"

"Penny and I'll hit it next week. Today is your and Dad's bronze anniversary, so we're prepping for the party this afternoon. I've planned everything and invited most of the people from Baker City. Twila Garvey is in charge of the cake and Pop MacGillicudy is bringing all the food. He says you're his daughter too. Reverend Tommy is announcing the festivities after his sermon."

Debbie blinked, then glanced over her shoulder when Rex entered the room. "Did you know about this?"

"Know about what?" He crossed to her. "Give me a sitrep, Ramsey."

"I forgot our anniversary and the kids are giving us a party." Heaving a sigh, she looked up at him. "I'm sorry."

"Nothing to be sorry about." He kissed her forehead. "I looked it up on my phone and for the eighth anniversary, symbols also include linen and lace. I'm sure we'll manage to improvise. I can think of several things you can give me."

Heat flooded her face, and she elbowed him. "Just for that, I'm letting you take me into town for breakfast and leaving the stable to your kids."

"Rory would say, 'yours' too, New Mom," Scott teased. "We'll have everything ready when you get back."

"I was afraid of that," Debbie said.

Once they were ensconced in the front seat of his pickup truck, she kissed him. "Why do I think I know what you want?"

"What we didn't do last night." He feathered his thumb across her lips. "Now, I know why the sisters of your heart, Nolan and Castenada told me they'd be here today when they couldn't make the show."

"And I know why West said he wasn't due back at the base until tomorrow afternoon." Debbie sighed, pressing her cheek against Rex's chest, and listened to his heartbeat. "I never thought I'd have what you've given me."

"What's that, Ramsey? Unconditional love."

"Well, that comes first. I love you so much, Rex Sinclair. You gave me a family. I didn't know I wanted one, didn't know I'd ever have one after the way I grew up. I do. We have each other and even more we have our kids. All five of yours and—"

"And your boy and Celi too."

"And a home in Baker City. Always. I'm so good with always."

"That makes two of us."

THE END

Don't miss out on your next favorite book!

Join the Satin Romance mailing list
www.satinromance.com/mail.html

THANK YOU FOR READING

Did you enjoy this book?

We invite you to leave a review at your favorite book site, such as Goodreads, Amazon, Barnes & Noble, etc.

DID YOU KNOW THAT LEAVING A REVIEW...

- Helps other readers find books they may enjoy.
- Gives you a chance to let your voice be heard.
- Gives authors recognition for their hard work.
- Doesn't have to be long. A sentence or two about why you liked the book will do.

ABOUT THE AUTHOR

Josie Malone lives and works at her family's riding stable in Washington State. She's taught children to ride and know about horses so long that she often discovers she's taught three generations of their families. Her life experiences span adventures from dealing cards in a casino, attending graduate school to get her Master's in Teaching degree, being a substitute teacher, and serving in the Army Reserve all leading to her second career as a published author.

Contact Josie at:
josiemaloneauthor@outlook.com

Find her on Online at:
www.josiemalone.com

Join her Newsletter:
https://sendfox.com/josiemaloneauthor

facebook.com/JosieMaloneAuthor

instagram.com/josiemaloneauthor

goodreads.com/shannonkennedy

amazon.com/Josie-Malone/e/B006HC9VMI

ALSO BY JOSIE MALONE

Baker City Hearts and Haunts

My Sweet Haunt

More Than A Spirit

Family Skeletons

Ghost of the Past

Kindred Spirits

Merry Ghostmas (Coming Soon!)

———

Liberty Valley Love

A Man's World

Cowboy Spell

The Marshal's Lady

Hero Spell

A Trail Through Time

Time In Between

Kitchen Witch (Coming Soon!)

www.ingramcontent.com/pod-product-compliance
Lightning Source LLC
Chambersburg PA
CBHW030938260626
47169CB00002B/528